The JEWEL *of*
GRESHAM GREEN

Books by
Lawana Blackwell

The Jewel of Gresham Green

THE GRESHAM CHRONICLES
The Widow of Larkspur Inn
The Courtship of the Vicar's Daughter
The Dowry of Miss Lydia Clark

TALES OF LONDON
The Maiden of Mayfair

www.lawanablackwell.com

LAWANA
BLACKWELL

The JEWEL of
GRESHAM GREEN

BETHANYHOUSE
Minneapolis, Minnesota

Published by Bethany House Publishers
11400 Hampshire Avenue South
Bloomington, Minnesota 55438

Bethany House Publishers is a division of
Baker Publishing Group, Grand Rapids, Michigan.

Printed in the United States of America

Library of Congress Cataloging-in-Publication Data

Blackwell, Lawana.
  The jewel of Gresham Green / Lawana Blackwell.
    p. cm.
  ISBN 978-0-7642-0511-8 (pbk.)
  1. Children of clergy—Fiction. 2. England—Fiction. I. Title.
  PS3552.L3429J47   2008
  813'.54—dc22

                                              2008014235

To Margaret Blackwell and Barbara Schmitt

Marriage made us sisters-in-law.

Thirty-plus years of birthday parties, lunches, family reunions,
movies, weddings, funerals, trips, chicken dances, hospital sits,
advice, crawfish boils, a few tears, and much laughter
made us friends.

Chapter 1

15 April 1884
Birmingham, England

Stitch and turn, stitch and turn, stitch and turn . . .

Jewel Libby folded the raw edges of silk into narrow hems as her feet pumped the treadle. Monotony was what made the job dangerous. Most scarred fingers belonged not to the newest workers at J. Mobley, *Elegant Corsets for the Particular Woman*, but to those who had spent enough time in the sewing room to forget that the needle could hypnotize just before it bit.

That same necessity to be alert took away temptation to chat with the women nearest her for the six days weekly, ten hours daily Jewel sat among them. Besides, socializing could get a person sacked, and then how would she feed her daughter?

Mr. Fowler's whistle shrilled. Machines hummed into silence. Forty sets of eyes mirrored Jewel's own puzzlement, for no evening sunlight slanted through the west windows.

The manager jumped up onto a chair and clapped his hands;

an unnecessary action in the tense stillness. "On account of the birth of Mr. Mobley's second granddaughter, you may all go home!"

"Four hours early!" Jewel said to another worker while joining the applause.

"God bless the child!" someone exclaimed.

"If she'd only been a grandson, we'd have been given the whole day," Mrs. Fenton said sagely during the homeward trek up Steelhouse Lane.

Jewel sent a look over her shoulder before risking a guilty smile. Not that Mr. Mobley would be anywhere in the vicinity. She had seen the factory owner once during two years of employment.

"Why are boys more valued than girls, do you think?" Jewel asked the older woman.

"Rich folk care about carryin' on the name. We poor need sons because we can send them out to work earlier than girls. And they're paid more."

Jewel gave her a sidelong look.

Mrs. Fenton shrugged. "Life's hard, if you ain't noticed."

They hurried past Perseverance Iron Works, its chimney belching smoke into the already pewter sky. Windows sent out ripples of heat. Jewel wondered how many sons of the poor sweat inside.

Thank God I have a girl, Jewel thought. Not that raising a daughter was easy. Most of her worries centered around Becky. Particularly of late.

They turned onto Vesey Street, then Halls Passage. Three-storey tenement buildings rose on both sides, identical in their stained brick, filth, foul odors, and weed-choked courtyards.

"I've got it!" a young voice called.

"Over here!" piped another.

Sixty feet ahead in the lane, five young boys played a game of catch with a ball. Near the arched entrance of the building on the right, a man stood holding a small girl's hand. Jewel's breath caught in her throat at the sight of the girl's berry-red hair, so like her own.

"Do you see—" Mrs. Fenton began.

"Becky!" Jewel gathered her skirts and ran.

Mr. Dunstan dropped her daughter's hand. He was forty or so, tall and solidly built, with blue eyes that could have been handsome if not set above a vulgar smile. He called out, "You'll be hurtin' yourself if you slip on them cobbles, Mrs. Libby."

Automatically Jewel slowed her steps, the immediate danger past. She drew close enough to take four-year-old Becky's hand. The small palm was clammy from the rent collector's grasp, and she had to fight the urge to wipe it against her skirt.

"It's just that she's not supposed to be out here without Mrs. Platt."

The corner of her eye caught movement. Mrs. Fenton, slipping into the building. That stung, but how could Jewel fault a woman who was the sole support for her aged mother? When these were the cheapest tenements within walking distance of the factory? When Mr. Dunstan wielded the power to toss a person out into the street?

"Why are you home early? Got one of those woman complaints?"

Jewel's cheeks burned.

Becky held out a pigeon feather, her face pinched with worry. "I found this for you, Mummy."

"It's lovely, Becky," Jewel said, grateful for the excuse not to reply to his coarse question.

That was the most maddening thing about being in the company of Mr. Dunstan—having to maintain the charade that he was just an ordinary decent person. To pretend not to notice the lust in his eyes, bad enough when directed toward her, but terrifying when fastened upon Becky.

Rumors added fuel to that fire. Such as the reason the Kents moved out last month, with their two young daughters. Mr. Kent's job at the foundry paid twice what Jewel earned at the factory, so they could afford that luxury.

"Good day, Mr. Dunstan," Jewel forced through a tight smile, while thinking, *Norman would wipe that leer from your face!* But two years ago he and another bricklayer had perished when scaffolding collapsed at the unfinished Castle Maltings building on Tower Street.

She dragged Becky by the hand, up the steps and through the doorway. Without knocking she turned the knob to number seven and entered. Mrs. Platt sat rocking a pair of sleeping infants. A tot squatted in a corner, picking at the straws of a broom. Another lay upon the filthy threadbare rug, playing with his own feet. Both ceased activity to send Jewel open-mouthed stares.

"Mrs. Platt!" Jewel said with a shaking voice. "Becky was outdoors!"

"Mrs. Libby, mind you'll wake the babies," the woman said through teeth as gray and crooked as old gravestones. "She whined to play with the older 'uns. She's too big for the babies. What was I to do?"

"What I pay you to do, that's what," Jewel said with less volume but more intensity. "Mr. Dunstan had her hand! God alone knows what would have happened if I hadn't come home early."

One infant stirred and whimpered. Mrs. Platt frowned above its downy head. "There you go again, harpin' on Mr. Dunstan, when he's the soul of mercy."

"*Mercy?* He pays too much attention to little girls."

"You should be grateful . . . your poor fatherless baby." A bony hand moved from the infant's back to shake a crooked finger at Jewel. "If you'd been here in Mr. Archer's time, you'd appreciate Mr. Dunstan. Gin on his breath, even in the mornings! A hairsbreadth late with the rent, and you're out on your ear."

"I *don't* appreciate having my instructions ignored. Keep her with you, or I'll find someone else." As if she had not already tried, but Mrs. Platt did not have to know that.

Grimy landing windows provided the only illumination on the staircase, sticky and reeking of urine and sour spilled beer. Those forced to take the steps at night carried candles or lamps. Chest burning, Jewel hitched Becky up to her hip and kirtled her skirts with her left hand.

"I'm sorry, Mummy," the girl said halfway up the staircase.

"Don't speak now, Becky," Jewel said.

In the corridor, she set Becky on her feet and fished the key from her pocket. The door to number twenty-one opened to a tiny parlor that led to a smaller kitchen and still smaller bedroom. Washing up was done in the scullery, with water carried up from a tap in the piece of bare earth that served as the courtyard. Chamber pots saved nighttime trips to the privy, only yards away from the tap. Furnishings were sparse. Shortly after Norman's burial, Jewel was forced to sell off most of their secondhand furniture before moving herself and Becky from the small but cozy back-to-back house on Hurst Street.

Jewel locked the door behind her and turned to Becky. The tears brimming in the brown eyes, the trembling lips, broke her heart. Had hardship driven from her all memory of what it was like to be a child?

"Ah, Becky," she said, kneeling to pull her into her arms. She stroked her back as sobs wracked the small frame. "My dear, brave little girl. I love you so much."

"I don't like to go to Mrs. Platt's!" Becky sobbed against her shoulder.

"I know, I know." Jewel's voice thickened. "But Mummy must work."

She held her daughter until the sobbing ceased. Tempting as it was not to distress her any more, Jewel unwound her arms and moved her back a bit so that she could meet her eyes.

"Becky," she said, gently, but with a sternness born of fear. "You're old enough to remember that you're not to go outdoors without Mrs. Platt."

"But she never goes," the girl said through trembling lips. "And the boys are allowed."

The unfairness of it tugged at Jewel's heart. But safety came before fairness. "You *must* stay with Mrs. Platt."

She swallowed, dreading the answer to the next question. "How long was Mr. Dunstan there?"

"Not for a long time. He's not a bad man, Mummy. He said he wished he had a bright girl just like—"

Jewel groaned as a shiver snaked up her spine. "Just because someone smiles and speaks kindly doesn't make him good. Did you go anywhere with him?"

The brown eyes evaded Jewel's. "He said there were toys and peppermints in the cellar."

"Becky!"

"But I said I wanted to stay outdoors and watch the boys play."

"God help us," Jewel moaned. She got to her feet. "Mummy has to go somewhere for a little while."

"Are ye sure ye trust me with her?" Mrs. Platt sniffed.

"Yes," Jewel said, adding mentally, *What choice have I?* "I'll try to return within the hour."

Fortunately, Mr. Dunstan no longer lurked outside. Jewel hurried up the lane. Cabbies avoided Halls Passage, but she would have walked the nine blocks anyway to save a shilling. On Great Russell Street, a well-dressed woman held a laughing small boy up before a toy display window.

"Oh, now it's a train you want for your birthday? What will it be tomorrow?"

Jewel envied not her finery but the unhurried enjoyment of her son, the taking for granted that there would be plenty of such moments.

Outside Great Russell Street police station, she brushed a wrinkle from her faded calico. If only she had taken time to change into her Sunday gown! Few in authority took seriously the poor, the illiterate, which was why her trip to this same station last month did no good.

Chin up, she ordered herself. *Look them in the eyes.* For Becky's sake, she must set aside her natural meekness, her feeling of inherent unworthiness, and present herself as a citizen deserving attention. At least she spoke proper English, having absorbed its importance when employed as a maid in the household of the headmaster of King Edward's School.

"As I said last time, Mrs. Libby," said Constable Whittington, "we cannot arrest a man who's done naught."

"He was holding her hand," Jewel argued, attempting to keep her tone steady.

"Not a crime, Mrs. Libby."

"He asked her to go to the cellar with him."

"Aye?" An eyebrow raised. "Did she go?"

"No. But—"

"Bright girl. And so he didn't forcefully carry her, did he?"

"He may have, if I hadn't arrived early."

"Mrs. Libby, if we arrested for *may haves*, we'd have to build more jails. Why do you not find another place to live?"

"I've tried to find one as cheap."

"What about your family?"

"I've no family, sir."

"None at all?"

She held back a sigh. Did the *wheres* and *whys* have any bearing upon the situation? Norman's childhood was spent in the Asylum for the Infant Poor on Summer Lane. She knew not the whereabouts of her father, whose drunken ways had contributed to the premature death of her mother when Jewel was twelve.

"None," she repeated.

"Then marry again," he advised in a fatherly, not familiar manner. "A smart-looking woman such as you should have no trouble finding a husband."

How many times had Jewel been so advised? She was no fool. She knew a husband would indeed take the load from her shoulders. Norman would have forgiven her. But the corset factory sewing room was shy of men, and those living in the tenement were either married, layabouts, or drunks.

Don't give up! said a little voice inside. "Sir," she said, "have you a daughter?"

The constable's weary gray eyes studied her.

Jewel held her breath, cautiously hopeful.

He sighed. "What's the name of the gent who owns your building?"

The hope wavered. "I-I don't know. We have dealings only with Mr. Dunstan."

"Well, I'll look him up in the town records, pay him an unofficial call. May be that other tenants have complained."

"Oh, thank—!"

He held up his hands. "Now, don't go thanking me. I can't guarantee he'll give a hedgehog's fleas about your problem. Some are like that . . . don't want to be troubled by the folk who put bread on their tables."

But at least it was some action. Despite his protest, she thanked him again.

"Will you tell me a story, Mother?" Becky asked in bed that evening, after a supper of potatoes and cabbage, followed by baths in the kitchen using flannels.

Jewel smiled in the darkness. Times like this, with her daughter curled beside her, she could almost forget Mr. Dunstan even existed. Almost.

"Which story?" she asked.

"Um . . . 'Silverhair and the Bears'?"

"Very well." Another gleaning from the educated household was the wealth of stories stored in Jewel's brain, for both the headmaster and his wife had read to their children.

"Once upon a time, a wee girl named Silverhair was told to stay indoors while her mother worked at the corset factory. . . ."

Not the headmaster's version, but Jewel had to seize any teaching moment available. When her daughter drifted off to sleep, Jewel prayed, *God help us*. Ofttimes that was all she could manage before succumbing to fatigue, but this night she added, *Please make the owner listen to the police.*

She could hear Becky's soft snoring and the scurrying of rodent feet in the attic. An infant wailed from the flat below. Somewhere down the corridor, a man began shouting. His words were muffled; the anger behind them was not.

And please . . . She swallowed saltiness as her eyes brimmed. *Help us have better lives one day.*

The following morning, she tucked her handkerchief-wrapped jam sandwich into an apron pocket and delivered a still-sleepy Becky to Mrs. Platt with a reminder to both that she was to stay indoors. And again, for ten hours she had to struggle to concentrate on the needle, so deep were her misgivings.

What if Mr. Dunstan is the owner's brother or some other relation? What if we're forced to leave?

Her fears were justified that evening, unhappily so, when she spotted Mr. Dunstan outside the factory.

"Oh dear," she said to Mrs. Fenton.

"I forgot my handkerchief," Mrs. Fenton said, turning back for the door.

Jewel attempted to hurry past him, lose him in the press of workers, but he fell in step beside her.

"There's been a misunderstanding, Mrs. Libby," he said. "I didn't mean to frighten you over your little girl."

Walking faster did no good. His legs were longer, and he was not even breathing heavily. "I'm truly sorry . . ."

Jewel swallowed a sob.

". . . so I need you to speak with Mr. Brown."

She did not ask who this Mr. Brown was, for she had no word to spare for Mr. Dunstan. Besides, who could he be but the owner of the blocks of flats?

"He stays late in his office. I need you to come with me . . . say you've made a mistake."

"No," she said tightly.

"Please," he cajoled with voice breaking. "I need my job."

She continued on, teeth clenched.

"I'll . . . cut your next month's rent by half, and cover the rest myself."

Jewel halted in her tracks, almost did not recognize her own voice for all the rage it held. "My daughter is not for sale!"

"Do you need help, Mrs. Libby?" came a voice from behind.

Jewel turned a burning face to Mr. Fowler and his assistant, Mr. Evans. "This man—"

But when she looked over her shoulder, Mr. Dunstan was making tracks.

"Coward." Mr. Fowler spat on the pavement.

The men turned back for the factory. Mrs. Fenton called out to her a moment later. Jewel waited, still sick at heart, but grateful.

"You sent Mr. Fowler out?" she asked.

"It was the only thing I knew to do."

Jewel squeezed her arm.

"Do you suppose he's been sacked?" Mrs. Fenton asked.

"I think so."

Mrs. Platt's aggrieved expression confirmed it was true when Jewel arrived to retrieve Becky. "Did ye hear?" she said, spotted hands worrying her frayed collar. "Mr. Dunstan's been sacked!"

Ironing her face of any expression, Jewel took Becky's hand. *Thank you, Father!*

Mrs. Platt's eyes narrowed. "Did you have aught to do with this?"

Jewel still needed her to tend Becky. Gently, she said, "I'm sorry you're displeased."

"You'll be, too, when they replace him with a heartless sot like Mr. Archer."

Jewel's lips tightened. *As long as he leaves Becky be, I don't care if he has a walnut for a heart.*

Chapter 2

21 April 1884
Gresham, England

"Hold still, dear," said seamstress Beatrice Perkins, on her knees pinning the hem of the gown.

"I'm sorry," Grace said. "There was a bird outside your window. It brought to mind a crippled sparrow I once nursed back to health."

"Betrothal makes you remember all sorts of things," Mrs. Perkins said knowingly. "Would you agree, Mrs. Phelps?"

"Yes, that's so," Julia replied, being pulled from her own memories of when the bride-to-be was a babe in her arms. When poised in the doorway to a new life, it was only natural to send some looks over the shoulder at the old one.

Mrs. Perkins returned her attention to the task at hand. "Now, if it seems too high from the ground, remember the six inches of lace. You'll not be flashing your ankles to the church."

"Her father will be happy for that," Julia said, causing Mrs. Perkins to chuckle. Grace smiled down from her perch upon the stool, a curly-haloed angel in white silk.

Several loud knocks sounded against a wall, and the angel lost her footing. Julia jumped to offer a steadying hand.

"Easy does it now," Mrs. Perkins said. "That's just my Priscilla."

A minute later the knocking came again, and more loudly.

"Shall I see about her?" Julia asked.

"That's very kind of you, but she'll stop when Frances brings up a tray." Mrs. Perkins glanced at the wall clock. "Half past nine? Ah . . . I remember. She wants to go to Shrewsbury for a bonnet. She doesn't usually raise her head from the pillow before eleven."

"I'm sorry," Julia said. But a sympathetic expression required some effort. Priscilla was, after all, a year older than Grace, and of sound body and mind.

Grace had enough sympathy on her heart-shaped face for the both of them. "Why don't you stop sending up trays, Mrs. Perkins?" she suggested, with the appropriate respect due the older woman.

"Why, she's got to eat."

"But if you didn't send up trays, she'd eventually have to come down."

"And then have her sulk all day?" Mrs. Perkins sniffed. "I admit I coddle Priscilla, her being the only child. Amos says it's high time she find either a husband or position. But easier said than done. Shropshire men don't take to high-spirited women. As to a position, she has no gift for sewing. And I'll not have my daughter slaving in the cheese factory."

Anwyl Mountain Cheeses, north of the River Bryce, was

named for the five-hundred-foot hill rising abruptly to the west. The thought passed through Julia's mind that it would be better for Priscilla's character to be making cheese than banging on walls.

Mrs. Perkins' lips tightened. "But you'd think she'd have some gratitude. Why, even with all the work I've got to do, she's got to have a new frock every month!"

"But she can't force you to—"

"Do stand straight, dear," Julia reminded Grace. "We don't want the hem uneven."

A half hour later Julia and her daughter were strolling homeward. The rainstorms of Easter week had dried, and the village abounded with sweet April color: yellow bellworts, red crown imperials, and violet corydalis nodded over white daffodils, blue anemone, and pink primulas. Green ivy and clematis resumed inching along weathered sandstone walls. Pear trees stood out like lights, with snowy blossoms against pale green leaves. Pink-faced women pegging out fresh laundry or pottering in gardens called out greetings.

"I should get your father some tonic," Julia said as they neared a rosy stone building on the corner of Market and Thatcher Lanes. The bell over Trumbles' door tinkled as they entered. Jack Sanders sent a smile from the postal and telegraph end of the shop as his hands continued sorting envelopes. Orville Trumble ceased arranging cards of needles upon a rack and hurried around the counter.

"How may I assist you, Mrs. Phelps and Miss Hollis?"

"I believe Andrew is almost out of—"

"Smith's Patented Stomach Soother," he finished for her. He swiveled to take an amber bottle from a shelf and slipped it into a small paper bag. His blond hair had thinned to a fringe, but his walrus mustache was in full glory, quivering with each word, legitimate or otherwise.

"My dear wife's mother," Mr. Trumble continued. "After meals, the pain was so bad she would become *historical* until we gave her a dose."

"I'm so sorry," Julia said. "But Andrew's isn't severe. It's usually after a heavy meal, and he has learned to lessen his portions."

The shopkeeper patted his stomach. "That's a *lessen* we should all learn."

Jack Sanders chuckled. Julia and Grace smiled, not so much at the humor but because they were genuinely fond of Mr. Trumble.

On Church Lane they passed the grammar school, where son-in-law Jonathan would be filling thirty-four young heads with knowledge. In the garden of the cottage to their left, Mrs. Shaw left off pruning a forsythia shrub to amble to the fence. Julia asked about her feet, which were apt to swell.

"Much better since I started propping them up three times a day." She was not one to go on about her health problems, but she did offer a bit of advice to Grace.

"Mind your spending, dearie. A woman can send out more with a teaspoon than her husband can bring in with a shovel."

"You'll be getting more and more of that," Julia said when they were out of hearing range. "It's natural for people to want to pass on to the young what they've learned."

"I don't mind," Grace said, and hesitated. "In fact, I had hoped you would offer some advice."

"To Mrs. Shaw?"

"Mrs. Perkins. She works so hard. And to have Priscilla abuse her so."

"Yes," Julia agreed. "There was a stout wind when the apple fell from that tree."

"Apple?" Grace caught on, laughed guiltily, sobered. "But shouldn't you have offered advice?"

"She didn't ask for any, dear."

"You could have helped her. You know more about rearing children than anyone in Gresham."

Julia smiled. "You may be prejudiced, do you think?"

"We turned out to be decent people."

"Oh, indeed. But Priscilla Perkins is twenty-one. It's a bit late for child-rearing advice."

"How can she take advantage of her mother like that?"

"Because Mrs. Perkins allows it. That will never change, as long as she gains something from it."

Grace turned to face her, emerald eyes wide. "What could she possibly gain from it?"

"Well, the feeling of being needed."

"But every mother wants to be needed. Don't you?"

Julia cast about in her mind for the right words. Grace had much still to learn, simply because twenty years was not long enough for the whole curriculum of human nature. Even at forty-six, Julia was still learning.

"Of course I do," she replied. "But when that becomes a mother's primary objective, then she cripples her children. They either become weak and passive or demanding tyrants."

After a thoughtful silence, Grace sighed. "I shall never be as wise as you, Mother."

"Oh heavens, daughter," Julia said. "You're far wiser than I was at your age."

For one example, Grace had gone against the village norm of marrying directly out of school, aware that she was not prepared for the leap into adulthood. Julia had married shortly after her seventeenth birthday, blissfully unaware that she was still a child.

Secondly, Grace was marrying her dearest friend. Thomas Langford, youngest graduate of the Royal Veterinary College, and recently attached to a practice in Telford, was neither the most handsome nor dashing young man to set his cap for Grace. But he was thoughtful, honest, industrious, shared her fondness for animals, and made her laugh.

Julia, on the other hand, had been unable to see the character flaws in her first husband, a charming surgeon whose gambling debts had left her and their three children virtually penniless after his death.

And yet, in spite of it all, God made gold from the rubble, Julia thought. Here she was, married thirteen years to Andrew Phelps, vicar of Gresham and the kindest man on earth. And, as Grace had said, her three children and two stepdaughters had grown into decent adults.

Arm in arm they walked up shady Vicarage Lane. The snug two-storey vicarage rested on a grassy knoll, a stone's throw from Saint Jude's. A white picket fence enclosed the garden, where sat one of those decent adults, Andrew's eldest daughter, Elizabeth. Doctor Rhodes' stooped frame rested in the wicker chair beside her. Some twenty feet behind them, three-year-old twins Claire and Samuel played with croquet balls and mallets.

Elizabeth waved. From the distance, and even up close, she seemed younger than her thirty-three years. Her hair was still golden in the sunshine, the dimples still curved around her smile. She and her younger children visited almost every day of late.

Julia understood her need to get out of the house. Her step-daughter was going through a difficult time, having miscarried a fourth baby the previous Christmas. Thankfully for Elizabeth's sake, the summer holidays were just around the corner, when Jonathan and eleven-year-old John would be home all day.

Samuel's mallet fell to the ground. He headed toward the gate, flaxen curls bobbing, short legs pumping the grass. "Grandmother! Aunt Grace!" he cried, as if he had not sat between both in church just yesterday. By the time Julia opened the gate, Claire had joined her brother.

Julia opened her arms, leaned into their embraces. The two could hardly be taken for sister and brother, much less twins. Samuel was solidly built, with blue eyes. Claire, lithe and an inch taller, had her father's dark hair and gray-green eyes.

"Good morning, sweethearts," Julia said with a peck for each forehead. As Grace kissed the same foreheads, Julia looked past to see Doctor Rhodes making pains to get to his feet. She advanced to the setting of chairs. "Please, don't."

He sank back again. "My aged limbs thank you, Mrs. Phelps."

"Are you here to see Andrew? Is he all right?"

"No, this is a call of another nature." He squinted at the parcel in her hand. "But if he is still having those pains . . ."

Julia sat in a wicker chair, leaned to prop the parcel at her feet. "Very rarely, since he started taking smaller meals, as you suggested. But he does want his tonic available. He doesn't care to suffer one second longer than necessary."

"Nor do any of us. Well, send him over to see me if they grow in intensity."

Julia had to smile. That would be some task.

Doctor Rhodes smiled back. "Or send word, and I shall gather a dozen strong men to drag him in with ropes. A man his age cannot afford to take any ache for granted."

The message in his eyes sobered Julia. What he meant was *a man in his condition,* for at fifty-seven, Andrew was years away from rocking chair and shawl. But just last summer he was diagnosed with a heart murmur, by both Doctor Rhodes and his Shrewsbury colleague, a Doctor Johnson.

Elizabeth had obviously caught the look in his eyes, too, for she leaned forward with furrowed brow. "Is Papa all right? Is his heart . . ."

"Your father is fine, child," Doctor Rhodes answered.

Grace, released from the embraces of the children, walked over and leaned to kiss his lined forehead.

"Were you lovely in your wedding gown, Gracie?" he asked, taking her hand. He had a special place in his heart for her, having, with God's help, snatched her from the jaws of death when she contracted scarlet fever at age ten.

"Mother says I was a princess."

"An angel," Julia corrected.

"I'm quite sure you were both," Elizabeth said without a smidgen of jealousy. "Papa has Titus Worthy and Mrs. Draper in the parlor. Doctor Rhodes and I wonder if there's to be another wedding in the near future."

"Titus Worthy?" Julia was not sure if her ears had heard correctly.

"The old saying is true," Doctor Rhodes said, a glint in his eyes. "There is someone for everyone."

"Now, now," Julia said. "I think that's marvelous. He's a decent man, if a bit rough around the edges."

"Yes, yes. Aren't all we men? If you'll forgive my changing the subject, I have something important to discuss."

"What is it?" Julia asked.

"I'm thinking of giving up my practice."

"Surely not," Grace said, with Elizabeth echoing the same.

"I'm too old to be climbing out of bed at three in the

26

morning to deliver—" His face fell. He looked at Elizabeth. "Forgive me, dear."

She gave him an understanding smile. "Go on, Doctor Rhodes."

He nodded with a grateful expression. "We have a nice little nest egg. I wish to spend the years I have remaining pottering about in the garden. Reading novels. And chiefly, annoying Mrs. Rhodes."

Ophelia Rhodes was Gresham's veterinary doctor for decades, but a trembling palsy had caused her to turn her practice over to a Mr. Beddows eight years ago.

"Good for you," Julia said. "Not the 'annoying Ophelia' part, mind you."

He laughed. "She would not feel loved if I did otherwise."

"But I can't imagine having another doctor," Grace said.

"Well, this person would have to be very special. I have an obligation to my community. Now that I'm long in the tooth, I receive letters from young doctors inquiring about my practice. But given Philip's connection to Gresham, I would first like to ask if he would be interested."

Silence followed. Elizabeth spoke first. "Wouldn't that be wonderful?"

"Wonderful," said Grace.

Both faces mirrored the hope Julia felt. Before entering the University of Edinburgh's College of Medicine at seventeen, her son's biggest dream was to practice medicine in Gresham. But practically on the eve of graduation, a guest lecture by Scottish surgeon Lawson Tait steered Philip's interests toward surgery. Would he have any desire to leave a successful career in the most exciting city on earth for the snail-paced dairying village of his youth? And the decision was not only Philip's to make. Loretta should have a say.

Loretta.

Who, on her one visit to Gresham with Philip four years ago, had rarely left their room. Who had enthused verbally over her parents' wedding gift—a house on Pembridge Gardens—but sat silent when Philip reminded Julia and Andrew how much they appreciated their gift of Royal Doulton china. And whose father was chief surgeon at Saint Bartholomew's Hospital, where Philip practiced.

"All you can do is write and ask," Julia said, as her hopes sagged.

"I hoped you would offer to write. Coming from his mother . . ."

"And that's why I must not." She gave him an apologetic smile. "You understand."

"Yes." The old man sighed. "You're right, of course. Perhaps I should wait until the wedding. Approach him face-to-face."

He got to his feet, and Julia walked him to the gate. On her return, she looked past Elizabeth. "Where are the children?"

There were days when the story simply wrote itself. Aleda Hollis unrolled the page from the Sholes and Glidden typewriter and added it to the growing stack. She inserted a clean sheet, moved the carriage to the right, and attacked the keys anew with her fingertips.

Was ever a night so dark? The fog muffled all sound but the infernal footsteps. They rasped against the damp grass, deliberate, closer and closer. Captain Jacobs' heart swelled in his chest, pounding agai—

"EEEE!"

Aleda's own heart lurched; she jammed the *s* and *t* keys.

The scream dissolved into giggles as she swung open her door. Two faces whipped toward her.

"Samuel found me!" Claire exclaimed, emerging from the linen cupboard.

"I'm a . . . good finder!" Samuel confirmed between hiccups.

Aleda scooped a folded pillowcase from the landing rug and stashed it back onto a shelf. "And what's the rule about playing upstairs?"

A guilty flush spread across Claire's cheeks. Samuel put a chubby finger to his lips. "We must be silent as mice."

"No, the rule is that you must not play upstairs while Aunt Aleda is writing."

"We didn't know you were writing," Claire said. "Your door was closed."

"That's how you know I'm writing. And you're being very naughty, making noise while your grandfather has guests in the parlor. Where is your mother?"

"In the garden," Claire replied.

Aleda guided the children downstairs, past the parlor, through the door, and across the porch. But the wicker chairs sat empty.

"There they are" came Elizabeth's voice as she, Mother, and Grace appeared from the side of the house.

"These little moppets were crawling into cupboards!" Aleda grumbled.

Elizabeth advanced, frowning. But instead of scolding the children, she looked Aleda up and down and said, "Mercy, sister! Do you dress blindfolded?"

"Elizabeth . . ." Mother said.

Because Aleda had actually forgotten what garments she

had thrown over her body that morning, she looked down at her ink-stained chartreuse blouse and red skirt.

"I happen to be too busy to labor over my wardrobe. And there is the matter of the children?"

Finally her stepsister directed her attention where it belonged. "Who gave you permission to go indoors?"

"We wanted to ask Mr. Smith for a ride on Belle," said Claire, the more verbose of the two. Luke Smith was the vicarage caretaker. "But he wasn't in the stable. We looked in the kitchen—"

"We looked in the kitchen," Samuel echoed.

"—but he wasn't there, either," Claire finished, and lowered her eyes. "I'm sorry, Mother."

Samuel mumbled something equally apologetic if indiscernible.

Elizabeth's voice softened as she patted their heads. "Well, just be mindful next time."

It was just as she would have expected, Aleda thought, accompanying the group to the chairs and dropping into one.

"What do you say to a turn around the green?" Grace asked the children.

They were reduced to quivers of eagerness, with Claire pressing hands together and Samuel hopping on one foot. They turned to Elizabeth. "May we, Mother?"

"Very well. Mind you obey your aunt Grace, and stay away from the river."

The two practically pulled Grace from the garden. Elizabeth touched Aleda's elbow. "I'm sorry they interrupted your work."

Aleda's martyred feelings crumbled. How could she fault Elizabeth for her softness with the children? How fragile they must seem, when Elizabeth's own womb had not afforded safety to the ones she had lost.

She shrugged and smiled at her stepsister. "It's no bother. I would be coming down for lunch in an hour anyway. Who does Father have in the parlor? I heard voices."

"Titus Worthy and Mrs. Draper," Elizabeth replied with eyes shining.

"You jest?"

As if on cue, the door opened and Father stepped out onto the porch with the couple. Titus Worthy and the widow Mrs. Draper were as different as chalk and cheese. Yet, something had changed. Aleda blinked. Gone was the gamekeeper's tangled beard. His matted hair was cut close to the head and appeared clean. A well-pressed suit replaced wrinkled dirty clothes.

Mrs. Draper, tidy as ever in a pale blue gown, returned Mother's wave but continued down the flagstone walk, her arm linked through Mr. Worthy's. Father accompanied them to the gate, then advanced toward the chairs, smiling so widely his hazel eyes crinkled, and the dimples were visible beneath his blond beard.

He was actually Aleda's stepfather since she was twelve. Like Grace and Philip, she adored him for stepping into the void left by their own father; a void present long before his death.

"Where are the twins?" he asked, settling into a chair.

"With Grace," Elizabeth answered. "Don't keep us in suspense, Papa."

He glanced over at the lane to make certain the couple were out of hearing. "Yesterday the squire gave Mr. Worthy permission to move in with Mrs. Draper, after they're married. The gamekeeper's cottage is too small for six children. He can perform his duties from her home just as well."

"He can perform them from Africa just as well," Aleda

31

quipped. No one understood why the squire even retained a gamekeeper, once his diet became limited to bland foods. Mr. Worthy's job basically was to keep poachers with their guns out of the woods nearest the manor house. But what few poachers there were preferred the north woods across the river, not crisscrossed by paths and invaded by berry pickers and mushroom gatherers.

"They wish to move the date closer?" Mother asked.

"I hope it doesn't conflict with Grace's wedding," Elizabeth said.

"What date did they set?" Aleda asked.

Father smiled. "A quarter of an hour ago."

"I beg your pardon?" Julia said.

"I pressed Luke and Dora into service as witnesses."

"So that's where Luke was," Elizabeth said.

"But why the hurry?" Aleda asked.

"They feared the squire might change his mind. His disposition has become worse, according to Mr. Worthy."

"The poor man," Julia said.

"Tragic," Elizabeth murmured.

Aleda arranged her face into a sympathetic expression. She really did pity Squire Bartley. But she could not stop her thoughts from racing toward a certain cottage in Gipsy Woods.

Chapter 3

The red sandstone manor house had been as unapproachable as a prison ever since the squire's wife, Octavia Kingston Bartley, slipped out of life while tending her precious roses five years ago. So it was with some flutters of nerves that Aleda trod the winding stone path through Squire Bartley's austere gardens.

She was dressed smartly for her mission. Even Elizabeth would approve. Housemaid Wanetta had ironed and starched her white blouse, and her skirt of tan Irish poplin with blue print flowed fluidly from her wide leather belt. While she wore a petticoat for modesty's sake, she did not even own a bustle. She adored her mother and sisters, who wore them, but was embarrassed for her gender that such a fashion even existed. What man would be so foolish as to attach a wire frame contraption beneath his trousers to exaggerate his bottom?

A gardener planting bulbs ignored her, and a young man

picking up sticks from the grass merely touched the brim of his hat, which gave her some courage. *Fear makes the wolf bigger than he is,* she reminded herself.

She mounted the porch, rapped the knocker, and was shortly face-to-face with the housekeeper, bosomy and round shouldered, dark hair peppered with gray, and keys hanging from her waist. Aleda knew her to be Horatia Cooper, a relation of Philip's school chum Jeremiah Toft, who now worked as the squire's groomsman.

"Good morning, Mrs. Cooper. May I ask a moment of the squire's time?"

Mrs. Cooper shook her head. "I'm afraid he's not seeing visitors, Miss Hollis."

This was expected. He no longer accepted even Father's calls.

"But I'm not exactly a visitor. It's more of a business matter."

"All business matters are handled by Mr. Matthews. He manages the factory."

"It doesn't have anything to do with the cheese factory," Aleda said while frustration gnawed at her insides.

Mrs. Cooper shook her head again. "I'm sorry, but I have my orders, miss."

That quelled all argument. Desperate as she was, Aleda could not ask this woman to risk her position. It was an ill-conceived idea anyway. Caught up in a surge of disappointment, she said, "I so desperately wanted to buy the gamekeeper's cottage."

"Titus Worthy's? But he informed us but an hour ago it's to be empty."

"Yes. And I practically ran all the way here. The thought of so much lovely privacy . . ."

But what was the use of standing there, rattling like a pebble in a jar? Aleda sighed, took a backwards step. "Forgive me for taking you from your duties. But . . . if you ever hear the squire mention the cottage, will you put in a good word for me?"

Mrs. Cooper pressed her lips together thoughtfully, glanced over her shoulder, and lowered her voice. "I'm very sorry, but the squire cannot be disturbed while he takes his tea in the conservatory. This very moment."

Dumbstruck, Aleda stared at her.

Mrs. Cooper's voice returned to its former level. "So as you can see, no visitors are allowed. I must ask you to leave."

"Yes, of course." Aleda reached out for the woman's work-worn hand, squeezed it. "Thank you."

She rounded the corner to the south side. In view were the stone smokehouse and dairy, barn and piggery, carriage house and stables. Some sixty feet away, a laundress pegged out wash, taking no notice of her.

The glass-and-wood-frame conservatory jutted out from the west side, no doubt added midcentury or later to the Georgian house. Aleda and her mother and sisters had once taken tea with Mrs. Bartley here. Aleda braced herself at the glass door. A five-foot monkey puzzle tree hindered her view. She could not tell if the squire was indeed inside.

"Miss? If you please?"

Aleda held her breath, turned. The laundress was striding toward her.

Oh dear. Aleda sent her a casual wave, as if perfectly in her place, and turned the knob in her hand.

"See here, miss!" she heard, louder.

Aleda flung open the door and hastened inside. *In for a penny, in for a pound.* Even as her heart hammered, she could appreciate the sweet musty scents of soil and living things: gardenias, mystic ferns, roses, orchids, hydrangeas.

"Who is there?" That unmistakable voice. Vocal cords made of flint.

"Aleda Hollis, sir," she replied, edging around the tree.

She met a pair of scowling gray eyes topped by tufts of white brows. The squire's tall frame seemed to have shrunk, or perhaps the wheelchair and lap rug made it seem so. Otherwise, he seemed not to have aged in the five years since Aleda had last clapped eyes upon him. But then, he had always seemed ancient, with his bald head and lined face. A tray rested upon an occasional table beside him. Precisely arranged were a saucer and cup filled with what appeared to be more milk than tea, a small pink china teapot, and a dish holding two bland-looking biscuits.

"Why are you here?" he demanded.

Behind her, Aleda heard the door open, the maid's voice. "Squire! There's a woman came—"

"I wouldn't disturb you, but I desperately wish to buy your gamekeeper's cottage."

"Miss, you must leave!" came from her right.

"It would be the most tranquil place to—"

"Shall I get Mr. Toft, Squire?" asked the maid.

The squire stared up at Aleda as if trying to decide.

"Please, sir."

"No." He blew out a pained sigh. "Leave her be. For now."

Finally Aleda risked a look to the right, expecting a venomous expression. But the young maid seemed too stunned for anger. A second later she was gone.

"Thank you, Squire." Aleda cleared her throat, stepped closer. "How are you keeping?"

"Marvelously. But you'll forgive me if I don't rise. I

danced the night away, drank to excess, and now must pay the piper."

He was mocking her. Aleda nodded. "I'm sorry, sir."

A pale spotted hand lifted, dropped back to his lap. "Your stories are quite entertaining."

"You read them?"

"I have subscribed to *Argosy Magazine*, among other publications, for decades."

"You're very kind."

"How long have you wanted to write?" he asked, ignoring the compliment.

"Since I was a girl."

"You write like a man. All those adventures. Not a lot of flowery words."

"I've also had stories in *Blackwood's Edinburgh Magazine* and *The Cornhill Magazine*."

"I have seen some. How does that happen to a girl from Gresham?"

"Well, I did graduate from Newnham College. But I got my start in *Argosy*. A dear friend introduced me to the editors."

"Ah . . . connections."

Defensively, Aleda added, "Even they wouldn't publish them if they were inferior."

"Of course not. Do sit. My neck grows weary. There is a stool somewhere to your left."

Aleda located the stool near a small apricot tree, placed it three feet directly in front of the squire so that his neck could be relieved of turning duty, as well.

"So you're here to inquire about the gamekeeper's cottage. Why do you wish to live in the middle of the woods?"

"It's not in the middle of the woods." The path from East Church Street to the cottage meandered only about a hundred feet. Far enough for seclusion, yet close enough to the manor house to ensure no poachers with guns. "But I would relish the privacy."

"For writing."

"Yes. The vicarage has too many callers. It's time I left the nest anyway. And I've loved that cottage since I was a child."

"Slipping out to play in my woods, no doubt?"

The worst he can do is order me away, Aleda reminded herself. "All children play in the woods, sir. Didn't you?"

He snorted a sharp laugh. "When I last set eyes upon it, it was not fit for a lady, due to Titus Worthy's slovenly ways. I can only assume it has declined since then."

"I like rustic. And I can hire any cleaning necessary."

"It has no water closet."

"A privy was good enough for Shakespeare."

Again he chuckled. "Why do you not stay at the Larkspur Inn? Your mother still owns it, correct?"

"Yes. I gave that a try. Too many people. It was not conducive to writing."

"Why not take rooms in the city?" the squire asked. "No one bothers another person in the city."

"On the occasions I come up for air, I want to be with family. It has to be Gresham."

His eyes scowled under their thatching of white brows. Yet his voice was amiable as he said, "You are tenacious, Miss Hollis. You should consider going into business if you ever tire of writing."

Aleda smiled, any remnants of fear gone. "I take that as a compliment, Squire Bartley. Now, as to your cottage . . ."

"How is your family?"

She was at his mercy. "They're well, thank you."

"I've heard something from my servants about a wedding."

"Yes, sir. Grace marries Thomas Langford on the seventeenth of May."

He shook his head wonderingly. "Little Gracie."

"She's twenty."

"Ah, time flies."

Not quickly enough. Aleda risked a glance to her watch. A gift from her parents upon graduating from Newnham, it was of pure gold with tiny diamonds circling the face.

"You would be more than welcome at the wedding," she said.

"I think not. I tire too easily. But give her my best wishes. Grace was Octavia's favorite."

"She's everyone's favorite."

"Does that make you envious?"

"Not at all." Aleda gave him a sincere smile. "She's my favorite, too."

"And your brother? Philip?"

Aleda was not so pleased with him. But that was not for public consumption. "He's a surgeon at Saint Bartholomew's."

Squire Bartley tapped his temple. "Bright young man, he always was. Any children?"

Just his wife. "None so far."

"And Vicar Phelps's daughters?"

"They're well. Elizabeth is busy with three children. Laurel's in Ceylon, where her husband, Ben Mayhew, is building a hospital."

"Ceylon." He shook his head. "Humidity and mosquitoes, I should imagine."

"They write that they're happy. They have a baby girl. Abigail."

"Indeed. Everyone starting families but you."

Give me patience, Lord, Aleda thought, shifting on the stool.

On the heels of that thought came awareness. There was only one reason he would drag out the conversation. Loneliness. But why, then, the self-imposed exile? Was the sympathy of friends so odious that he preferred to grieve alone?

"Yes. I'm not married," she confirmed.

"And how old are you?"

"Twenty-six."

"Are there any prospects?"

"Just the prospect of happy solitude."

He actually cackled. "And what has soured you on men?"

"I'm not sour on men. Half of my favorite people are men."

"And children?"

"I adore them," she replied, and thought, *Even those who hide in linen cupboards.*

"Then why do you not wish to marry?"

"Well . . . autonomy."

"Explain?"

Aleda drew in a deep breath, eased it out. "I've become too fond of coming and going as I please. Saving or spending my wages at my own discretion. Traveling at my own whim. And if I shut myself up to write for three days running, I don't have to worry about a husband getting into a huff over being ignored."

"In other words, you're selfish."

"I'm realistic, sir," she argued. "Why embark upon a venture that is contrary to my nature? That will ultimately make not only myself miserable but some other innocent person."

"Will you not mind being referred to as an old maid?"

"I don't mind tossing the village wags a crumb."

This brought on still another laugh. "We are kindred spirits, Miss Hollis."

Not even remotely, Aleda thought before realizing there was some truth to his statement.

It wasn't until her Newnham College years that she realized what a loner she was. While she enjoyed the company of her schoolmates, her sanity was maintained by seeking out an empty lecture room now and again for simply sitting and allowing the solitude to wash over her. Perhaps she had inherited this trait from her birth father, who probably never should have married, for all the notice he took of his family.

She pulled herself out of her thoughts and realized the old man was wiping his eyes with his fingertips.

"May I find you a handkerchief, sir?" she asked.

"I was just thinking of how, in my old age, I found myself unable to bear spending one day apart from my dear Octavia."

"Yes," Aleda said softly. "I'm sorry about Mrs. Bartley. She was a dear soul."

"Thank you." After several seconds, he shook his head. "I cannot sell the cottage. Seven generations of Bartleys would roll in their graves if I parceled out part of the land."

"But you once sold some pastureland to Seth Langford."

"Property I acquired separately, not attached to the estate. The ghosts of my forebears will take issue enough with me when I leave all to my sister's son, Donald, thereby tossing the family name into the ash bin."

"I see." That was that. Aleda sighed, got to her feet. "Thank you for your time."

But the squire continued speaking, as if she had merely risen to pour herself a second cup of tea. *If* she had been offered a first cup.

"I have no more relations, to my knowledge. The Bartleys have never been a prolific lot."

"I'm sorry."

"You may rent the cottage," he said.

Aleda sat again. "I may?"

"I say nothing I do not mean."

"Yes." The hope that rose in Aleda's chest sank just as quickly. The squire was practically leaning against heaven's gatepost. What if she were to spend money readying the cottage, only to have the nephew evict her?

"You're concerned about Donald, aren't you?" he asked.

"I am," she admitted.

"My solicitor—Mr. Baker—comes up from Shrewsbury the first Friday morning of each month. I shall have him draw up an agreement granting you exclusive rights to the cottage and garden. The standard rural lease is for twenty-one years, or you may renew your rights for two more terms at signing . . . meaning sixty-three years."

She blinked at him.

"The first choice implies that I shall be alive in twenty-one years to renew your lease. If it helps you decide, I don't feel well most days."

Aleda nodded. "The latter would be best. Thank you, Squire."

"I'm being entirely selfish, Miss Hollis. I want you to continue writing your stories." He eyed her. "How does three pounds per annum strike you?"

Her breath caught in her throat. "Three pounds?"

"You said yourself, the cottage needs repairs. And I like the thought of my nephew having to honor the agreement as long as he lives." He smiled to himself. "Now, you may take your leave. Go through the house this time. And inform Mrs. Cooper I wish to take my nap."

"Yes, sir." Aleda rose, thanked him again. At the door leading into the house, she hesitated, turned.

"I could visit now and then, read my stories to you."

"No," he said. "If you aim for solitude, take your solitude. I can read to myself just fine."

Guiltily relieved, she had her hand on the knob when he added, "But Vicar Phelps may visit, if he still has a mind to."

Aleda turned again, smiled. "He would like that."

"Perhaps your mother would care to come along." He gave her a sheepish look. "She's fond of chocolate cake, as I recall. I could have Cook bake one."

"They'll be pleased," Aleda said. "With or without cake."

She broke the news to her parents and Grace at the supper table, over dishes of rump steak pie, spinach, and poached eggs.

"You're leaving?" said Father. "Again?"

"I stayed at the Larkspur only a week," Aleda said. "You speak as if I flit about from place to place all the time."

"Oh, well a week's not flitting, is it?" he teased.

She made a face at him.

"But alone in the woods," Grace said. "They're so dark at night. Will you not be frightened, Aleda?"

"I don't think I will," she replied. "I'll lay in a supply of lamp oil."

Her mother had made no comment, and rose to dish out servings of lemon blancmange at the sideboard. Warily, Aleda watched her straight back. Her stepfather and Grace followed her gaze.

"Mother?" Aleda asked.

Her mother turned, smiled. "You're old enough to know your own mind, Aleda. If it doesn't suit you, you can always move back home. Now, who'll have pudding?"

Chapter 4

On the morning of the twenty-fifth of April, Julia and Andrew set out in the phaeton behind Belle, their gray Cleveland Bay mare. Now that the children were grown, Julia had fallen into the habit of accompanying her husband on his calls to parishioners. He would never have asked. His view was she was not married to the church and had the right to pursue her own interests.

Pursue them she did: grandchildren, gardening, reading, and the Women's Charity Society. But her inherent empathy and Andrew's nature made her desire to spend even more time with him, and he was of course pleased with her company.

He automatically gave the reins a gentle tug outside a certain low stone wall at the village crossroads. Belle slowed from a trot to a walk. Julia rested her eyes fondly on a well-tended garden before a rosy sandstone building.

The lodging house had started out as a thriving coaching inn, before the Severn Valley Railway laid tracks twelve miles to the south in Shrewsbury. Fifteen years ago the Larkspur sat in a state of profound neglect, and thus the London bankers who had seized even her wedding ring to pay her late husband's debts had shown no interest in it.

It was here that Julia, her children, and loyal housemaid Fiona O'Shea had fled after the foreclosures, armed with a loan from her late husband's butler. They refurbished the place and advertised a lodging house for those wishing the sedate way of life that a dairying village could offer. Companionship with like-minded people was a draw, as well, with the happy by-product being a marriage now and again.

Including Fiona's, to actor Ambrose Clay. Their rooms over the stables sat empty during the run of a play but would be again filled with their sweet voices come July, when *Anne Boleyn* was set to close in New York.

"Do you ever miss running the Larkspur?" Andrew asked. When Julia married him and moved into the vicarage, she had hired Mr. Jensen, the butler who had lent her the money. Even in his old age, he managed the inn with genteel efficiency and was now married to the former Mrs. Dearing, one of the first lodgers.

"It had its moments," Julia said, and squeezed his arm. "But I'm content where I am, Vicar."

"I'm glad to hear it, Mrs. Phelps," he said. "I hope you're of the same mind when the nest is empty."

And that day was coming soon. At this moment, Aleda was arranging with Squire Bartley's solicitor to lease the gamekeeper's cottage. They would have Grace at home for only three more weeks.

"It'll be an adjustment," Julia admitted. "For both of us. We've been parents for over half our lives."

"At least they're not moving away, like Laurel, and Philip."

"I'm grateful for that."

"So am I." He smiled. "And we'll have our own adventures. Just like the children."

"We're too old for adventures," she teased.

"Not at all. You're not officially old until you stop seeking them."

Belle's hooves rang against the stone bridge over the blue waters of the Bryce. Northwards was where most of the dairy farms were situated, where black-and-white Friesian cows grazed in fields bordered by hedgerows. Presently they turned eastward along Milkwort Lane, named not for the dairies but for the profusion of wild flowers flanking both sides.

They stopped outside a stone cottage with washhouse, privy, and smokehouse, and two pigs in a sty. Andrew held open the gate leading through a garden filled with lilacs and laburnum and pinks, squeezed in by the more important rows of broccoli and onions, parsnips and lettuces, young bean and cucumber plants, and potato vines.

"Why, good morning, Vicar, Mrs. Phelps," said Margery Stokes, rising from a stone bench. Beside her, a boy who could have been anywhere from nine to thirteen sat with one foot tucked behind the other. He was as thin as a reed, with hollow cheeks and wide uncertain eyes. His shirt and trousers were clean, if worn, castoffs from an older child. The blond hair and pale skin, however, reeked from the familiar odor of sulfur and lard. Most of the street waifs Mr. Stokes brought back from London after his biannual meetings with bankers were afflicted with lice of head and body.

"This is Gerald," Mrs. Stokes said after the exchange of greetings. In the boy's lap lay open an alphabet picture book. Most of the new arrivals were illiterate. To spare the older ones the humiliation of towering over wee classmates in the infant school, Margery Stokes tutored them until they could manage at least the primary lessons in the grammar school. She turned to the lad. "Will you say good morning to Vicar and Mrs. Phelps, Gerald?"

He ducked his head. Mrs. Stokes gave his larded tresses an understanding pat, then wiped her hands with her apron. "Poor mite, having to bear this muck for a whole week."

Julia smiled. Margery was as rough as she was kind, having spent much of her childhood on a milking stool. She was large-boned but not stout, with beautiful brown eyes and ash brown hair twisted into a convenient knot.

Her husband, Horace Stokes, Squire Bartley's accountant, kept an office at the cheese factory. As the story was told, he had worked as an under gardener at the manor house until age fourteen, when in a puzzling act of philanthropy, the squire paid to have him articled to a prominent Shrewsbury accountant. He showed such a gift for numbers that when the longtime accountant was pensioned from the cheese factory, Mr. Stokes overtook his position at the tender age of twenty-three.

Perhaps it was because he and his wife had both known poverty as children that they took in boys and girls like a widow takes in stray cats. Sixteen thus far, including three of their own making.

"Will you come in for some tea?" Mrs. Stokes asked.

"No thank you," Andrew said, and gave Julia a meaningful look. "At least, none for me. What say I help Gerald finish his book while you ladies chat?"

The lad's shoulders rose and fell sharply, and he appeared

poised to sprint, but only inched away to the far edge as Andrew settled beside him.

"Mind you don't get any of the grease on your clothes, Vicar," Mrs. Stokes warned. "It's a right chore to get out."

The parlor and kitchen were tidy, as Julia had expected. The children had duties both in house and garden but were allowed playtime as well. As Jonathan had said, it was a joy to watch pale, timid creatures blossom into rosy-cheeked children.

"Gerald is the last," Mrs. Stokes said, bringing the kettle to the kitchen table. "I've warned Horace not to bring any more home. We're bursting at the seams."

Julia smiled, raised her brows, and sipped her tea. Mrs. Stokes stared at her for a moment, then laughed.

"Yes, I know I said that before Nancy. And Tom."

"And Alma," Julia reminded her.

Mrs. Stokes winced. "But this time, it's got to stick."

Julia allowed a second to pass, two, before broaching the reason for their call. "I spoke with Mrs. Perkins recently. If you'll bring the children by as soon as possible, she'll have time to make each a set of school clothes before next term." She drew in a breath. "And two Sunday gowns for you."

"She will, you say?" Mrs. Stokes set her cup down sharply. A drop of tea sloshed over the rim and into the saucer. "And who's to pay for this?"

"The Women's Charity Society is not involved," Julia said quickly. The word *charity* was as distasteful to the Stokes as any oath.

"So, it's a ghost, then?"

"No, of course not." Julia sighed. "It's Andrew and me."

Already, Margery was shaking her head. Julia reached over to lay a hand upon her sleeve. "I understand how you feel. But I'm asking you not to allow pride to stand in the way. . . ."

"Pride?" Margery said. "You weren't raised poor. You don't understand how handouts tear down your very soul."

"I wasn't raised poor," Julia agreed. "However, my first husband's death left the children and me with nothing. If we hadn't had the Larkspur, we would have had to ask for parish assistance."

The gambling debts which caused such deprivation were not important to the matter at hand. Julia had her own issues with pride.

"I'm sorry that happened to you," Margery said. "But Horace draws decent wages. It's just that we have—"

"So many children," Julia finished for her, and softened her voice. "Mrs. Perkins is willing to keep to herself who settles the bill. Andrew and I don't think of you as charity cases. We simply hope to share in the joy you get from providing for those sweet children. Would you rob us of a blessing, Margery?"

Margery opened her mouth to argue, closed it. "Horace will never agree."

"Andrew will be visiting his office this afternoon. It would go a long way if he could say you were willing."

Another pause, and Margery nodded. "Thank you, Mrs. Phelps."

Julia squeezed her hand. "It's our pleasure."

"But no Sunday gowns. You've got to allow me some pride."

"Very well," said Julia, disappointed but understanding.

When they stepped outdoors again, Andrew was beaming and held up the small leather-bound notebook he carried in his coat pocket. Even the boy looked timidly pleased.

"Would you look at this?" Andrew said. "I asked if he could write his name."

With pencil the boy had expertly sketched Belle and the

carriage beyond the gate, and even the skeins of white clouds in the southern sky.

"Amazing," Julia declared, taking the notebook. The corners were greasy, but she had to trust that there was enough sulfur to kill any of the little crawlies.

Even Margery was surprised. "Why, we've got us a Mozart here."

Julia caught the glint in Andrew's hazel eyes. Not for all the gold in Shropshire would either have corrected her. Nurturing orphans covered a multitude of factual errors.

"We should stop at Mrs. Hopper's," Julia said back in the phaeton. "She'll be hurt if she spots us."

Andrew groaned. "She wasn't in her garden."

"And how would you know? You kept your eyes straight ahead."

He reluctantly agreed, but then the discussion was moot. A hundred yards back up Milkwort Lane, Mrs. Hopper stood at the gate of her tidy and symmetrical garden, beckoning. She welcomed them into a parlor as orderly as a museum, offered pleasantries about the weather and cups of good strong tea.

Julia was not fooled. The path from Mrs. Hopper's mind to her lips was a straight track, an express train bypassing such stations as discretion, compassion, and judgment. It would be somewhat understandable if she were elderly, beset by ailments and harsh memories, but Mrs. Hopper appeared to be only a few years older than herself. Few gray hairs stood out against her dark topknot.

"The Stokes have took in another stray," Mrs. Hopper said.

Julia's sociable smile faded.

"Mrs. Hopper . . ." Andrew said with brows meeting. "Animals are strays."

51

"Well, they behave like animals. Spilling out in the lane every afternoon, chasing each other, riding that pony back and forth!"

"Their land is taken up with crops," Andrew said with terse gentleness. "And between school and chores and supper, how long can they be out there?"

"Long enough to be a nuisance!"

I moved from Worton Lane for some peace, Julia thought, and waited.

"I moved up from Worton Lane for some peace!" Mrs. Hopper said.

I can hardly keep my mind on my needlework, Julia thought.

"I can hardly keep my mind on my Bible pages," Mrs. Hopper said.

Shrewd, Julia thought. But Mrs. Hopper was mistaken if she thought throwing in a little piety would sway Andrew.

Her husband leaned forward, resting elbows on knees. "Mrs. Hopper, when you read in those pages where Jesus says to suffer the children to come to Him, do you think He referred only to the children milling about Him that day?"

Mrs. Hopper opened her mouth, closed it, opened it again. "I don't know."

"I strongly believe He was sending us a message, as well. The Stokes bring those children to church, pray with them, demonstrate God's love to them in a hundred different ways. I think it's grand that you live close enough to witness all this. Why, you could become like a doting aunt. How full your life would be."

For only a fraction of a second did her expression soften. Her lips tightened again. "If I wished to be a doting aunt, I would have stayed in the house Mr. Hopper and I shared, between his sisters, when he passed on. Will you speak with them or not?"

"I will ask them to have the children play farther down in the other direction." Andrew sighed and got to his feet. "Though I must add, it will make it harder for Mr. and Mrs. Stokes to keep an eye out for them."

"Thank you," Mrs. Hopper said, nonplussed.

Julia stood, as well. "Thank you for the tea."

"Why, you're welcome. It's Twinings. The only brand I buy." Their hostess had slipped back into her public persona.

"I pray that's not Aleda in twenty years," Julia said when the carriage was out of earshot of the sterile little cottage.

"I don't think you have to worry," Andrew assured her. "Aleda's mind may be insular, but her heart is kind."

She squeezed his arm. "It's a shame about the boy's foot."

"What do you mean?" Andrew asked.

"Mrs. Stokes said he has a clubfoot."

"My, my." Andrew shook his head. "Poor little chap."

"But at least he has a home now," Julia said. "Do you think you can talk Mr. Stokes into accepting the clothes?"

"I believe so," Andrew replied. "Mrs. Stokes is his chief obstacle. He doesn't wish to look small in her eyes by accepting charity."

"Small," Julia echoed wryly. "They're the biggest people I know."

She did not mean in size. But there was no need to explain to the man beside her. *God, keep him healthy,* she prayed. The heart murmur worried her, and now the stomach pains, though he claimed to feel fine today.

It was Andrew who had asked her not to sell the Larkspur when a London investor offered a goodly sum. It comforted him to know she would have a place to go without being beholden to the children. Vicarages were for ministers, not their widowed wives. And the income from the Larkspur, while not a fortune after salaries and supplies, provided a bulwark against misfortune. Even if Andrew were to live a long life, vicars' pensions were barely adequate. It was nice having breathing room and the liberty to be generous with others. God was so good.

"Fancy a stop at Trumbles?" he asked.

"Of course," Julia replied, concerned anew. Andrew cared for shopping almost as little as for going to the doctor. "You haven't finished that bottle of tonic already, have you?"

"Tonic? I've not even opened it. I want to buy paper and pencils for that boy." He pursed his lips in thought for a second or two. "What do you think of watercolors, as well?"

Julia smiled at him. "Wonderful."

⁓∞⁓

The man for whom the cottage was built—Squire Bartley's great-grandfather's first gamekeeper, was married with children, and thus rated a shelter more accommodating than most gamekeepers' huts. The rosy stone cottage, situated in a hollow and embosomed by trees, was small by village standards but more than large enough to suit Aleda.

Kitchen, larder, and open parlor took up the ground floor. A wooden staircase led up to two bedrooms and loft. A chimney rose above the two dormers in the gray slate stone roof.

Aleda hired Mr. and Mrs. Summers, cheese factory workers who took on odd jobs after their shifts. For four days, in the remaining daylight, Mrs. Summers scrubbed the rooms to shining.

Her husband hacked away and mowed the weed-choked garden, leaving only the gooseberry shrub against the back fence, per Aleda's orders. She had neither time nor inclination to coddle plants that were not edible, but the pale green rob-in's egg-sized fruits would be a refreshing treat when summer came.

Mr. Summers also hauled away Mr. Worthy's scant furnish-ings. The crude furniture reeked of tobacco and mouse drop-pings, and the new Mrs. Worthy had understandably barred them from her home.

Mr. Croft and his sons did some carpentry repair work, replacing the front door, a half-dozen oak floor planks, and several fence pickets. The privy had to be torn down, as well, not only for rotten boards and ant infestation, but for Aleda's peace of mind. She could not bear to think of occupying the same space where Titus Worthy had heeded nature's calls, no matter that his personal hygiene had suddenly improved.

When Mr. Croft informed her the cistern could supply enough rainwater for a pump toilet and bathtub, Aleda was all nods. She reckoned Shakespeare would have made the same choice, had it been available. The roomy water closet was an add-on, adjacent to the back door, but beneath a new porch roof built for inclement weather. The Crofts also built a medicine cabinet over the sink, and a stand for a small kerosene heater.

Aleda raided vicarage and Larkspur attics for furnishings. She purchased four wicker garden chairs and tea table from the Keegans, Irish basket weavers. From a gallery in Shrewsbury, she purchased a framed print of Frederick William Watts's *Thames Near Henley* because it reminded her of the River Bryce. She splurged, as well, on new colorful rugs and curtains, throws for the sofa and chair, and coverlets for two beds.

The latter had required thought. Aleda had no intention of sharing her refuge with houseguests. That was what the Bow and Fiddle was for. But her plenary nature could not abide the thought of the spare bedroom sitting empty, incomplete.

She chose the west-facing room for herself, simply because she did not want the sun to wake her too early. The window commanded a view of an ash tree standing out against the yews, oaks, and alders. The contrast between the tree's delicate green foliage, dead-black bulbs, and ash-gray bark served as a reminder that the ink-born people in her stories must have contrasts of character to seem authentic. Even Napoleon Bonaparte was fond of dogs.

Aleda was not, however. But she liked cats and would need one to keep vermin at bay. Audrey Herrick, the Larkspur's cook, took care of that problem by gifting her an older tabby kitten, descendant of Aleda's first cat, Buff. She named her Tiger. She asked Mr. Croft to cut a little swinging opening into the back door so that the cat could do her business outside.

Though she could afford a cook and housemaid, she decided to give keeping house herself a try. She could always hire Mrs. Summers for a scrubdown now and again. Simple meals she could prepare herself; sandwiches and cheese, eggs and porridge, boiled vegetables, and fruit would tide her over between Sunday dinners at the vicarage. She did not think she could manage laundry, however, so hired longtime laundress Mrs. Moore to send her grandson by on Mondays and Thursdays to pick up and deliver.

The first night in her own bedroom, she lay on her pillow listening to leaves rustling and branches swaying, crickets chirping and tree frogs singing, owls hooting and cushats cooing, nightjars churring and turtledoves trilling. Through the window wafted the sweet earthy fragrance of sleeping trees and apple blossoms from the squire's orchard.

Edward Gibbon's quote came to mind: *I was never less alone than when by myself.*

She would have to add . . . with a cat sleeping at my feet.

She smiled in the darkness. She had achieved autonomy. Life would be very peaceful from now on.

Chapter 5

Jewel sat on the side of her sagging mattress, pulling her brush carefully through pillow snarls. Her hair was still damp from last night's washing. Her mother had often related how, when she was born, the midwife exclaimed, "What a little jewel, with that garnet-red hair!" *Garnet* did not appeal to her mother as a name; hence she was dubbed Jewel. With a pang she recalled how Norman had loved gathering her curls with his callused hands.

"Mummy, I'm all dressed. But look. What's wrong with this stocking?"

Snapped from her reverie, Jewel smiled and opened her arms. Becky stepped forward, and Jewel hefted her onto the bed beside her. "There is just one problem, mite. You see this bump? That's where your heel's supposed to be."

The girl laughed, touched Jewel's cheek while her stocking was adjusted. "Why do you have freckles, Mummy?"

"I swallowed a pound and it broke into pennies." Something else her own mother used to say.

"And why do I have them?"

Jewel thought fast. "They're where angels kiss you as you sleep."

"They kiss me?"

"How can they resist? You're so sweet." Jewel turned her face up to plant a kiss upon Becky's forehead. "And there's one from me. Now, let's hurry or we'll be late."

Jewel helped her into a crisp pink muslin, slightly faded from having been passed down through Vicar Treves' four daughters. She dressed herself in a navy-and-gray striped poplin, purchased from a secondhand stall on Market Street. The cuffs were frayed, but it was nicer than the two dresses she rotated on factory days.

She gathered Becky's hair with a ribbon, and her own into a straw bonnet.

With Saint Philip's Chapel being in a poor section of Birmingham, Jewel would have felt out of place clad in finery, were she to possess any. Even Mrs. Treves did not wear Parisian fashions, though she probably could, for rumor was that the vicar's family had wealth. In the vestibule, Mrs. Treves leaned to slip a peppermint into Becky's pocket.

"I trust you'll save that for after the service, little lady?"

"I shall," Becky said, and pleased Jewel by adding, "Thank you, ma'am."

Mrs. Treves smiled. Well past thirty, and plump from having birthed seven children, she was a beautiful woman, with jade green eyes and strawberry-blond ringlets. She was known for compelling merchants to give discounts so as to stretch the poor-box pennies as much as possible.

"Mr. Chandler's boy will be here with a cart of eggs and butter afterwards." Mrs. Treves leaned close so as not to embarrass Jewel, in spite of the fact that several others would be extended that same charity. Even the most desperately poor had their pride. Not the sinful pride stemmed from arrogance, but that of not wishing to be pitied.

Jewel thanked her. For Becky's sake, she would take any charity offered. The vicar's sermon, "The Hope of Heaven," from the first book of Thessalonians, was so encouraging that she could actually sense Norman and her mother watching them from above. Also encouraging was the generous parcel of butter and eggs she carried home. After a lunch of cold mutton and potatoes, followed by the luxury of Sunday luxuries, a nap, she stood in the queue twice at the communal tap to fill water buckets while Becky still slept. Afterwards she escorted the girl down the corridor to see the Bell family's kittens.

"Mayn't they open their eyes?" Becky asked with such concern on her little face that Mrs. Bell laughed. Back in the flat, Jewel taught her daughter how to make shortbread with some of the butter. The day was so fine, so perfect, that she was able to keep the familiar nagging fear at bay.

But in the dark of night, the fear swooped through her with renewed strength. Over two weeks had passed since Mrs. Platt gave her the news that Mr. Dunstan had been sacked. But did men like him slouch away quietly?

Father, please keep him away from us, she prayed, and wished she had the faith to push him from her mind completely.

Monday morning, she carried still-sleeping Becky downstairs as usual, murmuring, "You'll be too heavy to do this before long." In Mrs. Platt's parlor, Jewel deposited her and her little blanket onto the worn horsehair sofa and kissed her forehead.

"What's this?" Mrs. Platt said when Jewel took a handkerchief-wrapped bundle from her pocket.

"We made shortbread last night."

"Ah, you know my weakness!"

"I do *now*," Jewel quipped, and they traded smiles. She stepped out into the corridor with her heart lighter than it had been in ages.

Mrs. Fenton waved her down from just inside the entrance door.

"He's out there."

Jewel's throat tightened. Mrs. Fenton eased open the door a bit. In gaps between laborers rushing to their jobs, she could see Mr. Dunstan, leaning against the tenement building across the lane with arms folded, as if waiting for someone.

Me.

"Just pay him no mind," Mrs. Fenton said. "Let him rant and rave all he wants, get it out of his craw."

"Are you sure?"

The older woman peeked through the gap. "Come along . . . too many men out there for him to try anything. As I say, he's got to rant."

Jewel's heart hammered in her chest as Mrs. Fenton opened the door, then threaded an arm through hers.

"Mind you don't look at him."

Jewel followed that advice down the three steps, bracing herself for the rail of abuse, the embarrassment of having passersby witness a row.

When it did not come, her relief was overwhelming.

And short-lived.

Why wasn't he saying anything? Twenty feet up the lane, Jewel looked over her shoulder. Only the position of his head had moved. Their eyes locked. His eyes narrowed over a smile that chilled her to the core.

Mrs. Fenton tugged at her. "Forget him."

Jewel took two more steps, halted, whispered, "I can't leave Becky."

"Nip back and warn Mrs. Platt to keep her inside."

"I've done that. But she's too sympathetic toward him. What if she lets him visit?" She unwound her arm. "You go on."

The walk back to the building was the longest Jewel had ever taken. She did not have to look at him to know his eyes followed her.

"What's wrong?" Mrs. Platt asked. The mother of one of the infants looked at her curiously, as well.

Becky lay on the sofa, still asleep. She blinked as Jewel lifted her.

"Mummy?"

"Yes, it's me, Becky." To Mrs. Platt, Jewel said, "I won't be going in."

"You'll still owe me for today."

"Of course." At the moment, that was the least of her worries. By the time she had Becky upstairs, the girl was wide awake.

"I'm staying home with you," Jewel said.

Becky's blue eyes brightened. "All day?"

Jewel combed a hand through her red curls. "All day."

She went into the kitchen, slowly moved aside the curtain. Mr. Dunstan stared up at her with his maddening, knowing grin. She dropped the curtain as if it were on fire, stepped backwards.

"What's wrong, Mummy?"

Jewel turned to her. "Shall I tell you a story?"

She had recited "The Cinder Maid" so many times that her mind was able to churn over other things while Becky listened intently. Was his plan to lurk outside all day? Hopefully Mrs. Fenton could smooth over Mr. Fowler's ire. After all, this would be her first absence. Mourning her husband, stomach cramps, a bout with ague, and maddening worry when it moved on to Becky had not given her excuse to miss.

To keep from pacing the floor, she occupied herself with little tasks: mending the quilt that had been her grandmother's, tightening up buttons on clothing. By lunchtime, the knot in her stomach made the thought of food nauseating, so she fed Becky the cheese sandwich she had packed for the factory.

"May we visit the kittens?" Becky asked after her nap.

"I'm afraid not," Jewel said, trying to maintain the illusion that this was just a normal day. "The Bells will be at work."

Hours later, as she trimmed eyes from the last of the potatoes for boiling, someone knocked, and Mrs. Fenton's voice called, "It's me, dearie!"

"Keep an eye on the potatoes for me, but don't go near the stove," Jewel said to Becky before stepping out into the hallway and putting a finger to her lips.

Mrs. Fenton nodded, whispered, "He just left."

Relief made Jewel's knees buckle.

"But . . . he gave me a message for you." She bit her lip. "He said you did him a favor, that he found a job as night watchman that pays more than rent collecting. That he gets plenty of sleep and gets off just in time to come 'round to bid you good morning."

Now Jewel's knees went weak for another reason. She put a steadying hand on the doorframe. "How long does he intend to do this? I can't miss work again."

"No, you can't. Mr. Fowler says a dozen women a day ask about hiring on. If you don't go in tomorrow, you'll be sacked."

Frantically, Jewel thought. "Do you think your mother would—"

"She can't abide children," Mrs. Fenton said with a head shake for emphasis. "She couldn't even abide her own. I'm the only one who has aught to do with her, but . . ." She shrugged. "She's my mother. And I must go now. I'm sorry to bring you bad news."

Hours passed before Jewel was able to drift into fitful sleep. Early the next morning, she carried a pot of water into the parlor for her bath, even though Mr. Dunstan would have to be fourteen feet tall to peer through the threadbare curtains. After dressing, she braced herself to ease aside a corner to have a look. The sun's tepid rays diluted the darkness to the color of weak tea. Even so, from the far side of a stream of day laborers, she could see him. Looking up. He touched the brim of his hat.

I hope your neck gets a crick, Jewel thought.

What to do now? She would have to confront him, however dreadful the thought.

The stream of humanity would dry up very soon. Trying to keep the fear from her voice, she roused Becky and said, "Come, Becky. Let's dress."

Quickly she led the half-sleeping child through the morning ritual: taking her to the water closet, sponging her with a flannel, pulling a dress over her head and arms, combing her hair.

"I need you to wake now, Becky," Jewel said, easing her down at the foot of the stairs. "I can't carry you the whole way."

Becky yawned and looked up the staircase. She was awake

63

enough to know that they had passed Mrs. Platt's. "Where are we going, Mummy?"

"For a walk," Jewel said through chattering teeth.

Suddenly wide awake, she did a little bounce and said, "May we go to the park?"

"Not today." Jewel took her hand.

If walking past Mr. Dunstan yesterday morning was terrifying, it was doubly so with Becky beside her. She kept the girl to her right. Fortunately, Becky was too busy chirping her happiness to look around her skirts.

"I thought I was dreaming when you said that, Mummy! Will you stay home again?"

"I'm afraid not, mite," Jewel told her. If the police were to take Mr. Dunstan in this very morning, she would have to deliver Becky back to Mrs. Platt and hurry to the factory. She would still be late, but if she begged hard enough, perhaps Mr. Fowler would extend mercy.

Please, God.

"And what did the man say to you?" Constable Whittington asked, unable to disguise his pained tone.

"Nothing to me directly, sir," Jewel admitted. "But he bade a friend tell me that he would return to bid me *good mornings*."

"And he has not approached, nor laid a hand on you?"

Jewel shifted her weight upon her feet. If only there were a chair facing the sergeant's desk so she would not have to stand there like a worker called up for slacking. If only Becky weren't standing right beside her, taking everything in through wide eyes. But there was no way she would allow her daughter out of her sight.

"Why would he be there, sir, if not to intimidate me? He knows I won't leave Becky if he's out there."

"Again I say, it's no crime to stand in front of a building. And we *didn't* give the owner your name when we spoke with him—for which you seem to have no gratitude."

"I'm grateful, sir. More than you can know. But my daughter's safety outweighs even gratitude."

He sighed. "I'm not unsympathetic to your plight, Mrs. Libby. But the law—"

"Then it's the law that's unsympathetic," Jewel said, voice shaking from humiliation and desperation. "If I were the lord mayor's daughter, I believe you would find a way around the law."

"Now, see here!"

But what was there to see? She took Becky's hand, walked back on Great Russell Street. The bells of Saint Mary's chimed eight o'clock. Shop fronts and carriages blurred. She blinked salt tears.

"Are you crying, Mummy?" Becky asked.

"No." Jewel sniffed, lowered herself to reassure her daughter. "Well, a bit. But you mustn't worry."

Becky pressed hands against Jewel's cheeks. The smallness and coolness were a balm. "He's a bad man!"

"No, Becky. He's a good man. He's just done a bad thing."

Visions tormented her, of losing her job, of turning Becky over to an orphanage just to put a roof over her head and food in her stomach. *Father, please don't let it come to that!*

"Will we go home now?" Becky asked.

"Not now." But where to go?

Saint Philip's snug vicarage appeared younger than the

chapel in whose shadow it rested, but the worn stones had seen their share of decades. A round-faced housemaid led them through a narrow hallway and out to a compact garden where Mrs. Treves sat in dressing gown and slippers.

"Why, good morning," said the vicar's wife, rising from a cast-iron bench. "I was just collecting my wits after the mad rush to send the children and Paul off to—"

She paused, jade eyes meeting Jewel's.

"Mrs. Libby? What's wrong?"

Jewel opened her mouth but could not force out the words. Her eyes, however, had no difficulty producing tears.

Mrs. Treves eyed her for a second, then stooped to touch Becky's shoulder. "Mrs. Exter's making gingerbread. Why don't you go and watch?"

The look Becky gave Jewel was half hope, half worry.

"Go ahead, dear," Jewel said, forcing a smile.

Mrs. Treves nodded at the maid, who led Becky back into the house, saying, "Mrs. Exter bakes the best gingerbread in England, lamb."

"Now, come sit and tell me what's happened," Mrs. Treves said.

With such kind prompting, Jewel spilled out the story. "*If* I still have a job, I'll be docked yesterday's and today's wages. I'm barely hanging on as it is."

"Why haven't you come to us before?" Mrs. Treves asked.

"We were getting by. And you have so many parishioners worse off than us."

Mrs. Treves shook her head. "When Paul returns from his morning calls, I'll ask him to deliver you to the factory and speak with your employer. Becky may spend the day here."

Jewel let out a relieved breath. But on the heels of that relief came a terrifying thought.

"But what about tomorrow? And the next day? Mr. Dunstan's never going away. I saw it in his eyes."

The maid returned with tea. Jewel took three sugars. Sympathy and sugar. Both immensely comforting, but what she needed was a solution.

"You must stay here with us tonight," Mrs. Treves declared. "However long it takes. Paul will help us figure out what to do."

Again, the swallowing of pride. But relief helped it go down easier.

"How can I ever thank you?" Jewel asked, her voice thick with emotion.

Mrs. Treves patted her arm. "You would do it for us."

"I—I would hope so."

"I know so," Mrs. Treves said. "Which is *not* why we're helping, mind you. It's our Christian duty. But I've known you long enough to recognize the quality of your character, Jewel Libby. And I believe you would help anyone within your power to help."

It had been far too long since Jewel had heard anything so kind said of her. The words caused fresh tears to threaten her eyes.

But she would hold them in, lest she lay yet another burden upon Mrs. Treves' kind shoulders.

Chapter 6

"Can you go any faster?" Philip Hollis leaned out of the coach window and cupped his hand beside his mouth on the morning of the seventeenth of May. "I'll pay double!"

A snap of the whip and a jarring burst of speed jolted him back into his seat, tumbling his portmanteau to the floor. Fear that he would miss his sister's wedding set his heart pounding as fast as the sixteen hoof beats against the macadamized road.

His heart quickened even more when the Anwyl rose into view. Named from an old Celtic word for *beloved*, it was actually a hill of some five hundred feet. Soon the coach was turning up shady Market Lane. The shops were closed, unusual for a Saturday morning, but then, most villagers would be at the wedding.

He took a half crown from his pocket and, when the village green came into view, pulled the bell rope. Alighting, he pushed the money into the cabby's outstretched hand.

The shadow of Saint Jude's steeple stretched out across a green gilded with buttercups. As Philip ran, portmanteau thumping his side, lungs straining for breath, he prayed he would not be too late.

"Will you, Grace Lilleth Hollis, take Thomas Norton Langford as your lawfully wedded husband?" Andrew asked.

"I will," she answered.

The couple stood at the altar hand-in-hand. They were a study in contrasts: she fair skinned, petite and dark haired, he tall, blond, bronzed by the sun.

From the front row, Julia could see Andrew's eyes shining. She glanced across the aisle at Thomas's parents. Seth was blinking, Mercy wiping her eyes with a handkerchief.

Thank you, Father, for happy tears.

And some poignant ones. Laurel's absence was felt, but five-month-old Abigail was too young to be taken halfway around the world. Philip and Loretta, while not hindered by great distance, had yet to appear by the time Grace was to walk up the aisle.

When did you grow so distant, Philip? How easy it would be to blame Loretta, but he was old enough to make his own choices.

Only when she heard the piano and violin's opening notes did she realize Ira Johnson and his sister Helen had stepped up to the platform to sing.

My love is like a red, red rose . . .

Grace's wedding day is not for brooding, Julia reminded herself.

That's newly sprung in June.
My love is like the melody . . .
That's sweetly played in tune.

"Uncle Philip's here, Grandmother," Elizabeth and Jonathan's son John leaned over Aleda to whisper. "Standing in back."

"Did you hear?" Aleda whispered. Her mauve silk gown—the same she had worn for commencement at Newnham College four years ago—had a small scorch mark on the upper sleeve. But at least she had taken pains to iron.

"Yes," Julia whispered back, her heart filling with blessed relief.

"I'd wager the prima donna's not—"

Julia silenced her with a shake of the head, and smiled up at Grace and Thomas, poised to take their vows.

"With this ring, I thee wed," Andrew said.

"With this ring, I thee wed," Grace echoed, smiling up at Thomas.

Thomas expressed the same intent to Grace, and then Andrew pronounced them husband and wife. "You may kiss your bride."

After a short, sweet, and smiling kiss, they marched back down the aisle, hand-in-hand, to Mendelssohn's "Wedding March." Julia and her family followed, along with Seth and Mercy Langford and their daughter, twelve-year-old Amanda. In the vestibule, Philip was already embracing Grace, murmuring something to her, and then he shook hands with Thomas. He turned to Julia.

"Mother."

A lump welled in Julia's throat. But for the auburn hair, he could have been her first husband, staring at her through cobalt blue eyes. Yet he looked weary. Thinner. Older.

"I'm so sorry I'm late," he said.

She took him in her arms, kissed his cheek. "But you're here now."

"Forgive the stubble," he said, rubbing his face. "I didn't have time to shave."

She smiled and looked past him. "Where is Loretta?"

He shook his head. By then, the vestibule was filled and Julia was swept up into post-ceremonial activities.

Thankfully, an obliging sun and benign white clouds allowed benches to be set up on the green outside the village hall. Inside, tables groaned with food prepared by the cooks at the Bow and Fiddle: cold chicken, small minced veal pies garnished with rolled bacon, curried rabbit, new potatoes, cucumber salad, and baked macaroni with cheese.

Julia and Andrew followed Seth and Mercy outside the door and arranged themselves with the married couple to greet guests. Parishioners and shopkeepers, servants and farmers, old friends and new filed by to clasp their hands.

"I only caught sight of Philip," Andrew leaned close to say during a gap in handshakes and best wishes. "Did you speak with him?"

"Yes," Julia replied. "He's over there with the girls and Jonathan."

"Sans Loretta," he said.

"Yes."

He touched her elbow, concern for her in his hazel eyes. "It's still a lovely day."

She smiled back at him. "A lovely day."

"Hernia surgery with complications," Philip explained to Elizabeth and Aleda. "My train arrived in Birmingham too late to catch the one to Shrewsbury yesterday evening."

In his arms he held Samuel, whom he had not seen since Christmas, when he came up for the day to deliver gifts. Claire stayed close to her mother's skirt but did peek out to give Philip a timid smile.

Elizabeth's expression softened. "Did the patient come through all right?"

"He did."

Aleda's green eyes were still hard. "Did Loretta have to perform surgery, as well?"

"She would have liked to come," Philip said, ignoring the hurtful barb. "But she woke with a severe headache."

"Well, there you are!"

Philip felt a pounding on his back. Jonathan Raleigh grinned, eleven-year-old John at his side.

"How long has it been?" asked Jonathan.

Philip's insides tightened.

"Five months," Aleda said sharply. She turned and walked away.

"She misses you," Elizabeth said softly, taking Samuel from his arms, setting the boy's feet upon the ground. "We all do."

"I'm sorry. I miss all of you, too."

His stepsister smiled, but there was an aching doubt in her eyes. "We need to feed the children now."

"Will you join us?" Jonathan asked.

Philip eyed his mother and Andrew, greeting guests at the door.

"Thank you, but I'm not hungry."

Of truth, he was ravenous. However, his reluctance to face his stepfather was stronger than his hunger.

"Hello, young man" came a familiar voice from behind.

Philip turned, smiled. "Doctor Rhodes. How good to see you."

"And you're a sight for sore eyes." The stoop-shouldered

old man rested a hand upon his back. "Might I have a word with you?"

After the feast, when guests began filtering away, Thomas turned to Julia and Andrew, and cleared his throat.

"I want you to know I shall always take good care of her."

Julia embraced her new son-in-law. "Yes, Thomas, we know you will."

The married couple was about to face their first separation. Thomas left with his parents and sister to change his clothes and finish packing. Grace and her family returned to the vicarage.

In Grace's bedroom, Elizabeth began unfastening two dozen pearl buttons running up the back of the wedding gown while Aleda gathered last-minute items such as toothbrush and comb into a valise—the trunk was already loaded onto the coach Squire Bartley had lent for the journey to Shrewsbury Station.

For Julia's part, she simply propped weary feet upon a footstool and watched her daughters interact.

"You're not . . . afraid, are you?" Elizabeth asked.

"Of Scotland?" Grace asked with a little glint in her emerald eyes.

Julia smiled to herself.

"No, of—" Elizabeth glanced sideways at Aleda. "Would you mind stepping outside for a minute?"

"Heavens, Beth," Aleda said. "I haven't lived in a cave for twenty-six years."

"You would like to have," Elizabeth said with a little laugh.

"Now, there's a happy thought," Aleda replied. "Mother explained all that business to me when I was fourteen. But you're embarrassing Grace."

Grace shook her head. "I'm not embarrassed. As Mother said, all God's gifts are good. My only fear is of missing the train."

Elizabeth resumed unfastening buttons, and Aleda went over to the bed and picked up Grace's going-away gown, of yellow cambric with narrow white stripes and knife-pleated trim at the bottom of the skirt. She and Elizabeth helped Grace slip it over her head.

Footsteps sounded on the stairs, a knock, and then Philip's voice. "Please inform Cinderella her coach awaits."

"Almost ready!" Elizabeth called, combing Grace's mussed curls while Aleda fastened buttons.

Philip's voice came again after a pause. "May I come in?"

"No!" Aleda replied.

"Yes!" Grace called.

The door opened. He entered, smiled at his youngest sister. "I hope Thomas tells you every day how beautiful you are."

"He already does," Grace said, and opened her slender arms and took a step toward him.

Philip made the rest of the distance, gave her a quick squeeze and peck on the lips. "Don't want to detain you. I'm sorry I haven't had the chance to get a gift."

Aleda frowned and opened her mouth. Julia sought in vain to catch her eye. But before whatever recrimination could be let out into the room to spoil this bit of family harmony, Philip withdrew an envelope from his pocket and pressed it into Grace's hand.

"Please buy something . . ." His voice broke, and he looked away for a second.

"Thank you, Philip," she said softly.

He smiled at her again. ". . . something nice for yourselves on your trip."

The family stood outside the gate to wave the couple down Vicarage Lane—even Dora, Wanetta, and Luke, though they had been given the remainder of the weekend off. When they were out of sight, the men and John started setting up the badminton net. Aleda announced she would return to her cottage.

"You're leaving?" Elizabeth said.

"I've a story to finish."

"I'd like to speak with you," Julia said, and turned for the vicarage, trusting she would follow. As they stood in the vestibule, she took her daughter's hand and said gently, "We can't have hard feelings at him for not visiting, but then treat him harshly when he does."

"He could have made her come with him."

"How? Bound her in chains? This isn't the sixth century. And she had a headache."

Aleda let out a bitter laugh. "That's up for debate. How long will we allow her to spit upon our family, Mother?"

"We won't allow that. But she has not crossed that line so far. Please bear in mind Philip's caught in the middle. Have some pity for him."

"He put himself in that position."

"Then have some pity for me," Julia said, touching her arm softly. Tears pricked her eyes, born of all the emotions of the day. "I'm caught between two children I love more than life itself."

Aleda's frown wavered. Her expression softened. "I never thought of it that way."

"I understand that."

"But I'm still going home."

Julia closed her eyes, felt the tears course down her cheeks. Then Aleda's fingers brushing them away.

"To change my clothes, Mum. I can't play badminton in this."

Julia laughed. "You're a good daughter."

"I have my moments," Aleda said, heading for the door.

Over her shoulder she said, "Anyway, I'm rather glad the prima donna's not here. I just didn't want you to be hurt."

Julia shook her head as the door closed. But how could she have chided Aleda anyway, when she herself was glad they had Philip all to themselves?

She wondered much later, when the game was over and Philip and Jonathan raced around the net with Samuel and Claire up on their shoulders, if Loretta's presence would have put a damper on the fun.

But Philip would have been happier, she thought.

Would he? He seemed very much at ease now.

Until Andrew spoke his mind in the parlor that evening as he, Philip, and Julia sat with dishes of leftover wedding cake.

"Have we done something to offend Loretta?"

"Of course not," Philip replied. "She loves all of you."

He was too adamant on this point, almost as if trying to convince himself, as well.

"She barely knows us," Andrew said.

Stop, Andrew, Julia urged with her eyes. Yet how could he, when she had poured out her heart to him over this matter so many times? Like Aleda, he wished to protect her.

"She didn't plan on a headache." Philip set his dish of half-eaten cake upon an occasional table with a sharp *click*. "You know, you could visit us once in a while."

They had, less than a year after the wedding. Never had Julia felt so unwelcome in a house. Philip had been gracious, but fair or not, it was the woman who set the tone of a house. The few times Loretta had consented to occupy the same space with them, it was as if she had sent her body in for duty's sake but left her mind in another room. Questions put to draw her out had been answered in monosyllables, unless she was boasting about her parents' social status and wealth.

Yet how could Julia confess what was in her heart, and possibly damage Philip's marriage? He obviously loved Loretta.

And he obviously had thought back to that visit, for he said, softly, "We were practically newlyweds. Loretta was anxious over making a good impression."

"Of course," Julia said, so willing to forgive.

"It'll be different when you visit again. You'll see. And Loretta and I . . . we shall be more faithful about visiting and writing."

"That would be very nice, Philip," Andrew said, and smiled.

They spent the remainder of the evening catching him up on village news, even some that Julia had already written about in letters. Aleda's cottage. Gresham's placing second in the archery tournament. John's violin lessons. Squire Bartley's finally welcoming their visits, and his declining health. The Perkinses opening up Gresham's first millinery shop and staffing it with their daughter, Priscilla.

Philip spoke animatedly of his surgeries and responsibilities at Saint Bartholomew's Hospital, sparing them any unpalatable details. He did not speak again of his wife.

Nor did he speak of Doctor Rhodes having approached him. Though she had tried not to get her hopes raised, Julia felt keen disappointment.

Chapter 7

Rainstorms drenched Gresham almost daily the final week of May, but spirits were not dampened, partly due to Parliament's passing of the Third Reform Act. For the first time, men living in rural areas of England would have the same voting rights as those in towns.

It took four days for the ground to dry. After breakfast on the third of June, Julia pulled a smock over a house dress and began thinning onions and carrots in the kitchen garden, while Luke planted a row of long pod beans.

"I said to Wanetta that we must take the newspaper now," the gardener said. "A voting man should keep hisself informed."

A gap between his teeth caused a whistle to accompany the words *said, must, newspaper,* and particularly *hisself.*

Twelve years ago he had finally asked for the vicarage house-maid's hand. He and Wanetta and ten-year-old Lucas lived a stone's throw away, in the cottage they rented from Squire Bartley.

"That would be a good idea," Julia replied. "Good for Lucas, too."

"Is that so?"

"My father read the newspaper to me. Not front to back, mind. But interesting bits. It's a memory I cherish."

"I should have been doing that long ago," Luke said with forlorn voice.

"You're a good father, Luke."

"Why, thank you, Mrs. Phelps," he replied, and though his back was to her, she could hear the blush in his voice. Along with the whistle.

As usual, she had had to bully herself past Luke's reluctance for anyone to share his chores. But there was still plenty for him to do. Not only was he gardener and groomsman, but he also kept the vicarage in good repair.

The sound of hoofbeats did not cause her to cease pulling plants. She had no vanity about being seen with dirt-stained smock and fingernails. Anyway, most callers were for Andrew. Wanetta would see whoever was there to the study. Andrew planned for interruptions, the reason why he began writing his sermons on Mondays.

Carrots and onions thinned, she moved on to the parsnips. She understood the proverb *A garden is the poor man's apothecary*. At the end of the row she straightened slowly, pressed both fists behind her hips to quell the dull ache. *But it's not kind to a woman's back.*

Luke straightened just as slowly and began carrying his shovel over to the potting hut. "Fine work, Mrs. Phelps."

"Thank you, Luke." She looked up at the sound of the kitchen door. Andrew was descending the stone steps.

"Hallo, beautiful!" he called.

"Aw, Vicar . . . most kind of you," Luke said from the shadow of the hut. "But I fear my nose is too big."

Andrew squinted in his direction, chuckled. Julia laughed, as well. The moment was made funnier by the fact that Luke was most times contentedly stoic.

The rider had been Jack Sanders, Andrew said as he drew closer with a piece of paper in hand. Julia's breath caught in her throat. Laurel, little Abigail, Ben? Grace and Thomas? Philip and Loretta? Telegrams never brought good news. But Andrew did not look grim; in fact, he still wore the smile left over from Luke's quip.

"What is it?" Julia asked.

"Well, a mystery. We're to give the servants the day off and wait."

"I beg your pardon?"

"That's what it says."

She took it with her dirt-stained fingers. To the word, it said, *Give servants day off. Wait for delivery.*

"Did Jack say who sent it?"

"All he knew was that it originated in the Liverpool office, just after opening this morning."

They knew not a soul in Liverpool. The fact that it was the main shipping terminal in Britain meant it could be someone newly arrived from overseas. Just Friday past they had received a letter from Laurel, saying they anticipated returning to England in January if Ben's project was concluded upon schedule. And the Clays were not due to arrive for eighteen more days.

"What shall we do?" Julia asked.

"I've given Dora and Wanetta the remainder of the day off. Dora's about to set out for the lending library and to visit her parents. Wanetta asked me to inform Luke."

He turned again toward the hut. Luke was coming back through the door with pruning shears in hand.

"Did you hear, Luke? Take the day off."

"Why, thank you, Vicar," he said, and ducked back into the hut. As he entered the garden again, without the shears, he said, "I'll fetch Lucas. It's a fine day for fishing."

"I wouldn't plan on that, good man. Wanetta said something about a long overdue visit to your mother."

"Ah." Luke shrugged and started for the kitchen steps.

"Poor Luke," Andrew said when the door closed behind him.

"And poor Lucas," Julia said. Mrs. Smith was a self-absorbed woman, hedged about with complaints.

"Poor Mrs. Smith," Andrew added. "To conduct yourself in such a way that it's a chore for your own children to visit."

Julia thought of Philip once again.

The sympathy in Andrew's expression melded into anticipation. "I wonder who sent it. We didn't expect our adventures to begin so soon, did we?"

He was as pleased as a dog with two tails, almost giddy. She narrowed her eyes. "What have you cooked up, Andrew Phelps?"

He put a hand to his heart. "On my life, I'm as in the dark over this as you are."

Whatever was going to happen, she should not meet it with dirt beneath her fingernails. She went upstairs in the empty house, washed up, and changed into a simple gown of raspberry muslin shot with blue.

"What shall we do now?"

"Sit in the garden and wait, I suppose."

And thus they shared a bench, watching Vicarage Lane, as if that would cause the mystery person or persons to materialize.

The village was as serene as usual. Cows lowed on their way from milking to pastures. Childish voices were raised in play. River grasses rustled on the banks of the Bryce. A breeze sifted through the leaves of the chestnut tree shading the front gate.

"I should get my novel," Julia said, thinking of the half-finished copy of Wilkie Collins' *The Woman in White* in the parlor. "Shall I bring your sermon notes?"

He thought for a moment. "I doubt I could concentrate."

She sat. "Me neither."

By half-past eleven, she began to wonder if Andrew had been too hasty in sending Dora away. "Perhaps I should make some sandwiches. Just in case."

"Another half hour?" Andrew asked.

"Very well."

By noon, he had checked his watch five times. He heaved a disappointed sigh, looked toward the house. "You don't suppose we've been duped, do you?"

"Why would someone go to that trouble and expense?" Julia asked. "And it's not a very rewarding prank if you aren't nearby to see the results."

"Five minutes more," he said with a little frown. "And then we'll make those sand—"

"Listen." Julia touched his hand and held her breath.

There came the sound of wheels and hooves heading slowly eastward up Church Lane, then turning up Vicarage Lane. Four horses and a coach broke through the shade. Julia and Andrew rose, walked to the gate just as the driver reined the team to a stop. White letters on the door spelled out *Maxwell Livery*, used fairly often by visitors from Shrewsbury to Gresham. No luggage was tied to the usual place atop—only a large hamper. To add further mystery, curtains covered the windows.

"Good day to you, sir . . . madam!" exclaimed the driver, gray haired but spry enough to hop down from his box and fold down a little step.

"Good day," Andrew replied, opening the gate. "And whom do we have here?"

The driver simply smiled, opened the door, and offered a hand to someone inside. Julia caught sight of a sleeve and then Fiona Clay's smiling face.

Andrew burst into laughter. "My word!"

Ambrose Clay stepped out to join his wife.

"I can hardly believe this!" Julia exclaimed, embracing Fiona.

Her closest woman friend was exquisitely stylish in a gown of amethyst *gros de Londres* that enhanced her violet eyes. A narrow-brim satin straw hat trimmed with brown velvet nestled among coils of sable brown hair. Ambrose was as aristocratically handsome as ever, even with an extra stone's weight to his medium frame and gray hairs mingled with the brown.

The men helped the driver lower the hamper. Ambrose paid him, and obviously quite handsomely, for the man gaped appreciatively at his palm. "Why, thank you, sir!"

The kitchen seemed a more appropriate and intimate setting for an indoor picnic. Julia covered the table with a cloth, set out salt cellar, pepper grinder, and butter dish, while Andrew laid dishes and fetched bottles of seltzer water from the pantry.

"Our trunks are coming by wagon," Ambrose explained, the actor's cultured voice betraying a faint Cornish drawl. He helped Fiona withdraw one brown paper–wrapped package after another from the wicker hamper.

"We wanted some private time with our dearest friends," Fiona said.

Julia was touched, and understood the reason for subterfuge that went beyond Ambrose's dramatic nature. The Clays were the most popular couple in Gresham, esteemed even by those who had never set foot inside a theatre. The telegram would have been read by at least one person, Jack, and possibly Mr. Trumble, which would be entirely in his rights as postmaster. Word would have spread rapidly through the village, stifling any hope of privacy.

They had left Liverpool that morning and spent only enough time in Shrewsbury to order the picnic from the Lion Inn. It was a delightful feast: lamb cutlets; plover eggs; cucumber salad; tongue; curried lobster; Gruyère cheese; seasoned new potatoes; a loaf of rye, wheat, and barley bread; coconut cake; a dozen beautiful Montreuil peaches; and even four bottles of Welsh nectar.

"How did you come to leave New York early?"

Wood scraped against flagstones as Ambrose pulled out chairs. "Our hotel clerk telegraphed the White Star Line and discovered a liner was to leave the very next morning after closing night," Ambrose said as they settled into chairs. "We traded in our tickets for the HMS *Republic*."

"But you were to stop in Cornwall to visit your family," Andrew said.

Ambrose's smile faltered. "We shall go another time. We were too long from home."

Poor Ambrose, Julia thought. His gray eyes said it all. He was suffering one of his episodes of despondency, which made it all the more touching that he would seek their company before even the refuge of their rooms over the Larkspur stables.

He obviously read her thoughts, for he smiled and said, "But it's the first I've suffered in weeks."

"And why is that, do you suppose?" Andrew asked.

Ambrose hesitated. "As simple as this seems, I reduced my usual dozen or so daily cups of tea to one, in the morning. Gradually, mind you, so as not to get headaches."

He had gotten this piece of advice from Ada Cavendish, the British actress who played Anne Boleyn to his Henry VIII at Madison Square Theatre.

"A beautiful lady," Fiona said. "But suffering the same bouts of despondency as Ambrose. A friend's aunt, a midwife, had recommended the cutting back."

"It worked for her," Ambrose said.

Fiona nodded at her husband. "I'm very proud Ambrose was open-minded enough to give it a try. I was skeptical."

Fiona was protective of Ambrose, she being of stronger temperament.

Julia was proud of Andrew, too, for so many reasons. At this moment, it was for the modest amount of food on his plate against such extravagant temptation. He had not needed a dose of stomach tonic for several days.

After the meal, the Clays insisted upon leaving the leftover food.

"Have it for supper," Ambrose said after covering a gusty yawn. "Once Mrs. Herrick gets sight of us, she'll be disappointed if she's not allowed to feed us at least one meal."

"We'll help you tidy up." Fiona smiled at Julia.

Julia took her by the shoulder, pointed her toward the door. "I'll take care of this."

"And I'll drive you home," Andrew said. "Perhaps you'll squeeze in a nap before supper."

Julia tidied up and decided to allow lunch to digest a bit before returning to the garden. She was on the parlor sofa reading her novel when Andrew returned.

"Well, that was nice, wasn't it?" he said, sitting beside her.

"Very nice," she replied. "You were right, Vicar. We still have some adventures left in us."

He chuckled. That was when Julia noticed the sound of paper rustling. She dipped into his coat pocket, brought out a small paper sack.

"You bought tonic? But there is still a half bottle upstairs."

"Well, I wasn't sure . . ."

The bottle in his pocket had been opened, a liberal dose missing. "You couldn't even make it home? You're to go to bed. I'm going for Doctor Rhodes."

"No." He shook his head. "I'm much better. It must have been the lobster. Curry has never agreed with me."

"Still, you should have him check you out."

"I've done that, sweetheart. And he'll simply say I must cut back on rich foods . . . something I already know. I shall lie down for a half hour."

Julia sighed. "I may as well argue with a gatepost."

He touched her cheek. "Ah, but a gatepost can't tell you how beautiful you are."

"If you think flattery—"

"It's not flattery when it's true. Anyway, Mrs. Cooper was in Trumbles, and says the squire seems to have taken a turn for the worse. I need to visit him this afternoon."

It was pointless to argue. But at least she could watch over him. "Take your nap, Vicar. I'll wake you in an hour. And I'm going with you."

⁓

"I dreamed again of Octavia last night," Squire Bartley said from his wheelchair. Gnarled fingers clutched the lap rug close, though a fire hissed and snapped in his library fireplace.

This was probably the only chimney in Gresham with smoke rising, Julia thought. She and Andrew sat in chairs facing the squire. She wondered how Andrew could bear the heat in his suit, for sweat dampened the hair at the nape of her neck and trickled down her bosom.

Still, she smiled and asked, "Was it a good dream?"

A wistful smile touched his lined face. "It was, Mrs. Phelps. Octavia did not speak, but held my hand. When I asked to go with her, she shook her head."

He turned his face toward Andrew. "Do you imagine I'm close, Vicar, for such dreams to visit so often of late?"

"You may be, Squire," Andrew replied, gentle but frank. "I've known others who have had such dreams before slipping into eternity."

"Ah . . . I hope so."

"Are you prepared, my dear man?"

"To meet God?" Squire Bartley nodded. "I am a believer. Still . . ."

The old man fell silent, as if collecting his thoughts. Tears stung Julia's eyes. She looked at Andrew. He gave her an understanding nod. He was used to counseling people on their deathbeds. The longcase clock ticked away seconds. How many did the squire have remaining to him?

"I have been a selfish man," he said at length.

"Squire?" Andrew said. "You've been generous with the village. You donated a school."

Founded thirteen years ago, the Octavia Bartley School of Learning had filled a gaping need for children in the upper six forms.

"You provide jobs," Julia reminded him.

"I could have done more." His voice thickened. "I sit on a fortune, while Horace Stokes grows beans in every inch of space to feed his orphans. My factory workers live in hovels with no running water. The farmers must scrape up the rent even in years milk production is down."

This was so. Julia knew Andrew would not argue otherwise to comfort a dying man. Instead he said, still gently, "If it troubles you, it is not too late to repair this."

"Yes. That is my desire. It is also what Octavia would have wanted."

He attempted to tug the edge of the lap rug up toward his face. Andrew rose, withdrawing his handkerchief, and handed it over. The squire wiped his eyes and nodded as Andrew settled back into his chair.

"But how important is keeping a vow to a sister?" the old man asked.

"We are beholden to all our vows, Squire."

He nodded resignedly. "I was reared on the principle that family is everything. That blood is thicker than water. Yet I see how the Stokes love their orphans, how Seth Langford reared Thomas to be a fine young man. How you, Vicar and Mrs. Phelps, have taken each other's children as your own."

"Some families spring from the same root," Andrew said softly. "Some are grafted."

"There is no entail to this estate," the squire went on. "I am legally free to dispose of it as I wish. I promised my dear little sister, Emmaline, that my sole inheritor would be her Donald, the unexpected blessing to her late years. Yet he became anything but a blessing: shaming his parents, breaking their health, and then squandering the inheritance when they were gone. I hear the only way he maintains his hedonistic ways now is to borrow against his expectations for my estate. This home, this land

Emmaline loved and roamed so freely as a girl, will ultimately
fall into the hands of creditors under Donald's ownership."

Julia shook her head.

"How tragic," said Andrew.

"There is more. Something that happened . . . long ago."
The squire closed his eyes as a soft groan escaped his lips. "I
cannot bear to speak of it. Suffice to say that more wealth at
his disposal will add to Donald's ruin."

He fixed watery eyes upon Andrew again. "And so I ask
you, Vicar . . . am I beholden to that vow?"

"I don't know," Andrew admitted. "God knows we don't
live in a perfect world. For example, He does allow the marriage vow to be broken in the case of adultery. Yet . . . this is
not the case."

The heat of the room contributed to the aura of hopeless-
ness. Julia thought, *What will happen to Gresham?* Once the
leases on farms and factory workers' homes expired, surely the
squire's nephew would have the power to raise rents. Perhaps
he would lower factory wages. Money was a terrible weapon
in the hands of a bad man.

The old man heaved a great sigh. "It would have been better if I had been poor."

Silence ticked on. Andrew tapped fingertips against his
beard, thoughtful. Eventually he leaned forward. "What you
just said . . . there is your solution."

The squire's bushy eyebrows raised.

"Your vow was to leave to Donald all that you have *remaining* at the time of your passing. If you give most of it away
beforehand, you can still keep that vow by leaving him a legacy
that will take care of him—in modest comfort—the rest of his
life."

"Ha!" the squire said. "You mean enough for him to lose in a hand of cards."

"But he would have been given the chance to do otherwise. And your vow would have been unbroken."

Hope flooded the aged face. "I shall do that when Mr. Baker calls Friday. You've given me a way to leave this life with conscience clear. You're a wise man."

"Heavens, no." Andrew shook his head. "Just ask Mrs. Phelps."

"He's very wise," Julia said. "Except in the case of seeing the doctor."

That made Squire Bartley smile. "Your health is an estate you must manage wisely, Vicar. Now, good friends, return to your other duties. Leave an old man to rest."

⁓

Wednesday morning, Julia woke on the sofa—she often slipped down to the parlor to escape Andrew's snoring—to the sound of knocking. At least she assumed it was morning, though darkness still pressed against the windowpane. She pulled on wrapper and slippers and felt for the door. The hall was illuminated as Dora came from the kitchen side, also in wrapper, and holding a lantern.

They gave each other grim looks. Just like telegrams, visitors in the wee hours seldom brought good news.

"I'll answer," Julia said.

Squire Bartley's driver and groomsman Jeremiah Toft stood on the porch, cap clutched in hands.

"Sorry to disturb you, Mrs. Phelps."

Julia's knees weakened. "It's the squire, isn't it?"

"Yes, ma'am. He's suffered an apoplexy."

"Oh dear." She put a hand to her heart, turned to Dora.

"Did you hear?"

"I did," the cook said, the lamp casting shadows upon her face.

"Doctor Rhodes asks that the vicar come quickly," Jeremiah said. "I brought the dogcart."

"Yes, of course." Julia took a backwards step. The *quickly* part struck her. "You mean he's still alive?"

"For now."

Chapter 8

"No-no-no-no!"

Anyone passing the half-timbered cottage at the corner of Church and Bartley Lanes would have thought someone inside was being beaten.

"Now, now," Jonathan coaxed, holding the squirming, howling Samuel in his arms. "Grandfather hasn't even touched your finger. Just let him see it."

"No!"

"Really, Jonathan . . . Father," Elizabeth said. "Can it not wait a day or two?"

"It cannot," Jonathan replied with strained voice. "Leave the room if you can't bear it! We can't risk infection and lock-jaw."

"I don't want Samuel to get mockjaw!" Claire sobbed.

"Lockjaw," older brother John corrected.

Julia took Claire up into her arms. "It's just a splinter, Claire."

"What's that?" she sniffed.

"A bit of wood in his finger."

"Should I get you a knife?" John suggested, crowding closer to the men.

"NO KNIFE!" Samuel shrieked.

"John! Outdoors!" Jonathan barked.

The boy reddened, obeyed. It was disconcerting to Julia's ears, hearing Jonathan speak to his family so sharply, but he appeared close to tears himself.

That morning Samuel had sneaked into the gardening hut to surprise his mother by fertilizing the flowers, something he had watched her do. It was while attempting to raise the lid from the barrel containing Webb's Manure and Phosphate of Lime that he encountered the splinter.

Jonathan was not normally overprotective of the children, which was a good thing. Country children were prone to scratches and bumps. But last year a farm worker, George Fletcher, had tragically died from pneumonia induced by tetanus, brought on from a splinter from a cow yard gate. Thus, any splinter suffered by his children, or even students, was an enemy that must be wrenched out at once.

Forehead furrowed, Andrew bent closer to the boy's hand. "Just hold steady one . . . there it is!"

He held up the tweezers.

Samuel, sniffing and panting for breath, gaped at his finger. "All gone?"

"All gone, my little man!"

The boy grinned. "It didn't hurt!"

Andrew chuckled. Jonathan squeezed Samuel, looked up

at Elizabeth with glistening eyes that begged forgiveness. "Will you take him and clean it?"

"Of course," she said, returning the smile.

He stood and turned toward the door. "I need to apologize to John."

Thus, lunch got off to a late start. But Mrs. Littlejohn, spry in spite of graying hair, laid a fine meal on the cloth: asparagus soup, boiled beef with young carrots, new potatoes and suet dumplings, and for dessert, boiled gooseberry pudding and plain cream.

"We sent John to invite Aleda this morning," Elizabeth said, cutting Claire's beef on her plate. "But she told him she's in the middle of a story."

"Now, there's a surprise," Andrew said as he forked a dumpling. "Excellent meal, Elizabeth."

"Thank you. It's all Mrs. Littlejohn."

"How is Squire Bartley?" Jonathan asked.

"The same," Andrew replied. "We shall visit him when we leave here. But we never know if he recognizes us."

Five days had passed since Jeremiah Toft knocked on their door. A massive brain hemorrhage had paralyzed the squire's right side. On the two occasions Julia had accompanied Andrew, the squire seemed not to know they were present.

"You know," Jonathan said thoughtfully, "when my grandfather Hall suffered the same affliction, Grandmother read the newspaper to him every day, even though he showed no sign of hearing her. When he regained cognizance four months later, the first question he asked Grandmother was if she thought Disraeli would resign, now that the Liberal Party had been victorious over the Tories in the general election."

To John's questioning look, he explained, "It was something Grandmother had read to him. Anyway, he credited hearing her voice every day to clearing the fog in his mind. I'm not sure if his doctor agreed, but . . ."

Julia met Andrew's eyes across the table.

"Have you a *Shrewsbury Times* lying about?" Andrew asked Jonathan.

"Yesterday's," Jonathan replied.

"The squire won't know the difference."

"Good afternoon, Vicar . . . Mrs. Phelps." Mrs. Cooper stepped back to open the door wider. "Do come inside."

As she took Andrew's hat, her face was tight, her eyes anxious. Had the squire taken a turn for the worse?

Julia was opening her mouth to ask when footsteps sounded in the hall. A man who could have been anywhere from thirty to forty approached, dressed impeccably in gray double-breasted frock coat and striped wool trousers.

"More visitors for my uncle, Mrs. Carter?" he asked.

"Yes, sir. Vicar and Mrs. Phelps."

His straight coarse hair was as dark as ink. Two slashes of dark brows were set over brown eyes, and a handsome aquiline nose jutted out over a mustache that curved downward over the corners of full lips. His voice was polished, as smooth as his gold silk cravat. And clearly he had had a gentleman's upbringing, for he made a little bow to Julia. "It's good of you to come. I'm Donald Gibbs."

"Julia Phelps." And annoyed that his mere presence would so intimidate the housekeeper into not correcting her own name, she took the liberty. "And . . . this is Mrs. Cooper, by the way."

"Ah, yes!" He winced and turned to the housekeeper, charmingly. "Mrs. Cooper. I do beg pardon."

"It's nothing, sir," she said.

"I only arrived two hours ago. So many names to learn, and

I have never been good with them." Mr. Gibbs smiled as he and Andrew shook hands. "Of course, you have a whole village of names to learn, don't you? I could never be a vicar."

Your lips to God's ears, Julia thought.

"Please come with me," he said.

They followed him up the wide staircase leading from the hall. "I wanted to leave London as soon as the telegraph arrived. But I thought it prudent to conclude some vital business dealings so I could focus my sole energies upon my uncle."

"In what business are you engaged, Mr. Gibbs?" Julia asked.

"This and that. It would bore you to explain."

"I don't bore easily."

Andrew cast her a warning look.

They followed Mr. Gibbs down the upstairs corridor. He took the knob. "Don't be disappointed if he doesn't respond to you."

We know that more than you do, Julia had to bite her tongue from saying. It so irked her that this coxcomb was playing lord of the manor, after having waited five days to appear. Far worse, he stood to inherit everything, when so many good people in Gresham could have benefited.

The squire's bedroom was opulent and massive, with Constable landscapes upon olive-green walls, gold satin curtains, and a marble-tiled fireplace that was, thankfully, not lit. Chambermaid Mary Johnson dropped a spoon into an empty soup bowl. She was about thirty, gaunt and plain as a rail fence, and of a good heart. The perfect person to care for the squire.

"Good afternoon, Mary," Julia said.

"Good afternoon, Mrs. Phelps . . . Vicar." She made a little bob and sent Mr. Gibbs a rapid curious glance. "I've just fed him his broth and bathed him."

The squire lay propped upon pillows, his frail body covered with blankets and dwarfed by six-and-a-half-foot walnut bedposts. His skin as white as his sheets. Half-open gray eyes stared out at seemingly nothing; his mouth gaped. Julia went over to the bedside.

"Hello, Squire."

His eyes shifted, but she could have been a ghost for all the recognition in them. Julia stroked his cheek, turned to Mary. "You shaved him."

"Yes, ma'am. This morning."

"Very good, Mary," said Donald Gibbs. "You may go now."

A muscle twitched in her cheek, as if she were taken by surprise. "Begging your pardon, sir, but he must be turned."

"Why don't I do that?" Andrew said.

"Yes, sir," she said, and fled the room.

Andrew went over to the bed, gently pulled four pillows away, and handed them to Julia. She placed three out of the way at the foot of the bed.

"Why take his pillows?" Mr. Gibbs asked, hands in his pockets.

"To prevent bedsores," Julia replied, watching Andrew turn down the blanket and roll the man gently to his side. "A raised head causes the rest of the body to rest heavier on the mattress."

Andrew took the fourth pillow from her and placed it between the squire's legs. Anticipating Mr. Gibbs' question, he said, "This one is to keep his knees from pressing together. The skin thins as we age. Bedsores can lead to fatal infection."

"And the turning is for the same reason, I gather?"

"It is," Andrew said. "It must be done every two hours,

night and day. I'm sure the servants will update you on his treatments. And Doctor Rhodes visits every Friday."

"Good. I have so many questions." Mr. Gibbs hesitated. "Do you think my uncle will ever regain cognizance?"

Andrew glanced at the bedridden man. "We must treat him as if he will."

"I absolutely agree." There seemed genuine concern in his voice, which caused Julia some guilt over her immediate dislike of him.

Andrew took the folded newspaper from his coat pocket. "Would you mind if we read to him?"

"I beg your pardon?"

Andrew related what Jonathan had said over lunch.

Mr. Gibbs inclined his head thoughtfully. "It's worth a try. I'm most grateful for any time you can give him. But I still have some unpacking. If you won't mind showing yourselves out . . ."

"We don't mind," Andrew assured him.

They took turns reading for an hour. Julia's mouth became dry, but at least the room was not heated. She hoped the squire was comfortable, temperature-wise. If he could feel temperature. If he could feel anything. For though his eyes sometimes moved in their direction, they were blank.

"I'm not discouraged," Andrew said softly on the way down the corridor. "We just have to be consistent, like Jonathan's grandmother. And a couple of hours daily—not just from newspapers, but also books."

"But how?" Julia asked, pausing on the landing. "As much as we care for him, we have other responsibilities."

Andrew scratched his beard. "We could ask others to help. Take turns."

"That's up to Mr. Gibbs now."

"I'm sure he'll be open to the idea."

You're more charitable than I am, Julia thought.

Mrs. Cooper appeared when they reached the hall downstairs. After thanking her for his hat, Andrew said, "May we trouble Mr. Gibbs once more?"

"I'll ask, if you'll follow me. He's in the library."

She ducked inside briefly, opened the door wider, and nodded on her way out. The oak paneled room smelled of fine leather, old books, and smoke. Mr. Gibbs rose from a leather chair as he put aside a copy of *The Gentleman's Magazine* and extinguished a cigarette.

"Any luck?"

Andrew did not wince, though Julia knew he despised the word and all forms of superstition. "I'm afraid not."

"Ah." Mr. Gibbs clicked his tongue, motioned to a settee. "Would you care to . . ."

"No thank you, but we'd like to ask permission to have others come and read to him."

"Others?"

"Trusted people, well acquainted with him," Julia said. "We could design a daily schedule with Mrs. Cooper."

"How kind of you. Do you think it will do any good?"

"I'm optimistic," Andrew said. "The mind is a remarkable creation."

"Then of course you may. My uncle is fortunate to have such good friends."

During the homeward stroll up Bartley Lane, Andrew said, "You don't like him."

"Not in the least," Julia admitted. "I think he's full of wind. I doubt he even looked in on his uncle until we arrived. Mary had no idea who he was."

"But we don't know that. She could have simply been nervous for having a new master."

"What about those things the squire told us? Did you not believe him?"

"I did. But I also know he had harsh opinions of people at times. Didn't he dislike you when you first moved here?"

"Well, yes," Julia admitted. "But only because he missed a chance to buy the Larkspur for a pittance."

Gently, Andrew said, "Should we not give Mr. Gibbs the benefit of the doubt until we know otherwise?"

Sometimes it was a pain, being married to a vicar. Especially when he was right. Julia sighed. "Of course. It's the notion of so many good people losing out that has me bitter."

"I've grieved over that myself. We just have to trust that the squire will recover and continue with his plan. Until then, it will do us—nor the squire—no good to antagonize Mr. Gibbs. He could forbid us to visit."

That sobered Julia. "Oh dear, Andrew. I didn't mean to be a liability."

Andrew chuckled and linked his arm through hers. "Liability? Every man should be blessed with such a liability."

She leaned her head briefly upon his shoulder. "Who do you think would be willing to take turns reading?"

He thought for a moment. "Surely Ambrose and Fiona."

"Aleda could come out of her shell once in a while," Julia said. "Considering what the squire did for her. And I believe Mercy Langford would be willing."

"Don't forget Jonathan, now that school's on holiday. After all, he gave us the idea."

It so happened that they had reached Church Lane at that moment. Their son-in-law was outdoors, installing a lock on the gardening hut door.

"I'll be happy to read to him," he said.

But the following afternoon, Jonathan appeared at the vicarage just as Julia and Andrew were setting out to pay calls.

"I was turned away at the door," he said.

I shall die of boredom! Donald thought, pacing the library rug.

Aside from a few current magazines, nothing but ponderous old books. The conservatory was quite pleasant for sitting and smoking Gold Flake cigarettes, but a man could not spend all his hours so engaged. The stables still boasted four fine horses, but he did not ride saddle, a secret he guarded closely. When he was eight, his own horse had bolted with him at Hyde Park, eventually rearing up and tossing him off as if he were a rag doll. His broken shoulder had healed, but now thirty years later, he still suffered limited range of motion in his left arm.

When Mrs. Cooper brought tea, he asked, "How would I go about buying a billiards table?"

"You would have to go to Shrewsbury," she replied. "I've never seen one in the local shops."

"Hmm." He stirred milk into his tea. "Is there some household money put away somewhere?"

"Why no, sir. Anything we need from the shops is put to the squire's account, to be paid by Mr. Stokes at the factory."

"*Horace* Stokes?"

"Yes, sir. He pays our wages, as well. Perhaps you could ask him for the funds to buy the table?"

Donald studied her face for any sign of mockery. Her expression was as guileless as a baby's. Uncle Thurmond had had another housekeeper twenty-one years ago. Perhaps the old gaffer had indeed managed to hush up the incident that sent Donald repacking for London.

And obviously Horace had benefited.

Even so, Donald would have to be completely desperate to ask him to advance him so much as a shilling.

An idea struck him. Perhaps he could persuade one of the local shopkeepers to order the table and put it on account. It could not hurt to drive the dogcart into the village and inquire. He had a way of charming people into doing what he wished.

He sighed, remembering he was housebound, for he expected a visit from the vicar sometime today. Tempting as it was to hide from confrontation, it was best to get it over and done with.

"Vicar Phelps is at the door, Mr. Gibbs," Mrs. Cooper informed him a half hour later.

In the foyer, Donald was satisfied to see the housekeeper had followed his instructions not to ask for his hat. The sooner this affair was concluded, the better.

"It's good to see you again, Vicar," Donald said, pretending surprise, offering his hand. He was still a gentleman, after all.

"Thank you," said Vicar Phelps as the housekeeper slipped away. "But I'm afraid I don't understand. Mr. Raleigh, my son-in-law, wasn't allowed to see the squire."

"Yes, yes," Donald said. "Nice fellow. I hope he wasn't offended. I fear I did not explain myself satisfactorily to him."

"I believe that to be the case."

"You see, after you and Mrs. Phelps left yesterday, the thought struck me that I could read just as well to my uncle. Why inconvenience you and everyone else?"

"It's no inconvenience."

"But it is less of an inconvenience to me. What else have I here to occupy my time?" He smiled. "Or is it my reading ability that troubles you? Shall I fetch a book from the library and prove my literacy?"

"No, that's not necessary," the vicar replied with a polite

little chuckle. "But I had also hoped having a variety of visitors would stimulate your uncle's mind."

This was something Donald had not considered, forcing him to think fast. Fortunately, he had always been skilled at landing upon his feet—not counting the time the horse threw him.

"At what cost to his body? As you have witnessed, he hangs on to health by a thread. His resistance is obviously low. I should think the less exposure to visitors, the better. Can you not see my reasoning?"

Vicar Phelps hesitated. "Ah . . . well . . ."

Weary of standing there, Donald decided it was time for the *coup de grace*. "It was so good of you to come. Please tell Mr. Raleigh I meant no disrespect. And if you'll excuse me, I must see to my uncle."

He reserved his chuckle for the staircase.

Poor vicar, he thought. Mr. Phelps seemed a decent fellow. Down to earth, not lofty like his predecessor, Vicar Wilson.

His smile faded. Vicar Wilson, whose letter to Saint John's College had made him unwelcome at Oxford.

As irony would have it, the seeds of his piety and his bitterness were planted in the same ground when his parents sent him to Gresham at age seventeen. Uncle Thurmond had insisted he accompany him to Saint Jude's. Under Vicar Wilson's preaching, Donald found himself swept up in the desire to serve God. He became quite pious, devoting long hours to the Bible.

But that desire did not replace the other one, the reason he was banished briefly from London. And it was not long before that desire crept back from the mental closet to which he had confined it.

His problem, as in London, was choosing the wrong recipient of that desire. Haste and lust, yoked together, always outpaced judgment.

Chapter 9

"Liver and bacon, carrots and peas,
Bread pudding too, as rich as you please,
We must keep Aleda fat and well fed . . ."

Singing to the tune of "The Daring Young Man on the Flying Trapeze," Aleda waltzed into the larder on the nineteenth of June with a covered pot sent over from the vicarage. Full to the brim, she was, and here was enough left over for supper.

She paused on her way back into the kitchen.

Bed? Said? Red?

Finally something came.

"So stories will grow in her head . . ."

Not quite Gilbert and Sullivan. But she'd like to see those two pen a story about shipwrecked survivors and Komodo dragons.

A knock sounded at the door. All windows were open.

Heat flamed her cheeks; she thought of easing her way back into the larder.

"Aleda? It's Jeremiah."

Aleda blew out her cheeks, went over to the door. *You laugh once, Jeremiah, and I'll box your ears.*

The distress in his usually placid face sent that thought flying.

"What is it, Jeremiah?"

He looked over his shoulder, to where one of the squire's black horses was tied to the gatepost, and raked a hand through his brown hair. "I'm meant to be giving Shadow a run. If anyone asks, I stopped to ask for a drink of water."

She reached out and took his arm. "Come in, come in. What's wrong?"

He waited until she had closed the door. "It's Mr. Gibbs. He's mistreatin' the squire."

"How?"

"Well, he allows none but Doctor Rhodes to visit. . . ."

Aleda was aware of that, having been turned away by Mrs. Cooper four days ago. She had thought it might do the squire some good to hear her latest short story, "The Stowaway."

"Father says Mr. Gibbs is worried someone might infect him with a cold or something worse," Aleda said.

"Ha!" As if shocked at his own outburst, Jeremiah glanced at the door, lowered his voice again. "Mr. Gibbs has put Mary back to cleaning rooms that ain't even used. She's only allowed to change the squire's nappy and bathe and feed him, in the mornings and at night. We take turns flopping him over every two hours. But as soon as that's done, we're to leave. The curtains are open only when the doctor's expected. The squire spends most of his days and nights alone in that dark room."

His voice broke. "Mr. Gibbs says the squire needs his rest,

that he ain't aware of what's going on about him, but how does he know that? What if the squire's mind's working fine, and he's trapped by his body?"

"That's . . . so sad," Aleda said.

"We've been warned that anyone who carries tales will be sacked without pay. Can you get word to the vicar, without saying who it came from?"

"Yes. I'll leave now."

"No! Give me ten—fifteen minutes."

He gave her a miserable, helpless look. "We need our jobs. All of us. I've a wife and baby."

"Of course." She rested a hand upon his shoulder. "You did right, Jeremiah. I'll wait. Now go, before you're discovered."

The manor house boasted eight bedrooms. Donald had chosen the last chamber in the west corridor. He wished to be as far away from his uncle as possible when death came creeping up the staircase. It was a smallish room, perhaps originally intended for a child, but had a comfortable bed and good-sized writing desk. It was here that he penned a letter, the second in the eleven days since his arrival.

Enclosed you will find a cheque for twenty-three pounds, the remainder of my bank account after this month's mortgage. My uncle's end is imminent. I ask you again to be patient. I regret you're bored. When I come into my inheritance, we shall have all the money we desire. How does a tour of the pyramids strike you? But again, you owe me patience. I shall be very angry if you persist in visiting those dark little places on Cleveland Street. Think back to from whence you came, before I rescued you.

Lips pressed, Donald penned one final line.

Would you rather go back to shoveling out stables?

By then, his ire was so great that he did not sign the page, but stuffed it into the envelope and addressed it.

He should have forced Reese to accompany him there, he thought. As a friend. But his uncle, should he recover, would figure out the score in a heartbeat. He was almost disinherited at seventeen. He could not risk it again.

He was just as angry at himself. His inability to turn down a game of cards had landed him in this quagmire of debt, forcing him to mortgage his family home in Kensington Gardens and sell off most of the furnishings—even coach and horses, and the double box in the Lyceum Theatre. Once he returned to London for good, he would never go near the gambling salons again.

He opened his door. Mary was lugging mop and bucket up the corridor. He cleared his throat. She looked at him, her face a mask.

"Mary. Have I missed the postman?"

"Yes, sir," she said.

Donald blew out a breath. "What time does the post office close?"

"Five o'clock, sir."

"Please go have someone bring around the dogcart. I shall be downstairs in ten minutes."

She blinked at him. "Jeremiah or Osborn can deliver your letter."

"No. I can use the drive."

Ten minutes later he was crossing the porch. Black horse and dogcart waited, tethered to a carriage post. No sign of the two groomsmen. The staff had their ways, but dared not risk outright hostility.

He regretted their sullen disapproval. Who wanted to be the object of so much dislike, even from servants? He could not enjoy meals without wondering if they had been tainted. In his imagination, cutlets were dropped upon the floor, spittle stirred into the gravy. Or worse. Yet he had to eat. He did not even possess the funds to take regular meals at the Bow and Fiddle, for the old miser had not been a patron and thus had no account.

His mistake was underestimating the affection the servants felt for his uncle. In his memory, the man was a sharp-tongued old blister who kept the servants hopping. Never did he say please.

Perhaps he should call them all together when he returned from the post office. Announce that when the estate was settled he would double their wages. He untied the tether and smiled. *Triple. Quadruple. Hundredfold.* What did it matter?

So deep was he into his thoughts that it was only as he swung up into the seat and picked up the reins that he realized a carriage drawn by a pair of horses had turned down Bartley Lane. He frowned as it drew closer. Vicar Phelps and Doctor Rhodes sat in the front. He caught only small glimpses of the two in the rear seat. If he were a betting man—and he was—he would wager this meant bad news.

"We need to examine the squire, Mr. Gibbs," Doctor Rhodes said without formality as the men alighted the barouche. He introduced a graying bearded man in dark suit as Mr. Baker, the squire's solicitor, and a ferret-looking man in tweeds as Constable Reed.

No one offered a hand, so Donald did not offer his. He suspected it would be refused.

Stand your ground, he ordered himself. *You've done nothing.*

The longcase clock ticked a thousand seconds. Finally the four men filed into the library. Donald ceased pacing the carpet.

"Please have seats, gentlemen."

They took to the sofa and chairs. Without preamble the solicitor, Mr. Baker, said, "We suspect you of neglecting Squire Bartley. In light of our concerns, Constable Reed intends to order a postmortem when he passes on."

A nerve flicked in the corner of Donald's mouth. He hoped they had not noticed.

"And I intend to file a motion against the will, accusing you of hastening his death. Even if the postmortem clears you, I assure you the motion will tie up your inheritance for months and months. The Shropshire courts are notoriously slow."

"Gentlemen." Donald dropped into a chair and put a hand upon his chest. He could feel his heart thumping against his breastbone. "I fear you are correct. I've done my uncle grave harm."

Four sets of eyes traded glances.

"What do I know of nursing the infirm? I never had the opportunity to take care of my sainted mother and father, who drowned when the *Atlantic* sank eleven years ago. I only thought a quiet room, peaceful surroundings, would induce my uncle—my only living relation—to health."

It was difficult to tell if they believed him. But at least no more accusations came forth.

"I'm grateful to you for drawing this to my attention," he went on. "Please tell me . . . what can I do to atone for my error?"

Constable Reed spoke up. "We insist Doctor Rhodes examines him three times weekly."

"But of course. I welcome that."

"His bedchamber must be aired out," Mr. Baker said. "And he must have around-the-clock care. That means overnight as well."

"I'll see to it."

Through the whole visitation, Vicar Phelps had sat with tight lips set into a face that seemed a little pale. Finally he spoke. "That will benefit you, as well, Mr. Gibbs. Doing unto others as we would have them do unto us does not exclude family."

"Yes, thank you," Donald said humbly.

After a stilted silence, the men rose as one and started for the door.

"Good day, Mr. Gibbs," said Constable Reed.

"Good day, gentlemen." Donald turned to the solicitor. "Ah . . . Mr. Baker? May I have a moment?"

When they were alone, he said, "I realize this isn't the appropriate occasion to address this. But I have no idea when we shall meet again. I'm completely strapped for funds."

Mr. Baker's brown eyes were devoid of any warmth. "You're free to charge against your uncle's account in any shop in the village."

"Yes, yes. I understand that. But I . . . left behind some debts in London. Is it possible to have an advance . . . against my . . ." He cleared his throat. This was not the best time. But what choice did he have?

"Against your expectations?" Mr. Baker said flatly.

Donald hung his head. "Yes."

"I believe you have already borrowed against them."

My uncle and his big mouth! "Yes, some."

Mr. Baker shook his head. "Squire Bartley's instructions concerning his will were very clear. Not one inch of land, not one stick of furniture, not one penny is to be transferred until his death."

"But I stand to lose my house in London! The house my parents—" He jerked a nod toward the ceiling. "The house *his own sister* lived in for over thirty years."

And he stood to lose even more.

The solicitor shrugged. "I can only do as my client demands. Perhaps he'll rally, now that you're to be taking proper care of him. Then you may have a long conversation over your debts."

Donald did not miss the sarcasm in his voice, however impassive the solicitor's face.

Chapter 10

All things work together for good to them that love God. Jewel had heard the Scripture read in church several times over the years, but never understood it until she landed in the vast basement of Stillmans, the largest emporium in Birmingham, boasting twenty-thousand feet of floor space, electric lights, and, wonder of wonders, an elevator.

Her responsibility was to unpack and press dresses, blouses, and skirts for the Ladies' Department, hanging them with wooden hangers onto a rack on wheels that the shop assistants came for at the end of the day. She earned seven shillings and sixpence more than the corset factory had paid, enough to enroll Becky in Mrs. Mitchell's Infant School on Cornwall Street, just two blocks from the department store. For an extra two shillings weekly, Mrs. Mitchell kept the children of employed mothers past six o'clock, and fed them a substantial tea at four.

The housing situation had improved, as well. Vicar Treves had found her and Becky a room in a small back-to-back cottage on Waterloo Street. Mr. Turner was a night-shift worker at the gasworks, and Mrs. Turner feared being alone with only her five-month-old son. Kitchen privileges and the use of the water closet and tiny garden were included, and the rent was lower than at the previous flat.

Furthermore, Mrs. Turner was delighted to have Becky home Saturdays to help amuse Carl, a pleasant baby who smiled and pumped his chubby legs into the air whenever anyone spoke cooing noises to him.

Jewel even had new clothes. Or at least, new to her. Because she would be working somewhat in the public view, Mrs. Treves had given her five lovely dresses, a cashmere wrapper, and two nightgowns from a wardrobe she had decided to hoard no longer.

"If I'm ever slim enough to wear them again, they'll be woefully out of style," she had said. "Others can put them to use now."

The only fly in the ointment was that in order to be out of Mr. Dunstan's range, they had had to resettle across town. Vicar Hansford's sermons at Saint Martin Church were almost as inspiring as Vicar Treves', if his demeanor was not as warm, with his impersonal "Good day" at the church door. But this was a fair price to pay for safety, and Jewel would never feel comfortable near her former neighborhood.

The dozen or so denizens of the basement were friendly. Those closest to her work station were Mrs. Macey, who talked a blue streak while unpacking housewares, and Miss Hill, who went into long stories of her childhood while unpacking toys. Jewel found the chatter refreshing, after so many months of silent fixation upon a sewing needle.

"It's best if you've got a slice or two of bacon," Mrs. Macey said five weeks into Jewel's employment, while wiping sawdust from a Blue Willow teapot. She claimed her green pea soup recipe, clipped from a magazine, was the same served to the queen in Buckingham Palace, and Jewel was extremely fond of soup.

"The more bacon the better, to give it a bit of smoky flavor."

"That's so," Miss Hill said. "My mother added it to hers, whenever we could afford it."

Miss Brent from the Ladies' Department entered the basement and looked at Jewel.

"Mr. Clements is asking for you."

"Me?"

"Yes." Miss Brent turned, expecting her to follow.

Shop assistants were, as a rule, snooty when they came downstairs to collect merchandise. This had never distressed Jewel, for she only had contact with them those ten minutes daily. But today, the aloofness in Miss Brent's manner was almost devastating. Swamped with nervousness, Jewel did not risk a look over at the other workers lest she see pity and give way to the threatening tears.

What have I done? Please, Father, I can't lose my job, she pleaded beneath her breath while leaden feet climbed the service staircase.

"We're impressed with your work, Mrs. Libby," said fatherly looking Mr. Clements in his office. "Would you be interested in filling a vacancy in Ladies' Leather Goods?"

When Jewel could speak, she assured him that she would indeed. She was turned over to Miss Brent again, whose frozen haughtiness thawed somewhat as she fitted Jewel into a white

115

blouse and brown poplin skirt, the uniform of all female shop assistants.

"You'll be given two sets today," Miss Brent said. "And you might think of buying another blouse or two later, to keep ahead of the laundry."

Thank you, Father, Jewel prayed, carrying the parcel containing her uniforms back downstairs. Her joy was tempered at the sight of her co-workers. Poor Mrs. Macey, nine years in the basement. Five years for Miss Hill.

She did not anticipate their congratulatory smiles.

"So, they've promoted you!" said Mrs. Macey.

"To Ladies' Leather Goods," Jewel said uneasily. "But how did you—?"

"You think you're the first?" Miss Hill asked. "And when they sack one of us, they just send a messenger down with wages in an envelope."

"I'm so sorry . . ."

"That it's you and not us?" Mrs. Macey shook her head. "We would trade places with you in a heartbeat and have your red hair to boot, but we don't have it so bad. They want the pretty people toutin' their wares upstairs."

Miss Hill nodded. "Just don't turn all uppity when you come down here."

"Never," Jewel promised, embracing both.

⁂

Sunday morning, she roused Becky earlier than usual. "Good morning, mite."

Becky's eyes opened. Her lips formed a half smile that faded as her eyelids drifted downward again.

Jewel stroked her hair. "Would you like to take an omnibus ride?"

This time the eyes opened and stayed open. "Yes, Mummy! Where will we go?"

"To church. Our old church."

Just this once. She was bursting to tell the Treves her good news.

She ignored the little warning voice in her mind. Never had she seen Mr. Dunstan in the vicinity of Saint Philip's. Even if he had known of their attendance, five weeks' absence would have told him that they were gone.

She took precautions. She bound up their telltale red hair into the same bonnets they wore on the way to school and work. They sat on the lower, enclosed level of the omnibus, even though Jewel would have loved showing Becky the city from the upper level. As they alighted and walked the half block more, she scanned the faces of passersby, even those in the distance.

"How good to see you," Mrs. Treves said, drawing them aside in the vestibule.

"May I have a peppermint?" Becky asked.

"Becky . . ." Jewel scolded.

The vicar's wife laughed and produced a sweet from her bag.

"Thank you, ma'am," Becky said, redeeming herself.

"I just want to thank you and the vicar," Jewel said. "The Turners are kind, and Becky likes school. And . . . I've been promoted to shop assistant."

"Wonderful! I can't wait to tell Paul . . . or rather, *you* must after service."

Jewel smiled. "I was afraid you would be upset at our being here."

Mrs. Treves gave her a quick embrace. "Not at all, dear."

"We won't make a habit of it."

"That would probably be best. The man would have to be insane to hang on this long. Still . . ."

Jewel nodded. It was the *still*s you had to watch.

⁓

Patrons ambling toward the east corner of Stillmans' ground floor caught the aroma of fine leather before catching sight of tables of purses and card cases, satchels and valises, skate bags and pocketbooks.

"The buckles on this Gladstone Bag protect it from flying open in the hands of even the clumsiest porter," Mr. Houghton, head of Ladies' Leather Goods, said to Jewel on Monday. "The inside is lined with satin."

"I've never seen anything so nice," Jewel said, running a hand along the fine leather.

Mr. Houghton gave her a sober look. He was not much older than Jewel, though his authority made him seem older. "Remember, Mrs. Libby, you are selling, not buying."

"Ah . . . sorry, sir."

"Don't be." He winked. "Enthusiasm is contagious. You'll do fine."

Indeed she made her first sale that afternoon, a calfskin toilet case containing scissors and comb, plate mirror and nail cleaner.

She fairly skipped the block over to Cornwall Street. Mrs. Mitchell's stucco terrace house was conveniently situated across the street from Cornwall Square. A house servant escorted the children there twice daily for play and, Jewel suspected, to give Mrs. Mitchell a moment to prop her feet up. As Vicar Treves had explained, she charged such a low fee because she considered her school a mission. Becky had already memorized five Scripture verses and her alphabet, and absorbed lessons in manners and hygiene.

Jewel smiled at the memory of her daughter's demonstration of the proper way to clean teeth. Who knew that the toothbrush was supposed to go up and down, not side to side? Even the Turners were impressed, except for little Carl, who happily drooled upon Jewel's sleeve.

Her happy reverie dissolved at the sight of Mr. Dunstan, loitering at the pillar-box outside Mrs. Mitchell's.

"Why are you here?!" she demanded, trembling.

His brows raised with his smile. "Why, Mrs. Libby, is it? Fancy meeting you! Ain't it a small world?"

Anger, fear, and nausea churned inside, so that every step drawing her closer took every ounce of courage. "Why won't you let us be?"

He put a hand to his chest. "I'm doing naught but standing on the pavement, Mrs. Libby. My right as a taxpayer. You know about taxes, don't you? They pay for roads and pavement. And the police."

Tears filled her eyes. "I wouldn't have gone to them if you would have stayed away from my daughter."

"What did you do? Weep to them as you're doing now?" His mocking smile took a downward curve. "I never did no harm to her."

"You were looking for the chance."

"Well, what means *harm* might be different for you and me."

Jewel's blood chilled. "I'll go back to the police!"

"And what? Try to get me sacked again? My employer won't care, long as I do my job." His eyes narrowed. "I've had enough of this conversation, Mrs. Libby. Just remember, you spoke to me first, so you can't accuse me of harassment."

Jewel had had enough as well. She needed to make sure Becky was all right, get her home, figure out what to do next.

She was three steps away when he said to her back, "By the way, that's a pleasant little park across the street. It does a man's heart good to see little ones romping out in the sunshine."

"Did the woman who kept Becky at your former place know you were a parishioner here?" Vicar Treves asked in the vicarage garden. Becky was indoors, playing with the children.

"Mrs. Platt. She did." Jewel's throat ached from weeping herself dry. "After all you did to keep us safe . . . to give us a better life. I had to ruin it. I'm so sorry."

"Now, now," Mrs. Treves consoled, but with worried expression. "You mustn't blame yourself. But we have to assume he knows where you live, as well. You must stay here tonight."

"I'll ride over and inform the Turners," Paul said, rising. "Tomorrow morning we'll visit the police, and then I'll drive you on to Stillmans."

"You're too kind," Jewel said thickly, despising herself for causing so much trouble. And another, terrible, thought struck her. "We took a hansom here, but what if Mr. Dunstan followed? He surely knows you've helped me. What if he tries to hurt your children? What have I done?"

"We'll keep an eye on them," Mrs. Treves said, and put a hand on her shoulder. "You need to calm yourself, Mrs. Libby. God will not fail us."

Jewel held Becky close and slept not one wink, though the small bed in the garret room was comfortable. Attempts at faith were overwhelmed by the sick feeling that, even with Vicar Treves beside her, the police would be as ineffectual as before.

Sure enough, Constable Whittington said, wearily, "We'll

send an officer 'round to give him a stout warning. But standing on public property's not a crime."

"So we must wait until he harms Mrs. Libby's daughter?" said Vicar Treves.

"No offense, Vicar, but I'd wager my last farthing he'll not harm her, not with our knowing his identity. He just wants to frighten Mrs. Libby."

"Intimidation is harmful, too," Vicar Treves argued, but to no effect.

"We'll never be free of him," Jewel said with bleak voice back in the carriage. "He's twisted. We can't hide ourselves at your house forever. And there's no place in Birmingham where he won't find us."

As he reined the horse up Great Russell Street, Vicar Treves gave her a thoughtful, but odd, look, and then another. Finally he spoke.

"This Mr. Dunstan is employed somewhere as a night watchman?"

"Yes, sir."

"So that's his Achilles' heel."

"What do you mean?"

"Well, that he has a weakness."

"I know what it means, Vicar," Jewel said respectfully. Her former employer, the headmaster, had loved to speak of the Greeks.

The vicar looked a little sheepish. "I beg your pardon."

Jewel shook her head. Of all people, he owed her no apology. "But how is his job a weakness? If anything, it gives him power, to lurk in the streets while I'm at mine."

Vicar Treves reined the horses to a halt near the department store entrance. "I have an idea. I'm not completely certain it has merit, so I must first speak with Noelle."

"What should I do?"

"Sell pocketbooks, Mrs. Libby. For today. But I must ask you this. How attached are you to Birmingham?"

"I've . . . never lived anywhere else."

Birmingham was home, for all its frantic pace, smokestack-tainted air, slums jostling for space with factories. But that was not his question.

"I would live on the moon to keep Becky safe."

The vicar smiled. "I don't know about the moon. But we shall see."

❧

The moon factored into Vicar Treves' plan after all. It was after sunset Wednesday that a hired coach, better equipped for gaslit streets, stopped by the Turners' for Jewel's battered tin trunk, then made the journey to the Queen's Hotel across from New Street Station. Jewel and Becky followed the Treves through the arched entrance with eyes wide. The foyer was a palace, with shining marble floors, red velvet draperies, high columns, and chandeliers.

"Does the queen live here?" Becky breathed.

Vicar Treves chuckled, and Mrs. Treves replied, "No, dear."

"It's too grand," Jewel said. "We'll wait in the station."

"You'll not spend the night on a bench," Vicar Treves said, nodding toward the reception desk. "My parents are paying for this."

"Why should they—"

"We told them of your situation," Mrs. Treves said. "They wanted to help. You wouldn't want to rob two dear old people of a blessing, would you?"

The young man behind the desk wished them good evening

and asked Jewel to sign the registry, as if she were as entitled to a room as any upper-class guest. The porter who had brought in the trunk politely waited to the side for farewells.

"Tickets . . . instructions . . . money for meals and a coach . . . it's all enclosed," said the vicar, handing Jewel a packet.

Mrs. Treves embraced her. "Godspeed, Mrs. Libby . . . Becky."

Words were inadequate, but they were all Jewel had. She thanked them with a voice thick with emotion, promised to pray for them every remaining day of her life.

"This way if you please, miss?" the porter said as the Treves left to return to their home and children.

Again, Jewel did not expect to sleep. Too much had happened today. She had had to turn in her uniforms at Stillmans and suffer the disappointment in Mr. Houghton's face. Explain to Mrs. Mitchell why Becky had not returned to school and caution her to keep an eye out for Mr. Dunstan, for revenge was not his sole motivation for stalking little girls. Apologize to Mrs. Turner for leaving with so little warning, give Carl one final cuddle. And there was the unfamiliar future rushing toward her.

But she had not reckoned with the power of lavender-scented sheets on a goose down mattress in a half tester bed.

Early the following morning, she and Becky stared out of the train window at passing farmhouses and pastures, cottages and hills, hedgerows and trees, as the Severn Valley Railway chugged westward.

"Mummy, why is it all so green?" Becky asked.

Jewel gave her a squeeze. "This is what God intended summer to look like, mite."

Chapter 11

Julia and Elizabeth were preparing the vicarage for a morning meeting of the Women's Charity Society. As a man would be in the way, even shut up in his study, Andrew decided it was his duty to go fishing. Jonathan and John were at archery practice, but he found a willing accomplice in Ambrose Clay.

The waters of the Bryce slipped along with patches of reflected sunlight mingling with shade from the willow trees. The two men stood on the bank, engaged in a favorite guessing game while watching their lines.

" 'The robbed that smiles steals something from the thief,' " Ambrose said.

"Give me a minute," Andrew said.

"No one's rushing you."

Andrew made a tentative guess. "*Hamlet*."

"Not *Hamlet*."

"Hmm."

In a silence enhanced by birds calling to each other in the branches, faint lowing of cattle being led to pasture across the river, the clicks of the reel as he wheeled in his line, Andrew mentally traveled back in time to his university days.

At length he turned his head to smile at his friend. "*Othello.*"

Ambrose smiled back. "Correct. Your turn."

"Very well. 'Let your moderation be known unto all men.' "

Ambrose's brow furrowed over his slate gray eyes. "Did you not preach that one a few months ago?"

"January past."

"It sounds New Testament."

"You're warm."

"Saint Paul to Timothy."

"Very good."

The game was interrupted when Ambrose's cork disappeared beneath the water. He let out a whoop and reeled in a grayling of at least three pounds. As it flipped about in the pail, he said, "Now I need at least two more. I promised Mrs. Herrick I would bring back enough for supper."

"Weren't you being rash?" Andrew asked.

"Not at all." Ambrose grinned. "If I don't make my quota, I'll stop by Temple's for some salmon."

"Crafty you."

"Fish is fish. Now, whose turn?"

"Yours."

"Hmm." Ambrose pursed his lips thoughtfully, but not from any strain of memory, Andrew knew. He had played so many Shakespearean characters that the library in his mind was vast.

The pause came from finding a quote that he had not already mentioned in their game.

Andrew checked his line. The hook had been stripped clean by some crafty fish. He could smile, just as Shakespeare had advised. He was having a good time.

Later that day he would step back into the role of minister. Ezra Towly lay dying of lung cancer, and his five grown children were already dividing up the cattle and household goods. Jessie Sykes' wife, Nora, had delivered a fine baby girl yesterday, the first after three boys. The Hayes were spreading word all over Gresham that the Sloans' Labrador retriever, Dusty, had killed two of their chickens, when their own Alsatian, Bob, padded about the village with a knowing canine smile.

And there was the matter of yesterday's telegram from Birmingham.

Woman daughter need job home escape. Can you help?

Escape? Had the woman broken out of prison?

Of course not. He trusted Paul Treves not to involve him in a crime. And so there was naught he could do but reply yes, until Mr. Trumble pointed out that he should add two more words, for the minimum price was set at three.

Yes of course.

He expected a reply from Vicar Treves soon, hopefully with meatier details. But for this moment, he was simply a man with a fishing rod, a good friend, and a cloudless morning.

Ambrose gave him a gleeful smile. "You'll never guess this one."

"Not if you don't speak it." The water dimpled where Andrew's hook sank.

" 'Our doubts are traitors,' " Ambrose said, " 'and make us lose the good we oft might win by fearing to attempt.' "

Andrew repeated the line. "That's a great one, Ambrose."

"Take all the time you need," Ambrose said graciously.

Smiling to himself, Andrew thought how easily his friend fell into the acting role, for patience was not one of Ambrose's virtues. It was a wonder that he enjoyed fishing.

"What have we here?" Ambrose said, and reeled in a bream, too meager for Mrs. Herrick's table.

"You'll be patronizing Temple's after all," Andrew said, just before a great wave of pain rolled through his midsection.

"It is no shame to contribute to the village economy." Ambrose baited his hook, whistling Verdi's "La Donna è Mobile" between his teeth.

Andrew clutched his stomach with his left hand.

"Say, old man, are you thinking?" Ambrose said.

Sweat trickled down Andrew's temple.

Ambrose cast his line back into the water. "Would you care for a hint?"

A groan rose up from Andrew's stomach, pushed through his lips.

"As you wish, but there is no shame in getting a hint."

Andrew groaned again.

Ambrose jerked his head in his direction, threw down his rod and reel.

"What is it?" Ambrose asked, taking the rod from his hand, helping him sit on the grass.

"Tonic," Andrew said weakly. "I need—"

"You need the doctor." Ambrose crouched before him, felt his forehead. "You're sweating like old cheese. Will you be all right while I get help?"

"Yes," Andrew replied. And indeed, the pain was subsiding. "I think it's better. I just need a minute."

"Not on your life. I'll be back." Ambrose straightened, started toward the vicarage.

"Wait!"

Ambrose turned back to him, face tight with concern. "What is it, Andrew?"

"The line . . ."

"It's over there in the grass. I'll gather it all up after—"

"No." Andrew shook his head. "Shakespeare."

Ambrose gaped at him. "I can't believe you! It's from *Measure for Measure*! Act one! If you're dead when I return, I shall carve it on your gravestone!"

Andrew chuckled, listening to the fading footfalls against the earth. Only a true friend would make such a morbid joke.

If he passed on this very moment, he would not hold it against God, for he had been blessed with good friends and loving family. A fulfilling vocation. The most loving wife a man could ask for.

Julia, he thought, and closed his eyes.

But if you would kindly grant me just a little more time . . .

"May I bring you up some tea, Mrs. Phelps?" Dora asked from the landing.

"No thank you," Julia replied. "I'm sorry your lovely treats are wasted."

"They'll make a fine lunch later, anyway. How is the vicar?"

"I don't know yet."

What Julia did know was that it was absolutely useless to pace outside the bedroom door, but she could not tear herself away. She was grateful that Elizabeth and Fiona and Ambrose were downstairs to explain to the ladies arriving that the meeting would have to be postponed.

The door opened and Doctor Rhodes stuck his head through the gap. "Come back inside, Mrs. Phelps."

Julia entered. Andrew sat on the side of the bed, buttoning his shirt. He smiled at her. "I feel much better. Don't look so worried."

∽

"Over there! Directly east!" cried first mate Harris. He hopped to his feet and waved his arms. "We'll gather sticks . . . build a fire!"

"Wait!" Captain Jacobs ordered. "We don't know who they are."

"Who they are? After two years on this blasted island, I don't care if it's Napoleon Bonaparte!"

Captain Jacobs drew his pistol, aimed it at Harris. Just two bullets remained. The rest rusted in the carcasses of Komodo dragons that had feasted on three of his men.

"Lay low, Harris, or I'll plug you and leave you for the lizards!"

That got the first mate's attention. He dropped to the ground.

"There's a good man," Jacobs said. How could he fault Harris, with his young wife and two children waiting? Perhaps if he himself had someone to return to, he would not be so cautious.

He raised his field glasses to his eyes. The Union Jack flapped from the mast. Jacobs smiled.

"Build your fire, Harris."

What Captain Jacobs could not know was that Indonesian pirates had commandeered the ship. *Another one in the oven*, Aleda thought, unrolling the page and its carbon copy.

She would not trade places with anyone. In what other vocation could one be paid for sitting in the cool window breeze, sending daydreams to the fingers to type? For changing from nightgown at one's leisure, sometimes not at all when a deadline loomed near.

130

As she wrapped and tied the original pages for mailing, she wondered how long she could stretch out the story. She would send the hapless crew of the HMS *Sphinx* home eventually—minus the poor trio eaten by Komodo dragons and however many would perish battling pirates. But Harris and Captain Jacobs would come out alive. Readers would want Harris reunited with his wife and children and Captain Jacobs to find romance.

That gave her pause. What if in next month's installment those same pirates had on their ship a beautiful daughter of a lord, captured for ransom?

Hmm. Aleda chewed her fingernail. Captain Jacobs would have to be over forty to have participated in the siege of Petropavlovsk. The woman should be in her thirties.

She could be the widow of a lord . . . who was recently murdered by the pirates.

But this lord would have to have been corrupt, perhaps have attempted to do business with the pirates. He would have mistreated his wife, or readers would not accept her falling in love with Captain Jacobs so soon into her widowhood.

She had a month to sort it all out. She pushed back her typewriter on her desk, filled her Waterman fountain pen. Whatever time her bread-and-butter stories did not demand was devoted to her novel. *Wharram Percy* was set in an actual abandoned village in the Yorkshire wolds, and filled with stories of characters who might have lived there. She had visited the site and surrounding area five times over the past four years. Last year, she had tied plots and subplots into a proper ending. Even so, the story stretched out before her like a road dipping over the horizon.

Her pen was the tortoise on that road. The typewriter was too impersonal. Completion was impeded by such things as side trips to chapter six to enhance the dialogue between the constable and his errant child, chapter ten to trim superfluous adjectives from a sunset.

Critics, somewhat forgiving with newspaper serializations for the masses, could be brutal with novels. Aleda had felt just enough critical jabs from her stories to know that she would not surrender her heart, her passion, for public viewing until every word, phrase, and paragraph was the best it could possibly be.

Knocking sounded downstairs. She picked up her watch from her desktop.

Twenty past nine?

Mrs. Moore's grandson, Vernon, would be delivering clean laundry today, but he usually came just before noon. She pushed out of her chair and slipped dressing gown over nightgown. She could only find one slipper, so padded downstairs in bare feet.

"Aunt Aleda?"

She recognized John's voice through the door.

"Come in!" she called, halfway across the kitchen.

He opened the door and entered. The eleven-year-old had inherited Jonathan's dark hair and compact build, but the good-natured hazel eyes were handed down from Andrew. Today they were filled with worry.

"Is it the squire?" Aleda asked.

He shook his head. "Mother says come. It's Grandfather."

"Well, it's an ill wind that blows no good," Father said from his parlor chair. "It's good to see you, daughter. Did you finish your story?"

But for paleness to his cheeks, he seemed well. There was more distress in the faces of the other occupants of the parlor—Mother, Elizabeth and Jonathan, Ambrose and Fiona Clay.

"Yes. John says you're ill. What is it?"

"Gallstones," her mother said gently, sitting on an ottoman at his side, holding his hand.

"What does that mean?" asked John.

Father smiled at him. "That I've got too much gall, John. Can you believe it?"

"Grandfather will be fine," Elizabeth assured her son. "The stones just need to . . . come out."

The boy's eyes widened. "How?"

"Well, in hospital."

"It's done all the time now," said Mr. Clay, but the assurance in his voice did not travel up to his eyes.

The parlor table was set with teapot and two trays of sandwiches and assorted treats. They looked barely touched, and must have been intended for one of her mother's charity meetings. Aleda was famished, having subsisted on bread and cheese and gooseberries for the past week. But nothing could have induced her to eat. She crossed the carpet and stood before her stepfather with arms folded.

"We will *not* allow Doctor Rhodes to put a knife to you!"

A gasp came from behind. She twisted around and realized John had followed her across the room. Jonathan got up from the sofa to put an arm around the boy's shoulders. Elizabeth, rising too, shook her head at Aleda as if to reassure her that she had done nothing wrong.

"Why don't you take him home?" Mother said gently. "See about the twins. Mrs. Littlejohn and Hilda will be tired."

Jonathan and Elizabeth looked at each other. The message traveling between the two sets of eyes was as distinct as if spoken. When Jonathan did speak, it was simply confirmation for the rest of the people in the room.

"We'll go," he said softly to Elizabeth. "Stay here awhile."

She touched his sleeve and returned to the sofa. Aleda moved to sit beside her.

"Doctor Rhodes recommends a well-reputed surgeon at Saint John's Hospital," Mother said. "He's telegraphing to inquire for Monday."

"Monday?" Fiona Clay said.

"That was the first attack I've had in a couple of weeks," Father said. "I feel right as rain now."

"Right as clouds, you mean," Aleda said. "You're white."

"Mother?" Elizabeth pleaded.

"I agree he shouldn't wait," she said with pained tone. "But we may as well argue with a gatepost."

Father nodded. "I appreciate all of you. And I don't wish to cause you worry. But I've had these attacks for months now. Four days will make no difference. I've promised to baptize the Coggins' grandchild, and have already written my sermon. As I shall be laid up in bed for weeks afterwards, I intend to be in the pulpit on Sunday."

It was useless to argue. Aleda could hardly blame him. If she were told she required immediate surgery, she would argue for a couple of days to get her manuscripts in order, adjust to the idea. But there was another question no one had asked—at least not in her hearing.

"What about Philip?" she asked.

"Yes, Andrew," Mr. Clay said, starting to rise. "I'll telegraph him at once."

"No," Father said. "Doctor Rhodes says this other man is good. I'm satisfied."

"But, Father," Elizabeth said, "Philip was at the top of his class."

"And you have that heart murmur," Aleda reminded him.

"He wouldn't have time to arrange for someone to cover his absence."

"Shouldn't that be his decision?" Mr. Clay said, seated again but looking prepared to hop up at a moment's notice.

"No. It should be mine." Father looked from face to face. "I appreciate all of you. More than I can say. But I shall be very hurt if any of you go against me and contact him."

Silence followed, with most eyes staring down at hands.

This is insane. Aleda cleared her throat. "Will you even inform him, Father?"

"Of course. Tonight I'll write to him, as well as to Laurel and Grace. Now, noon is only forty minutes away. What say we pass those dishes around and have lunch?"

"Yes," Mother said, rising. "We have so much here. Oh, but Jonathan and the children . . ."

"I'll just pack a hamper and join them at home," Elizabeth said.

"I'll help you." Aleda got to her feet and gave her mother a regretful look. "I've lost my appetite."

Chapter 12

Aleda and her sister walked in silence, holding the hamper between them, until out of earshot of the vicarage.

"What do you think?" Elizabeth asked.

"I think Philip ought to know."

"But Father would be incensed."

"And to what end?" Aleda gave a dry chuckle. "His sermon Sunday past was on forgiveness."

Elizabeth's eyes grew wide. "Oh, Aleda! Are you thinking of telegraphing him?"

"Absolutely."

"I'm so relieved. I won't tell anyone." A little sob broke her voice. "I couldn't do it myself. I've always been afraid of disappointing Father. Not that he's harsh, but because his opinion of me matters so much. When you lose one parent . . ."

She hesitated. "Forgive me. You lost a parent, too."

"You have nothing for which to apologize," Aleda assured her. "I barely knew my father."

"Was it the same way, having only a mother? Did you care terribly what she thought?"

Aleda mulled over that one. "I cared. I've always adored my mother."

"Of course."

"But I don't know if I had the overwhelming *drive* to please that you describe. That seems to be more particular to daughters and fathers."

"Thank you for doing this for him," Elizabeth said hoarsely. "I know you and I haven't been terribly close because of the age difference. But I'm so glad you're my sister."

"It's nothing," Aleda said, embarrassed by the sentiment while blinking the sting from her eyes.

As they reached the cottage gate, Aleda smiled at the sight of Jonathan romping with the children in the garden.

"Jonathan's a good father, too."

"Yes, he is." Elizabeth took the hamper and reached for the latch, but then turned back around with a knowing smile.

"What is it?" Aleda asked.

With lowered voice, her sister said, "Can you bear another niece or nephew?"

Aleda stared at her, noticed the bloom in her cheeks. "Are you serious?"

"I'm three months along. We haven't broken the news to anyone yet. We want to give the baby time to grow. I've not even written to Laurel."

The fact that she had just been honored did not escape Aleda. "Thank you for telling me." She reached for the hamper. "But here, you shouldn't be carrying that."

Elizabeth moved it aside. "Exercise is good for me. That's

been my mistake, coddling myself, taking to bed. I started reading up on childbearing after the last—"

Aleda nodded, stepped over to embrace her. "I'm happy for you."

"Aunt Aleda!"

The twins were sprinting toward the gate. Aleda surrendered to both sweaty embraces and smiled when their attention leaped from her to the hamper.

"Ooh, what have you, Mother?" Claire asked.

"Lunch!" Elizabeth said, producing more exclamations of ecstasy.

Aleda waved at Jonathan and John, and set out again. Her ears barely registered distant hoofbeats and the rumbling of wheels. Her mind was going over her conversation with Elizabeth.

She had noticed the unique bond between daughters and fathers long ago. She suspected most writers were lifelong people watchers. Living in the Larkspur as a girl, the vicarage later, and Newnham College as a young woman had provided a wealth of material for her ink-drawn characters.

That habit of studying people was what propelled her toward Trumbles. She was quite certain she had seen through her stepfather's refusal to telegraph Philip.

Andrew was the most decent man she had ever known, but he was not above a little vindictiveness when a loved one was hurt. Aleda had heard the stories of how he had tormented a younger Jonathan when he came to Gresham seeking Elizabeth's forgiveness for his indiscretions.

What better way to bring Philip up short for hurting Mother, for not taking the time to write a single letter during the five weeks since Grace's wedding, than to have him receive Andrew's letter *after* the surgery? Even she herself found some smug satisfaction over the notion.

But teaching a lesson was one thing. Safety was another. Philip would go the second and third miles to see that their stepfather got proper care.

At least the old Philip would. The pre-Loretta Philip. She could only hope that part of him would not have changed.

"How is the vicar?" Mrs. Shaw called from her garden, pushing back her bonnet. She wore the look of someone about to amble over to the gate.

"He's better, thank you," she replied with a little wave, to get the point across that she would not be stopping.

"Too bad about the surgery. But he'll come through fine."

Aleda's steps faltered briefly. But of course. Doctor Rhodes' telegram to his colleague. Trumbles was a cake of yeast in Gresham's lump of gossip dough. "Yes, thank you," she said with another wave.

A pair of horses and coach broke into sight beyond the elm trees. She paid it no mind, but then the horses slowed to a halt. The driver doffed his cap.

"Pardon me, miss, but will you direct me to the vicarage?"

"The vicarage? Why?"

"My passengers here say they're to report to Vicar Phelps."

A young woman stared from the window, seeming so much like a frightened rabbit that Aleda stepped close and said with softened voice, "My stepfather is the vicar. But he's not well."

"Oh dear," the woman said.

"What's the matter, Mummy?" came from inside. Another

head squeezed into view, smaller, with the same red curls peeking from a straw hat.

"Miss?" the driver said.

"A moment please," Aleda said to him, and turned again to the woman. "Why do you wish to see him?"

"I've a letter from Vicar Treves in Birmingham asking him to find a job for me. I'm sorry he's ill. Will he be all right?"

"Miss?" the driver said impatiently.

Aleda sent him a glare. He shrugged and took a pipe from his pocket. To the woman she said, "He needs surgery."

"Oh dear."

The concern in her voice seemed genuine. For herself and the girl, yes, but also for her stepfather.

"Can you come back in a month or so, when he's recovered?" Aleda asked.

The woman's face clouded. "I've nowhere else to go."

Aleda stifled a sigh. What to do? She looked about. Mrs. Shaw had apparently retreated to her cottage. Should she send the pair to Elizabeth's? On her return from telegraphing Philip, they could deal with the matter without involving Mother and Father. Elizabeth was a member of the Women's Charity Society, and Jonathan knew almost every person in Gresham.

But wait, she thought. Elizabeth had enough on her hands, especially in her condition. No matter what she said about exercise, Aleda was quite certain mental strain was a detriment to pregnancy.

Her spirits sagged. She would have to take charge. She opened the door, called up to the driver.

"Please continue on until I call for you to stop."

The woman moved over, looking both frightened and hopeful. The girl, leaning against her mother, stared. Aleda gave both a resigned smile.

"Good day. I'm Aleda Hollis."

The woman's reddish brows lifted. "The writer?"

"Yes, I am. Vicar Treves told you?"

"Mrs. Treves did."

"She gives me peppermints," the girl piped.

Aleda had to laugh. "Is that so? And what might your names be?"

"Where do you want this?" the driver grunted, bent under the weight of a battered tin trunk.

"Just inside here," Aleda replied, moving aside the umbrella stand, almost tripping over the canvas bag of laundry Vernon Moore had delivered three days ago.

The driver set down his burden with a thump. Mrs. Libby had apparently already paid him, for he touched the brim of his cap and said to her, "Good day."

"Thank you," she said. She stood in the corner of the cottage kitchen, holding her daughter's hand. Thankfully, the day was still young. After telegraphing Philip, Aleda would figure out what to do with them.

An idea came to her. She could make up for most of her lost time.

"Wait!" she said to the coachman. "Will you drop me off at the crossroads?"

"For a shilling."

"Very good. I just have to fetch something."

He pursed his lips. "A florin, then."

Halfway up the staircase, she thought of her temporary guests and turned to say, "The water closet's through the back door. And please help yourselves to the gooseberries on the table."

She might as well mail her manuscript, too, Aleda thought.

It was as she tied it with paper and string that a more potent thought struck her.

If she sent the telegraph from Trumbles, her father would know within the hour. Given his stubbornness, he could possibly move up the date of his surgery. It depended upon which was more important to him, having to turn his pulpit over to a curate one Sunday earlier or having Philip not involved.

Only a few yards away waited transportation to Shrewsbury. She should send it from the railway station.

That thought led to another. Why not speak directly with Philip? Shame him for so neglecting his family that their stepfather would not even venture to ask his opinion about the surgery. If Philip was so cowed by Loretta as to refuse, he would have to do it looking in her eyes, not holding an impersonal piece of paper.

She looked at her watch. If she hurried, she could make the five o'clock express to London and be back by tomorrow evening.

You're insane, she told herself, even while shoving her toilet kit, nightgown, and manuscript into her satchel. She changed into the same olive green cashmere traveling suit that had served her well for four years. She would simply wear the same clothes home tomorrow.

Downstairs, the driver munched gooseberries at the table, while Mrs. Libby and Becky did not seem to have moved.

"Will you drive me to Shrewsbury Station?"

"Cost you a crown," the driver said between chews.

Highway robbery, given that if she didn't go, he stood to make nothing for the return journey. But her only alternative was to inquire if Mr. Pool's coach was available, and his nephew sober enough to drive. And of course, the whole of Gresham would know, and Father would suspect her mission.

Aleda approached Mrs. Libby. "I apologize for running out on you like this, but I've an important errand. We'll figure out what to do with you when I return. But for now, make yourselves at home."

"Oh, thank you!" Mrs. Libby gushed with shining eyes.

But there was no time for sentiment. Aleda went on. "There's a guest room upstairs. You'll find some bread and jam and cheese and an egg or two in the larder. The potatoes may still be good. The cat fends for herself, but give her some cheese and change the water bowl. And there are lots more gooseberries on the bush at the bottom of the garden. I've meant to shop for days. But that should do until I return tomorrow evening."

"I've some money. We can buy—"

"No," Aleda said. "Stay away from the shops. I doubt anyone will stop by here, but if so, you're to say I'm not available. It won't be a lie, and will be absolutely believed."

Once settled back in the coach, Aleda closed the curtains lest even Elizabeth spot her. The fewer people involved, the better.

"Was that lady angry?" Becky asked on the way to the water closet.

"Oh no, mite," Jewel replied. "Just in a hurry."

"Where did she go in the coach?"

"To Shrewsbury Station. You know, where we left the train?"

"Why?"

"I don't know. But she's to return tomorrow."

"Who is she?"

"She's the daughter of the vicar we came to see. Her name is Miss Hollis, remember?"

The girl had more questions as they came back through the parlor. "Is this our new home?"

Her young voice begged reassurance. She had been uprooted too many times of late. But any false assurances would later chip away at the small bit of security she possessed.

"No, sweetheart," Jewel replied. "At least not this house. But Miss Hollis didn't send us away, so I think we'll be allowed to stay in the village."

She did not wish to raise her own hopes, either. But she had seen enough from the coach window to believe that Gresham was a harbor of peace and serenity, with its cottages and gardens, blue sky and dainty shops, leafy trees stretching branches across quiet lanes.

And most pleasant of all . . . no Mr. Dunstan lurking about with a lewd eye on her baby.

Thank you, Father. I'll work very hard to deserve this.

Becky yawned, looked about. "What will we do now?"

"Are you hungry?"

"No."

"Then it's high time for a nap."

"I'm hungry," Becky amended quickly.

Jewel smiled. "After your nap. Help me find our bedroom."

That piqued her interest. Her boots made eager little clicks on the wooden staircase. She disappeared through an open doorway off the landing.

"A cat! Here, kitty!"

A tabby cat scampered from the room just as Jewel went through the doorway. Bed sheets, pillows, and coverlet were twisted into a heap. Dust particles danced in sunlight slanting from the window to a desk boasting a typewriter and littered with papers and teacups. Stockings lay heaped upon a chair cushion. The dress Miss Hollis had changed from was draped over the chair's back. A lone slipper lay on its side on the rug.

"Doesn't the lady know how to tidy up?" Becky asked, leaning to peer under the bed.

"We mustn't say that. She's probably very busy writing her stories."

"There's dust under here, Mummy . . . and a shoe!"

"Come away from there now," Jewel said as Becky's head disappeared beneath the mattress.

She obeyed, bringing out a kidskin slipper. Jewel brushed the dust from her bodice, then the slipper, to set it beside its mate near the bed's edge. She picked up the gown from the chair. It seemed hardly worn, so she hung it in the wardrobe.

"What's in there?" Becky asked, weaseling beside her to see.

"Clothes, Miss Nosy." Jewel closed the wardrobe and led her daughter by the hand back onto the landing.

Becky pointed to the only other open doorway. "Is that our room?"

"We shall see."

The second bedchamber was simply furnished, with iron bed, table, chair, rug, and cupboard. A fine layer of dust covered everything. Jewel folded the coverlet, set it upon the chair to take outside and shake later, stripped Becky to chemise and drawers, and tucked her between the sheets.

"Sleep tight."

Becky yawned. "What will you do, Mummy?"

"Oh, I'll find something."

"Will you leave the door open?"

"I will."

What Jewel found to do was stand before a fireplace

begrimed with soot and wonder if she should obey the impulse
to clean.

There were three reasons she should. Gratitude was foremost. Secondly, it would prove that she was a hard worker so
that Miss Hollis could enthusiastically recommend her to others.
Thirdly, she could not stand to be idle for too long.

The lone reason against it would be that her hostess might
take offense. Three outweighed one, so she looked through
the kitchen cupboard for some rags.

Chapter 13

At seven o'clock in the evening, when Gresham lanes would lie silent, London's streets were thronged with carriages and coaches, horses and wagons, omnibuses and hansoms. On the pavement, clerks streamed from offices, hawkers sold wares, beggars held out hands, and shop assistants fastened shutters onto windows.

The frantic pace became calmer once the horse-drawn hansom cab turned up Notting Hill Gate onto Pembridge Gardens. The ecru stucco terrace houses presented a unified front of anonymity: three narrow storeys, bow windows, service entrances, and cast-iron railings.

The horse stopped before number twenty-three. Aleda stepped down to the pavement and paid the cabby. A woman answered, wearing black alpaca and a white apron. Olive skin and dark eyes hinted of Spanish ancestry.

"Yes?"

"I'm Doctor Hollis's sister Aleda. May I speak with my brother?"

The maid welcomed her into a foyer papered with greens and golds. Ahead rose a staircase; to the left, an open arched doorway revealed a drawing room.

"Doctor Hollis is at hospital," she said with an accent that confirmed Aleda's guess. "And Mrs. Hollis is at dinner with friends. I think the Grand Hotel."

Aleda did not give a fig at which trough Loretta dined and could only imagine her friends as shallow and slavish to fashion as she.

"Do you know when to expect Doctor Hollis?"

The maid shook her head. "Would you care to wait?"

"Yes, please."

"May I take your bag?"

"No thank you." She set her satchel to the side, out of the way. "I'll find a hotel after I speak with my brother."

"A hotel? But Doctor Hollis would expect you to stay here."

"I don't think it's a good idea."

The maid nodded, motioned toward the drawing room. "This way, please?"

To Aleda, drawn to simplicity, the drawing room was as oppressively frantic as the streets, with its floral wallpaper and tables laden with bric-a-brac. She sat on a chesterfield sofa uphol-stered in tufted red velvet, folded her hands in her lap.

"May I bring you tea?" the maid asked.

"That would be nice," Aleda replied. "And . . ."

"Yes, madam?"

"I'm quite ravenous."

"Rav-in-ous? Does that mean you are hungry?"

"No. Hunger means your stomach moans because it's empty. Ravenous is when your stomach howls like a banshee, and you may just start gnawing on your shoes."

The maid laughed, a rich sound. "I do not know what a banshee is, but it does not sound pleasant. Cook is out, too, but I will find you something in the kitchen better to eat than shoes."

"I'll go with you," Aleda said. "No sense in your having to go back and forth."

"Oh, but you must not—"

"I insist."

"Doctor Hollis has a picture of you in his study," the maid said, leading Aleda past a dining room and into the kitchen in back of the house.

"He does?"

"When you were a girl. With your sister . . ."

"Grace."

The maid turned, smiled. "Is it she who married last month?"

"Yes. And we have two stepsisters."

"One is in Ceylon."

"Laurel." She could only have gotten this information from Philip, for Aleda could not fathom Loretta chatting about the peasants related to her husband.

Aleda would have starved rather than ask Loretta for food, but the kitchen belonged to Philip, as well, no matter that Loretta's parents had paid for it. The fact that the maid was friendly did not hurt.

Aleda asked her name.

"Ines," she said, pouring Aleda a beaker of milk to accompany a generous slice of cold rhubarb tart.

"This is so good," Aleda said between bites.

From up front came the sound of the door opening and closing, footsteps. In spite of her professed courage, Aleda froze in mid-chew. Even Ines seemed uneasy.

"I hope I haven't gotten you into trouble," Aleda said. But then the footsteps seemed decidedly male. Aleda smiled at the maid, went through the dining room, and called, "Philip?"

There was a pause, and then, "Yes? Is that . . . Aleda?"

They met in the hall. He looked weary, with shadows beneath his eyes, black coat open and white shirt collar unfastened. Every lecture Aleda had rehearsed during the journey, every biting sarcasm died inside, and she threw her arms about him. "Oh, Philip! We need you!"

"Of course I'll go," Philip said as Ines sliced another wedge of tart. "I shall speak with Doctor Trask and hopefully be ready for the four o'clock train tomorrow."

He looked at Ines. "Please pack for me in the morning."

"Yes, sir," she replied, handing him the dish. "How long will you stay, Doctor Hollis?"

Philip looked at Aleda. "At least three weeks. I want to see that he's well recovered."

Almost weak with relief, Aleda would have gotten up and embraced him again if Ines had not placed another slice of tart in front of her.

But there was a question that begged to be asked. "What of your patients?"

"Saint Bartholomew's is a teaching hospital. There is no lack of surgeons." He gulped down a long drink of milk, and said, "Are you settled in? Am I needed to carry any luggage upstairs?"

"All I have is a satchel," Aleda replied, and traded glances with Ines. "And I'll find a hotel room."

"But why?"

"I . . . don't want to be a bother." She could not bring herself to say, *Because your wife treated our parents coldly when they visited and I'll not allow her to do the same to me.*

Philip chuckled. "Bother? You're my sister. I insist you stay, silly goose. Anyway, it's dark outdoors."

She did not fancy waving down a hansom so late, and besides, how long had it been since she and her brother had had time to themselves? If Loretta turned up with her nose in the air, Aleda could stomach it for the short time she would be there.

They sat upon the drawing room sofa later, their feet sharing an ottoman.

"Do you remember when everyone thought the Larkspur was haunted?" Philip asked.

"Jake Pitt," Aleda said, smiling. "The spirit of some poor knife sharpener who had died there, I think."

Philip chuckled, then sobered. "Why didn't Mother telegraph me? Why did you have to come? Not that I'm not overjoyed to see you . . ."

She frowned. How to answer? How would she want unsettling news put to herself? *With all frankness.*

"Because Father forbade it."

"But why?"

She took a breath. "He said he doesn't want to burden you. But I believe he resents how you've slighted Mother. He's very protective of her."

To her brother's credit, he made no denial. Only sighed and said, "He's right. I've never been good about writing."

"And that's your reason?" Aleda said, irritated. "So a wastrel who bankrupts his family is excused by saying he'd never been good at paying bills? A mother with malnourished children may simply declare she was never good at cooking?"

He groaned. "Aleda . . . you cut me to the core."

"A few lines once a week would work wonders. It's not the length of the letter that counts as much as the proof that you care."

"Yes, you're right. I promise, Aleda. I'll do better by them."

But she was not finished. She had gone beyond warming to the subject, to absolute heat. "And with the express train, you've no excuse not to make at least an overnight visit. Do they chain you to the surgery table at that hospital?"

"No, of course not." He swallowed audibly, turned his face toward her. "Believe it or not, sister, I seldom visit because I don't wish to hurt them. Every time I go alone, I have to make excuses for Loretta. Eventually they'll assume she doesn't care for them."

"Assume?" Aleda barked a bitter laugh.

He closed his eyes for several seconds.

Had she gone too far?

When he opened them again, they stared into hers, shining with tears and misery. "My family . . . all of you . . . you're an extension of me. And it's me she doesn't care for."

Somehow, this did not surprise Aleda. But she ached for him no less. She threaded her arm through his and rested her head against his shoulder. "Oh, Philip."

"I know I've been a bad son. I promise to do better. But just the act of stepping into this house saps me of strength."

Aleda hesitated. "But what happened?"

"Well . . . there's someone else."

She gasped, raised her head again.

"I don't mean an affair. It's someone she has never gotten

over." He blinked, twice, and said thickly, "I do love her, Aleda. How I wish to God I did not."

Loretta adored Gilbert and Sullivan. Not like stuffy Verdi. Which was why she consented to accompany her friends to the Savoy after dinner, even though she had seen *Princess Ida* twice already. She sang softly, peering from the coach window at the gaslit Strand.

"Whene'er I spoke sarcastic joke
replete with malice spiteful,
This people mild politely smiled
And voted me delightful!"

Wryly, she thought, *That'll stick in my mind for days.*

She loved London, as well, with a passion. The fashions and culture, museums and restaurants, promenading at Hyde Park, rowing in the Serpentine. Friends.

Distractions.

Too soon the pair of horses came to a halt, rocking the coach slightly back upon its wheels. The house looked ghostly in the lamplight. The weight lifted by Gilbert and Sullivan and girlish chatter over dinner settled upon her shoulders again.

Marry in haste, repent in leisure, she thought.

Haste brought on by pain. Even when she marched up the aisle at Saint Peter's on her father's arm over four years ago, she had had to force herself not to look to the row where sat Conrad Lockhart and her sister, Irene.

Six years ago, the young army captain had practically dominated her dance card at Aunt Helen's birthday ball. Tall and bronze he was, with broad shoulders and high forehead from his English father, sensitive gray eyes and poetic soul from his French mother.

He called at least twice weekly after the ball and wrote her wonderful letters filled with poetry. Her parents permitted them to take unchaperoned strolls up Park Lane, her hand tucked into the crook of his arm. Carriage rides on Rotten Row. He spoke in vague terms of their future, as if reassuring himself that she was of the same mind before approaching her father with a question. She was nineteen, and very much of the same mind.

The question never got asked. At least not in reference to herself. Her sister, Irene, chose that inopportune time to return from Girton College for Easter holiday. Her *younger* sister, eighteen, whose wild brown hair, tanned skin, and tall athletic lankiness were no matches for Loretta's platinum curls, ivory complexion, and petite frame. Irene, who was too high-spirited to give any man a second glance. Until her eyes locked with Conrad's.

It was as if a spell was cast upon the sitting room. Loretta had tried to break it, chatting frantically about anything that would jump into her mind. Conrad began inviting Irene to join them on walks, for games of whist in the parlor. And once Irene returned to Cambridge, his visits to the Park Lane house ceased.

The memory of that spring was still a knife in her heart.

She could neither eat nor sleep, losing so much weight that her parents spoke of sending her to a sanitarium near Salzburg. She had protested so adamantly that they abandoned the idea upon her promise to take regular nourishment. It was essential that she stay in London, for surely Conrad would come to his senses. She had to continue her morning watch from the library window so that she could meet the postman at the gate.

A believer since early childhood, she had made promises with God. *Make Conrad love me, and I'll never complain of*

*anything again, spend my life helping the poor, read ten pages of
my Bible daily. Twenty!*

When Irene returned for summer holiday, she also looked
drawn and undernourished. But for a different reason. Letters
had traveled almost daily between London and Cambridge. She
and Conrad were in love, she admitted tearfully.

Their father had refused Loretta's demand that he bring
charges against Conrad for breach of promise. "There was no
overt promise made," he had said, and then drew her into his
arms to add, gently, "You cannot make someone love you,
daughter. And if you could, what sort of marriage would that
be?"

Loretta was forced to watch the courtship progress. Smile
through their wedding, lest tongues wag that she was bitter.
Hold back tears as the two stared up into each other's faces
and pledged their troth. Wonder if the stone that had replaced
her heart would ever heal.

A few months later, her father brought Philip home to
dinner, touting him as the highest-ranked graduate of Edinburgh's esteemed medical college and the latest member of
Saint Bartholomew's surgical staff. He was neither as dashing
nor poetic as Conrad, but he was kind and seemed to enjoy
her company.

Her father continued inviting him over, throwing them
together. It mattered not at all that Philip's father, also a surgeon, had died with so much gaming debt that his family lost
their home. Here was a balm for her wounds. The agonizing
love she carried about for Conrad could be transferred. Or so
she thought.

"Mrs. Hollis?"

She broke out of her melancholy thoughts and looked up

at Tom, coachman and groomsman, holding open the coach door.

In the foyer, Ines asked, "Did you have a lovely evening, Mrs. Hollis?"

"Yes," Loretta said. She felt a twinge of conscience for Ines having to wait up so late after a long day, but she could not unfasten the two dozen tiny pearl buttons running up the back of her satin gown without assistance.

"I'll sleep in the guest room," she said with a hand on the balcony. "So as not to wake Doctor Hollis."

It was unnecessary for her to state her intentions to Ines, but acting the charade had become a ritual, like cleaning her teeth.

"But Doctor Hollis is still awake, madam," Ines said softly. "He only went upstairs minutes ago. He sat up and visited with Miss Hollis . . . who is in the guest room."

"Miss Hollis?" Loretta whispered. She was about to ask which sister until she remembered Grace had recently married.

Aleda. Who wrote stories. A spinster, which was no wonder. Loretta remembered the open dislike in her expression four years ago.

"You may retire now, Ines," Loretta said.

Philip sat with ankle propped upon knee, unfastening a half boot. He looked up when the knob turned and door opened. Loretta stepped inside, a vision in pearl gray satin, her flaxen hair bound up in ringlets that teased her bare shoulders.

"I thought I heard you," he said.

She dropped bag and wrap onto the settee at the foot of the bed, then sat down herself. "Your meeting went well?"

"Fairly. The annual look-over of applications. Paper never

tells you enough about a person, but it's a start. How was your night?"

"Nice. We saw *Princess Ida*."

A shoe thumped softly to the carpet, and then he began on the second. "Again?"

"But you see? It's my dream that Leonora Braham *and* her understudy take ill one night and it's announced that they have to cancel the show. I pop up from my seat and declare, 'The night is saved! I know that part!' "

He chuckled. "That's a nice dream. As long as Miss Braham recovers the next morning, there's no real harm done. I would pay to see you."

"I just have to find a way to get to their food."

He feigned a look of shock. "What sort of woman have I married?"

They held the shared smile for a couple of seconds, and then she shifted her eyes and yawned. "But all the commotion has given me a headache."

"I'm sorry," he said. But he was not surprised. Funny how the headaches never prevented her from going out with friends. "Do you need some medicine?"

"I'm sure a good night's sleep is all."

"Of course. But I must discuss something important with you first," he said, setting the other shoe down by its mate.

"Will you unfasten my dress and pearls at the same time?"

"Of course."

He left the chair and crossed the carpet. She got to her feet and turned her back to him. First he unfastened the clasp to her pearl choker. A small cameo of onyx and ivory dangled from the front. It was a wedding gift from her grandparents that she wore often, while the jade and gold necklace he had given her had not seen the light of day for months.

He never asked about it. Perhaps she did not care for the style. "Aleda's here."

"Yes, Ines said so," Loretta replied.

"Did she say my stepfather needs surgery?"

"No. Oh dear."

He could see the two of them in the cheval glass as his fingers gave the buttons the same concentration they gave to his work. Just touching her unyielding back brought on an ache that no light banter could heal.

"If he suspects Aleda came for me, he may do something rash. The sooner I leave, the better. I hope tomorrow."

"Yes, of course," she said, obviously attempting to hide the relief in her voice. "Leave in the morning. I shall explain everything to Father."

His fingers briefly stopped. "No. I'll speak with him."

"But he never refuses me anything."

"I'll speak with him," he repeated. A pause, while he unfastened another button. "And I hope you'll come with me."

"To see Father?"

He could not hold back a sigh. "To Gresham. It would mean a lot to my family. To me. Please."

Loretta turned, even though only half the buttons were unfastened. "How long do you intend to stay?"

"Three weeks, at least. I want to make certain he's healing before I return."

"I can't possibly. We committed ourselves to the croquet party at the Allens' on Saturday next. They have been so kind to us, sending flowers when I had that sore throat."

"They would understand."

"And I promised to call on Mrs. Dutton, Vera's aunt. She

becomes quite disheartened when the family's in the country. And there is—"

He shook his head. "Never mind, Loretta. I'll go alone."

Feebly she said, "If I only had more notice . . ."

"Well, sickness is like that. Turn around, please."

They stood in stilted silence while he finished unfastening the dress. He then scooped his slippers from beneath his side of the bed and took a folded nightshirt from his chest of drawers.

"I'll sleep in the drawing room."

"You don't have to do that, Philip," she said, but not forcefully.

"It's better for your headache." He turned at the door. "By the way . . . gallstones."

She stared at him. "I beg your pardon?"

"That's why my stepfather requires surgery. You didn't ask, so I wanted to spare you from wondering later."

Chapter 14

Short in stature, Principal Surgeon Reginald Trask sat high in his chair behind a massive oak desk. His prematurely white hair flowed back from his forehead like plumage on an officer's cap. Philip had gotten on well with Doctor Trask from their first meeting. Both having received their medical training in Scotland had served as an immediate bond.

"You do not trust any of the Shrewsbury surgeons, Philip? I daresay I may have trained some."

"Yes, sir," Philip replied. "I'm sure there are competent ones. But none that will care so much about the patient as I do."

His father-in-law rested his chin upon steepled fingertips. "Is caring on the same level as skill?"

"I don't know," Philip confessed. "I only know that I must go. I regret very much the hardship this will cause."

"We shall cope," said the older man. "And *I* regret Florence and I were in Italy that time your parents visited. I enjoyed my chats with Vicar Phelps during the festivities surrounding your wedding. He must have been a good stepfather to you."

Philip nodded as a memory swept over him. "Did you go to boarding school, Doctor Trask?"

"Of course." He frowned, grew pensive. "A breeding ground for bullies. I was, naturally, smallish. I may as well have painted a target on my jacket. I wept into my pillow every night. They were the darkest years of my boyhood."

"I had the same experience," Philip said, "and was ashamed to tell my mother, when she had sacrificed so much to enroll me. One day I was out running laps around the building for simply defending myself, and a carriage pulled up in front of me. Andrew got out, said he was taking me back to Gresham."

Doctor Trask's brows raised. "What a wonderful kindness."

"He wasn't even my stepfather yet. Do you see now why I must be there for him?"

"I do," Doctor Trask replied, his eyes actually watering behind the spectacles. He glanced away for an instant, cleared his throat. "Then I'll detain you no longer. I know you want to look in on your cases. I'll need to send a messenger to Florence. She'll want to bid Loretta farewell."

Philip hesitated. "Loretta isn't coming."

"But why not?"

"She has several appointments in place."

Doctor Trask opened his mouth, closed it. Just when Philip was wondering if he should himself break the stilted silence, his father-in-law said, "Perhaps the time away will benefit you both. My prayers for Vicar Phelps go with you."

Saying farewell to Ines and slipping out of the house before Loretta could wake, Aleda walked down to Notting Hill Gate and found a hackney cab. After dropping off her manuscript at the *Argosy* office on Oxford Street, and staying there much longer than she had intended, she gave the cabby an address on Bloomsbury Square, one block east of the British Museum.

Gabriel's butler answered the door to the terrace house. "Why, Miss Hollis, is it?"

"In the flesh, Mr. Smithson," Aleda replied.

"Mr. Patterson's in the garden. Shall I lead you to him?"

"How about if I make my own way?"

"I shall bring out tea."

"And some toast or cheese, perhaps?"

"Very good, madam."

She was getting good at asking for food. Perhaps she was a beggar at heart. She walked through Gabriel's tastefully appointed home, past a drawing room with overstuffed chairs and landscapes on serene teal green walls, a dining room with Belgian rug, oak table and chairs. Double French doors opened into a cozy world of greenery and trellises, flagstones and wooden benches, fish pond and vines creeping up stone walls.

She saw Gabriel Patterson's thinning brown hair first, then the back of his portly frame, swathed in dressing gown and ensconced in a lawn chair. As she drew closer she could see his left hand penning lines across a folded sheet of foolscap.

"Gabriel?"

His shoulders jumped a little before he turned to face her. He smiled and rose, drawing the sash tighter around his middle.

"Aleda! I had the oddest feeling last night that I would see you soon, and here you are. Are you visiting Philip and Loretta?"

"Philip," she replied. "And just last night. I slipped out of the house this morning before the duchess came down."

He winced. "Aleda . . . she's Philip's wife."

For how long? she thought. But not wishing to waste precious time with Gabriel on the subject of Loretta, she said, "I spent much of the morning in the *Argosy* offices. When my editors realized I was there to drop off my manuscript, they wanted to discuss extending the serial—about sending Captain Jacobs off to some new adventure."

"Well, good for you." He opened his arms. "And it's wonderful to see you."

She fit comfortably into his arms, then stepped back, lest she give him false hopes. They had gotten all that business settled two years ago.

"Don't grieve yourself, Aleda," he said lightly. "Friends embrace, too."

Embarrassed and relieved at the same time, she said, "Then I'll have another."

But instead he smacked a kiss upon her forehead and said, "Naughty girl. You've caught me in my dressing gown. Can you entertain yourself while I change?"

She strayed a glance to his manuscript pages. "I'll think of something."

"Sorry, no peeking before it's polished. I don't want you to think I'm a hack."

As if, Aleda thought. Gabriel could write circles around her. And the popularity of his novels, adventures set in Roman Britain, proved it.

He was wealthier than Croesus, and generous to a fault. Representatives of charities called often, well acquainted with his philanthropy. Sometimes she thought she was foolish for not accepting his proposal of marriage. He would make a wonderful husband.

But just as Brutus had said of Caesar and Rome, it was not

that she loved Gabriel less, it was that she loved independence more.

Was there not any sharp London woman willing to look beyond the less-than-perfect physique and value the gold of his heart more than his bank account? But where would he have met her? His forays beyond his house were limited to Bloomsbury Chapel and occasional ambles through the museum or an art gallery. Philip was practically his only caller, besides the charity representatives and his editors from Macmillan Publishers.

He returned in black trousers and white shirt, as she was munching happily on a croissant with a generous slice of ham tucked inside.

"You're still against typewriters?" she asked.

He settled into a chair beside hers. "Shakespeare never owned one."

"He never owned a water closet, either," Aleda said, grateful for the opportunity to use the quip a second time.

Gabriel made a face at her. "Besides, you use a pen for your novel yourself. You've admitted such. How is it progressing?"

"I'm still polishing."

"How many polishings does this make now?"

"Um. . . . I don't remember."

"Interesting," he said.

"You're not going to suggest that I don't want to finish."

"I only suggest that you're more gifted than you think. That you do not have to fear editors. Or critics."

Aleda bristled. "I'm not afraid of critics."

"Then I'm mistaken," he said graciously.

She loved him for it. They both knew the truth. Of what use to belabor it?

"Just bear in mind, I'll be happy to read it and give you my opinion any time you wish."

"Thank you," she said, just as she said every time he made the offer.

He shrugged, and asked why she had come to London. He was saddened when she told him. "I've envied you and Philip . . . having such a father."

It was rare that Gabriel spoke of his parents. But she had learned the family dynamics years ago, when fifteen-year-old Philip returned from a fortnight with the Pattersons in Birmingham. Doctor Patterson had praised her brother's sports prowess and aspirations toward the medical field, while making barbs about Gabriel's weight and desire to write.

Mrs. Patterson was as bad in her own way, cautioning Gabriel against exerting himself physically as if he were fragile, pushing food and sweets upon him as if a famine were imminent. It was a wonder he was able to break free to attend Oxford, and no wonder that he moved to London straight after commencement.

Later, over a simple but delicious lunch of asparagus soup, baked sole, crusty brown bread, and salad, and the anticipation of a not-so-simple chocolate cheesecake ahead, Gabriel asked about her cottage. She took him audibly from room to room.

"You must come see it sometime." She frowned. "I just hope my belongings are still there."

"Go on . . ."

She told him of happening upon the coach, and Mrs. Libby and her daughter.

"Brummies?" he said, referring to the nickname often given to Birmingham natives. "How interesting. But you just left them, knowing no one?"

She slurped a spoonful of soup. "I was pressed for time."

"Hmm. What if this Mrs. Libby manufactured the whole

situation? What if she's an aspiring author, intent upon stealing your manuscript?"

"But how would she know of my family's friendship with Vicar Treves?"

"Let's see." Gabriel mused for a second or two, then snapped his fingers. "She was a servant in his household and heard your family being spoken of as she served tea."

Aleda nodded. "And in the course of dusting his desk, she copied his signature and forged a letter."

"She's so desperate that she stole an orphan from the streets. Who could turn away a mother and child?"

"I'm not sure about that one. They both have very red hair."

"Orphans can't have red hair?" Gabriel countered.

"Touché." They exchanged smiles of mutual fondness, and Aleda thought it was a pity that she did not live in London. With her determined nature, she could find him a good wife.

Double pity, that she could not do the same for her brother.

Gabriel's voice cut into her thoughts. "Do you mind if I accompany you and Philip back to Gresham?"

She straightened in her chair. "You'd be most welcome."

"Not to be in the way, mind you. But I'd like to be there for your father's surgery. I'll stay at the Bow and Fiddle."

"You don't have to—"

"Your parents don't need houseguests. And you already have some."

Aleda sighed. "I'll just put them up at the inn until we figure out what to do with them."

"Yes?" Gabriel's brows lifted. "And have it bandied about that you've an unchaperoned gent under your roof? *That* would hasten your father's recovery. I'll be happy with the inn. That's what it's there for."

"Very well," she conceded.

"And as long as I'm there . . ."

"Yes?"

"You might reconsider allowing me to read a chapter or two of your book?"

"Gabriel . . ."

"Just give it some thought. You have to put a toe in the water sometime, Aleda."

Chapter 15

After a simple lunch of potato soup and weak tea, followed by an hour-long nap, Andrew insisted he was in no pain and would read over his sermon. Julia finally felt confident enough to leave him in the care of Luke, Dora, and Wanetta.

"Mother?" Elizabeth said, stepping back from her front door to allow entrance. "Is Father . . . ?"

"He's all right. He's in his study. But you were so worried yesterday, I just wanted to be sure *you're* all right."

Elizabeth embraced her. "You're so dear, Mother. I'm fine. We had such fun after breakfast. Jonathan gave the ensemble permission to practice in the schoolhouse, and we all walked over to listen. They plan to start Sunday afternoon concerts on the green very soon. Danny Perkins is so gifted with his violin that we said he should try out for the London Symphony Orchestra. It's hard to believe he's but sixteen."

Her tone was too chirpy, too cheerful. Julia hoped Elizabeth was not acting brave for *her* sake. By then, the twins had heard her voice and rushed into the parlor. Julia planted kisses upon soft cheeks, listened to their plans for the day, and finally continued down Church Lane.

As she neared the end of the path, she caught sight of pillows draped over bedroom windowsills. Aleda must have hired Mrs. Summers again to clean, she thought. She opened the gate and noticed a thin red-haired girl in a wicker chair, bare feet dangling halfway to the ground, a hand stroking the cat curled in her lap.

"Why, good morning," Julia said, entering the garden.

"Good morning," the girl replied, and grinned proudly. "The cat jumped up here when I sat down."

"Yes, I can see that." Julia walked over to scratch between the animal's ears. "She won't go to just anyone. She likes you."

"It's a girl?"

"Yes. Her name is Tiger. My daughter said it's easier to say twenty times a day than Tigress."

The girl tried both names, softly. She had a faint accent that Julia could not quite place. Perhaps the Summerses had family visiting from another part of Britain.

"I'm Mrs. Phelps," Julia said. "And you must be Mrs. Summers' granddaughter."

"Who's Mrs. Summers?"

"My mistake. What's your name, dear?"

"My name's Becky. Mummy's cleaning the water closet. She said I could play outdoors if I stay inside the fence."

"I see. It's a pleasure to meet you, Becky. Is Miss Hollis upstairs?"

"No, ma'am. She went to that place where the trains stop."

The sink, bathtub, and floor shining, Jewel eyed the medicine cabinet again. There was a difference between cleaning and meddling, at least for a guest. While the oak door shone from her polishing, the inside was a mess. A half-dozen cakes of Pears soap, a box of Beecham's indigestion pills, a jar of glycerine hand salve, four hairpins, and a comb lay helter-skelter. A tin of tooth powder sat open, with white powder spilling onto the shelf.

She sighed, closed the cabinet door, and gathered cleaning rags into the pail. She had just entered the kitchen when a woman stepped through the kitchen door.

"Good morning."

Jewel froze. The pail bumped the side of her knee.

"I've startled you . . . forgive me," the woman said, and looked around. "Everything smells so clean."

This was surely Miss Hollis's mother, with her auburn hair and green eyes. Her open, friendly expression would have set Jewel at ease were she not bound to her hostess's instruction to declare her unavailable.

"Are you Mrs. Phelps?" Jewel asked.

"Yes, I am." She stepped closer with hand extended.

Jewel set down the pail to shake her hand. "I'm Jewel Libby."

"It's a pleasure to meet you. I've met Becky. She's quite smitten with the cat."

"She's always wanted one. How is your husband?"

"He's fine for the moment, thank you." Mrs. Phelps inclined her head thoughtfully. "I'm acquainted with two people who speak with your accent. Vicar Paul Treves is one. May I assume you and Becky are the subjects of his telegram?"

"Yes, ma'am," Jewel replied. "He didn't realize your husband was ill. But we happened upon Miss Hollis on the roadside, and she offered to help us. So please don't trouble yourself."

"She has a good heart. Pray tell . . . why is she at Shrewsbury Station?"

Jewel swallowed and felt heat rise to her face. Did Miss Hollis's demand for secrecy include her own mother?

"Becky said she's at the railway station," Mrs. Phelps said, as if not certain Jewel had understood her question. "The closest is Shrewsbury . . ."

"I'm sorry, Mrs. Phelps. But all I can say is that she's not available."

"I beg your pardon?"

"Please forgive me, but I can't take advantage of her hospitality and ignore her wishes."

"Her wishes . . ."

Shifting her weight on her feet, Jewel endured the bemused scrutiny of the older woman.

Seconds later, Mrs. Phelps said, "Why don't we sit?"

They pulled out chairs. Julia folded her hands on the table. "I try not to meddle in my daughters' affairs. I seldom visit Aleda. But yesterday she was anxious over her father's upcoming surgery. I'm only here to see if she's all right."

"Yes. I'm quite sure she is."

Mrs. Libby's evasiveness brought to mind Elizabeth's artificial breeziness. Like game pieces lining up perfectly on a draughts board, the answer fell into place.

Aleda had gone to telegraph Philip!

She would know the folly of doing so from Gresham. It was so like her to take command of the situation, like her fictional Captain Jacobs.

A weight lifted from Julia's soul. Andrew would be angry, but he wasn't the only person involved. She needed him. So did the children and grandchildren. So did Gresham.

She smiled. "Don't worry. You don't have to say any more."

The young woman sighed. "Thank you, Mrs. Phelps."

"Now, what is it that brought you and Becky from Birmingham in such haste?"

Mrs. Libby glanced toward the staircase. "I have a letter."

Becky was still in the chair, softly singing and stroking the cat. Jewel smiled and turned from the open door to light the stove jet beneath the kettle.

"This is actually from Noelle Treves," Mrs. Phelps said with a rustling of paper.

Jewel returned to the table. As the letter was addressed to Vicar and Mrs. Phelps, she had not thought it proper to open the seal.

"You were right to get far away from that man."

"Thank you," Jewel said as gratitude for Mrs. Phelps washed over her. Gratitude for not taking the danger lightly, as had the police. For agreeing that Becky, as any child, was worthy of protection.

At the stove again, she poured boiling water into the teapot.

Mrs. Phelps surprised her by coming over to fish mismatched cups and saucers from the dresser and take a tray from the top of the cupboard. "And of course Aleda persuaded you not to contact us."

"She was only thinking of you. Your husband . . ."

"I believe that." Mrs. Phelps paused from scooping sugar from crock into bowl. "And it's true. We're self-absorbed for now. But once the surgery is over and he's on the mend, I'll be happy to help her find you a position."

God is so good, Jewel thought. The decent people He had put in hers and Becky's lives outnumbered the bad. "You're very kind."

"Only on my good days," she quipped on her way into the larder, causing Jewel to smile again. A second later she came out. "I'm afraid there's no milk."

"I usually drink mine plain," Jewel assured her.

"But what about your supper? There's not much of anything in there."

Jewel had boiled the eggs for their breakfasts, and made cheese sandwiches for lunch. But she was used to making meals from dabs of this and that. "Please don't worry. We'll make do."

"Perhaps Aleda plans to bring something from Shrewsbury. What time did she leave?"

Heat returned to Jewel's face. If only Miss Hollis would return and put an end to this confusing secrecy.

The vicar's wife nodded. "Being caught in the middle is never pleasant. But for the sake of Aleda's safety, I must ask how long she's been away."

"Since yesterday, just before noon," Jewel murmured, crumbling in the face of this motherly concern. After all, she was a mother, too. "She's to return sometime today."

The kettle hissed. Jewel turned off the jet.

Mrs. Phelps stared at the cloud of steam continuing to rise. Seconds later she said, "I'm afraid I can't join you for tea after all."

Dora's rolling pin made muffled *whumps* as it swooped down

upon the dough at all angles. A smile widened her round face as Julia entered the kitchen.

"Did you enjoy your stroll, missus?"

"It wasn't quite a stroll. I met the mother and daughter of Paul Treves' telegram. A Mrs. Libby and Becky."

"Ah. But where are they?"

"They're staying with Aleda for now."

"Indeed? Did you learn why they had to leave Birmingham?"

Dora was practically family. Julia told her, briefly.

The cook clucked her tongue. "I'd like to introduce his head to my rolling pin!"

However much Julia would enjoy hearing the ways Becky's tormentor should be punished, she had a more pressing task outside the kitchen.

"Will we have enough supper to share?"

"But of course. You know I always cook enough for drop-ins. And with the vicar limited to soup, there's to be even more." The cook raised sparse brows. "Are the mother and daughter here now?"

"No. I'll ask Luke to carry it over. Aleda asked them not to stray from the cottage until she returns."

"Returns? But where is she?"

"Unless I'm very, very wrong . . . London."

Though she had the right to open the door to the study at any time, Julia always knocked. Privacy was worth little when it could be barged in upon without warning. Besides, Andrew counseled the occasional parishioner, who would need to know that his privacy was respected, as well.

She knocked softly and heard "Come in" from the other side.

Andrew's absorbed voice. Julia could picture him reading his sermon notes, his mind only half aware of his mouth speaking the invitation.

Sure enough, when she entered, he looked up from his sermon notes as if surprised.

"Why, Julia. I didn't realize you'd returned."

"Only a little while ago. Is your studying going well?"

His smile made shadowy dimples behind his beard. "I'll be preaching from the third chapter of Saint John. Jesus and Nicodemus."

Julia closed the door and sat in the horsehair chair facing the desk. "But wasn't your sermon to be on loyalty? David and Jonathan?"

"I've put it aside for another time. I felt a strong urging from God to give a Gospel message. Just in case . . ."

He hesitated, as if expecting her to chide him for his morbidness.

"Very good," she said simply, earnestly. "For as long as I've known you, you've kept an ear turned up to heaven."

He gave her a grateful smile. "I'm afraid I don't always hear Him."

"But you try." She moved up to the edge of the chair to reach across his desk.

Automatically he clasped her hand. "Are you all right, Julia?"

"That depends upon you."

"It does?"

"I believe Aleda went to London to speak with Philip."

His cheeks flushed above his beard as his smile faded. Softly but firmly he said, "I made my wishes quite clear, Julia."

"Perfectly clear. And yet Aleda chose to defy them. How she must loathe you."

He blew out his cheeks. "It's not that I don't appreciate her concern."

"But you want to show Philip just how much we don't need him."

"That's not why—"

"Isn't it?" Julia shook her head. "Vindictiveness is unbecoming in a minister, Andrew. Or in any Christian. Yes, he's hurt us. But not from any malice. I suspect any energy not consumed by his job is drained by his marriage. I'm asking you to listen to your own sermons and forgive him."

Andrew looked wounded. "You think I'm trying to punish him?"

"Aren't you?"

He shook his head. Tears lustered his hazel eyes. "I'm . . . afraid that if anyone asks, and he refuses, I shouldn't be able to bear it."

He was unconsciously squeezing her hand to a painful degree. With her other hand, Julia touched his, and he released her. She rose, went around the desk, and cradled his shoulders.

"If Aleda went for him, he'll come," she murmured. "If she didn't, I'll telegraph him, and he'll come. Either way, he'll be here for you. I don't know everything in my son's heart, but I do know he loves his father."

Chapter 16

Gresham rested in that twilight time between day and night, the sun painting the sky orange and pink and purple as it poised to dip below the Anwyl. In the carriage drive of the Bow and Fiddle, the coachman handed a gladstone bag down to Gabriel.

"Are you sure you won't come with us?" Aleda asked.

"They would love to see you," Philip said.

Gabriel shook his head. "We'll catch up tomorrow. As gracious as your family is, I would feel like an intruder when you have such weighty matters to discuss."

"But the night is still young," Philip continued. "Will you not be bored?"

"Not at all. I'll write for a while."

Aleda could not help but feel a bit of relief. Gabriel's presence would inhibit Father from expressing his feelings. If there was to be a scene, it should be gotten over with as soon as possible.

She stood on tiptoe to kiss his cheek. "I'll join you here for breakfast. Then you must see my cottage."

"Very good," he said, and bade them good evening.

As the coach continued eastward, Aleda's brother looked at her and said, "Gabriel's a good man."

"One of the best," Aleda said.

Philip hesitated. "You still feel nothing for him but friendship?"

"Nothing but friendship? Since when is friendship a 'nothing'?"

"Point taken." He gave her a contrite smile. "I just want you both to be happy."

Aleda thought, *As you are?*

Philip's expression sobered, as if the same thought crossed his mind.

She elbowed him in the ribs. Now was not the time to be thinking of Loretta.

"Watch that!" he said with mock scowl.

"Why don't we get out at the lane and surprise them?"

"Won't they be surprised enough when we come rolling up?"

"Please?"

"You'll have to carry my medical bag *and* your satchel, if I've got to lug my portmanteau," he grumbled.

But at least the sober look had been replaced by one of anticipation.

Creeping along the corridor in her stocking feet, Aleda smiled at lamplight spilling from the parlor doorway. A rustle of papers met her ears, then her mother's voice.

"I wonder why the navy stopped giving them lemons in the first place."

"I don't know." Father's voice. "Three, four generations pass, and they forget all about scurvy."

Aleda stepped into the parlor. The two sat on the sofa, each with a section of *The London Times*. Mother looked up over the page and smiled. "Aleda?"

Father lowered his newspaper. "Why, good evening, daughter."

Aleda took a breath. "Now, stay calm. I have a surprise."

She turned to motion to Philip. He slipped into the room beside her. "Hello, Mother and Father."

It was Mother who reacted first, pushing aside the newspaper. A second later, she was standing with her arms around him. "So, you came!"

"How could I not?"

Aleda turned again to Father. His eyes met hers. She braced for the worst, but inexplicably, he smiled at her. Then he shifted his gaze back to Mother and Philip. They were turning toward him with arms linked.

He rose from the sofa with eyes filling. "Son."

Philip moved from Mother's arms to his. "I'm going to take care of you. You'll be fine."

Aleda wiped her eyes with her fingertips and left to collect her shoes from the vestibule. She walked on down to the kitchen and was fishing a pot from the rack when Dora padded inside, wearing her wrapper and with hair rolled in papers. "What's going on?"

"I thought to make some hot chocolate."

"Not in my kitchen, you won't. That's not even the right pot."

"Then I insist on serving it, at least."

The cook was vain over being seen in curling papers and would need to go to the trouble of taking them down if she brought in a tray herself. Opening the lid of the cocoa tin, Dora said, "Very well. And for how many?"

"Four." Proudly Aleda added, "Philip is here."

"Mr. Philip? How grand! So, that's why you went to London. By the by, Luke carried some lamb stew and asparagus and half a currant pudding over to your guests for supper. Milk for the girl, and a jar of lemonade, too."

Aleda froze. "How did you know I had guests? And that I went to London?"

"Well, your mother went over to your place. I suppose they told her."

"Was she upset?"

"Not that I could tell. Why should she be?"

Dora was right, Aleda realized. Father was the only one who had not wanted to contact Philip. She sometimes forgot that her parents were two individuals, not always of the same mind. "May I rob you of some bacon and eggs for their breakfasts?"

"Of course. I'll set some out for when you leave."

Minutes later, Aleda carried the tray into the parlor, where Mother sat alone on the sofa.

"Philip wanted to examine your father," she said, clearing newspaper pages from the tea table to make room for the tray. "They won't be long. He said Gabriel came with you?"

"Just until a day or so after the surgery."

"He could stay here."

"He insisted on the Bow and Fiddle." Aleda set down the tray and sat beside her. "You knew I was in London."

"Well, yes. Mrs. Libby followed your orders, so you mustn't blame her."

Aleda could not remember even mentioning her plan to

Mrs. Libby. Leave it to Mother to figure it out. "I won't. But you seemed genuinely surprised when we popped in."

Mother smiled and rested a hand upon her shoulder. "While I was quite certain what was going on, there was that tiny bit of uncertainty. It was good of you to do that. And very good of you to take in Mrs. Libby and Becky, with your privacy meaning so much to you."

"It was my pleasure," Aleda said lightly while basking in her mother's praise. Regardless of what she had said to Elizabeth, she realized even grown daughters appreciated a *well done* from their mothers. "Thank you for sending food over. I didn't have time to restock the larder or even find out why Vicar Treves sent them."

As her mother told her of the letter, chills prickled Aleda's arms. She had heard of such twisted men from a couple of her Newnham College mates in late-night whispering sessions.

When the men entered again, Father wore dressing gown and slippers and a pleased expression.

"Philip wants to bring me back here as soon as possible."

"How soon?" Mother asked.

"I must speak with Doctor Rhodes first," Philip replied, "but hopefully . . . two days after the surgery."

"Isn't that risky?"

"The greatest risk is infection. There is much less chance of that here at home. We'll put a padded stretcher in Mr. Pool's coach and walk the horses the whole way. We'll first have to bring one of the spare beds down here, for he'll not be able to take the stairs for some weeks."

"You're agreeable to this?" Aleda asked. A silly question, given Father's serene expression, but the concept was quite radical so she wanted to hear it from his lips.

"Most agreeable. I dreaded the weeks in hospital more than the surgery. It's a relief to have Philip here to take charge."

Aleda busied herself pouring hot chocolate. She could not help but feel a small slight. Philip deserved his status as the knight in shining armor who would save the day. But did Father even appreciate her part in this?

She handed over his cup—or rather, half a cup, per Philip's orders. "Careful," she cautioned.

He smiled up at her. "Thank you, daughter."

The warmth in his hazel eyes was clearly meant for more than the cup in his hands.

⚬∞⚬

The chimneypiece clock had just struck eleven when Jewel heard a squeaking sound. She held her breath, listened. The gate? Hours ago she had tucked Becky into bed with the cat curled at her feet. She sat in a parlor chair, reading Miss Hollis's stories in copies of *Argosy*.

The adventures were quite good. Norman, who had never been to school, would have enjoyed having her read them to him; especially the latest, with a ship's crew stranded on an island battling all sorts of hardships.

She heard cat feet thumping down the staircase, and then footsteps outside the kitchen door. She replaced the magazines in their basket and crossed into the kitchen.

"Now get some rest!" a feminine voice called out.

Jewel hurried to open the door. Miss Hollis came through it, carrying satchel and basket. She set both upon the table. "I was afraid you'd wait up. My brother insisted on walking me to the gate."

"Is he to perform your father's surgery?" Jewel asked.

Miss Hollis gave her a bemused look. "Why, yes. Did my mother tell you about Philip?"

"No, Mrs. Treves did." Jewel gave her an apologetic look. "But I did meet Mrs. Phelps. I'm sorry if I gave away your whereabouts."

Tiger was yowling for attention. Miss Hollis lifted him into her arms and smiled. "You didn't, really. Mother figured everything all out herself. And actually, it gave her the opportunity to prepare my father. He wasn't keen on having Philip do the surgery."

Jewel did not quite understand but was glad she was happy.

"It smells so clean in here." Miss Hollis eyed kitchen and pantry. "You even put away the laundry?"

"It was the least I could do to thank you for taking us in."

Aleda's insides cringed. *Taking us in* sounded permanent. She felt such pity for this mother with her young daughter. But the solitude she had gotten so used to seemed in danger of slipping away.

Carefully she said, "You understand it's only until we find you a position and place to stay?"

Mrs. Libby nodded. "I believe in paying my own way, Miss Hollis."

The cleanliness of the cottage validated that statement. And, Aleda discovered minutes later, so did the bedclothes turned back upon her tidy bed, and the pair of slippers greeting her upon the rug.

She opened her wardrobe doors and noticed the sharp creases in sleeves. *She even ironed!*

Chapter 17

Philip woke before sunrise, as was his habit. A cuckoo's notes tolled from the garden, clear and sweet as a silver bell.

The snores from the next room were not so sweet, but twice as endearing.

He dressed quietly and carried a lamp downstairs into the parlor to retrieve his cravat and pin. Something stirred; he directed the lamp closer to the sofa. Mother rose to her elbow, squinted into the light.

"I'm so sorry," he whispered.

"Is it morning?"

"Yes, but the sun's not up yet. Go back to sleep."

"I'm glad you woke me." She yawned and swung her feet around to sit. "Time to go back upstairs."

"Why didn't you go to Aleda's old room?"

"Habit. I started coming down here when your sisters were still here. This sofa's comfortable."

"What will you do when we move Father's bed down here?"

She smiled. "Not sleep?"

"We'll take turns."

"We'll see. Must you leave so early?"

"I want to see what sort of arrangements Doctor Rhodes has made. He's an early riser, too. Don't plan on me for lunch. I'd like to ride down to Shrewsbury and look over the surgery facilities."

"You're a dear."

He left through the front door instead of the kitchen. Dora had hearing like an owl and would try to push breakfast on him. Walking around the house to the stable, he wondered how long his mother had been slipping out of her bedroom to escape the snoring. He had a feeling Father was blissfully unaware. This latest example of their mutual devotion was touching, and yet brought a stab of pain. Would Loretta do such a thing?

Actually, she did it all the time. Just not for the same reason.

A mist lay upon the grass, to be burnt away later by the warmth of the sun. In the near distance, Saint Jude's stood in a solemn quiet of its own, as if to guard the repose of the sleepers in its hazy shadow. Belle was eager to be out and away, and took bridle and bit with no resistance. Her hooves fairly danced across the cobbled stones as she pulled the carriage. Gresham rested dew-spangled and tranquil against the first low rays of the sun. Past the rooftops, the Anwyl dawned a soft azure.

A thousand memories swept over him. This village had nurtured him when he needed it most, after his father's death. It was here that Mother had met and married Andrew Phelps, and doubled the number of his sisters. They teased him sometimes, tormented him others, but never had he doubted their love. And even later in Edinburgh, when so absorbed with texts and lectures and dissections that some days he did not even think consciously of his family, he carried them in his heart.

And then, to be loved by a beautiful woman! Not in the tranquil way of family, but with the excitement of Columbus finding the New World. When Doctor Trask introduced them, Loretta seemed as smitten with him as he was with her. In fact, she had almost frightened him away with the intensity of her dedication, the hints she dropped of marriage. He knew his faults. Could any woman, so willingly blind to them, be stable?

The scales were tipped by her father's position at Saint Bartholomew's. Not that Philip sought to advance his career, for his work spoke for itself. But to have such a respected man treating him as a son was a heady thing, adding to the allure of the daughter. Only fractionally, however, for Doctor Trask did not accompany them on their honeymoon, a month in Tuscany that was almost magical.

Within weeks of returning to London, however, she was giving off signs of disappointment with him. Making little complaints. She hated his beard, which he had cultivated for the Edinburgh winters and retained because he disliked shaving. He gave up cigarettes. They were a nasty habit anyway, picked up to ease the rigors of medical school. He ceased balking at her parents' insistence on paying for a coach, horses, and a coachman's wages, even when accepting the gift of the house had made him feel less than a man.

No amount of praise from his peers and superiors at Saint Bartholomew's could compensate for coming home and finding his wife absent. Even when she was present. When he questioned what was wrong, her stock answer was "nothing."

Their conversations eroded to either trivialities or banter. They excelled at the latter. Humor was a great distancer.

He felt his cheek. His auburn hair was fine, and so the stubble barely stood out against his fingertips. In his haste to leave the vicarage, he had not shaved. But then, perhaps he would not tomorrow, either.

Sunlight through the gap in the curtains was warm on her face. Jewel slipped out of bed and into her wrapper. Becky snored softly on her side, her curls tumbled about the pillow.

On the landing, Jewel was relieved to hear movement in the other bedchamber. Even though Miss Hollis was meeting a friend for breakfast, she might care for a cup of tea.

The kettle was boiling when Miss Hollis came downstairs, fastening the cuff buttons of a crisp white poplin blouse. "No one will recognize me without the wrinkles. Tea? Wonderful! I tossed and turned so."

"I'm sorry." Jewel poured her a steaming cup.

"My fault. I can't drink hot chocolate in the evenings." She covered a yawn, then took a sip. "It's useful, when I must work all night, but not when I want to sleep. Will you have some?"

Jewel poured herself a cup and joined her at the table. "Thank you for the eggs and bacon. And I'd like to buy some food."

"Yes, of course. I'll get some money. . . ."

"I have money," Jewel said respectfully. Only two pounds, but with her usual frugality at the market, she could stretch it for a while.

"I'm not going to allow you to do that."

"I can't do all the taking, Miss Hollis. Will you tell me where to go?"

Miss Hollis sighed. "Take the southward path around the

fence until you reach Church Lane. Set out to your right, and you'll eventually come to the crossroads. Any of the shops there will deliver if you need them to."

After breakfast, Jewel and Becky set out on foot. The village was twice as charming as it had seemed from the coach. Tree branches meandered over the lane. Stone and half-timbered cottages boasted flower gardens and pots of geraniums in windows. The shade-cooled air felt invigorating. A farmer passing in the lane doffed his hat. An elderly woman waved from her garden. Becky skipped along at her side, chattering happily.

"I hear a cow, Mummy. Do you?"

Jewel cocked her head to listen. "I do. But not just one. Miss Hollis said there are dairy farms here."

"What's a dairy farm?"

"Where people keep cows for their milk."

They passed a schoolyard, where four children were sending up squeals from a merry-go-round. Becky sent a half-shy, half-longing look that caused an ache in Jewel's heart. They were no longer in Birmingham, but not quite part of Gresham, either. Even though school was not in session, were only students allowed to play here?

"Why don't we look for some cows?" she said impulsively.

"Oh, may we?" Becky clapped her hands.

Jewel smiled. There was no hurry to return; the cottage was almost spotless. Outside the cluster of shops at the crossroads, she asked directions of a barber sweeping the pavement. Before even reaching the stone bridge to the north, they could see black-and-white cattle grazing in distant rolling pastures.

"This is far enough, mite," Jewel said. "I don't want to have to carry you back the whole way."

"Just to the bridge? To look at the water?"

"Very well." Truth was, Jewel was having just as much fun. Once she found a position, the opportunities for exploring might be limited. But leisure time was an abnormality, as stiff as a pair of Sunday shoes.

At length they returned to the shops. Jewel purchased bread from the baker, soup bones from the butcher, potatoes, onions, carrots, and peas from the greengrocer. The parcels in her arms were bulky, but manageable.

Near the end of the path, Becky hurried ahead. "I'll open the gate."

"There's a good girl."

Seated in the wicker chairs were Miss Hollis and a large, pleasant-faced man wearing a gray tweed suit. He rose to his feet and advanced.

"Please allow me, Mrs. Libby," he said in a familiar accent.

"You're very kind, but I can manage."

Miss Hollis said from her chair, "Mr. Patterson has few opportunities to play the gentleman. You may as well humor him."

"Aleda exaggerates. One can be a gentleman even while alone. How very good to meet a fellow Brummie." Taking the parcels, he inclined his head toward Becky, gaping up at him. "*Two* fellow Brummies, that is."

Jewel could not help but smile.

"Please, sir, what's a Brummie?" Becky asked.

"Why, it's the nickname for those of us from Birmingham." He smiled. "Allow me to introduce myself. I'm Gabriel Patterson. And you are, of course, Mrs. Libby and Becky."

"We're pleased to meet you," Jewel said. "Where in Birmingham do you live?"

"Ah, but I fled Birmingham over a decade ago. It's a good place to be *from*. If you'll pardon me . . ."

He turned toward the steps. Jewel realized she should follow, to open the door. Behind, she heard Miss Hollis ask, "Did you enjoy the shops, Becky?"

"I liked the cows and the bridge more."

"Well, sit here and tell me about it."

Mr. Patterson set the parcels upon the table. Jewel was not quite sure what was expected of her, given her position as part servant, part houseguest. She thanked him again and offered her hand.

Two fleshy paws engulfed it. "My pleasure."

He was not handsome in the classical sense, with his thinning, dun-colored hair, full cheeks, and girth. But the kindness, humor, and intelligence in his face were pleasing to the eyes.

"Was there nothing about Birmingham that you liked, Mr. Patterson?" she found herself asking.

"That's a very good question. There was plenty to like, but I didn't like who I *was* when I lived there. Does that make sense?"

She thought of herself, one of a multitude trudging from factory to slums to factory, with only Sundays to brighten the weeks. "It does, Mr. Patterson."

"Will you join us in the garden?"

"Thank you, but I must start making soup." She would call Becky indoors, as well, and not take advantage of his courtesy.

He nodded. "It was good to meet you, Mrs. Libby."

Miss Hollis came inside an hour later, as Jewel swept stray vegetable peelings from the kitchen floor, and Becky sat at the bottom of the staircase tying bows with string from the parcels.

"My brother abducted Gabriel to go to Shrewsbury with him and look over the hospital." She went to the stove and lifted the lid from the pot. "Soup?"

"I'm afraid it won't be ready until tonight. But there is still plenty of lamb stew left."

Miss Hollis patted her stomach. "I overdid breakfast."

"See, Miss Hollis?" Becky said, holding up one of her string bows. "You only have to pull an end to make it come apart."

"Clever girl. Do you like to draw?"

"I do."

"Sit at the table. I'll be back."

She went upstairs, and returned with a stack of paper about six inches thick.

Surely not! Jewel thought, and was opening her mouth to protest when Miss Hollis peeled off four sheets from the top and placed them before Becky. She handed her two pencils, winked at Jewel, and left for the garden with the bulk of the stack.

Lost in her story, Aleda was startled when Mrs. Libby appeared with a beaker on a tray.

"What time is it?" Aleda asked.

"After one o'clock. I thought you might care for some lemonade."

"What a coincidence. I was just reading about lemonade. . . . Here . . . my characters are drinking lemonade at a May Day picnic."

"Perhaps you're a psychic?" Mrs. Libby lowered the tray.

Aleda laughed, a little surprised, given Mrs. Libby's factory and service background.

Her expression must have revealed so, for Mrs. Libby

explained with no rancor, "My first employer was a headmaster. They entertained often, and I learned much from discussions while helping in the dining room."

Aleda took a sip from the beaker. "Very good. But perhaps *you're* the psychic. You knew I was thirsty."

"You don't really believe in that, do you, Miss Hollis?" Mrs. Libby said carefully.

"My stepfather's the vicar. What do you think?"

Mrs. Libby laughed, and was turning toward the cottage when Aleda said, "Where is Becky?"

"Napping. Is there something you wish me to—?"

"No, pour yourself some lemonade and join me."

She sent an uncertain glance toward the chair beside her. "Join you?"

"To chat. You know, as people do. Don't look so uneasy."

Minutes later, when Mrs. Libby had settled with her drink, Aleda asked, "Do you miss Birmingham?"

"There are some things I miss. Saint Philip's Chapel. Vicar and Mrs. Treves. Fidget pie. The places my husband and I took walks. Our first little house, even if it was a back-to-back."

"Do you hope to return one day?"

"Never." Her red curls bounced against her shoulder with her headshake. "I do miss those things I mentioned, but I suppose if you grew up in a hole in the ground, you'd recall some things fondly, too."

Amused, Aleda said, "Such as dirt? Grubs? Worms?"

Mrs. Libby smiled. "If that's all you knew."

"It took great courage for you to leave your 'hole in the ground,' knowing so little of the place you would land."

"Thank you, but I never felt courageous. It's just that my fear of the known was greater than my fear of the unknown."

They sat in companionable silence for a while, sipping lemonade. Mrs. Libby looked at the stack of papers on her lap and said, "I read some of your stories last night. They're very good."

"Why, thank you."

"Is your novel an adventure, too?"

Aleda shook her head. "It's set in a village, much like this one. A bit of humor, a bit of romance. And well, yes, some adventure, but no Komodo dragons."

Mrs. Libby smiled. "May I ask why you've written it in script, when you have a typewriter?"

"Well, because it's closer to my heart than my magazine stories. The pen is more personable than tapping it out on a machine."

"A labor of love?"

Aleda sighed. "When it's not a labor of hate."

Mrs. Libby's reddish brows lifted.

Aleda was astonished at herself for revealing so much. But having an impartial listener, with no emotional stake, was refreshing.

"I wrapped up all plots and subplots into a tidy ending long ago. But I can't bear the thought of bad reviews from critics . . . or worse, having it rejected, so I won't submit it for publication until it's perfect. Or at least as close to that as possible."

"Is it almost there?"

"Every time I read it over, new flaws stand out. But it'll be worth it in the end. Samuel Johnson said great works are performed not by strength, but perseverance."

"Has he read your story?"

"He was a famous writer of the last century," Aleda said, trying not to sound condescending.

Nonplussed, Mrs. Libby said, "He must not have come up in the dinner conversations. So, no one else has read it?"

"Heavens, no. Mr. Patterson has offered, which is why I brought it out here to look over. But I don't think it's ready, even for him."

"But wouldn't he be kinder than the critics?"

Aleda hesitated before admitting, "That frightens me more than their opinions. I don't want his pity if it so happens that I'm meant only for magazine romps."

Mrs. Libby took a sip from her glass, chewed her lip thoughtfully. "Pardon me for asking, Miss Hollis, but . . ."

"Go ahead."

"I don't know anything about writing. But could it be that you've looked for the bad parts so many times that you can't recognize the good? Like having a spot on your face. . . . It's all you see in the mirror, but no one else does because they're looking at the color of your eyes?"

Aleda felt a tinge of annoyance. Mrs. Libby was obviously intelligent, but as she had just admitted, what did she know of the complexities of emptying one's heart onto paper? "It's not that simple."

"Of course. My apology." Mrs. Libby got to her feet. "Would you care for more?"

"No thank you." Aleda handed over her empty beaker, gathered her manuscript into her arms, and rose. "And I must return to my story. Make up for time lost in London. Will my typing wake Becky?"

"It won't. She's a heavy sleeper, and her door's closed."

But just in case, Aleda closed her own door, softly. Odd, but a sheet of paper lay draped over her typewriter carriage. She moved over to her desk, lifted the page, and smiled at the stick figure standing beside a stick cat. *Miss Hollis* and *Tiger* were spread across the top of the page in wavering letters, as if an adult hand had helped guide the pencil.

Tiger was probably napping at Becky's feet now. Aleda did not mind. Animals seemed to prefer children when they weren't the sort who grabbed and teased. That would have been terrible, having a brat under her roof.

She rolled a sheet of paper onto the carriage and began.

> *Lady Kempthorne raised her chin, as salt breezes toyed with the golden ringlets about her face. "I owe you my life, Captain Jacobs. But not my affection. You forget how recently I was widowed."*
>
> *"How could I forget," the captain replied tersely, "when your husband was so eager to trade you to the pirates for his freedom?"*
>
> *"We're not to speak ill of the dead."*
>
> *"There is speaking ill, and there is speaking truth. And ofttimes they are the same."*

Should he kiss her now? Probably not, Aleda thought. Even though her late husband had been a scoundrel, she was indeed a recent widow, and Captain Jacobs, a gentleman.

But what would her readers want?

She sighed. A kiss, passionate and fierce. Followed by a slap from Lady Kempthorne's soft white hand. Leave any reader under the age of twelve assuming she hated him.

Her eyes strayed to the stack of hand-scripted pages.

Gabriel would be kind in his critique, but he would also be honest. He would love her no less if the book was no good. She thought of Mrs. Libby setting out with no more than a letter and a little money, a battered trunk and a daughter depending upon her. What had she said? *My fear of the known was greater than my fear of the unknown.*

By clinging to her manuscript she was staying in Birmingham. Or worse, in the hole in the ground. She could see herself years from now, still pruning and grafting and fussing over her story, until she became an odd little woman hiding her treasure away in a cupboard until the pages yellowed.

But at least it would be safe from criticism, she thought wryly.

I have to do this.

Remarkable, that someone she barely knew had nudged her out of her inertia.

She had to thank her. She opened the door, softly again, and went downstairs. Savory aromas drifted from the pot on the stove. Mrs. Libby stood at the table over the assortment of household lamps, drying their globes with a tea cloth.

"You'll work yourself to death," Aleda said.

The streak of soot on her cheek curved with her smile. "I'm not tired."

"You're not my slave, either. I'm beginning to feel I'm taking advantage of you."

"Advantage?" Mrs. Libby waved a sooty hand. "You've given us shelter."

"I'm happy to do so." She would be happier when that was no longer necessary, but that was beside the point. "Just promise me you'll do something with Becky when she wakes? She obviously enjoyed your morning stroll."

Opening her mouth as if to offer more protest, Mrs. Libby leaned her head in thought. "If I'm making you uncomfortable . . ."

"You are."

"I'll take Becky for another walk when she's up."

"There you are. Explore the woods a bit. They're quite lovely, and you can't get lost if you stay on the path."

And as long as she was having her say, Aleda thought, she may as well address another issue.

"And you mustn't buy any more food. Make a list of what we need, and I'll have it delivered."

Mrs. Libby's blue eyes clouded.

"Now, no more of that." Aleda smiled. "You think you're doing all the taking, but it's just not so. Besides giving me the cleanest house in Gresham, you've helped me come to a major decision."

"I have?" Mrs. Libby gave her a hopeful look. "You'll allow Mr. Patterson to read your book?"

"With fear and trembling, but yes."

Chapter 18

"He could hang on like this for weeks," Doctor Rhodes said in the corridor with lowered voice.

Why whisper? Donald thought. His uncle's mind was gone. Circus acrobats bouncing over his bed would have been met with the same drooling, blank stare.

Doctor Rhodes surely accepted this, too, for he no longer pressed him to allow visitors other than Mary Johnson, who napped in a cot when not attending to his needs.

"I appreciate your concern over germs," the doctor went on, "but it would do him good if you stuck your head in the room more often."

Donald's teeth clenched. Mary and her big mouth! But what could he say? He needed Doctor Rhodes on his side, should the will be contested. He put a hand upon the old man's shoulder.

"It's just that it pains me so to see him that way. But you're right, and I shall."

That should have satisfied him, but maddeningly, the doctor went on. "One thing more. Miss Johnson looks exhausted. She cannot possibly be giving him decent care with so little sleep. You *must* get her some help."

"Yes, of course."

When he was gone, Donald ambled out to a bench in the rose garden. Fragrant breezes pawed at his hair. Like his uncle, his mother had loved roses. If he closed his eyes, he could picture her bringing a tray of milk and biscuits out to the garden when he was a boy, coffee when he was older. With biscuits. How many British childhood memories were centered around biscuits?

He sighed and rubbed his eyes. There was no use scolding Mary Johnson, and have another episode of his private business spread all over Gresham. But Doctor Rhodes was wrong. He had once stuck more than his head through his uncle's door when Mary was at lunch. He had combed every inch of chest of drawers and wardrobe. No money was tucked away. Not even a ring or watch, cuff links or tie pin that he could slip over to a pawn broker in Shrewsbury.

Was the old man really that tight? Or had the servants beaten him to the goods? Frustrating that he could not level any charges without revealing just how he knew the valuables, if they existed, were absent.

Just before coming to Gresham, he had lost his watch and jewelry in a game of twenty-one in one of the lesser salons, a foolish attempt to raise enough stakes to save his house.

He could not carry off any household treasures—such as the ten-inch jade statuette of a Japanese geisha in the library—from under the eyes of servants who dusted daily. The housekeeper kept the silver locked when it wasn't being used, polished, or counted. Pathetically, he had almost been reduced to stealing the spoon from his uncle's tray outside the door and allowing Mary to take the blame. But how much would that have landed him?

Smothering his uncle with a pillow would have been a mercy. Who would wish to live that way? But firstly, the threat of a postmortem hung over him. Secondly, as his luck was running of late, he was certain he would be caught. Thirdly, he was not sure his hands could perpetrate the act. Wishing someone to die was one thing. Overt murder was another.

He blew out his cheeks. Poverty was no less grinding when it was temporary. He *had* to get to London for a couple of days, which not only required train fare but enough for theatre tickets and lobster dinners, perhaps a bauble from Harrods' jewelry department. He would need to leave some money, too, lest Reese grow restless again.

He heard some tune being whistled and spotted the postman walking up the carriage drive with sack slung from his shoulder. Here would be another to benefit from his uncle's shuffling over to The Other Side. It seemed Uncle Bartley subscribed to every magazine in England. The unread stack in the library grew taller every week. Too bad he could not sell those, but even so, how much could one earn from out of date, and soon-to-be out of date, publications?

A thought sparked in his mind. He sat up straight. On his second morning in Gresham, before the servants had begun to dislike him, Mrs. Cooper had offered him a magazine to read, saying that the author of one of the serialized stories rented the old gamekeeper's cottage. That she was Vicar Phelps's daughter, a spinster with a cat.

An author. Having serials published, which meant steady

income. And no one to spend it on but her spinsterish self and the cat.

He knew he was handsome. The mirror did not lie. Nor did the looks sent his way whenever he strolled down the London pavement. Or drove his barouche, before he lost it, along with the team of ash gray Welsh cobs.

He groaned, shook the thought from his head. No sense beating himself up over that again. He had used his looks and charm in the past for financial gain. It could be a tedious process, depending upon the particular whims of the object of his attention. And he took no pleasure in it. But for now in his desperation, it seemed Miss Phelps was the only game in Gresham.

"Miss Phelps?" Mrs. Cooper said to his query. "There's no Miss Phelps in Gresham, sir. The two girls married some years ago."

"But did you not say one of the vicar's daughters leased a house from Uncle Thurmond?"

"That would be Miss Hollis. She's actually his stepdaughter."

Apples and oranges, Donald thought. Still, she had something there. Women were flattered when a man took pains to learn a little something about them. Should he not read some of her stories before introducing himself?

He was on his way into the library when another thought struck him. If he were to pretend surprise at learning of her profession, she would have no reason to suspect he was interested in her money. And for that reason, he chose his plain tweed coat, though he did clean his teeth and comb his hair.

He set out without informing the servants where he was going. *Let them wonder!* But then again, they were probably dancing, thinking of new ways to taint his food. How satisfying it was going to be to sack all of them!

The path wound through the woods across Church Lane, just as he remembered. He saw movement and stopped to peer through the branches of a yew. Over the picket fence, a glimpse of red hair. That made him feel better. He adored red hair, the contrast it made with fair skin. Miss Hollis wore an apron over a dress of violet-and-pink checks, and was sweeping the cottage steps. Not a very writer-worthy activity, but when one chose to live alone, one had to look after oneself.

"Mummy, may I pick more berries?"

His eyes found the source of the voice: a girl, with the same red hair. Was this her actual reason for seclusion? A vicar's daughter, with a base child?

"No, mite, you've had quite enough."

Quite met his ears as *quoit*. He would know that flat accent anywhere, having enjoyed a two-year liaison with a member of the Royal Opera House chorus who hailed from Birmingham.

Yet oddly, Mrs. Phelps, who would be her natural mother, had not shared the accent.

The plot thickened. Perhaps Miss Hollis had lived long enough in Birmingham to pick up the accent—and a child—before returning to self-exile on the fringe of the community.

He smiled to himself. *He* should be the writer. He stepped out from the tree. His mission might have been unsavory, but at least it proved to be interesting.

"I'm finished sweeping. If you'll fetch your boots, we'll explore a bit."

Becky's face brightened, and she darted into the house.

Jewel smiled. The trees were so fragrant, and this was Becky's first experience with a forest. Jewel had fond, vague memories of visiting her mother's parents on the outskirts of Chelmsley Wood.

She heard movement. Footfalls in the grass. Panic was her immediate reaction. *He doesn't know where we are,* she had to remind herself.

"Good afternoon, miss," said a voice, male, but decidedly not Mr. Dunstan's. Nor Mr. Patterson's. Perhaps Miss Hollis's surgeon brother?

A dark-haired man stepped up to the fence, with a good-humored face that made up for the fierceness of his black mustache. "I've startled you. I should have given warning. Whistled, or sang a song. Only, I have a tin ear, so you might have thrown a stick at me."

Jewel smiled. "No, that's quite all right, sir. I'm just a bit skittish this afternoon."

"Ah." He nodded. "Strangers popping out of the woods will do that to you. So please allow me to introduce myself. I'm Donald Gibbs, the squire's nephew."

"I'm pleased to meet you," she said, also pleased that he kept himself on the other side of the fence. But surely he was harmless, related to a village squire as he was. And he did not leer at her. She was about to introduce herself when Becky came running outdoors with boots flapping.

"Will you fasten them, Mummy? Who is that man?"

"Mr. Gibbs, Becky," Jewel replied, and wrapped an arm around her shoulder to draw her to her side.

"I've been staying with my uncle for the past three weeks," he said.

"We're to walk in the woods," Becky said as if they had not gone through such an ordeal over the last strange man to show interest in her.

"What fun! I used to wander up the path to pick blackberries

208

when I was young. Should they be ripe now? No, it's a bit early in the season."

"I don't know, sir," Jewel replied. This Mr. Gibbs was a little too friendly for her comfort. "I'm suddenly fatigued. I doubt we'll walk after all."

"Please, Mummy," Becky pleaded.

Mr. Gibbs unhooked his hands from the fence and took a backwards step, clearly understanding. "Pity, on such a lovely day. I'm rather fatigued myself. I hear a nap calling back at the house. Perhaps you'll have the energy for your walk later."

"Good day, sir," Jewel said, not sure if this was a ploy, hating the cautious eye she would be forced to cast upon men, when most were surely decent.

"And to you." He paused in midturn, brow furrowed but voice gentle. "I realize you're my uncle's tenant, Miss Hollis. But that does not obligate you to address me as *sir*. In fact, it causes me discomfort, considering the circumstances."

"Your uncle owns this cottage?"

"Of course. How . . . could you not be aware of that? Are you not Miss Hollis?"

Relief flooded Jewel, that he had come with a legitimate purpose. "I'm Mrs. Libby."

A pause, and then, "Are you her housemaid?"

"Oh, no sir. But she's offered to help me find me a position."

"Are we to take our walk now?" Becky asked.

"Shush, child."

Mr. Gibbs scratched his head. "Where is Miss Hollis, then?"

"She's at the vicarage. I'm not sure when she'll return."

"I see." He folded his arms. "You're not from Gresham, are you?"

"No, sir."

"Your accent—Birmingham?"

"Why, yes. We came up just two days ago."

"How are you acquainted with Miss Hollis?"

"My minister gave us a letter introducing us to Vicar Phelps. But he's unwell."

He nodded. "I thought he looked peaked that day. Are you saying you're not acquainted with *anyone* in Gresham?"

"Only Miss Hollis and Mrs. Phelps."

"And you're looking for a position?"

"Yes, sir."

"Do you keep your word, Mrs. Libby?"

The question surprised her. "I do my best. It's a sin not to."

"My uncle is dying."

Jewel put a hand to her heart. "I'm sorry."

"He requires a day nurse who would be willing to move into the manor house. If I were to hire you, could you refrain from gossiping to the servants, or anyone else, what goes on? He was always a private man. Out of respect for him, I don't want it bandied about the house and village what he's going through."

"I can do that, sir." He had not asked if she had experience, but she thought she should add, "I cared for my mother for eight months when I was twelve."

"Very good."

"I would have to have my daughter with me."

"Fine. I'll send someone for you in the morning."

In the morning? Could this not wait until after church? But illness was no respecter of time. And the way the job was offered to her, out of the blue, surely this was from God. Had she not prayed for a position?

210

Thank you, Father!

Jewel and Becky were sitting across from each other at the table with bowls of soup when Miss Hollis returned with Mr. Patterson.

"We've interrupted your supper," he said.

"We've only just sat down. Would you care for some soup?"

"No thank you," Miss Hollis said on her way to the staircase. "We've been helping rearrange furniture at the vicarage, and Dora brought out sandwiches. Gabriel's just here for my manuscript."

"I'm afraid she'll change her mind if I wait until tomorrow." Mr. Patterson pulled out the chair beside Becky and sat. "And what did you do this afternoon, Miss Becky?"

"She drew a lovely picture for me," Miss Hollis called down from the landing.

Beaming, Becky said, "And we saw a rabbit in the woods."

"How exciting!" Mr. Patterson said.

She nodded. "And Mummy has a job."

"What was that?" Miss Hollis said, halfway down the staircase with her manuscript in her arms.

Jewel looked up at her. "I'm to be the day nurse for the squire. His nephew, a Mr. Gibbs, came by. I start tomorrow morning. I hate to miss church, but hopefully we'll have other opportunities to go."

At the bottom of the staircase, Miss Hollis turned to set her manuscript upon a step. She walked over to the head of the table and sat adjacent to Jewel. With an eye toward Becky and voice low, she said, "Mr. Gibbs has a reputation."

Another Mr. Dunstan? Sickening chills ran up Jewel's back.

"I've not met him, but it's all over Gresham that he had to be goaded into providing decent care for the squire. And that he only allows Doctor Rhodes to visit."

Jewel pursed her lips. "But if he's hiring me as nurse, would that not mean he intends to give him proper care?"

Miss Hollis rolled her eyes. "Have you considered that he may have taken a fancy to you?"

"To me?" Jewel shook her head.

"You're quite pretty."

Mr. Patterson nodded somberly.

"I would have known. He didn't look at us that way at all."

"Are you sure you want to do this?" Miss Hollis asked.

"Yes. This seems an answer to prayer."

"Well, you can always come back and we'll start all over if it's not a good situation. And if this is your going-away supper, I believe I'll have some soup after all." She pushed out her chair. "Gabriel?"

"It does smell good," he said. "A half bowl?"

Jewel started to rise, but Miss Hollis patted her shoulder. "I think I can find the bowls and spoons."

"Delicious," Mr. Patterson said after a taste. "Have you worked as a cook?"

"Only a kitchen maid, when I was young."

"Mummy sewed corsets," Becky piped.

"Becky . . ."

Mr. Patterson laughed. It was a wonderful, joyous sound, and contagious, for Miss Hollis joined him, then Jewel.

"How did you come from sewing corsets in Birmingham to making soup in Gresham?" he asked, wiping his eyes.

"It's a long story," she said respectfully. "And best forgotten."

"Bad Mr. Dunstan wanted me to go to the cellar with him," Becky supplied with childish frankness. "Mummy, what are the green things?"

Mr. Patterson's round face filled with distress and compassion. His eyes shifted to meet Jewel's. "Men can be such beasts."

"Not all men," she said softly. "And we're fine now."

"You deserve to be."

She felt a flush to her cheeks and looked again at her daughter. "They're peas, Becky."

Interesting, Aleda thought.

After the meal, she watched Gabriel take Mrs. Libby's hand and wish her well, then pat Becky's head.

He took up her manuscript, and she accompanied him to the gate in the gathering dusk.

"Hurry, Gabriel, or you'll be caught in the darkness. Perhaps I should get you a lamp."

"And risk igniting these precious pages? Don't worry." He looked at the cottage. "You think they'll be all right?"

"I've not heard of Mr. Gibbs forcing his attentions on any of the women servants. Or children. And it comforts me to know she'll be tending the squire. She seems a compassionate woman."

"Yes, she does. But Becky . . . has she any toys at all?"

Aleda thought for a second. She had had little interest in toys as a child, so had not even noticed. "I don't think so."

"May I give you some money to buy some toys to send to the manor house? They must be from *you* or Mrs. Libby will think . . ."

"Yes, I understand. But I don't want any money."

"You've done a good deed, helping them. Please let me help, too." He patted the top page of her manuscript and grinned at her. "You do owe me a favor. . . ."

"Very well." Aleda tugged at his sleeve. "Now go, or I'll worry about you wandering about in the darkness."

She smiled on her way back through the garden. Perhaps it wasn't necessary to live in London to find Gabriel a wife after all.

By the time she reached the door, her practical side had elbowed its way past that fantasy. The two were barely acquainted, and one had only to look at Philip and Loretta to see the danger of wedding in haste.

But it couldn't hurt to keep both in her prayers and see what the future held.

Chapter 19

Andrew preached his sermon Sunday morning, baptized the Coggins infant, and made an announcement just before the closing prayer and doxology.

"As many of you are aware, I'm to have surgery tomorrow morning."

There was a faint ripple of voices, heads leaning together.

"Mr. Nicholls of Whitchurch will fill the pulpit for the month of July. I realize I do not have to ask that you show him the same courtesy you have shown me, for you are the kindest congregation I have ever known."

Julia smiled, remembering the grumblings fifteen years ago when Andrew and the girls arrived in Gresham. The general consensus was that no one could fill Vicar Wilson's shoes—nor his pulpit. It had taken Gresham some time to warm up to him, just as it had taken her time to see this thickset, self-deprecating man in a romantic light.

"Which leads me to this request I make of you, dear ones. My family will have the unenviable task of nursing me. I fear too many calls will tax their strength. We would be most grateful for some quiet time to heal . . . and above all, we would be grateful for your prayers."

Another ripple, accompanied by nods and smiles. He stood at the door twice as long, receiving handshakes and promises of prayers.

"If anything goes wrong . . ." Andrew said that night as Julia lay in his arms.

She put a hand up to his lips. "Shush, Vicar."

He chuckled under the faint pressure of her fingers, then mumbled, "I need to say this."

She moved her hand.

"I hope you'll move back into the Larkspur. I can't bear the thought of you in some lonely cottage while the children move on with their lives."

"Then I shall," she said.

"And if some old gent . . . perhaps one of your lodgers . . . takes a fancy to you, and you find yourself wanting to marry again, please know you have my blessing."

"Andrew. I'll never marry again."

"I thought the same after Kathleen died. You can't know what's around the corner. I just want you to know that . . . whatever you do, I approve. I never want you to be lonely."

"Very well," she said to appease him.

"Unless it's Donald Gibbs."

Julia smiled in the darkness. "There goes my manor house."

"M-m-m." He nuzzled the top of her head with his chin. "It's nice. Sleeping snuggled together like this."

"Very nice," she said. She did not plan to slip down into the parlor tonight anyway.

⁓

On Monday morning, Julia, Aleda, Elizabeth and Jonathan, Ambrose and Fiona, and Gabriel—who would be leaving for London later in the day—sat in Saint John's Hospital's waiting room on the ground floor, engaged in small talk and looking up whenever the door opened. Just before noon, Philip walked in, looking weary but pleased. He had taken the time to remove his apron, which Julia appreciated.

"He came through fine. The ether is wearing off, and he's resting."

Julia, able to retain her composure most times, melted into quiet tears. She soddened her own handkerchief, and the one Fiona pressed upon her. *Thank you, Father!*

Philip escorted her past a dozen beds, most occupied, and some with curtains closed. "Remember he's still coming out of the ether," he whispered as a nurse withdrew the curtain around the last bed. "He may speak out of his head."

Sheet up to his chest, Andrew gazed at her through half-closed eyes, as if trying to identify her. With Philip watching from the other side, Julia knelt, touched her husband's bare shoulder lightly.

"How do you feel?"

He gave her a weak smile and mumbled, "It's over?"

"Yes. Philip says you came through fine."

"Very good. Will you write to Laurel and Grace?"

"Yes. Tonight."

He closed his eyes, as if to rest a bit from the effort. Julia smiled up at Philip. The ether had obviously worn off, for Andrew was as lucid as ever.

Andrew opened his eyes again. "Will you write to Laurel and Grace?"

Or then again . . .

"Yes," Julia said. "Tonight."

"And when Philip comes for supper, please ask him not to marry that girl. I don't think she will make him happy."

His eyes closed. Julia went around the bed and laid a hand upon Philip's arm. "I'm sorry, son. As you warned, he may speak out of his head."

"It's all right, Mother. I realize I've given you both occasion to worry."

"Are . . . you happy?" She had to ask.

He smiled and patted her hand in the crook of his arm. "How could I not be, with such a wonderful family?"

It was an answer that made her smile, while making her profoundly sad.

✦

Donald woke from restless sleep on Tuesday, the first of July. That month's mortgage payment was due by the eighth. Driven to desperation, he had the dogcart brought around front, and took the reins.

He had always hated the cheese factory. The fathomless stone building reeked of sour milk. Today, however, it smelled of money. At least in theory, for there was one huge obstacle to overcome.

He asked a white-aproned worker for directions to the accountant's office.

"Come in" came from inside after his knock.

Donald opened the door.

Horace Stokes ceased penciling numbers into a ledger and looked up. "May I help—" His face tightened into a glare that would curdle milk.

"Good day, Mr. Stokes," Donald said, entering, closing the door.

In spite of the malice pouring from it, Horace Stokes's face was still handsome after twenty-one years, with its piercing blue eyes, aristocratic nose, and square jaw. At thirteen, he had had the looks of a Greek god, albeit a skinny one. The broad shoulders now filling out his shirt were a surprise.

"You've done well for yourself," Donald said, nonplussed by the hostility. Power, even delayed, was a fine antidote to awkwardness.

"Thanks to your uncle," Horace said coldly.

I deserve some thanks, as well, Donald thought. "Will you not offer me a seat?"

"I'm very busy, Mr. Gibbs. What is it you want?"

"I have a mortgage due in a week. Tending my uncle has devastated my income. I'm in need of ten pounds." He thought of Reese. "Fifteen."

"And why do you bring this to me?"

Don't play stupid, you under gardener! "Because my uncle has given permission to withdraw it from the household accounts."

"Have you that in writing?"

"You know I haven't."

"Then I shall have to speak with the squire."

Donald rolled his eyes. "As I'm sure you're aware, my uncle cannot speak. But he communicated his permission to me in a way only I understand."

"I cannot hand over his money without concrete proof of his consent. I suggest you speak with his attorney, Mr. Baker."

Donald leaned forward. "I was only seventeen. How long do you plan to nurse a grudge?"

Horace's eyes narrowed, condensing the hostility in them into hatred.

"Leave now, Mr. Gibbs."

"You're aware that this place will soon be mine?"

"It is a fact I live with daily. But I'll not dishonor the man who gave me this opportunity by going against his explicit rules."

"And what of your family? I will also own the cottage they call home. It would be a pity to see them turned out."

Horace's hands curled. Donald waited for the rants and railings sure to come. But instead, the man said through tight jaw, "Unlike you, I have a skill that I may take elsewhere. And my family and I would live in a tent rather than submit to your blackmail."

Blackmail! Donald frowned. "I resent—"

"But hear this, Mr. Gibbs," Horace went on. "I'm no longer a frail thirteen-year-old! On the day you turn us out, it will be my pleasure to thrash you within an inch of your life!"

∞

Aleda bolted up in bed Wednesday morning with heart pounding. She had slept through Father's return! She pulled in a deep breath. This was no frantic nightmare. She slipped out of bed, walked over to her desk, and looked at her watch. Twenty of eight. Plenty of time to dress and make it over to the vicarage, for Philip had said not to expect the coach before ten.

But it did not roll up Vicarage Lane, slowly, until half past eleven, with Mr. Pool at the reins. Philip, Jonathan, John, and Luke carried Father just as slowly to the bed in the parlor.

It was Aleda's first sight of her stepfather since Sunday

evening. And though he was dosed with laudanum for his pain and the journey, she pressed a hand to his bearded cheek and kissed his forehead.

Elizabeth did the same, tears trailing down her face. Dora knelt by his bed and said a quick prayer. Luke touched his hand. And then Philip asked everyone to leave the parlor so that he could check him over.

"Go home and write," Mother said to Aleda in the foyer. "Philip says he'll sleep most of the day."

"Will you not need me?"

Her mother smiled. "I need for you to write your story."

Aleda embraced her. "Thank you. I'll return tomorrow."

"I'll pack you a proper supper if you'll give me a moment," Dora said.

When Aleda stepped out into the garden, early risers John and Jonathan were relaxing in chairs while Elizabeth cut flowers under Claire's and Samuel's supervision.

"We're making a bouquet for Grandfather's room!" Claire chirped to Aleda.

"We're making a bouquet for Grandfather's room!" Samuel echoed.

"How lovely. Grandfather is very fond of flowers."

"What do you have in the basket?" Claire asked.

"Claire, let's not be nosy," Jonathan scolded gently, before Samuel could speak his line.

Aleda did not mind. She had great respect for curiosity. "My supper."

"But it's not dark," Samuel said in a surprising show of improvisation.

"I'm saving it for then."

"May I get the gate for you, Aunt Aleda?" John said sleepily, in a tone that begged refusal.

"No, thank you." She was switching the basket to her left hand so that she could unfasten the latch, and realized something was not as it should be. She pushed back her sleeve. Had she not worn her watch? But yes, she could remember fastening the catch after dressing.

She was casting about in vain for any memory of removing it in the vicarage, when she felt a touch at her elbow. Jonathan stood near, face filled with concern. "Aleda? What's wrong?"

"What's wrong, Aunt Aleda?" she heard Samuel say.

∞

Gentleman that he was, Donald had realized that he should not make another attempt to call on Miss Hollis until her father was on the way to recovery. She would be preoccupied and think him a cad. But when Mrs. Cooper informed him the vicar was to be home that morning, he realized the surgery must not have been as serious as he had thought. Desperation drove him to take another chance.

After lunch, he picked his way up the path bearing roses. Now that Jewel Libby had been in his employ for a few days, he could not pretend not to know Miss Hollis was a published author. So his story today was that he was calling only for Becky Libby's sake. Miss Hollis had kindly sent toys over, but shouldn't a child also have books?

Perhaps as a writer herself, Miss Hollis would be so kind as to advise him on some good picture books he could purchase. And of course, he would ask how the vicar came through surgery.

The roses? Why, they were a mere neighborly gift, but hopefully would continue to work on his behalf when they parted; a fragrant reminder of his thoughtfulness.

His right foot was closing down when a glint caught his eye. He pulled back, almost losing his balance. A gold watch!

He picked it up, brushed it against his tweed sleeve. A segment of fine chain dangled from one end of the open catch. Surely it was Miss Hollis's. And there was nothing like gratitude to hurry along a courtship.

Carefully he dropped the watch into his pocket, took another step.

It would command a pretty penny at a pawn lender's.

He was not a thief. He could redeem it once he came into his inheritance. Combing the house for his uncle's valuables was one thing—they were days away from becoming his. While he had cheated at cards before—but only when he was certain he could get away with it—he had never overtly stolen. Dare he do this?

While his mind wrestled with the question, his feet did a reversal and hurried back up the path.

Early that afternoon, Jewel's chair was pulled close to the squire's bedside. On the rug nearby, Becky held a tea party for her doll, with small china dishes, using toy blocks as a table. The squire's bedchamber door opened, and Mr. Gibbs walked inside.

"What are you doing?" he asked Jewel.

"Trimming his toenails."

He grimaced and looked away. "I've been called to London on urgent business. Remember, when Doctor Rhodes comes, you're to mention I look in on my uncle daily."

Which was true, though his visits lasted less than a minute.

"Yes, sir."

"And again, remember you're not to gossip."

His face lost some of its sternness when he looked at Becky.

"Are you enjoying your toys?"

"Yes, sir. I named my doll Lucy."

The sound of coach wheels and hoofbeats had barely faded from the open window when Mary Johnson opened the door and stuck her head round it. The chambermaid did not begin housework until after noon, after catching up on her sleep from sitting with the squire the night before.

"How is he?"

Jewel looked up at his face. On his left side, he stared listlessly across at Becky. But because she had no idea how much his mind retained, she said, "He's doing well. Aren't you, sir?"

Mary nodded grimly. "Would Becky care to help me change sachets in the linen cupboard?"

The girl sprang up from the rug. "Please, Mummy?"

"After you put your toys away."

"I'll help her," Mary said.

Perhaps because the atmosphere in the house was more relaxed with Mr. Gibbs away, that was the beginning of so many kindnesses by the other servants. Jewel had felt tremendous guilt over keeping her daughter cooped up in the room or waiting in the hall whenever she bathed or changed the squire.

Mrs. Wright invited Becky to help in the kitchen the following morning. Mrs. Cooper escorted her out to feed the goldfish, and then to pick strawberries from the kitchen garden. Parlormaid Annabel Tanner allowed her to move figurines while she dusted. Mary Johnson plaited her hair.

They popped in often to see about the squire, as well, sometimes pray at his bedside, though he merely gaped at them. Jewel allowed it because she had not been instructed not to. Surely the displays of caring were good for him. As were surely the frequent absences of a chattering four-year-old.

"One last bite, if you please?" Jewel said soothingly on Friday while holding a spoon of porridge over the bowl.

Propped up on pillows, the squire opened his mouth like a baby bird, and watched her as he chewed.

"Very good, sir." She set bowl and spoon upon the table. She moved the napkin from his chest and dabbed the corner of his mouth. "I'll just put the tray outside."

The wiry brows shot up, as if this distressed him. There seemed some question in his eyes.

"You don't wish me to leave? Very well. I'll do it later."

The eyes faded a little.

"You'd like more porridge? Is that it?"

If a sigh could be written on a face, it was upon his. His mouth opened to make the only syllable within his power. "Auh."

Jewel studied his beseeching eyes. "Shall I close the window? Are you cold?"

His aged eyes closed. Tears stung Jewel's. To be mute, and so helpless. Not even able to scratch an itch.

"Have you an itch somewhere?"

A faint moan rose from his throat.

He was almost totally dependent upon her. Mary's only duty was to turn him every two hours. He was so frail that a woman could do it easily.

She looked around the room. What was different?

"Becky?" she guessed.

His eyes opened again.

"You wish to know where Becky is?"

"Auh."

Jewel smiled. "She's helping Zinnia at the wash line. She hands her the pegs."

Everything clicked. She had assumed the squire's eyes followed Becky simply because she moved about so much, exploring the vast room, going from window to window, playing with her toys.

Was he fond of children? Or was there more to it? Did watching Becky ease the tedium of lying motionless, the humiliation of spoon feedings and nappy changes? She had never considered boredom as one of the trials of illness.

"You're bored to tears, aren't you?"

His mouth sagged, speechless, but the eyes said it all.

Dear Vicar and Mrs. Treves,

Jewel wrote that evening in the cozy attic room she shared with Becky.

I hope you and your children are well. Becky and I pray for you every night before we retire, and I add a silent prayer that Mr. Dunstan has not troubled your family.

You will be pleased to know that I was offered a position two days after arriving in Gresham. I tend an elderly man you may remember from your time here, Squire Bartley. His health is sadly deteriorated so that he cannot speak. This afternoon, I thought reading aloud might cheer him. I intended to ask permission to seek a book in the library, but while looking for a warmer pair of stockings in his chest of drawers, I came across a copy of Around the World in Eighty Days by a Mr. Jules Verne. The spine is creased as if it has been read before, but he seems to be enjoying it.

I do not know if you have been informed, but Vicar Phelps had surgery for gallstones on Monday past. I hear that he is recovering very well. His daughter, Miss Aleda Hollis, took us in when we first arrived in Gresham. They are a fine family.

Again, I thank you for rescuing us. The other servants are kind here in the manor house, and the meals are filling. Already I can see blooms in Becky's cheeks. May God reward you a hundredfold for your kindness to us and to others.

Chapter 20

Dear Loretta,

I received a kind letter Saturday from your parents, asking after my stepfather. I have just answered that he is recovering. Five days from surgery, he is still confined to bed. This morning I allowed him a slice of bread soaked in milk instead of the usual broth. He savored it slowly, as if it were ambrosia.

I am leaving him in Mother's care this morning, to watch over Doctor Rhodes' practice so that he may drive his wife to Shrewsbury, as she has dropped and broken her eyeglasses. He has asked again if I would take over his practice. I have asked for some time to consider this. I should like to know your wishes.

Since our marriage I have made excuses for your coldness to my family, believing the root lay in your fear that I might wish to move us to Gresham; something I would never do without your consent. I have come to understand that I am the only barrier to your happiness, even in your beloved city. How do you think that makes me feel, as a husband?

And so I must ask . . . Shall I accept Doctor Rhodes' offer?
Should I write a letter of resignation to your father? Will my absence
bring you the happiness my presence obviously does not?
Please let me know your wishes.

Philip signed and sealed the letter. Even though his heart ached terribly, a burden lifted from his soul. He scratched his fledgling beard. At least there would be a decision.

He dropped the envelope into the letter box and carried his black bag across the green to Walnut Tree Lane, the farthest north-south road to the west of Gresham. The Rhodes' cottage was a snugly thatched mixture of stone and cob. His knock was answered by housekeeper Mrs. Grimly, whose name was at odds with her jolly round face.

"Aye, they've already left," she said, allowing him entrance into a parlor filled with a comfortable but eclectic mixture of old furniture and scattered medical books. "And you've got Willet Sanders waiting."

Philip had forgotten how early dairy farmers rose. Mr. Sanders would have already done the morning milking. The odor of pipe tobacco wafted down the hall from the surgery, which had its own outdoor entrance beneath a fading green canopy. Sure enough, Mr. Sanders rose slowly from a chair in the waiting area, peered at him through thick-lidded eyes, and pulled his pipe from scowling lips. "Where's Doctor Rhodes?"

"I'm taking his place this morning, Mr. Sanders."

"Took you long enough to get here."

He's family, Philip reminded himself. His daughter, Mercy Langford, was adoptive mother to Grace's husband, Thomas. *Still . . .*

"You may not smoke in here, Mr. Sanders. There is an ash barrel in the corner."

The old man's leathery brow furrowed, as if he were

considering returning later to more amiable doctoring. And it seemed he would do so, for he went to the door. "I just put in a new wad of tobacco. I'll leave it on the step. You ain't gonter be too long, are you?"

Not a moment longer than I have to, Philip thought.

"My knees," the old man said in the examining room. "Can't hardly sit on the milking stool. Worse in the mornings."

Philip had him remove his trousers and boots and stockings. Mr. Sanders cried out as he probed a swollen knee.

"Sorry," Philip said, and moved down to his feet. Gingerly he moved the right big toe. Mr. Sanders let out an oath. Philip ignored it. Pain could sometimes thrash self-control, especially when the latter was weak from underuse.

"You have gout, Mr. Sanders," he said after helping the man dress himself.

"Gout? But thet's for rich folk."

"Not at all, Mr. Sanders. It affects mostly older men whose diets contain purine-heavy foods."

Another scowl. "You wanter say thet in English?"

Philip nodded, apologized again. Most of his surgery patients were unconscious. He would have to work on his bedside manner. "Do you eat a lot of organ meats? Brains, liver, kidneys?"

"Well, yes. All the time."

Philip went over to Doctor Rhodes' medicine cabinet. "I'm going to give you some colchicine, which will help. But you must change your diet or this will not go away. I'll write you a list of foods to avoid, and those you may have in moderation. And, by the way, no beer."

Mr. Sanders looked as if he'd been punched. "None at all?"

"Is it worth the pain?"

He expected more argument, but the old man shook his

head, even squeezed out a tear. "Nothing's worth this pain. I don't wanter spend my last days like this."

Philip patted his shoulder. "I think you have many years left in you. Let's just make them *good* years."

Later, he flipped through one of Doctor Rhodes' medical texts, between treating Mrs. Winters' sty on the eye with a warm compress and citron ointment, and setting twelve-year-old Alger Sway's left index finger, broken while trying to catch a rounders ball.

The best call of the morning came when young Boswell Jefferies carried his near-hysterical wife, Sally, in because the infant she had carried in her womb for eight months had not moved in over a day. Philip picked up a faint but healthy heartbeat with his stethoscope, and allowed the parents to listen. The tears in both sets of eyes caused his own eyes to blur and sting. He certainly never got that from a surgery patient.

ஒ

Mr. Nicholls of Whitchurch was an earnest-faced young curate whose barely audible sermon on Elijah and the widow put some of the elderly people to sleep, but at least none had the indecency to snore. There were a couple of snorts, which ended abruptly on up notes brought on by neighborly elbows.

When a marble rolled down the aisle, Mr. Nicholls took the hint and began the closing prayer. Some child—probably a boy—would get a paddling later. Aleda would have given him a shilling for his sacrifice.

"You can only strain to listen for so long before your ears give up trying," Elizabeth said in a hushed tone as the family strolled toward the vicarage. Jonathan was absent, having volunteered to sit with Father.

"He said *Elisha* twice," John said.

"Are you quite sure?" Philip said.

"I am, Uncle Philip."

"Young people have sharp ears," Aleda said. "He could have said *Father Christmas* for all I could hear."

"Father Christmas," Claire twittered sociably, for she and Samuel had been chattering on and paying no attention.

"Father Christmas," Samuel chortled.

"That's enough," Mother said firmly. "It's not fair to make comparisons. He was nervous. And your father has been a minister for thirty years."

She was right. All grumblings gave way to guilty silence.

In the parlor, Father was sitting up against his bed pillows with the expression of one who had counted the minutes. "Well, how was it?"

Mother went behind his chair, leaned to kiss the top of his head. "Fine. You may want to give Mr. Nicholls some fatherly advice when he visits."

He was staying at the Larkspur. One of the lodgers had left Thursday to visit family in Yorkshire, and offered her room. Aleda and Elizabeth exchanged knowing looks. By sunrise tomorrow, the poor man would have had his fill of preaching advice from the lodgers.

⸏

"We begin chapter eleven," Jewel said to the squire.

Becky looked up from the tower of blocks she was building upon the rug. "Mummy, do you think Mr. Fogg and Aouda will marry?"

Jewel stared at her. The child had not even been inside the bedchamber for every reading, for the women servants still sought her company. She glanced at the squire, and her surprise was even greater.

His eyes were smiling!

Jewel smiled, as well. "It's too early to tell, mite."

She cleared her throat and began reading.

" 'The train had started punctually. Among the passengers were a number of officers, government officials, and opium and indigo merchants, whose business called them to the eastern coast.' "

"Mummy? What's opium and indigo?"

"Opium is something bad that you must never, ever take. I don't know what indigo is, but if these merchants are selling it with opium, then it's bad, too. Now, you must be quiet and allow me to read."

She looked at the squire again. If his eyes were smiling before, they positively laughed now!

⁓

"No cheques," Mr. Maxwell of Maxwell and Son Livery Service said between puffs on a pipe, beneath a nose spidery with red veins.

"But it's drawn on the Bank of England."

"Don't mean there's money in it."

There was not indeed, but still Donald took umbrage. "I resent your implication that I'm not a gentleman, sir."

The man waved a spotted hand. "No implication, just policy from having been burned by too many 'gentlemen' in the past."

Were the man not at least twenty years his senior, Donald would have called him out. But even so, how would that get him up to Gresham? He did not fancy the idea of walking twelve miles.

He tried another tactic. "Have you heard of Squire Thurmond Bartley?"

Mr. Maxwell cocked his head. "Of the cheeses?"

"Indeed. He's my uncle, and very ill."

"I'm very sorry."

"And so you can see I must get to him straightaway."

The man nodded, pointed his pipe. "Then, nip a half block over to the warehouse, and you can catch a wagon on its return. They sometimes take on passengers to and from Gresham. I'll wager they won't even charge you the shilling."

"Pleasant day, ain't it?" said the driver as the wagon rumbled along the macadamized roadway.

"Lovely," Donald muttered. The money gleaned from the watch was gone. He would have been in deeper hot water had he not had the foresight to purchase a return railway ticket, and to pay the July mortgage before heading over to his Kensington house. Reese went through the rest like a sow through corn, even insisting on another velvet jacket, simply because the sleeves of the one purchased in February creased excessively at the elbows.

Why the need to dress so smartly, just for hanging about the house? Donald hated to guess.

"Was you away Friday?" The driver's voice cut into his thoughts again.

"Yes."

"Rained like the dickens. We couldn't even take out the wagons."

"How utterly devastating for you," Donald muttered.

This time the driver caught the sarcasm in his voice and made no more effort at conversation.

"The manor house, if you please," Donald said as cottages began popping up on either side.

The man did not argue that it was not on his route. By

now he had surely figured out that Donald would own his livelihood very soon.

Mrs. Cooper met him in the foyer, looking startled to see him. "I thought I heard horses, sir. Everyone's to lunch. Will you be wanting something to eat?"

"I'll ring for a tray in a couple of hours. I mean to rest a bit, after I look in on Uncle."

The housekeeper smiled. "You'll be pleased. He seems more alert now."

Donald stretched his lips into a smile. "Outstanding. You may return to your meal."

He did not even take the time to stash his portmanteau, but propped it against the wall beside his uncle's door. The old man lay facing the doorway. The eye not pressed against his pillow was closed.

Upon the bedside table lay a copy of *Around the World in Eighty Days*, he supposed from the library downstairs. He had not forbidden Jewel to read to his uncle, simply because it had not crossed his mind. Mary was illiterate, and he'd assumed anyone so desperate for a menial position as Jewel Libby was probably so, as well.

Uncle Thurmond lay so still. Did he even breathe? Donald leaned close.

The eye opened!

Donald gasped.

"Whoa! Uncle!" he muttered with a backwards step. He was just about to turn and leave when he realized the gray eye was focused upon him. Not just upon him, but piercing him, reading him like the novel upon the table. And sending forth beams of dislike, if not hatred.

Mrs. Cooper was right. Jewel was good for the squire,

whether because of the reading, or presence of a child, or constant attention, or all three.

What if his mind became so sharp that his power of speech returned? It was too late to play the part of the attentive nephew. His uncle was not stupid. What would stop him from demanding to see Mr. Baker?

She has to go, he thought back in the hallway. The only fly in the ointment was that she would run to Miss Hollis. She would take her side, of course. He must choose the lesser of two evils.

A mental picture of Uncle Thurmond, dictating a new will to Mr. Baker, nudged him into action.

Chapter 21

The day's fare in the servants' hall was hashed calf's head, green pea soup, and brown bread. Plain, but tasty. Jewel relished the one time daily she and Becky joined the others at the table. As much as she cared for Squire Bartley, it was refreshing to chat with adults who could chat back. She had even begun to see the gardeners and stable workers as decent men, though she could not bring herself to allow Becky to run about unsupervised.

"Yes indeed, the world is round," Mr. Rignold, chief gardener, was saying to Becky. "Round as an apple. Has your mother not told you?"

To the inquiring eyes sent her way, Jewel smiled sheepishly. "It never crossed my mind to do so."

"She'll be learnin' it in school," laundress Zinnia said.

"Anyhows, the world ain't round like an apple," said Lottie, the scullery maid. "Where would be the stem? Stickin' out the North Pole?"

The banter quieted when Mrs. Cooper walked back into the hall and resumed her place at the head of the table. "Mr. Gibbs has returned. I knew my ears weren't playing tricks."

"Meow," Osborn, the groomsman, said softly. "The cat's come home, then."

Mrs. Cooper looked poised to scold him, but then picked up her spoon.

"You rang, Mr. Gibbs?" Annabel asked inside the library doorway.

Donald looked up from the open atlas upon the table. "I'll have my tray now."

"Yes, sir."

"Oh, by the by," he said as she was turning to leave. "What happened to the statue?"

"I beg your pardon?"

He nodded toward a wall table and the bare space once occupied by the geisha. "I hope it wasn't knocked over. But jade is quite hardy, is it not?"

Her eyes widened, as well they should have, for the library was part of the parlormaid's responsibility. "Ah . . . I don't know, sir. It was there when I dusted yesterday."

"Hmm. Tell Mrs. Cooper I wish to see her."

She gaped at him.

Donald clapped his hands. "Chop-chop!"

The housekeeper took less than three minutes to appear, according to the longcase clock.

"Yes, Mr. Gibbs?"

He placed a finger upon the atlas page. "Do you know the location of Cameroon, Mrs. Cooper?"

She stared at him for a fraction of a second. "I do not."

"Nothing to be ashamed of. It's in Central Africa. I had to look it up myself after catching up on the newspapers and learning the Germans had taken possession of it."

"Annabel said something about the jade geisha being moved?"

"Missing, actually. Perhaps it's being polished?"

"Annabel polishes it right there, when she dusts."

"Well, then, we have a mystery. I've looked about in here. Please search the servants' rooms."

Her face clouded. "Surely you can't think . . ."

"Of course not. But that does not change the fact that it is absent, and there will always be that kernel of doubt until you've cleared everyone." He rose. "In fact, I shall help you. Now that I've located Cameroon."

"Hey diddle diddle, the cat and the fiddle,
The cow jumped over the moon. . . ."

Becky stood at the bedside, unabashedly piping nursery rhymes. The squire's gray eyes stared at the ceiling. Yet there was something in his stillness that gave Jewel reason to think he enjoyed the little entertainment.

"The little dog laughed to see such sport,
And the dish ran away with the spoon!"

"What should I sing next?" she asked.

"What would you like to sing?" Jewel said.

Becky walked around the bed and whispered into her ear, "Will 'Jesus Loves Me' make him sad?"

Jewel stroked her head. "Why would it make him sad?"

"Because I think he's going to be up with Jesus soon. Like Papa."

Jewel looked at the squire, hoping he had not heard. But then, surely his own mortality had crossed his mind, if his injured brain had allowed it. "I think he might like to hear it."

"Jesus loves me, this I know,
for the Bible tells me so. . . ."

The door opened. Zinnia entered with anxious expression. "Mrs. Cooper and Mr. Gibbs are asking for you in the library."

Jewel cast about for a response. "Shall I bring Becky?"

"I'm told to take her out to play in the garden."

"Do you know why?"

Zinnia bit her lip. "I think something's missing."

Donald wished he had thought of another plan when Jewel walked through the doorway, doe-eyed and pale. He had nothing against her, and of truth, enjoyed having a child lighten up this mausoleum of a house. He usually ended up regretting his impulsive actions. But with time of the essence, what else could he have done?

He expected Mrs. Cooper to lead, but she stood as ramrod straight and tight lipped as a palace guard. Donald sighed, nodded at the statuette standing upon the atlas table.

"Would you care to explain how this found its way into your trunk?" he said sternly, but not coldly, for after all, she was a human being. And innocent.

"It couldn't have been in my trunk," she said.

"I found it myself," he said gently. "I assume when you came down here for something to read to Uncle, it caught your eye."

"No, sir!"

"You're not used to nice things, are you?"

"I have never stolen anything . . . in my life!"

She buried her face in her hands and wept quietly, shoulders shaking. Donald could barely stand to look at her.

Be strong, man! Think of Reese! Think of your debts!

"Becky, perhaps?" Mrs. Cooper asked, finally breaking her silence. "Thinking it was a toy? She's so young. . . ."

"No! I never allow her to wander the house by herself."

"Well, I'm afraid you'll have to leave," Donald said.

A sob tore out of her. She gave Mrs. Cooper a beseeching look, and when the housekeeper looked away, she turned and fled the room.

Donald's heart raced. He felt ill. He despised scenes. "I assume she'll return to Miss Hollis. Please see that their things are delivered."

Mrs. Cooper raked him with her eyes. "Yes, sir."

The dislike emanating from such a stoic person shook him a bit. "And pay her whatever wages she's due. As you said, it could have been the girl."

And then to remind her that he was head of the house, he raised his chin and said coldly, "I never got my tray, by the way. Send an early supper in here."

Aleda's fingertips upon the keys could almost not keep up with the scene playing out in her mind. *This is good!*

Someone was knocking. With a sigh, she finished a sentence and then went downstairs to open the door. Her eyes took in Jewel Libby's red-splotched cheeks and swollen eyes. Becky, holding her hand, was trembling.

"I don't mean to be a burden," Mrs. Libby rasped. "But we've nowhere else to go."

"Come in, come in," Aleda said, her annoyance carried away on a tide of guilt and compassion. She moved ever-curious Tiger to the side with her foot and pulled out a chair. Mrs. Libby stood sniffing incessantly, with Becky pressed into her side.

Rather than abandon them to run upstairs for a handkerchief, she grabbed a tea cloth. She just had to trust the thoroughness of Mrs. Moore's laundry.

Mrs. Libby pushed it away, sniffed, "No, thank you. It's too fine."

"Blow."

When both noses were groomed, Aleda gently disengaged Becky from her mother, who seemed now in another world. She led the child up into her room, pushed back her typewriter—and half-finished page—and took a sheet of paper from the drawer.

"Why don't you draw your mother a picture?"

The girl looked back at the door.

"I think it will make her feel better. Don't you?"

She nodded and allowed Aleda to heft her into the chair. Aleda handed her two pencils. "A spare, just in case. I'll come for you shortly to bring you back downstairs."

"What should I draw?" the girl asked, thin fingers clutched around a pencil.

"Anything you like."

Downstairs again, she fortified Mrs. Libby with tea before sitting beside her and allowing her to give the story.

Once it was out, Aleda shook her head. "Rubbish!"

Mrs. Libby blinked swollen eyes at her.

"Donald Gibbs is just waiting for his uncle to die. You were obviously good for the squire."

"I think we were, Becky and me. Sometimes he communicated with us, as outrageous as it sounds." She put her hands to her face again. "Oh dear. Mary Johnson cannot read. He loved being read to, I could tell. If Mr. Gibbs hires another day nurse, will she?"

"I don't know," Aleda said honestly.

"And there will be that shadow over me. Who will hire me now?"

"He didn't send for Constable Reed, did he?"

She shook her head.

"And I'm sure by now the squire's servants have figured him out. Besides, my father's recommendation carries far more weight than Mr. Gibbs'."

"I just hate to be—"

"Yes, yes. But you're not a burden. In fact, you may keep house for me while we're looking. I rather enjoyed having everything tidy for a change."

Mrs. Libby closed her eyes, took in a long breath, opened them. Finally there was some hope in her face. "Thank you. But not for wages. It's enough that you've taken us in—twice."

Aleda shook her head. "You're quite stubborn, Mrs. Libby."

"Yes, ma'am. I've been told."

"Well, so am I. And I'll not take advantage of your situation. The laborer is worthy of his hire. Or *her* hire."

Mrs. Libby took Aleda's hand, kissed it. "May God bless you for this . . . not for my sake, but for my daughter's. I have prayed for your father. Is he still recovering?"

"Yes. He's been home for over a week now." Aleda pushed out her chair. "In fact, it's been a few days since I last looked in on him. Please make yourselves at home. If I know Dora, I'll be bringing back supper, so don't cook anything. And Becky's drawing a picture for you."

Out of hope and habit, she swept the path with her eyes. Jonathan, John, and Luke had helped retrace her steps several times. Mr. Trumble had allowed her to post a notice offering a reward. She could only hope someone would come forward.

Aleda's pace quickened on Bartley Lane, out of range of the lost watch.

The manor house loomed ahead.

Mrs. Cooper answered her knock almost immediately, as if expecting her. "How is Jewel?" she asked.

"She's crushed."

The housekeeper's lips all but disappeared in a thin line.

"But we'll take care of her."

"That's very good of you." Mrs. Cooper looked back over her shoulder, lowered her voice. "None of us believe . . ."

"I know." Aleda cut her off for her sake, lest Mr. Gibbs be skulking around the corner. "And she'll appreciate hearing it. May I speak with Mr. Gibbs?"

Again the lips tightened. "I'm afraid Mr. Gibbs is unavailable for the remainder of the day."

What a coward, Aleda thought. "May I leave a message?"

"Yes, ma'am."

"Please tell him I said he's a horse's rump."

The housekeeper nodded, a ghost of a smile at her lips. "My pleasure, Miss Hollis."

Chapter 22

What opium did for some and gin did for others, shopping at Redfern's did for Loretta. The shop assistant at the millinery counter tied the bow to the Marie Stuart–style bonnet fashionably below her left ear, and angled the standing mirror.

"Madam looks lovely," said the Frenchwoman, who could not have been more than eighteen, making Loretta feel old at twenty-five.

Sharon Fry sidled up to her. "That won't do. Too matronly."

"My thought exactly," Loretta said, offering her left cheek for the assistant to untie the bow.

Maud Caswell wandered over from the glove counter, a slender package tucked under her elbow. "Still at it? I wish I had a penny for every one you've tried on."

Loretta made a face at her. Maud had no use for hats,

choosing simply to ornament her wealth of golden brown hair with combs, ribbons, or even jewelry—depending upon her whims.

The two were her dearest friends, schoolmates from Blackheath Academy for the Daughters of Gentlemen, and though not even remotely kin, could have passed for sisters with their hazel eyes, brown hair, and angular faces.

Maud set aside her hat disinterest to help her select an ecru-colored hat of satin straw, trimmed with brown velvet and pale blue ostrich feathers, and a gray straw capote trimmed with emerald green velvet.

"Where to lunch?" Maud asked back on New Bond Street as her driver, Henry, took their packages and assisted them into the coach.

"I couldn't make another decision," Loretta said.

"May I have your vote?" Sharon asked.

"It's yours."

Loretta was instantly sorry for the light in Sharon's hazel eyes.

"Now you've done it," Maud groaned.

"We won't know if we like it until we try it," Sharon argued. "Besides, I have the votes."

"Our husbands will be livid if they find out," Maud said as the coach rolled eastward toward Limehouse. She winced. "Oh, Loretta. Forgive me."

"No offense taken," Loretta said, smiling to show she meant it. She was exactly where she wanted to be.

For she had replied to Philip's letter—as cordially as possible—that it would be best if he took Doctor Rhodes' offer. She had even wished him well.

That would give him the power to obtain a judicial separation after two years, possibly leading to divorce, but the stigma of being a divorcée could not be worse than this misery she carried around inside.

Surely her friends would never desert her. And unlike Sharon and Maud, she had no children who would be affected.

The irony of it, she thought, was that Philip would think it a great adventure, heading over to the Chinese section of Limehouse to sample Cantonese food for the first time.

Three hours later, she turned at her door and waved at her friends.

"Did you have a lovely afternoon?" Ines asked.

"It was an interesting one."

She was bursting to relate the whole experience to someone. *We were the only white faces in the crowded little place!* she might have said. *Maud had Henry join us for safety's sake. A group of men with pigtails bowed and gave us their table, and finished their meals standing. After the proprietor came to understand we could not read the menu, he brought out dishes of some sort of chicken sauce upon rice. And then . . . chopsticks! We made motions that we would like forks, and he either did not understand us or had none.*

One thing her mother had taught her at an early age was that servants were to be treated fairly and spoken to with courtesy, but that the social gap must not be crossed if the household was to run efficiently.

Someone knocked; Loretta assumed it was Henry. Had she forgotten something in Maud's coach? She waited at the foot of the stairs while Ines set the hatboxes on the hall bench and opened the door.

Her father stood frowning at her.

"Good afternoon, Doctor Trask," Ines said.

"Good afternoon." He stepped over the threshold, looked up at Loretta, and motioned toward the parlor.

Once they were alone, Loretta knew not to mention the Limehouse adventure. Not that she would have had the opportunity. He closed the door and turned to her.

"A letter from Philip was just delivered to my office, expressing his intention to resign and take over a practice in Gresham. He made no mention of this when he asked for time off."

He was staring at her, arms folded. Loretta waited for the question, then realized he had just stated it.

She sighed. "He didn't deceive you, Father. He was concerned about his stepfather. No doubt his family is pressuring him to stay. They're quite clingy."

He shook his head. "I did not perceive that when we met. Close, yes. Loving. But not clingy."

Perhaps she had exaggerated to a small degree, but she would not take it back. "I suppose returning to Gresham woke up his old dream of practicing medicine there."

"Then why become a surgeon? A gifted surgeon."

"A *dispensary* surgeon," Loretta reminded him. Trained for both surgery and general medicine.

"So what tipped the scales?"

A flush crept up Loretta's cheek.

"Loretta?"

She told him of Philip's letter, and her reply. "It's better this way, Papa. We've both been so unhappy."

He dropped to the sofa and put his head in his hands. "This can't be."

She was surprised when tears stung her eyes. She decided she may as well use them. They had served her well since she was a little girl, sitting on her father's knee complaining that her cousin Marie owned four dolls, when she owned only three. Those tears had netted her a trip to Lowther Arcade, two dolls, and a music box.

She sat beside her father, hands folded and head lowered, and squeezed out a few more. "I'm . . . sorry, Father. I know I've disappointed you . . . not being able to maintain his affection."

She could feel his eyes upon her, and waited for the touch upon her shoulder. Instead she heard a snort.

"Rubbish, Loretta. That man is head over heels for you. Bring me his letter."

She gave him as indignant a look as she dared. "*Father* . . ."

"You can't fire a cannon like that, sitting here in a house I paid for, and demand privacy. I insist on seeing it."

It was too late to claim to have burned it. He would be able to tell by looking at her. She fetched it from their bedchamber and handed it over.

He read it once and then again. "I see nothing about divorce in this letter. All marriages hit a rough road now and again. You'll go to Gresham. Patch things up."

"Impossible."

"You'll not simply throw up your hands and bring scandal upon our family. Pack your things tonight. Tomorrow, you'll disengage yourself from whatever commitments you have. I shall escort you to the station on Sunday morning."

It was time for the real waterworks. All she had to do to summon them was to think of herself in Gresham as a country doctor's wife. She put her hands to her face. Tears filled her eyes, flooded her cheeks.

"Now, now," her father said with an arm around her, gently pressing her head to his shoulder.

She sobbed and sobbed, and when she thought it was enough, found that she could not stop. When his shoulder as well as his handkerchief were sodden, and her throat felt almost as sore as it had the winter she had contracted scarlet fever, he patted her arm and began speaking, softly.

"I don't like to make you sad. Please hear me. You and Irene were enigmas. I had only brothers growing up, did not know quite how to treat you. I loved you dearly, could not bear to see you unhappy. But I left the everyday rearing to your mother and nursemaids. I was not the sort of father to bounce you on my knee. As a result, I think you picture me as only beginning to live once I became imprinted in your consciousness."

He was right. She had never thought much about his youth. Mother was the one who liked to tell stories of her adventures as daughter of the ambassador to Moscow.

"But my heart was broken terribly, before I met your mother."

She raised her head. Even if he were not her father, she could not picture him as the romantic type, with his smallish frame and white hair.

"She was a Scottish girl, a tobacconist's daughter in Edinburgh. I took up the pipe just to have reason to frequent his shop. As did many of my fellow students. When she became betrothed to the lord mayor's son, I thought I would die." He smiled. "As did many of my fellow students. But I had my studies to occupy my mind. The regimen of medical school kept me from floundering around, wondering what to do next."

"But you loved Mother when you met her. Right?"

"Absolutely. But you see? I met her four years later, when the shopkeeper's daughter was but a vague memory. I could appreciate your mother as the wonderful woman she was . . . not as a balm for a broken heart."

She would have been grateful for this opportunity to get to know her father better had she not realized this was a preamble to what he was about to say. She braced herself.

"I erred by allowing Conrad to court Irene so soon after your heart was broken. I was relieved when you seemed interested in Philip, and so I did all I could to encourage a romance. Inviting him for dinner, encouraging walks in the park. Your hurt had mended, or so I thought. My guilt was assuaged."

"Father . . ."

"Please allow me to finish." He cleared his throat. "Your mother and I tried to help make your marriage happy. Giving you this house. Hiring a coachman. But I see now that it only delayed the inevitable. Once you realized Philip couldn't take away your thoughts for Conrad, you began to resent him. You've never really put Conrad out of your mind long enough to appreciate your husband for who he is."

She had thought she was wrung dry. But even these fresh tears did not soften his resolution. She was going to Gresham.

Chapter 23

Aleda unwound the finished page from her typewriter and added it to the stack. The woodsy air wafting through her window was intoxicating. She decided that even if her book sold, and sold well, she would stay right there. If she purchased the largest house in Shropshire, she could find no more pleasant corner than where she sat now.

She looked over to the foot of her bed. "Don't you agree, Tiger?"

The cat looked up, but only because the kitchen door opened and closed. Footsteps sounded on the stairs, and Mrs. Libby appeared in the open doorway.

"Pardon me, Miss Hollis, but your sister sent some short-bread, still warm. May I bring some up to you, with some tea?"

"That would be lovely."

"Where did you see Elizabeth?" Aleda asked when she returned.

"Her son John came with an invitation for Becky to play with the younger children. I've just come back from delivering her. They're very sweet."

So was Elizabeth, Aleda thought. In spite of the wardrobe comments. She made room on her desk for the small tray. "I'm glad Becky has an opportunity to play, but she's no bother. She's not a boisterous child."

"I can take little credit. She learned to play quietly a long time ago. The woman who once minded her while I worked kept infants, as well."

"You're due more than a little credit, Mrs. Libby. I see how you are with her."

"Thank you," she said. Her face sobered. "May I make a request?"

Aleda bit into a square of shortbread. "You may make one, but there's no guarantee I'll follow it." Warm pastry brought out the tease in her.

Mrs. Libby looked startled for only an instant, then smiled. "With my being officially in your employ—at least for now—I wonder if you might use my given name? It'll be easier for you, and I'll not feel like a stuffy old aunt."

"Very well. If that's what you wish."

"It is, thank you. And I'll leave you to your work."

"Wait. Did you happen to check the letter box?" It was erected on Church Lane, for the Royal Post Office did not recognize the path into Gipsy Woods as a legitimate route.

"I'm afraid there was none." Jewel gave her a sympathetic look. "You're hoping to hear from Mr. Patterson."

"Which makes no sense." Aleda shrugged. "He has his own work, and besides, said he plans to hire someone to type mine. It's a strain to read someone else's script for the length of a novel. I don't expect to hear from him for at least a month."

Which meant, she told herself after Jewel left, she must stop wondering and leave it in God's hands. She wiped her hands upon the tea cloth and rolled another sheet of paper into the typewriter. For now, the magazine stories were her bread and butter. And if they ended up being all she had, her life would remain about the same anyway.

⁓

The Larkspur lodgers had obviously gotten to Mr. Nicholls, for Sunday's sermon, entitled "The Laborers Are Few," from the book of Saint Matthew, was far more pithy. He projected his voice more, sweat less.

Aleda, seated as usual with her family, looked back and smiled at Jewel and Becky, seated with Mrs. Cooper and a couple of other manor house servants. A person could not hide his true nature from his servants for too long, and they clearly knew Mr. Gibbs'.

After church, the family gathered in the dining room for the first time since Father's surgery. Philip helped Father to his chair, and Dora set before him vegetable soup pressed through a strainer, with bread for sopping. He was so overjoyed to be at the table that he clearly did not begrudge the others the usual Sunday cold meats and salad, or the two flaky giblet-and-potato pies Dora had stuck in the oven after church. The pies were reduced to crumbs when hoofbeats and carriage wheels sounded in the lane. Ever-helpful John volunteered to leave the dining room to answer the door, even though Mother was bringing a snow cake from the sideboard.

He returned with eyes wide and Loretta at his side.

"Good afternoon," she said sheepishly.

A benign north breeze carried across the Bryce the sweet aroma of newly shorn hayfields. The green was absent of romping children and gossiping housewives as the village respected Sunday afternoon. Philip and Loretta strolled along with a foot of space between them, like two acquaintances.

"Are you sure you're not hungry?" Philip asked.

"Mrs. Day packed sandwiches for the train." She hesitated. "How long have you been growing a beard?"

"Two weeks. It's finally out of the itchy stage." He rubbed his chin, smiled at her. "I know. You don't like it."

"No, it's not so bad. I don't know why I didn't care for it before."

Philip could take that two ways. Either she had missed him enough to where the beard no longer caused an annoyance, or she simply did not care.

Between seeing about his father and easing into Doctor Rhodes' practice, he had managed to push her to the back of his mind, but never out of it. She was as beautiful as ever in a tan traveling suit, her blond hair trailing to her waist from the back of a small narrow-brimmed hat.

They made small talk. He related Andrew's progress in healing, after she had the decency to ask. She told him of trying Chinese food in Limehouse, which made him laugh.

And then it was time for Philip to ask the hard questions. First, "Why are you here?"

She hesitated, slanted him a worried look. "Father . . ."

"I see." But of course. How foolish to think his letter had stirred the dying coals and ignited the love she had once felt for him.

Second, he asked, "Where is your luggage?"

She bit her lip. "At the Bow and Fiddle."

That stung worse than the first answer. And made him angry. But he managed to keep his temper from poisoning his voice. Softly he said, "Is the thought of staying with me so odious, Loretta? Have you no feelings for me at all?"

"No, it's . . ." She rubbed her temples, appeared to be casting for words as her eyes reddened. "I'm so very confused, Philip. I just need some time to think."

He resisted the urge to gather her into his arms, whether to comfort her or himself. "Then you need to go back. Do your thinking in London. I'll drive you to the station tomorrow morning so you may truthfully tell your father I sent you away."

She actually looked tempted. Another stab to the heart.

"No," she finally said.

"He would only send you back here, wouldn't he?"

Her silence said as much.

Despair tore at him. But emotion never solved a problem. Their marriage was diseased. He was a doctor. What was the best source of treatment? Surely it did not include living apart in the same village. They had practically done that in London, and where had it gotten them?

"Please move into the vicarage."

She began shaking her head before he was halfway finished.

"You may take Grace's old room. I won't bother you."

"And then what would your parents think? They already despise me."

"They don't despise you," Philip said. "They would like nothing better than to be close to you."

"I can't stay there," she said, adamant.

Awareness dawned. She simply planned to stay in Gresham long enough to appease her father, convince him she had attempted to mend the marriage.

Faint discordant notes met Philip's ears. Ahead to their left, people sat in chairs facing the village hall, while two members of Gresham's nine-piece ensemble began tuning trumpet and French horn. Gently Philip reached for Loretta's arm and nodded toward the river. She did not resist. As they stood between two willows, watching the blue waters of the Bryce, he mulled over the situation.

God, what should I do? he prayed. *Please show me where I'm failing as a husband. Please change her heart toward me.*

Yet how many times had he made those requests? Could it be that God wanted them apart? He could hardly believe that.

A violinist had joined the musicians when he turned to face her. "How long does your father expect you to stay?"

"He didn't say."

Long enough to mend the marriage, he thought. Doctor Trask's determination was legendary about Saint Bartholomew's.

"I don't give a tinker's big toe what people think of me," he said. "But I won't purposely bring gossip down upon my family. If you stay in the Bow and Fiddle, that will humiliate them."

"Perhaps if you moved there too?" she said with tepid enthusiasm.

Of course she meant separate chambers. He could see it in her eyes, and knew it was the next thing she would say. He shook his head. "Absolutely not. Housemaids talk; people are not stupid."

"Then what should we do?"

"I'll ask Aleda if we may borrow her cottage and she move back into the vicarage. We would have separate rooms, but as it's entirely remote, it would not set tongues to wagging."

A clarinet had joined the disjointed snatches of melody in the distance.

"Remote?" Loretta said, expression uneasy.

Had he never noticed how transparent she was? Or had he become so cynical that he assumed her every thought of him was negative?

"I would be away most of the day . . . assisting Doctor Rhodes, seeing after my stepfather. You would still be within walking distance to shops. And you wouldn't be alone. A young widow from Birmingham is keeping house for Aleda. We could ask her to work for us. She has a sweet little daughter."

"Aleda would never agree. She dislikes me most of all."

Philip could not debate that point. "I believe she would. She has a generous heart. The vicarage is quieter now. People are staying away, respecting my parents' privacy."

"For how long?"

He held in another sigh. Their marriage would now be reduced to dates circled upon a calendar. "One month? If you still don't wish to be married, I shall go with you to speak with your father. Set a divorce in motion."

"Very well," she said after a hesitation.

He took her hand, tucked it into the crook of his arm. "Now . . . Mother is saving slices of snow cake for us, a heroic feat in my family. And we have some arrangements to make."

"I do like snow cake," she said as they left the privacy of the willows.

"Of course you may use the cottage," Aleda said after Philip posed his question in the vicarage garden.

Loretta was resting from her journey upstairs in his room. Mother and Father were in the parlor, ostensibly reading newspapers, but probably wondering what was going on with Philip and Loretta. Elizabeth's family had ambled over to the village hall, bearing rugs. She imagined Claire and Samuel succumbing to naps as the notes to Schubert's Symphony no. 2 in B-flat Major floated over them.

He caught Aleda up in his arms, gave her a quick squeeze. "I can't thank you enough."

She smiled, and was truly glad for the relief in his countenance. What she would never say was that this favor was not for him, as much as she loved him. And certainly not for Loretta.

· Father needed this rare peace and quiet to continue. As Philip had explained to her a couple of days after the surgery, the gallstones and heart murmur were not related, but physicians were beginning to wonder if nerves had some ill effect upon the latter.

Mother needed the tranquillity, as well. She and Father were like two connecting spheres, with common interests in the middle and their own energy-building interests in the outer spheres. Mother would never admit it, but she appeared to be wearing down a bit.

⁓∞⁓

Loretta held her breath as she passed Elizabeth's cottage late Tuesday morning. Fortunately, while children's voices and other domestic sounds flowed past the flower pots in the windows, no one came out into the garden to invite her inside. She found Elizabeth's company more tolerable than Aleda's, but she was feeling too melancholy for idle chatter. Especially with Philip's family members, with their loving cords binding him—and now her—to Gresham.

The school building appeared vacant. A dozen children played in the yard, kicking up heels on swings hanging from elm limbs, squealing with delight on a merry-go-round, and simply running off energy.

Loretta begrudged them their joy. She wondered what Irene

and Conrad thought of her exile, for surely Father had informed them. Irene was probably relieved to have their parents to herself, without the tension that tainted every pleasantry. And it was unlikely that Conrad thought of her at all.

Was she the only person on earth to feel robbed of her youth and tormented by what might have been?

She turned southward down shady Market Street, toward the shops nestled cheek-to-jowl. A display of ladies' hats in a bow window jogged a memory. She went inside Perkins' Fine Millinery. The shop assistant behind the counter did not raise her eyes from her magazine.

Loretta cleared her throat. The woman held up a finger, read for another second, then looked up. She had a pleasantly rounded figure, soft brown eyes, and full lips. Her hair was swept up into a chignon, revealing garnet earrings. Her high-collared, low-waisted gown of navy tweed studded with red and white checks was the height of fashion. Loretta was so relieved to see someone in this village who was not three years behind London fashions that she forgave the snubbing.

"*Godey's Lady's Book*," the woman said in a voice as high-pitched as Becky Libby's. "I've got to keep up with the style."

"This is your shop?"

"All mine. My mum and father bought it for me, to give me some direction." She assumed a stern look and mocked a man's voice, as much as her high pitch allowed. "Daughter . . . no more of this sleeping in while life passes you by."

She giggled, motioned toward a half-curtained door behind her. "Father was miffed when I put a cot back there. I explained it's just for propping my feet for a minute when I have the monthly. That shut him up. But it's sort of nice, having my own business. One day ladies will be coming from all over Shropshire to buy from me."

That's debatable, Loretta thought. While the hat displays were reasonably attractive, the service was lacking. London shop clerks would have crawled over her as soon as she entered, like ants on an apple core.

"Do you block hats?" she asked. The gray straw capote she had purchased last week had gotten mashed after falling from its box on the train.

Without a word the woman disappeared through the curtained doorway. She returned with a circular wooden device and pursed her lips at it. "I believe that's what this is for. I'll ask my mum for certain."

And then, oddly, she stretched out her hand toward Loretta.

Loretta stared at her. "I beg your pardon?"

She blew out an exasperated breath. "The hat?"

"Not this hat," Loretta said, adding under her breath, *You twit!* "I shall have to bring it another day."

The woman looked aggrieved at the device in her hands, turned again toward the curtained doorway. Loretta chose that time to exit.

She received a better reception in Trumbles. As soon as the bell tinkled over the door, a doughy-faced man with walrus mustache turned from dusting cans. "Good morning, madam. Unusually dry July we're having, isn't it?"

"I suppose," Loretta said, approaching the counter. What did she know of Shropshire weather? "I would like some chocolates and something to read."

The man smiled, hooked his thumbs through the braces holding up his trousers. "Ah . . . nothing like chocolate and a good book for a phlegm-matic day."

Phlegmatic? Loretta wondered. She was quite sure that phlegm was mucus. Not a pretty mental picture.

"The only problem is," he continued, "while I can order books for you, I don't carry them, not since Mrs. Bartley—God rest her dear soul—added to the subscription library. You can't fault folks for not buying what they can borrow. That's just wise money mangerment."

Management?

She left with a small tin of Cadbury Fine Crown chocolates and the directions to Bartley Subscription Library, northwards on Market Street and almost to the river. She was relieved to discover the bookshelves were indeed well stocked. At least she would have something to do during her month of exile.

"We just got this one in," said a white-haired woman who introduced herself as Mrs. Jefferies.

Loretta paged through the copy of Henry James' *The Portrait of a Lady* with some reservations, for she had heard that the plot included an unfulfilled marriage. It looked interesting enough, but she also selected *Wives and Daughters* by Elizabeth Gaskell, just in case.

On a whim, she also chose *Wonderful Stories for Children*, the Hans Christian Andersen tales, evoking fond memories of Nanny Miriam reading at bedside to her and Irene. Perhaps Jewel would care to read them to Becky? If she could read, that is. At least the pictures were nice.

Having had three days to observe her, Loretta did not believe that Jewel would take this as a narrowing of the God-ordained gap between servant and master. Thankfully, the housemaid went about her work quietly in her presence. The snatches of mother-daughter conversations Loretta had overheard through walls and windows were subdued and sweet, and caused her to smile. And sometimes brought tears.

Young women tending small children and older women tending gardens sent her curious stares as she returned to the cottage, but most were accompanied by amiable g*ood mornings*. Loretta returned the greetings, even while counting the days until she could leave, counting the minutes until she would seek comfort in a novel and chocolates, and counting her hurrying steps past Elizabeth's gate.

Savory smells greeted her on the cottage path. Jewel turned from the kitchen stove. "I hope you like fried sole and potatoes and gooseberry pudding, Mrs. Hollis."

"Lovely," Loretta said.

Becky, playing with her doll at the foot of the stairs, looked up with brown eyes bright. "I helped pick the gooseberries. I was mindful of the thorns, just like Mummy said. You just have to be very careful."

Loretta laughed in spite of her heavy heart.

"You must pick up your blocks from the table so I can lay the cloth," Jewel said to her daughter. "Remember what I said about leaving your things lying about?"

The girl went over to the table at once. Intent upon helping her—for Becky was not a servant—Loretta picked up a block.

Jewel gave her an uneasy look. "Begging your pardon, ma'am, but she's got to learn to pick up after herself."

Loretta replaced the block and shrugged at the child.

One compensation for living in the cottage was that Philip took lunch at the vicarage or Doctor Rhodes'. Evenings after sharing supper, they gave each other dutiful kisses in the landing between their separate rooms. He was keeping his word, not crowding or pressuring her. Yet she knew that if she should receive a letter from Father tomorrow, giving her permission to return to London, she would be finding a way to Shrewsbury that same day.

Chapter 24

In her vicarage bedchamber late Wednesday morning, Aleda was halfway through another episode of Captain Jacob's adventures when Wanetta knocked and stuck her head around the door.

"There is a gentleman downstairs to see you, Miss Hollis."

"Me? Who is it?"

The maid gave her an enigmatic smile. "I'm not allowed to say."

Heart swelling with happiness, Aleda swung her chair around to face her. "Only Gabriel would try a stunt like that."

Wanetta blew out her cheeks. "Now, I didn't say . . ."

"Don't worry," Aleda laughed. "I'll pretend to be surprised."

It was as she fished her leather slippers from beneath her desk that she thought to wonder why Gabriel would pop out of the blue with no advance notice. He disliked writing letters, with so much energy going into his books, but even so, he'd always managed to send at least a telegram before one of his rare visits.

She could interpret this one of two ways. He had finished her novel, loved it, and could not wait to tell her. Or he was halfway finished, hated it, and must get the unwelcome chore of informing her over with immediately, as one pulls a splinter.

Worry accompanied her down the staircase. Perhaps Gabriel wasn't even the visitor after all, she tried to tell herself. Three feet before the parlor doorway, she stopped to listen.

"I'm glad to see how well you're recovering, Vicar."

Gabriel's voice. She said a quick prayer and stepped through the doorway. To enhance her air of unawareness, she looked immediately over to her stepfather's chair—pushed closer to the sofa to make room for his bed.

"Father, I wonder if I may bring you any—"

It was then that she allowed herself to glance at the sofa, where Mother and Gabriel sat, beaming.

She put a hand to her heart. "Why, Gabriel!"

He got to his feet. Smiling, she crossed the carpet to embrace him. "What a wonderful surprise!"

But when she stepped backwards, he studied her face and rolled his eyes. "You figured me out."

Aleda forced a laugh. "Guilty. How did you know I was staying here?"

A silly question, under ordinary circumstances, for he could very well have come to visit Philip. But these were not ordinary circumstances. Surely this had to do with her novel.

"Mrs. Pool informed me, when I dropped my satchel off at the Bow and Fiddle."

"You're most welcome to stay here, Gabriel," Mother said.

Gabriel gave her a tender smile. "Thank you, but I'm quite comfortable there."

Anxiety gnawed at Aleda's stomach. But the etiquette taught to her from childhood was so ingrained that she could not ask even such a good friend why he was there. And even if she could, moments later Philip arrived, and immediately engaged Gabriel in the male pounding-on-the-back and bantering ritual.

"London's not the same without me?" Philip said.

"Oh, have you been away?" Gabriel replied.

And then Dora announced lunch, and they were trooping down the corridor to the dining room.

Mercifully, Gabriel spared her suffering, once plates of roast beef and vegetables were filled from the sideboard and Father had prayed.

"I hope you'll forgive my springing myself upon you without an invitation. . . ."

"You never need one," Mother said.

"Thank you, Mrs. Phelps." He sent her another tender smile.

"Never," Aleda echoed, in the hopes he would turn his attention to her again and give her *any* scrap of information about her novel.

As it turned out, that was what was in his mind, for he winked at her and said, "As to why I'm here, I've had only two hours' sleep. On the train."

While Aleda held her breath, Philip said, half seriously, "Are you in need of a doctor, Gabriel?"

Gabriel laughed, and continued smiling at Aleda. "I received the copy of your *Wharram Percy* from the typist yesterday morning. I *literally* could not put it down. And I couldn't wait to tell you in person."

"Are you serious, Gabriel?" Aleda said in the hush that followed.

"Most serious. I'd like your permission to submit it to my editors at Macmillan's."

From childhood, any public display of tears was embarrassing to Aleda. But she found herself weeping into her hands, and happily so, as parents and brother took turns cradling her shoulders and congratulating her.

"There is no guarantee they will ask to contract it," Gabriel said softly, to bring everyone back down to earth.

Aleda smiled at him through her tears. While that mattered, it didn't matter so much as the fact that an expert and honest pair of eyes had traveled the length of her story and deemed it worthy.

Somehow they plowed through the rest of lunch, if only not to hurt Dora. Then Gabriel expressed need for a nap and insisted upon taking it at the Bow and Fiddle. Philip offered to accompany him on his return to Doctor Rhodes'.

For her part, Aleda went upstairs and fell to her knees. The only prayer she could utter was *Thank you, thank you, thank you*. . . . Over and over. But it rose from such a deep part of her, so connected her to God, that she knew He forgave her lack of originality.

"You have to return tomorrow?" Aleda asked in the vicarage garden three hours later, when Gabriel had returned. She had hoped for at least several long conversations in which he would point out exactly which parts of her novel he had most enjoyed.

"First thing in the morning. Alas, I've got to get back to my own story before it grows cold."

"I understand," she sighed. "And I do appreciate your devoting so much time to mine."

"It was my pleasure." He began fumbling with his cuff link. "Philip said Mrs. Libby now works for him and Loretta."

"I'm glad she got away from the manor house," Aleda said. "True to form, Mr. Gibbs was a horse's—"

"When will you tell her?"

"Why? If anyone knows it, she certainly does."

"Not about Mr. Gibbs." He shook his head. "About your novel. After all, she did influence your decision to have me read it."

His eyes shifted toward the pear tree. Aleda smiled to herself. He may be creative, but he should never try for the stage. So, the little spark she had sensed around the table in June had not been extinguished.

Adore him as she may, grateful as she was, she could not resist throwing a little torment his way.

"Hmm. I'd forgotten." Aleda nodded. "I'm sure I'll see her Sunday."

His voice fell flat. "Sunday."

"Or, we could do that now. If you're not fatigued."

"I'm not fatigued."

Arm-in-arm, they strolled down Vicarage Lane.

"You enjoyed that, didn't you?" he asked.

"Could you have resisted, if the situation were reversed?"

"No." He chuckled. "We're woefully immature, aren't we?"

"That's why we need mature people in our lives."

Elizabeth waved from her parlor window, then came out through the gate as they passed. She embraced Gabriel, and upon hearing Aleda's news, embraced her, as well.

"We're on our way to the cottage," Aleda told her.

"Will you invite Mrs. Libby to bring Becky over? The children will be waking from their naps any minute, and she's such a calming influence on them."

"Certainly," Aleda agreed. And then a better idea came to her. She could only hope Loretta had not chosen that day to repent of her antisocial ways.

And it was Loretta whom Aleda spotted first, seated in a wicker chair. Becky, arranging blocks on a bit of bare earth, hopped up from her knees and hurried over.

"Miss Hollis! Mr. Patterson!"

"Hallo, Miss Becky!" Gabriel said, leaning to clasp her little hand.

"I didn't know you were coming here today," she piped.

"Well, now you do." He cocked a brow at her. "Is that all right?"

"Yes, sir."

"Good day, Mr. Patterson," Loretta said, tucking a book under her arm as she rose.

"Good day, Mrs. Hollis."

Aleda held her breath.

Not even asking why Gabriel was in Gresham, Loretta offered him a limp hand and nodded at Aleda. "If you'll forgive me, I was just about to take my book indoors. My fair skin burns so easily."

And even more so if you were in sunlight, Aleda thought dryly, surveying the shade covering almost every square inch of her garden.

She could feel waves of gratitude coming from Gabriel when she said, "Would you mind asking Jewel if she'd like to come out and visit with us for a little while?"

If Loretta was curious, it was not evident in her unfaltering steps toward the door. "I'll send her out."

It had all happened so swiftly. One minute, Jewel was ironing. The next, she was out in the garden, Mr. Patterson taking her hand, Miss Hollis delivering her good news.

"It was you who convinced me to allow him read it," she said.

"You succeeded where others failed," Mr. Patterson said, beaming.

"It's the Brummie in me, sir," Jewel quipped. "We're a pushy lot."

That caused him to laugh until he wiped tears, and Becky, face pinched with worry, to offer him a peppermint.

"He's fine, Becky," Miss Hollis said, and asked Jewel if she could deliver Becky to Mrs. Raleigh's for her.

"You don't have to do that," Jewel protested.

"My insides are bouncing with joy. I can't sit still. Just keep Gabriel company until I return."

And so it was that the two occupied wicker chairs in the cool shade of the garden, three feet apart and facing each other. Mr. Patterson looked as stunned as Jewel felt, and how could she blame him, with Miss Hollis running off like that.

"Good-bye, Mr. Patterson!" Becky chirped just before they disappeared through the trees.

"Good-bye, Becky!" he called back. He smiled at Jewel, seeming to relax somewhat. "Elizabeth says your daughter calms her twins."

"That's very kind of her to say."

"Perhaps she'll calm Aleda on the way over."

That made Jewel smile. "It was good of you to read her book."

"I was happy to do it for her. Do you read much, Mrs. Libby?"

"I'm afraid not, Mr. Patterson."

He raised brows at her. "But why be afraid to say so?"

"Well, because you . . ."

"Because I'm a writer. If I were a turnip farmer, I shouldn't expect everyone to be turnip enthusiasts."

"It's not that I dislike reading," she said. "Not at all. But there just was never time when I was younger, and now that I have the time, it seems I can't be content unless my hands are busy. But I do enjoy Miss Hollis's newspaper stories. And I'm reading a book to Becky, that Mrs. Hollis checked out from the lending library."

"Will wonders never cease?" he mumbled with a look toward the house.

"Sir?"

He blinked at her, as if just realizing he had spoken aloud. "Forgive me. I shouldn't be so judgmental. But tell me . . . has Becky no books of her own?"

"Well . . . no, sir. But Mrs. Hollis said there are several in the library."

"That's well and good, but I can't help but believe a child should own at least a few, to read over and over through the years. My books were my best friends."

"I've never thought of that," Jewel admitted. She remembered the squire's well-worn copy of *Around the World in Eighty Days*. Perhaps no age was too young to take comfort from a collection of books that never had to be returned. She had a decent little nest egg now. When Miss Hollis returned, she would ask where to go about buying at least a couple.

"I don't presume to give you parenting advice," he added quickly.

"But I'm glad for the advice."

"You've done a marvelous job with your daughter."

"Thank you," Jewel said. "I hope so."

Silence eased into the space between them, but not an uncomfortable one. At length, Jewel remembered her manners. "Would you care for some tea?"

"No thank you. But please . . . have some yourself if . . ."

She smiled and shook her head.

He smiled back. "My cook, Mrs. Lane, has a granddaughter just a bit older than Becky. Patricia's her name. According to Mrs. Lane, she asks to be read to almost constantly. I could ask her what books she likes best."

"Why, that would be very kind of you."

She wondered when Miss Hollis would return. As unfailingly courteous as he was, surely Mr. Patterson was beginning to wonder himself. She cast about in her mind for something to say next, and came across a question she was genuinely interested in hearing answered.

"Have you always wanted to write?"

"Always," he replied. "A couple of my stories were published when I was a boy."

"Your parents must be very proud."

"They would be prouder if I were a doctor."

"That can't be so."

"I'm afraid it is. But not just any doctor, mind you."

"A surgeon?" Jewel asked.

"A *thin* surgeon."

Jewel shook her head. "I hope you're jesting."

"I wish I were. But forgive me; here I sit boring you with the Patterson drama. Tell me . . . what of your family?"

But she was not to be detoured so easily. Having spent half her life without parents, she imagined most felt about their children the way she felt about Becky. How could any mother or father be anything but proud of this kind and gentle and humorous man?

"If I may be so bold as to ask . . ."

"You may ask me anything," he said, and peered at her so intently that she had to look down at her hands.

"Have you told them how much this hurts you, Mr. Patterson?"

"It wouldn't make a difference, and would only cause hard feelings."

"But how can you know for certain?"

"Because overly critical people have thin skins." He smiled and wagged a finger at her. "You mustn't pity me, Mrs. Libby. How many people are allowed exactly what they wish to do? And now, I wish to hear about you. Are your parents still living?"

"My mother passed on when I was twelve. I've no idea where my father is."

"Was he lost at sea?"

"A sea of gin."

She could not believe she was sharing so much information. But Mr. Patterson's interest was a magnet.

"What a pity," he said, "to waste the one life you have down here."

"He will die one day. If he isn't already dead. And he'll leave not so much as a ripple."

"I beg to differ. What about you and Becky?"

"I suppose we're at least ripples," Jewel said.

That made him smile, and naturally she smiled back.

They were still chatting when Miss Hollis appeared again. "Elizabeth's walking them over to the schoolyard."

Jewel thanked her and glanced toward the cottage. "I must return to my work now."

"Must you?" Mr. Patterson asked, seeming sincere.

She stood, torn between relief and disappointment, and understanding neither.

He stood, as well, and clasped her hand. "I look forward to seeing you again, Mrs. Libby."

Again, a light in his eyes, a sincere tone that puzzled Jewel. She was just a housemaid, after all.

Later, Mrs. Hollis, without even being asked, explained the reason.

"Poor, pathetic Gabriel," she said in the parlor when Jewel brought her some tea. "He'll never give up."

"I beg your pardon?"

"Trying to win Aleda's heart. He knows her fondness for you and Becky. But Philip says Aleda's adamant that she has no feelings for him beyond friendship."

How sad, Jewel thought as she resumed ironing. Mr. Patterson was one of the kindest souls she had ever met. Was Miss Hollis waiting for someone like one of her fictional heroes to sweep her off her feet? It was never like that with her and Norman. Yes, there was romance to set her heart fluttering, but above that, a mutual fondness. Basking in the warmth of each other's company, even when absorbed in separate tasks at opposite ends of the room. And even the disagreements, which taught them both how to compromise and accommodate each other's personalities, had proven worthwhile.

Carefully, Jewel guided the iron over Doctor Hollis's shirt sleeve. She was not one to dictate to God. But she did not think it was too cheeky to pray that Miss Hollis have a change of heart. Miracles happened every day. She had only to picture herself back in the corset factory to know that.

"When will your publishers tell you if they're interested?" Aleda asked during the walk back up Vicarage Lane.

"It could take weeks," Gabriel said.

"Weeks . . ."

He patted her hand in the crook of his arm. Gently, he said, "Patience, love. You must understand that they're not sitting on their hands, waiting for your novel. They have other projects in the works."

Aleda sighed. "Of course."

"If they offer a contract, you must be prepared to go to London to meet with them."

"If they offer a contract, I'll walk the whole way. On my knees."

He chuckled. "Take the train. And . . ."

When the hesitation took longer than it should, Aleda nudged his side. "Yes?"

"And naturally you'll ask Mrs. Libby and Becky along? Surely Philip and Loretta can do without them for a few days, if they're still here." He gave her a self-conscious look. "In case you're lonely."

She grinned wickedly. "I'm never lonely on trains."

"Well, couldn't you be . . . just this time?"

She decided not to torment him. "I'll invite them."

"Thank you. I would enjoy showing them the sights while you're wrapped up with book business."

"That would be the thrill of their lives. But could you really leave your safe little world to escort them about London?"

Offering his arm again, he snorted. "Well now, they won't bring Buckingham Palace to us, will they?"

Thursday morning of the seventeenth, Philip looked down Andrew's throat, took his temperature, and inspected the surgery scar while Julia watched.

"I think it's time for a soak in the tub."

Andrew, sick of sponge baths, perked up. "Because the scar's better?"

"Because you smell like a goat."

Andrew roared, cuffed his arm. Julia ran the bath, but Philip insisted she move aside and allow Luke to help get Andrew to the tub. "We don't want to drop him and have him split wide open."

"You should work on your bedside manner," Andrew said, unruffled.

"Tubs-s-side manner," Luke quipped, which made Andrew laugh again.

Once Andrew was safely immersed, Julia chased the men from the water closet and washed her husband's hair. Afterwards, when Andrew was wrapped in a clean dressing gown and ensconced in his favorite armchair, Philip collected his medical bag from upstairs.

"Will you be back for lunch?" Julia asked in the hall.

"I will," he said with a peck on her forehead.

She did not ask if Loretta would be with him. In the four days since her arrival, she had shared but one Sunday dinner with them. Julia could only hope that Philip and his wife were trying to mend the obvious strain upon their marriage. Elsewise, why would she be there?

Later, over a lunch of rump steak-and-kidney pudding and asparagus, and pea soup with white bread for Andrew, Philip told of stitching Mr. Seaton's leg that morning.

"He fell into his pen, and his hog gashed him."

"Ouch," Andrew said, salting his soup.

"I wonder if revenge will make his winter ham tastier?" Aleda quipped.

"He didn't even groan while I stitched him."

"Those Wesleyans always were stoic," Andrew said, but not in a mocking way, because he got on well with Gresham's nonconformist pastors.

"Anyway," Philip went on, "their housekeeper is soon to be pensioned. I mentioned that Jewel Libby would be available soon. They're very interested."

"They're nice people," Julia said, and looked to Aleda. "This may be the answer to our prayers."

"Hmm," her daughter said, chewing.

"Their grandchildren live next door," Andrew said. "Little Becky would have playmates."

"She'll have plenty when school starts in September," Aleda said.

Julia studied her. "Are you thinking of keeping her on?"

Aleda's shrug was not as casual as she had probably intended. "I can afford to."

"But what of your privacy?" Andrew said.

"They're quiet. And I seem to write better . . . even think better, when everything is clean and orderly, and there are regular meals on the table."

"That's wonderful," Julia said. "When will you speak with her?"

"Soon."

"Becky's very sweet," Philip said. "She won't ask, but if you offer to read to her, she listens with her head angled, as if she's picturing it all in her mind."

"That's how you were," Julia said to Aleda. "Perhaps she'll become a writer."

This made Aleda smile.

"Loretta's growing fond of her, too," Philip went on.

It pained Julia how often he seized every opportunity to mention Loretta's good points. Not that a husband should not compliment his wife, but that there was a note of desperation about it.

"And I believe the feeling is mutual," he continued. "Just yesterday Becky picked a bouquet for her bedroom."

Andrew ceased tearing bits of bread into his soup. "You mean, for your bedroom."

Philip looked at him.

"The one you share."

"Father," Philip said softly. "We won't be discussing this."

"Very well. I beg your pardon."

After Philip left again for Doctor Rhodes' and Aleda had returned to her typewriter, Julia helped Andrew out to the garden bench and sat beside him. He closed his eyes, allowed the breeze to stir his hair and whiskers.

"I missed the outdoors."

"Yes. Me too."

He opened his eyes. "You don't think anyone who happens by will be scandalized? Seeing the vicar out here in a dressing gown?"

"Not as long as you mind how you sit."

"Philip was right . . . correcting me. I just don't understand what's going on with the two."

"Nor do I. I was encouraged when she arrived, especially when they wanted Aleda's cottage. Another honeymoon of sorts? But it seems less and less the case."

"Indeed."

What more was there to be said? Yet having bottled up her angst in favor of tending to Andrew, Julia needed to spill it out.

279

"I believe I'm fair-minded enough to give her the benefit of the doubt and not automatically take Philip's side. But I suspect she's here not by choice."

Andrew took her hand. "I suspect so, as well. I remember her father as a strong character. I can very easily see him getting involved."

"Yet that's exactly what we must not do. Other than pray. Between your surgery and Philip's marriage, I've done plenty of praying. I fear my faith must be terribly weak. I still long for something constructive to do."

Andrew studied her. "Actually, there is something. Why don't you pay a certain call?"

Julia raised eyebrows at him. "I just said we must not get involved."

"Not to Loretta. To Fiona."

"How will that change the situation?"

"It won't." He shook his head. "But it will help you. Nurturers need nurturing, too, and you need a shoulder."

"I have yours."

"Yes. But a feminine shoulder is softer. I believe God made them so, to better absorb another's pain."

The idea was tempting. "What about you?"

"Luke is in shouting distance if I need him. Just fetch my Bible and notebook for me, please."

Julia rose and leaned down to plant a kiss upon his lips. "I'll be away no more than an hour."

He gave her a mock scowl. "If you've returned in less than three, I shall be very angry."

Chapter 25

Jewel was standing at the table, slicing bacon, when Philip carried his medical bag downstairs. The bacon would be for the still-sleeping Loretta. He had instructed Jewel not to prepare two separate breakfasts. There was no sense in it, when his first stop was the vicarage, where Dora would consider it an insult for him to pass up her table.

Becky, still in her nightdress, sat in a chair cradling the cat. Her red curls lay haphazardly about her shoulders. She smiled when Philip wished her and her mother good morning.

"Good morning," she said. "Mummy says we may walk in the woods and see if the blackberries are ripe today."

"Excellent," Philip said. "But as a doctor, I have to warn you against eating too many."

Worry shadowed the young face. "Why not?"

"Because you could turn purple."

That made her giggle. He liked that about young children. Humor did not have to make sense, and silliness was just as valued as wit.

"Oh!"

Philip turned and saw the knife clatter to the table.

"It's only a nick," Jewel said, snatching up the end of her apron to press against her fingertip. "It just startled me."

He walked over to take her finger. It was indeed a small cut, but the bacon made it dangerous. With Becky watching soberly, he had her wash her hands; then he squeezed out more blood. He took a small jar of carbolic salve from his bag, smeared it on, and bandaged the finger. And against her protests, he sliced enough bacon for four or five days.

"You're very kind, sir," Jewel said as he washed his hands.

"Not at all." Drying his hands, he smiled at her. "I'll leave the salve. Keep it somewhere handy for future nicks—perhaps a shelf in the water closet. You may remove the bandage tonight and dab a little more on, then again in the morning."

He took up his bag and left. The air on the path was scented with sweet woodbine, dew-damp grasses, and trees just waking. He wondered what Jewel thought of the separate bedchambers. Fortunately, she went about her business with no indication of curiosity. Aleda had said she and the girl had suffered hard lives in Birmingham. He was glad his family was able to help them.

A new framed watercolor of Saint Jude's hung on the vicarage parlor wall. About the size of a hymnal cover, it was quite good, with muted impressionist-style lines. "Horace Stokes dropped that by yesterday evening," his stepfather said proudly. "Their adopted son Gerald painted it."

"The lad with the clubfoot?" Philip had noticed at church that the Stokes brood had gained a few more members since his last visit to Gresham.

"Why, yes."

"How did you guess?" Mother asked, tying off thread from a button she had sewn onto a shirt.

"Because doesn't it seem to follow that the most gifted artists have obstacles?" He took stethoscope from bag and listened to his stepfather's heart. "Speaking of obstacles . . . what do you think of giving the staircase a go after lunch?"

"A bath *and* the stairs, all in one week?"

"Only if you'll rest this morning."

"Very well. What joy!"

Philip smiled. "You're a man of simple wants, aren't you?"

"It takes illness to make us realize just how little we need to make us happy."

"I feel a future sermon in the works," Mother teased gently while folding the shirt.

"Not a sermon," Father said, and gave her a loving smile. "Just a request."

"What is it?"

"While I'm resting, will you go potter in your garden?"

Philip packed his stethoscope and closed the drapes. He and his mother happened to meet in the hall, she buttoning a gardening smock over her dress. They walked onto the porch together.

"Mother?"

"Yes, son?"

He hesitated. "Did you have an inkling how good you would be for each other, before you married?"

"Well, yes. Because we had become such good friends. When romance came, we had a solid foundation to build upon."

"I guess Loretta and I skipped over the friendship part."

She laid a hand upon his shoulder, her expression filled with

283

maternal understanding. And pain. "It's not hopeless, Philip. She's here."

"Her father ordered her."

"Oh dear."

"Please don't tell anyone."

"Very well." She shook her head. "I wish I could make it better."

"I shouldn't have brought it up. You have enough on your hands."

"No, I'm glad you did. Maybe now is the time you should devote to building a friendship."

"You don't think it's too late?"

"It's never too late to try," she said. "Perhaps it's good that you spend most of your day away. Forget rekindling your romance for the time being. She'll think more clearly without that pressure, and surely remember your good qualities."

He chuckled dryly. "I don't feel I have any good qualities at the moment."

She patted his bearded cheek. "Shall I make a list?"

He kissed the top of her head. And felt better. It was not right to burden her with his problems. But even grown men needed nurturing at times. He wondered if Squire Bartley, in his dreadful isolation of mind, longed for the touch of a maternal hand upon his forehead.

He went on to the surgery, where he and Doctor Rhodes played cribbage between his lancing a boil, setting a broken arm, and walking over to Walnut Lane to check on an infant boy he had treated for croup the day before.

"The baby's much better," Philip was pleased to report upon his return.

Doctor Rhodes yawned. "Very good. It's about time for my nap. Will you look in on the squire this afternoon?"

"My pleasure."

After lunch, his stepfather took to the stairs like a racehorse let out of the gate, until Philip warned him to slow down. "You can still burst your stitches."

That cooled his pace. He allowed the banister to take much of his weight, as instructed. "Does this mean no more sleeping in the parlor?"

"That's what it means," Philip said.

"Oh joy!"

On his walk to the manor house, Philip was tempted to make a small detour by the cottage to see how Loretta's day was going. His mother's advice rang in his ears, and he turned down Bartley Lane instead. He met Jeremiah Toft, sitting astride a black Cleveland Bay. His old friend dismounted.

"How good to see you!" Philip exclaimed, clapping his back as they embraced. "I hear you're a family man."

Jeremiah flushed with pleasure. After what seemed like perpetual bachelorhood, last year he had married Beryl Worthy, one of Grace's former playmates. "Little Jenny's three months old . . . and already she laughs when she sees me."

"Ben and I did that years ago," Philip teased.

Jeremiah cuffed him on the shoulder. "I should have thrashed you both when I had the chance."

Philip smiled and stroked the horse's neck. The animal snorted, but not in a panicked way.

"The squire sold off most of his horses a couple of years ago," Jeremiah said. "He was no longer taking the coach out. I'm just giving her a bit of exercise."

"Why don't you and your family come to dinner tomorrow night?" Philip said as his friend swung up into the saddle again.

"We'd like that," Jeremiah said.

Mrs. Cooper, whom he well remembered from church, asked Philip to wait in the foyer of the manor house. Presently a tall man appeared, with dark mustache and puzzled expression.

"And where is Doctor Rhodes?"

"He's resting," Philip replied. "I'm his associate for now. May I see the squire?"

"Very well." Mr. Gibbs nodded to the housekeeper. "I'll escort him upstairs."

"Are you any relation to Miss Hollis the writer?" Mr. Gibbs asked amiably on the staircase.

"She happens to be my sister."

Mr. Gibbs opened the bedchamber door and followed him inside. A thin young woman, whom Mr. Gibbs said was his day nurse, put aside some needlework and rose from a chair. Philip approached the bed, saddened by the state to which the old man had been reduced.

"Good afternoon, Squire," he said, leaning close. "Do you remember me? Philip Hollis?"

"Amm-grabeel," Squire Bartley growled, staring up at Philip as if wishing his eyes could speak.

"I wish I could understand what you're trying to say. It must be terribly frustrating. But I'm here to examine you."

"Grabeel."

Philip took his temperature, then listened to his chest with the stethoscope. "No fever. And your heartbeat's strong."

"My servants turn him every two hours, day and night," Mr. Gibbs said. It seemed he was speaking more to his uncle, as if wishing him to understand all that was being done for him.

"Very good," Philip said. "There is no sign of bedsores."

"MM-gale!" the squire said.

Philip smoothed the lined forehead. "I'm so sorry, sir. I

wish I could understand. But it's good that you're exercising your tongue, making syllables. The more you keep at it, the more control you'll gain."

An idea struck him. He turned to Mr. Gibbs. "May I have a sheet of paper?"

The nephew nodded to the nurse, who left the bedchamber.

"What is it?" Mr. Gibbs said.

"An experiment," Philip said, taking his pen from his bag. "He seems desperate to communicate. I'm not sure how much of his cognitive ability was affected, but if he can recognize the alphabet, he may be able to spell out words by grunting or blinking."

"Wouldn't that be a miracle, Uncle?" Mr. Gibbs said to the man, fidgeting with his own shirt button.

Philip jotted down the letters of the alphabet and held them close to the squire. The experiment was a failure. The squire either lay listlessly while Philip pointed to letters, or grunted at random for those which formed no words.

"What a pity," Mr. Gibbs said.

Feet propped onto a parlor footstool, Donald smoked two cigarettes in a row. He had not stuck his head into his uncle's room for a week, and was stunned by his intense drive to speak. If he had thought getting rid of Jewel and Becky would cause him to give up trying, he had not reckoned with the power of pure, unrefined revenge.

What were you thinking? Donald asked himself. *You imbecile.*

He had to appease the old man. Get him to sink back into complacency. He feared having Jewel at his bedside every day, as before. But would he calm down if she visited occasionally?

He rang for Mrs. Cooper. "I'm thinking I was too harsh with Mrs. Libby. And my uncle does seem to miss her and Becky."

"Yes," the housekeeper said crisply, as if to both statements.

Donald squelched his irritation. "Do you know what's happened to her?"

"She's housemaid for Doctor Hollis and his wife, while they're staying in the cottage."

"Indeed? Well, please ask her to visit my uncle now and again. I think it would calm him."

"I think so, as well," Mrs. Cooper said with hands clasped. "But I'll not ask."

Gaping up at her, Donald said, "I beg your pardon?"

"You discharged her. You ask her."

"You seem to forget that I can discharge *you*."

"Do what you must, Mr. Gibbs. I can move in with my sister, where I don't have to walk on eggshells."

She turned and left the room. Cheeks flaming, Donald was sorely tempted to act upon his threat. And then what? Run the house himself? Endure even more hatred from the other servants?

He went to his chamber for his tweed jacket and a hat, and set out on foot.

From the gate he saw Becky, using twigs to form squares upon the ground. A cat nuzzled its head against the girl's side, demanding attention.

"Hallo, Becky."

She stood and walked over to the gate. "I'm making a house, Mr. Gibbs."

"It's a fine house," he said, and for an instant regretted

that he would never have children. "Will you ask your mother to come out here?"

"Yes, sir."

She turned and trotted for the cottage. Only seconds later, Jewel stepped out, brushing hands upon her apron. She stared out at him, narrowed her eyes, and crossed the garden.

"What is it, Mr. Gibbs?"

He removed his hat. "I've come to apologize for . . . what happened. I was very wrong to think you capable of . . ."

"Stealing," Jewel said, blue eyes cold upon him.

"Yes. It was simply a misunderstanding."

"Begging your pardon, sir, but misunderstandings don't hide statues in trunks."

His temper sparked, and he had to remind himself why he was there. "You're right. I . . . should have investigated more thoroughly. Perhaps one of the other servants was jealous of your closeness with my uncle. But that's water under the bridge. My uncle misses you and Becky. Terribly."

Her voice softened. "The poor man."

"It would help so much if you would visit him."

"I have Sundays off. We will come after church."

"I was hoping you could come today. Wouldn't Doctor Hollis allow you to slip away for an hour or so? He's aware of my uncle's condition."

She hesitated, nodded. "Mrs. Hollis is napping. I'll ask her when she wakes."

He thanked her and turned for the path. He had taken only six or seven steps when he heard, "Jewel?"

Through the trees he spotted a woman with curls the color of corn silk walking toward a garden chair. He studied her for several seconds, watched her sit gracefully. She wore a simple yet elegant summer nautical costume of pale blue trimmed in white. Even from the distance, he could tell it was expensive.

"Will you make some tea?" Mrs. Hollis said from the chair nearest Becky's twig-house outline. A copy of *The Portrait of a Lady* rested in her lap.

"Right away, ma'am," Jewel said.

"And afterwards, will you go to Trumbles? Doctor Hollis and I have finished the Cadbury's. Of course, we had some assistance in the form of a four-year-old."

This was the most personable Mrs. Hollis had ever been with her. Jewel had to smile. Twice she had seen the doctor slip Becky chocolates.

Mrs. Hollis pursed her lips. "Actually, my taste buds are nudging me toward cake."

Jewel was about to suggest Johnson's Baked Goods when the gate squeaked open behind her. She looked over her shoulder. Mr. Gibbs was advancing.

"You must *not* entrust your taste buds to the local baker, Mrs. Hollis. Not when the manor house cook bakes a chocolate-plum torte that puts Bertolini's to shame."

Her whole countenance brightened. "Bertolini's? On Leicester Square?"

"Where else? It's my favorite after-theatre restaurant."

"You enjoy the theatre?"

"Was Guy Fawkes fond of gunpowder?"

Mrs. Hollis laughed. "You're from London!"

He made a little bow. "Please allow me to introduce myself. I'm Donald Gibbs, presently of Gresham, but my roots are firmly planted beside the Thames."

"I'm very pleased to make your acquaintance, Mr. Gibbs."

She extended her hand. Mr. Gibbs stepped forward to scoop it up as if it were a delicate orchid.

"If I may be so bold to ask a favor, my ailing uncle misses Jewel's company. If you would allow her and little Becky to visit the manor house, she could deliver a message to Mrs. Wright. Within a couple of hours—no less than three—you could be feasting on cake warm from the oven."

"Yes, of course," Mrs. Hollis said with a little wave in Jewel's direction. "Of what part of London are you from, Mr. Gibbs?"

"I own a lovely house on Kensington Square."

"Indeed? I live in Pembroke Gardens."

Waiting for a pause in the conversation, Jewel noticed the word *I*. In fact, she had not seen Mrs. Hollis so animated the entire week.

"Mrs. Hollis?" Jewel asked.

"What is it, Jewel?" she asked with a little dent between her brows.

"Shall I make the tea first?"

Now it was Mr. Gibbs who waved her on. "You must embark on your mission of mercy straightaway, Jewel. I shall make the tea. And then we two expatriates will reminisce."

Chapter 26

Annabel the parlormaid, happy for a break, gave Jewel and Becky quick embraces before exiting the room.

No matter what her misgivings were over Mrs. Hollis and Mr. Gibbs, Jewel was pleased to see the squire.

"You dear man," she said, holding his papery hand as Becky stroked his bald head.

He seemed pleased to see them, though the sounds he made were still unintelligible.

"Shall I fetch your book and continue where we left off?"

His eyes filled with dismay. Jewel squeezed his hand lightly. "Then we'll stay right here."

She told him whatever came to mind. Their train journey from Birmingham. Her duties at the cottage. She even confessed to laboring over *Mrs. Beeton's Victorian Cookbook* evenings to plan each day's meals, for she was used to plain cooking. Becky sang several songs.

Mrs. Cooper appeared.

"Would Becky care to look at the fish pond with me?"

Jewel was grateful. However much the child cared for the squire, the bedside vigil was too much for her tender age. When they were gone, Jewel got to her knees.

"Please heal our dear Squire Bartley, Father, or take him on to the place where he will be whole again. And above all, please grant him peace. Your will be done."

She could not be sure, but imagined she felt faint pressure of the squire's hand squeezing hers. Standing again, she did not imagine the tears filling his eyes.

When Mrs. Cooper returned with Becky and a basket containing the cake, Jewel kissed the old man's forehead and promised to return Sunday afternoon. She did not want to give him false hopes by promising any sooner.

"While I'm as fond of the Bard as any Englishman, I confess to preferring modern comedy for an evening's entertainment," Mr. Gibbs said over a third cup of tea.

"You're not alone," Loretta said. "Or else the Savoy operas would not be so popular."

"Um, indeed. But then there is all that singing." He hesitated. "I hope this doesn't offend you. . . ."

Loretta smiled. Entertaining her with talk of London and the theatre as he was, she would not take offense if he spit in her eye.

"I admire frankness."

"I sensed that deepness in you," he said, studying her face.

Which was unfortunate, because the compliment made her blush like a schoolgirl. To cover her embarrassment, she said quickly, "Are you aware that Ambrose Clay lives part of the year in Gresham?"

"The actor? In this stodgy old village?"

"I met him and his wife at our London wedding. They'll be at the vicarage for Sunday dinner. Perhaps I could wrangle you an invitation?"

He shook his head. "You're very kind, but I shall have to decline. My uncle becomes very moody when I'm not there to feed him his meals."

"It's good of you to care so deeply for him." Loretta had heard stories of heirs so overcome by greed that they lost all compassion.

He fell silent, as if battling some emotion. At length he said, quietly, "It's very kind of you to say so, Mrs. Hollis. I can hardly think what I shall do with myself when he's gone."

"I'll send Jewel and Becky over for a short visit every day. If you think it will help."

He pressed his hand to his heart, nodded.

Loretta was startled to hear Becky's childish voice in the near distance. Where had the time gone?

"Look, Mummy! A redbird!"

"Already?" Mr. Gibbs said, voicing Loretta's thoughts. He got to his feet. "How very rude of me, overstaying my welcome."

"On the contrary." She extended her hand. "In fact, I hope you will visit again."

He leaned down to take her hand and pressed a kiss to the back of it. "Nothing would please me more, Mrs. Hollis. You have provided a bright spot in an otherwise dark day."

It's an ill wind that blows no good, Donald thought, holding open the gate.

"Thank you, sir," Jewel mumbled, a basket in one hand, her daughter's hand in the other. The fact that she avoided his eyes did not damper his high spirits.

Hopefully his uncle would be appeased back into his near stupor. And he had finally met someone in this backwards place as sophisticated as he, and who shared his passion for London. It was a tonic to his soul, reliving his memories.

Carefully selected memories, of course. He would write to Reese and share his day.

When he stepped into the manor house, an envelope was propped upon the foyer table, the address written in the familiar uneven letters. He held it to his heart on the staircase, closed his door, and tore into the envelope.

Drained of strength, he dropped into his chair. The love of his life had left him for Mr. Angier, a married art appraiser who haunted the music halls in the hopes of picking up those as desperate and beautiful as Reese. Why, Reese had often mocked the man, prancing about with puffed-out cheeks and cushion-stuffed shirt!

But everyone had a price. Reese's was a posh flat on Wellington Street, in the thick of restaurants and theatres, instead of a silent house in Kensington. A day cook and maid instead of a half-empty larder and tin of matches for the stove.

Donald wept until no more tears came and his throat felt raw.

Life was not fair. Why had he even come here?

He would have to beg, borrow, steal, or grovel enough to return to London and woo back Reese.

He wiped his face with a handkerchief, rested his head against his chair cushion, and closed his sandpapery eyes.

At length, soft raps came at the door, then Mrs. Cooper's voice. "Shall I send up your supper, Mr. Gibbs?"

He opened his swollen eyes, blinked at the dimness of the room.

"Just some soup," he croaked.

The nourishment helped him to think more rationally. Of what use to win Reese back, only to be tossed aside again for the next man with money? At the risk of losing his house?

As much as it pained him to admit it, the more prudent action would be to keep up the mortgage. By the time he inherited and reclaimed all that was his, Reese would have grown weary of Mister Toad.

He had three weeks to raise his August payment. And his mind wrapped around a possibility. With a surgeon husband and parents residing on Park Lane, Mrs. Hollis had money. And she had enjoyed his company.

The fact that she was married was an asset. When he did not make advances, she would think him a gentleman.

But he must not attempt to plunge headlong into a relationship. Impulsive men looked desperate. The wealthy could smell desperation. He ought to know. He hailed from their ranks.

Having read from *The Portrait of a Lady* all through the following morning, and even through lunch, Loretta was sitting in the garden with head back and eyes closed when the squeak of the gate penetrated her fog.

"Mummy, may I pick some gooseberries?"

"Sh-h-h," she heard Jewel say.

Loretta opened her eyes.

"Sorry, ma'am."

"I wasn't asleep."

Jewel turned to her daughter. "You may pick one, if you'll be careful as I taught you."

"How was the squire?" Loretta asked as the girl skipped

over to the gooseberry shrub. The pale green fruit glistened like aquamarine gems through the leaves.

"He seemed pleased to see us again. But I must get into the kitchen and start supper."

"Doctor Hollis ordered from the Bow and Fiddle. He'll collect it on his way home. You have only to lay the cloth."

Jewel's shoulders relaxed visibly. "How thoughtful. I admit I was worried. I've never cooked for a dinner party."

"This will hardly be a dinner party," Loretta said dryly. "Did you see Mr. Gibbs?"

"Just briefly in the hall."

"Did he say anything?"

"He thanked us for coming."

How about thanking me for sending you? And he had seemed the perfect gentleman yesterday. Loretta had to remind herself, *He's distracted . . . concerned for his uncle.*

And of truth, she should have sent a note, thanking him for the cake. She would go inside and compose one for Jewel to hand to him tomorrow. She would mention how much she had enjoyed their conversation and extend an invitation to visit again. It was neither improper nor forward. She would write the same note to a woman. Courtesy was courtesy, no matter that he was a handsome, witty man who shared her love for London.

"My great-grandfather worked for the squire's grandfather," Jeremiah Toft said that evening, while grinding enough pepper over his roast beef to give everyone at the table sneezing fits.

"And then my grandfather for his son, who was the squire's father. My own father worked in the stables, before he passed on. And now me. And Beryl worked in the scullery before we married."

Loretta nodded politely and almost wished she were in the parlor, where Jewel and Becky had taken the infant.

Beryl Toft turned her face toward the cooings and soft laughter coming from the other side of the house and smiled. She was a smallish woman, with dark beady eyes, and wiry brown hair barely tamed by a comb. "But our Jenny won't work in nobody's kitchen. She'll go to college. Maybe even become a doctor, like you, Philip."

"There are women doctors now," Philip said, adding cautiously, "but you must be sure it's her wish and not yours. I've seen too many medical students forced into the profession by their parents."

"Philip's got a point there," Jeremiah said around a mouthful of beef. "She might even decide to become a writer, like Aleda."

She's three months old, Loretta thought. *Why are we even discussing this?*

The lack of respect was unsettling. Addressing Philip by his given name? While the pair had attended school with her husband, their paths had diverged years ago, both geographically and socially.

And as little as she expected of Gresham's collective sense of fashion, Loretta was stunned when Beryl appeared in a *gardening smock*, over a skirt of eye-assaulting yellow, and announced, "My regular clothes still don't fit. But at least this smock makes it easier for Jenny to get to her food."

She could only hope the woman would have the sense to go off in private, should that become necessary.

The manor house chocolate cake, every bit as delicious as Mr. Gibbs had described, was tucked away in the pantry to be savored, a sliver at a time. Bread-and-butter pudding from the Bow and Fiddle served as dessert. No sooner had they finished—Jeremiah wolfing down two servings before anyone else finished firsts—then he wiped his mouth on the cuff of his sleeve and thanked them for the evening.

"Jenny's just now started sleeping all night," Beryl explained. "We've got to get her home."

"We understand," Loretta assured her, and was so happy over not having to spend another hour in the parlor gushing over the baby that she embraced Beryl at the door, even said, "It was so lovely meeting you."

Though darkness had not yet settled, Philip escorted them to the lane. Jewel began clearing the table. Loretta took a cup of coffee into the parlor and found herself listening to Jewel's and Becky's voices among the clicks of china.

"I wish we had a baby like Jenny," Becky was saying.

"She was sweet," Jewel said. "I've only seen one sweeter."

"Me, Mummy?"

Loretta had to smile. Sometimes she felt a pang of envy at the pleasure mother and daughter took in each other. She had little use for babies, never having spent much time in their company, but knew that they were necessary in order to get to the "Becky" stage.

She heard the door open and close, then Philip thanking Jewel for serving and tidying up.

"I'm helping," she heard Becky say.

"Yes, you certainly are."

She could picture Philip patting her head. *Perhaps the head pats keep them from growing too swiftly,* she thought. *And perhaps you're a silly woman.* Relief over being shed of the Tofts was making her giddy.

Philip entered, sat in a chair, and smiled at her. "Thank you for being so hospitable to them. I realize I sprang this on you practically at the last minute."

She was mildly pleased that he had noticed. "You're welcome."

"They want to have us over soon."

"How nice," Loretta said while thinking, *When pigs fly.*

She had not suffered a headache all week, simply because Philip had not pressured her to make calls to his family, and more importantly, had kept to his own bedchamber. She would give the Tofts the power to decide when the next headache would strike. Three weeks remained of her banishment from London. Why surrender another evening to boredom, why cultivate a friendship she had no intention of maintaining?

Mr. Gibbs came again to mind. But that was different, she reminded herself. Here was a grieving nephew who needed the occasional uplifting conversation to divert his mind from his uncle's situation. Just because she had enjoyed his company made it no less of a charitable act.

Chapter 27

"The sermon won't be as grand as Saint Peter's," Philip warned during the walk up Vicarage Lane, as Saint Jude's bells tolled.

Imagine that, Loretta thought.

They were late; she had fussed over her hair a bit longer than necessary. Of truth, she wished to avoid the visiting on the lawn, being introduced to farmers' wives who would desire to make small talk and ask if they were moving there for good.

Jewel and Becky had gone ahead, to walk with some of the squire's servants. No doubt Mr. Gibbs would be staying behind with his uncle. He had that self-sacrificing quality about him. She could tell, from only one meeting.

Accompanying her husband up the aisle, Loretta could feel the envious glances sent her way. Whether because of her silken-blond hair and flawless complexion, her fashionable sea green gown with pointed bodice and the new accordion-kilted skirt, or her pearl choker and earrings, she could not know, but she would have guessed a combination of all.

She held her head higher. True, God had blessed her with good looks, but she also worked hard to project herself in a positive way. Most of the women she had passed were wearing what would almost be considered house dresses in London.

She sat between Philip and his mother in the family pew, and leaned forward a bit to smile at the others. At least Mrs. Phelps and Elizabeth were somewhat in keeping with the latest fashions, though Aleda's nutmeg-colored skirt clashed with a gray blouse with blue stripes.

Mrs. Phelps squeezed her gloved hand, which felt rather nice, for Loretta's mother was not keen on physical displays of affection. Loretta had to remind herself of how desperately Philip's family wished to keep him, and thus, her, in Gresham, and took her hand away on the pretext of adjusting her hatpin.

Philip was right. The curate was not polished. He mopped his brow several times while preaching a sermon titled "People of Vision" from the book of Nehemiah. Loretta felt a little sorry for him. Perhaps he also was not there of his own choosing.

An hour later, Loretta and Philip, Elizabeth and Jonathan, Aleda, Philip's parents, and the Clays were assembled in the vicarage dining room. The women were invited first in queue, to a sideboard set with dishes surprisingly plain for Sunday: cold roast fowl, boiled potato salad, pickled beetroot, breads and cheese, olives and radishes, and cherry tarts.

At the table, Loretta was pleased when the Clays chose chairs across from her and Philip. The actor wore an elegantly cut black suit and silk paisley cravat. Mrs. Clay was strikingly beautiful in a gown of pale green and white brocaded satin trimmed with tiny seed pearls. Loretta could hardly keep from staring at them. She imagined villagers gaped at them all the time.

Philip had told her the story, of how Fiona was once a family servant, and how Mr. Clay had come to Gresham seeking respite from dark moods. How anyone with his fame and fortune could suffer dark moods was beyond her, but then, she had suffered many herself since her sister stole her beau.

They're probably sitting down to dinner in my parents' dining room now, she told herself. *Chatting on as if there were no pain in the world.* When would hers stop?

She was blessedly distracted from that thought when Vicar Phelps asked Elizabeth from the head of the table, "Aren't you going to call in the children?"

"We sent them home with Mrs. Littlejohn and Hilda," Elizabeth replied. She picked up her fork. "Boiled potato salad. Don't tell Mrs. Littlejohn I said so, but Dora's is the best."

"But why?"

"I suppose it's the tarragon vinegar. Mrs. Littlejohn uses plain."

Vicar Phelps shook his head. "No, why did you send the children home?"

"It's nice just being with adults for a change."

"How does it feel to have solid foods again, Andrew?" Jonathan asked.

"Wonderful. So many things I took for granted. And it's bliss to be back in my suits. Although I must admit to missing the comfort of dressing gowns."

Mr. Clay raised an eyebrow at him. "I can help you there. I still have my kilt from *Macbeth.*"

Chuckles rippled around the table, Vicar Phelps's the heartiest before he replied, " 'Yet do I fear thy nature; it is too full o' the milk of human kindness.' "

"You've been studying while you were laid up," Mr. Clay said. "Not fair."

" 'Fair is foul and foul is fair.' "

"That will be quite enough."

Fiona Clay explained to Loretta, "They have an ongoing duel . . . Shakespeare versus Scripture."

"Are you fond of Shakespeare, Loretta?" Mrs. Phelps asked in a sociable tone.

"I'm as fond of him as any Englishwoman," Loretta replied, and realized she was almost parroting Mr. Gibbs, "but I prefer modern comedy."

"Which would you rather perform, Mr. Clay?" Aleda asked.

"Comedy. It's just plain fun. Although Shakespeare was no slouch in the wit department."

" .'Tis an ill cook that cannot lick his own fingers,' " said Vicar Phelps.

Loretta laughed with the others. She had dreaded this occasion, fearing group pressure. What a relief that her fears were unfounded. At least this time.

Later, as they sat with coffee and dishes of cherry tart, Elizabeth pushed out her chair and stood. Jonathan looked up and smiled, rose to stand beside her with his arm around her waist.

"We have an announcement," Elizabeth said. She smiled at the Clays. "And because you're practically family, this is the perfect occasion. We actually sent the children home because we want to wait a while to inform them . . . just in case . . ."

Vicar Phelps was already pushing out his chair.

"Oh, daughter . . . is it so?"

Tears filling her gray-green eyes, she nodded. "We'll have a Christmas baby."

Her father hurried around the table to embrace her, and even kissed Jonathan's cheek loudly. Mrs. Phelps moved over to the couple as well. Philip congratulated them with thick voice. Covertly, Loretta watched the Clays' reactions; Mr. Clay smiled and nodded, while his wife wiped her eyes with a handkerchief.

"Father, we humbly ask you to bless Jonathan and Elizabeth, to keep this child you have created healthy," the vicar prayed over clasped hands around the table. Loretta found her own eyes prickling.

As they strolled down Vicarage Lane, Philip walked close enough to Loretta to assist her if she should need it, but did not offer his arm. If she needed distance from him, it should be consistent.

"Why don't the Clays build a proper house here?" she asked.

"It was Mr. Clay's idea. He's reclusive during his dark spells, hence the rooms above the stables. All Fiona has to do is walk across the courtyard for companionship."

"But . . . over the stables? Odors?"

Philip smiled. "The stables were built for several horses, back when the Larkspur was a coaching inn. There are only two horses now, and Mr. Herrick keeps the stalls tidy. So it's not bad."

"Have you visited their London flat?"

"No. They don't entertain there. All of Mr. Clay's energies go to his roles, and all of Fiona's energies go to supporting him."

"The poor man. Is he . . . *that* weak?"

"Only in the sense that someone with heart or liver ailments is weak."

"But he's a Christian."

So are we, and look at our problems, he thought. Patiently he explained. "Organs have no religion. Just like the heart and liver, the brain can malfunction to varying degrees. Sometimes from injury, sometimes a chemical imbalance."

"Yet he's so clever and talented."

"Yes. And very kind. As is Fiona."

Loretta sent him a sidelong smile. "Can you imagine marrying out of servitude the way she did? It's a Cinderella story."

With increasing sadness, Philip listened to her description of the first time she saw Mr. Clay perform on an outing with her parents and sister, when she was twelve or thirteen.

"I believe it was *Hamlet* at Theatre Royal. Never did I dream that he would attend my wedding, or that I would sit across the table from him. I shall write to Irene tonight. She'll be green with envy."

They turned onto Church Lane. A horse-drawn trap rolled westward. Philip exchanged waves with Mr. and Mrs. Hayes.

"And I realize ladies' fashion is not in your field of interest," Loretta went on, "but trust me when I say Mrs. Clay's gown came from Paris. I wonder if he helps her choose—"

Philip could no longer restrain his tongue. "Loretta."

"—her wardrobe." She paused. "What is it?"

"Elizabeth and Jonathan shared incredible news just moments ago. After so many disappointments, they're bravely trying for another baby. My heart is filled with joy, as well as fear that they will be disappointed again."

"I hope all goes well, too, Philip."

"But . . . it seems that you hope in the way one hopes for a distant acquaintance. No genuine emotional investment."

She gaped askew at him. "How can you say such a thing?"

"Because you've spoken of nothing but the Clays since we set out. Elizabeth and Jonathan are your family. The baby is your niece or nephew. Yet their announcement appeared to make very little impression in your mind."

"You had to lend me your handkerchief."

"Indeed." He had watched her dab at her eyes after the prayer. Three seconds later, she had been complimenting Fiona's gown.

"It's painfully clear," he went on, "how much you loathe being here. But it's not my family's fault. And they're good people. If you got to know them better, you might enjoy their company."

"And that's been the plan all along, hasn't it?" she said with crimson staining her fair cheeks. "Separate me from *my* friends and family in the hopes I'll throw them over for this place?"

"Yes, Loretta. That's why I made my stepfather ill, and made your father send you here."

Immediately he regretted stooping to sarcasm, the weapon of the weak. He blew out a breath, calmed his voice. "I shouldn't have said that. But if you miss your friends, why not invite them for a visit? We could telegraph them in the morning, book a couple of rooms at the Bow and Fiddle."

She turned to face him as if he had lost his mind. "You think I'd allow Maud and Sharon to see where we're staying?"

Would it matter to true friends? he could counter. But he was weary of the whole argument. They turned up the path in silence; hers stormy, his resigned.

He was relieved that Jewel and Becky were absent from the garden and ground floor. Perhaps they were visiting the squire. Loretta went to the staircase without a word. Not quite sure what to do with himself, Philip watched her hurry up the steps. He winced as her door slammed.

Weeping sounds drifted downward. The old protective impulse nudged him up the staircase. But he paused at the top. The scenario would be the same. She would weep while he begged forgiveness for his insensitivity. She would eventually dry her eyes and forgive him . . . with a sulking, grudging forgiveness. There would be no mutual presenting of sides, no attempt to find a solution or at least a compromise. A little bit more of his manhood would be surrendered.

And he had a depressing feeling she wept not for the state of their marriage, but because she had to endure Gresham and his company for three more weeks.

"I'm going for a walk, Loretta!" he called through the door.

A *thump* came from her side of the door. A shoe?

He heard Jewel and Becky coming up the path. The girl, skipping ahead of her mother, spotted him first. "Mummy, here's Doctor Hollis!"

Odd, how being recognized with such delight by a child could make him feel better. How wonderful it must be, to be the hero to one's own child! Would he ever know that feeling?

"And where have you been, Miss Becky?" he asked, crouching to her level.

"To the big house to see the squire."

"Good afternoon, Doctor Hollis," Jewel said.

He returned her greeting and asked about the squire.

"He seems calmer than two days ago."

Perhaps Mr. Gibbs had some good in him after all. "I'm sure it's because of your visits."

"Perhaps so," she said with no false modesty.

"Did you see me wave to you in church?" Becky asked.

"Alas," Philip replied truthfully, "I did not. Or I should have waved back. But next Sunday I'll keep an eye out for you. Will you give me another chance?"

That reduced her to shyness, but she smiled and nodded.

"There's a good girl." He straightened to address Jewel

310

again. "My wife feels unwell. Please bring her a cup of tea in a little while?"

"Of course, sir," she replied with no hint of a question in her eyes. Surely there were several in her mind.

Such as, why would he walk away from an ailing wife? Why the separate rooms? Why were evenings spent in separate parlor chairs with polite conversation interspersed with pages of novels?

Why can't Loretta be more like her? he thought, continuing down the path. Jewel Libby radiated serenity, an evenness of mood, in spite of a cruel past.

Philip repented of the thought. He was married and had no business straying, even mentally.

Reaching Church Lane he turned eastward, avoiding the village proper. The lane narrowed, a cool shady tunnel embowered by meandering leafy limbs.

Three weeks, he thought, wishing he could see the future.

But God knew it, and could even affect it. He veered off the lane, found a patch of grass, got to his knees, and prayed for his marriage.

I beg you for a miracle, Father.

That was what it would take at this point.

Standing, brushing off his trouser knees, he turned again toward the cottage. Whether or not God would choose to grant his prayer, there was something he felt nudged to do.

Loretta sat in the garden, holding saucer and cup of tea balanced upon her knees. Her face appeared as one who had been beaten, face splotched and eyes swollen into slits. A pang stabbed his heart. To cause a loved one so much misery, just by the nature of his existence!

She turned her head as he came through the gate. He lifted another wicker chair, placed it adjacent to hers so that the arms almost touched.

"Loretta," he said gently. "Why don't you have Jewel pack your things?"

She turned her face to him.

"I'll take you home, help you face your father."

He could see the temptation in her swollen eyes. Mingled with worry.

"You mean, you would stay there, too?" she said with voice raspy.

"No. Not the way things are between us now. Just long enough to help explain to your father that it's over."

The fact that she even had to think about it was another stab to his heart.

She sighed. "You know how he is. He'll drag the vicar over, talk us to death to where we can't think straight."

Philip could picture him doing that. It was Doctor Trask's need to be in control at all times that made him a superior surgeon, but caused him sometimes to ignore the boundaries in his daughters' marriages.

"Then write to your mother. She has some influence with him. Ask her to plead your case and telegraph when it's safe to go home."

After several long seconds of thought, she stretched out her hand. He took it, but there was no warmth to it. It lay in his palm like a dead fish.

"I'm sorry, Philip."

Her image blurred as tears stung his eyes. He wished so much to tell her how much he loved her. But that would only distress her. So he simply nodded and held her cold hand, wondering if it would be his last time to do so.

Chapter 28

"No one's come forward yet," Mr. Trumble said with a nod toward the window, where Aleda's notice was propped along displays of lamps, cooking pots, and packets of flower seeds. "Perhaps if you upped the reward? Might give someone an inceneration to look for it?"

"I'll do that," Aleda said resignedly, for after almost three weeks, she held little hope. She borrowed Mr. Trumble's pen, crossed through the amount, and wrote in a new amount above it. A steep price, but worth every penny if the watch would be returned.

She purchased the tin of baking soda Dora had requested, the jar of Muscovite Lustre shoe polish for Father, and a half-dozen cakes of Pears soap for mother.

A tall man entered just as she turned from the counter.

"Good morning, Mr. Gibbs," Mr. Trumble said.

"Good morning." The man removed his hat for her sake. She pretended not to notice, and gave him wide berth. As she headed toward the door, she heard him ask Jack in a tone of faint desperation, "Is there a letter for a Donald Gibbs?"

Why would he come for the mail, when Mr. Jones delivered to the manor house?

I'm here for the same reason, she reminded herself. Wryly, she thought that perhaps Mr. Gibbs had also written a novel and asked someone to read it.

She turned northward outside, to head for the lending library for the copy of *Ben-Hur* Father had requested. Her eyes caught a flash of raspberry-colored movement ahead as a woman disappeared into Perkins' Fine Millinery. Loretta?

She paused to look through the window. Loretta indeed was setting a hatbox onto the counter while looking about. Her raspberry-check silk gown was more suited for London theatres than Gresham's shops. But then, Aleda was the last person to criticize another woman's wardrobe.

As if sensing she was being watched, Loretta turned and looked at her.

Aleda sighed. The longer she dallied around the shops, the greater her chance of encountering Mr. Gibbs again. So she simply waved and pushed on.

As little as she cared for Philip's family, it stung to have his sister brush her off so quickly. All the more reason to mail the letter to her mother that was in her bag.

Finally, a hand moved aside the curtain behind the counter. Priscilla Perkins entered, not bothering to cover a yawn.

Loretta took the injured hat from its box. "You said you could block this."

Miss Perkins shrugged. "I'll give it a try."

314

Stunned by the disinterest, Loretta noticed pillow markings upon one side of the shopkeeper's face. "It's an expensive hat. And I shall need it back within a day or two."

"Don't get your knickers in a knot. I said I'd try."

"Never mind!" Loretta dropped the hat back into the box. Tears blurred her eyes, from the frustration of dealing with unrefined people. She hurried through the door, holding the box by the string, and collided with a man in a tweed suit. The box flew to the ground and the lid popped open.

"Pardon me," he said, snatching the hat from the cobbled stones.

Mr. Gibbs!

He smiled down at her. "How lovely to see you, Mrs. Hollis. Or shall I say, 'to bump into you'?"

"It's good to see you, as well," she said. "How is your uncle?"

"Physically . . . no better. But his spirits have improved, thanks to you."

"To me?"

"For kindly allowing Jewel and Becky to visit. He's become much less agitated, even when they're not with him."

They stood before the millinery shop window. He handed her the hat. "Did you just buy this? I'm afraid the fall has dented it."

"That happened on the train," she said, setting it into the box he picked up and held out. "I meant to have it blocked, but . . ."

Inches away, the door was flung open and Miss Perkins rushed out.

"I'm so sorry, miss! I didn't understand what you meant. Please forgive my rudeness. I was feeling out of sorts."

"That's no excuse for what you—"

"No excuse at all. And I shall be happy to block your hat. At no charge."

She snatched the box from Mr. Gibbs and tucked it under her arm. Too bewildered to respond, Loretta watched her extend her hand to him.

"I'm Priscilla Perkins," she said with lashes fluttering like hummingbird wings. "You must be Mr. Gibbs. I've heard of you."

"You have?" he said, sending Loretta a dry smile. "Then you know what an ogre I can be if my friends are not given proper service."

"Yes, of course, I shall do my best. And I'll give you a discount on a man's hat, too."

"I'll bear that in mind." He took a backwards step to open the door. "And you'd best be at it if you're going to repair that hat, yes?"

"Ah . . . yes." Halfway through the door she turned. "Remember the men's hats."

"I shall think of nothing else."

Loretta held in her laughter until they walked a few paces to Johnson's Baked Goods. Not out of respect for Miss Perkins, but in case she was the vindictive sort who would damage her hat. Mr. Gibbs' laugh was as rich as his voice.

"She wouldn't last a day behind a counter on Regent Street," he said.

"She's the *owner*," Loretta said.

"You jest!"

"I'm serious."

He laughed again, sobered. "Don't you wish you were there now?"

"In my fondest dreams."

An older woman came out of the bakery, smiled, and said in passing, "Good day, Mrs. Hollis."

Probably someone who saw her at Saint Jude's with Philip yesterday, she thought.

"Are you heading homeward?" Mr. Gibbs asked. "I should be honored to escort you."

She happened to glance through the bakery window. A white-aproned man was wiping the counter, and lifted his hand in greeting. The friendliness of villagers—Miss Perkins notwithstanding—was increasingly annoying. While they could stroll down most London streets and passersby would neither know nor care about her business, she was in Philip's domain. Why, Aleda could pop out of one of the shops any minute!

What will he do? Divorce me?

She was not engaged in any immorality, simply enjoying the company of a friend with common interests. But she could not hand Philip ammunition to present to Father, should their marriage reach the bitter end it was racing toward.

"On second thought, why don't you come for tea this afternoon?" he said with understanding tone. "We can tell more London stories."

"Why don't you come to the cottage instead?" She nodded toward the bakery. "And this time, I'll provide the cake."

"I'm looking forward to it." He smiled, tipped his hat, and left.

On her way into the bakery, Loretta realized she had not mentioned a time. After two o'clock would be best, she thought. Becky would wake from her nap, and Jewel would take her with her to the manor house. She wondered if she should go back outside and try to wave him down.

But some instinct or intuition told her that he knew exactly when he should arrive. She smiled to herself. Just as she had when she'd slipped away to Limehouse for Chinese food, she was being daring without being naughty. Having an innocent adventure, in a place where few adventures existed.

"Mummy, when will we live in the big house again?" Becky asked after her nap, raising her arms for Jewel to slip her dress over her chemise.

"Probably never, mite." Jewel began fastening buttons. "We only go there to visit Squire Bartley."

"No, not that house. The big house where Mrs. Platt lived."

"Never, Becky. Do you miss it?"

"Not the house. Just Ricky. He was nice."

Jewel's insides froze. "Who is Ricky?"

"Baby Ricky. Mrs. Platt let me give him the bottle sometimes. He pulled my hair, but he didn't know any better."

Relief eased through Jewel. She even remembered Becky speaking about the baby. For how long would Mr. Dunstan's crimes make her view every male in her daughter's young life through a cloud of suspicion?

They descended both staircases, and had just reached the kitchen when Mrs. Hollis charged around from the parlor. She had changed into a silvery-blue gown with scooped neckline. Her pearl choker wound elegantly around the base of her long neck.

"Ah, there you are. You'd best be setting out. The squire needs you."

That was so, but some needs were more urgent than others. Jewel nudged Becky toward the parlor. "As soon as she goes to the water closet, ma'am."

Mrs. Hollis glanced at the kitchen door and sighed. "Very well."

Five minutes later, they were trooping up the path toward Bartley Lane, Becky struggling over the alphabet.

"*H-I-J* . . ." She looked up at Jewel.

"*K*. It makes this sound: *ca* . . . *ca* . . . *ca*. . . ."

"*K*." Becky nodded. "*L-M-O-P*."

"*L-M-N-O-P*," Jewel said gently. "Remember the *N*."

"What word starts with *N*?"

"Nose . . . nice . . ."

"Knees?" Becky asked.

"I'm afraid not, mite. There's a *K* in front."

"Why?"

"I haven't the foggiest," Jewel admitted.

They were on to *S-T-U* when they reached the gravel carriage drive. Mr. Gibbs advanced from the rose garden.

"Ah, there you are! Thank you for coming. And for goodness' sakes, go through the front door. You're visitors, not servants."

"I poured my heart out," Loretta said, "begging my mother to convince Father to allow me to come home. But then after all that business with Miss Perkins, I forgot to mail it."

They sat in the garden, as would any respectable married woman entertaining a man who was not her husband. Crumbs from a fairly decent almond cake and empty teacups rested upon the garden table.

"Perhaps it was fate," Mr. Gibbs said.

"Perhaps so. Anyway, I may not even mail it tomorrow. What good would it do? My father assumes his sheer resolve can force me to be happy again."

Mr. Gibbs listened thoughtfully, hat propped upon a crossed knee and elbows propped upon chair arms. "Forgive me . . . but is that a bad thing? Wishing to make you happy?"

"It is when it stems from guilt."

Because he was such an attentive listener, she found herself pouring out the story of Conrad and Irene.

Mr. Gibbs shook his head. "How sad. Having your heart broken in such a cruel way. There is no worse feeling."

"You know?" she said.

His eyes filmed over. "Quite recently. It rips your heart out."

The poor man. And yet, as sorry as she was for him, she was relieved that he understood her pain.

"Back to fate," he said when he had composed himself. "It's good that you did not mail the letter. If you decide for divorce, your parents will be more apt to understand and support you if you are able to prove you gave it a try."

That was so. She had known it all along in her head, but her heart was willful.

"You're fortunate to have your parents," he said. "I would give anything in the world to have mine."

Now Loretta's eyes misted. As infuriating as her father could be, she could not imagine life without either parent. "I'm so sorry."

"Thank you, Mrs. Hollis. The only thing I'm grateful for is that they did not live to see what a mess I made of things."

"What do you mean?"

He sighed. "I had started up a little import business. It was going well, but you can't up and leave it in the hands of managers and expect them to have the same visions. But no regrets! My uncle comes first."

"I admire your loyalty."

"My uncle has always been loyal to me."

A thought sparked in Loretta's mind. Would it be indelicate

to voice it? She'd told him practically her whole life story. Why would he resent her delving into his?

"Please don't take offense, but . . ."

"What is it, Mrs. Hollis?"

She hesitated.

"There is nothing you can say that will offend me," he said. "We are kindred spirits. I believe fate had a hand in our meeting, as well."

She smiled and thought what a difference having a friend made. But still delicately, she said, "You're your uncle's only heir . . . correct?"

"I would give it all up if it would buy him renewed health."

"I'm afraid that's not going to happen," she said gently.

He ran a hand through his dark hair. "Yes, you're right."

"It would surely comfort him to know that he'll leave you the means to restart your business."

"The business is beyond repair. Even after mortgaging my family home. I may as well have burned the money in the fireplace."

"Oh dear. But . . ."

"Yes?"

"At least your inheritance will pay off your mortgage?"

"And more. It's just maintaining the monthly payments that—"

He stopped, gaped at her with a horrified look. "Mrs. Hollis, this is unforgivable."

"I beg your pardon?"

"I've taken advantage of your kind sympathies in a most ungentlemanly way!" He took his hat from his knee and got to his feet. "I will trespass upon your company no longer. Good afternoon, dear lady."

"Wait!" She rose, caught up with him at the gate, and put a hand upon his sleeve. "You said fate had a hand in our friendship. You're going through a trying time, and so am I. May not friends bare their hearts to each other?"

"Oh, Mrs. Hollis," he groaned. "But a man has his pride."

"I led you into the discussion . . . remember? But if it humiliates you, we'll speak no more of money."

"Thank you. You are too good for this earth, Mrs. Hollis."

"My husband would argue with you there," she said dryly. "Will you call again tomorrow?"

He gave her an incredulous look. "You would wish me to?"

"Yes. You may even bring the cake." She smiled. "Though I fear this friendship may be too fattening."

He took up her hand and kissed it. "Then I shall bring strawberries."

She wished tomorrow were already there, but a small worry nudged her mind. She bit her lip.

"What is it?"

Loretta hesitated. "My husband's sister lives near Bartley Lane, and if she spots you entering the path . . ."

He smiled understanding. "Say no more. I played in these woods as a child, and there are bridle paths running behind the house that connect with this one farther along."

"Not that we're doing anything wrong," she hastened to say, lest he assume she intended more than friendship. "But you understand . . ."

"I absolutely do." He kissed her hand again and took his leave.

Her hand could still feel the faint pressure of his lips as she went upstairs to tear up the letter she had written to her mother. She had only entertained Mr. Gibbs' sentiments over fate for politeness' sake. But perhaps there was something to it after all.

As Jewel prepared supper that evening, Doctor Hollis returned to the cottage bearing a parcel about the size of two loaves of bread.

"I stopped off at Trumbles, and Mr. Sanders said it came in today's mail. He was going to send out a notice in the morning for you to pick it up."

"For me?" Jewel said.

Doctor Hollis grinned and set it upon the table. "Actually, for Becky."

"Me?" Becky said from the foot of the staircase, immediately putting Tiger to the side. "But what is it?"

Even Mrs. Hollis came from the parlor. Doctor Hollis took a knife from the dresser and cut the string. "That's for you to find out, don't you think?"

She tore into the paper with such joy that Jewel did not have the heart to instruct her to save it for future use, as she would have in leaner days.

"Oh, happy, happy, happy!" her daughter cried at the dozen children's picture books.

There was a brief letter inside.

Dear Mrs. Libby,

After my return to London, I realized my publisher, Macmillan's, also publishes children's books. I pray you do not mind my taking the liberty of asking them to send Becky an assortment. I hope you and Becky are well.

With highest regards,
Gabriel Patterson

"They're from Mr. Patterson, mite," Jewel said.

"Oh, I like Mr. Patterson!" Becky piped, picking up book after book.

Mrs. Hollis smiled. "He'll never give up, will he?"

"Give up what?" Doctor Hollis asked.

"Well, trying to impress Aleda."

"I don't think that's his reason," Doctor Hollis said.

Whatever he meant, whatever the reason, the happiness in her daughter's face prompted Jewel to write a note to Mr. Patterson that night, thanking him.

And she could not wait to tell Miss Hollis of his kindness. She was still praying for that miracle.

Chapter 29

On Monday morning a week later, Jewel passed through the parlor with her basket of cleaning soaps and rags, to happen upon Mrs. Hollis and Becky seated together upon the sofa. Still in dressing gown, Mrs. Hollis read from a book of nursery rhymes while Becky held Tiger in her lap.

"Solomon Grundy,
Born on a Monday,
Christened on Tuesday,
Married on Wednesday,
Took ill on Thursday,
Grew worse on Friday,
Died on Saturday,
Buried on Sunday.
That was the end of

Solomon Grundy!"

"What a morbid one!" Mrs. Hollis said with an exaggerated shiver, which made Becky giggle.

As any mother, Jewel was pleased with any proper attention shown to her child. "That's very kind of you, ma'am. But are you over your headache?"

She had lain up with one all day yesterday. Jewel had overheard her insist that Doctor Hollis go on to church and dinner with his family without her, saying Jewel could stay to bring up a tray. Which she did.

"I'm much better. I just feel like reading. She's such a bright little sprite." She waved a hand at Jewel. "Now, run along with you, so we may find some sunnier rhymes."

"I thought to pick some blackberries for tarts," Jewel said. "Perhaps I'll—"

"Oh, Mummy!" Becky exclaimed, torn.

"We'll wait till tomorrow," Jewel said. In a couple of hours she would have to prepare lunch, and then after Becky's nap they would be off to the manor house. Supper preparations and cleaning up would take over the remainder of the day.

"No, go with your mother," Mrs. Hollis said, nudging the cat from Becky's lap and helping her scoot forward on the sofa cushion. "We'll resume where we left off another time."

She was in the kitchen when Jewel came out of the pantry with the pail.

"I'm almost tempted to go with you."

"Please do, ma'am," Jewel said. "The woods are so peaceful."

"Perhaps some other time."

"If you change your mind, just follow the path to the left when it forks."

It was good to see her happy, Jewel thought as she led Becky up the dark, cool path. And yet her heart felt heavy. It was obvious her newfound happiness lay in Mr. Gibbs' daily visits.

From the evidence of tray and dishes left in the garden every afternoon, the two did not venture into the cottage. But for how long? And what of Doctor Hollis? She lived in the same cottage, and *knew* Mrs. Hollis had not informed him of these afternoon teas.

They filled their pail, or rather, Jewel filled the pail and Becky filled her stomach. On their walk home, she realized she had not reminded Mrs. Hollis that it was laundry delivery day. But Vernon Moore usually came later in the morning, when she was starting lunch preparations. And so she was not surprised when the canvas sack did not rest beside the umbrella stand.

"Let's brush your teeth before they stay that way," she said to Becky.

"Yours are purple, too, Mummy."

Jewel laughed. "So we both can use some grooming."

When they reentered the kitchen, Mrs. Hollis had come downstairs trailing perfume, her fair hair pinned up into ringlets, her slender figure draped in blue silk with ruffled bosom and waterfall bustle. She admired the bucket of blackberries, which pleased Becky.

"Shall we read some more while your mother prepares lunch?" she said.

Jewel thanked her, happy for the distraction, for Becky's eager help in the kitchen made it twice as difficult to cook.

Today's lunch would be salmon with caper sauce. She was beginning to enjoy experimenting with recipes as her confidence increased. It helped that Doctor Hollis usually took breakfast and lunch at the vicarage or at Doctor Rhodes', and that Mrs. Hollis wanted only tea for breakfast, sometimes with toast. She and Becky were content with cheese and fruit in the mornings, with the two regular meals coming later. They ate far better than they had in Birmingham. And there were no rats in the walls! God had answered her prayer, and then some.

As she dotted bits of butter onto the salmon in the pan, she could hear Mrs. Hollis's voice from the parlor, faint, but clear enough for the words to be recognizable.

> *"Mary, Mary, quite contrary,*
> *How does your garden grow?*
> *With silver bells, and cockle shells,*
> *And pretty maids all in a row."*

An unsettling thought struck Jewel. While Mrs. Hollis had always been kind to Becky, today's doting had almost a frantic feel about it. As if the hours lay so heavy that she felt pressured to fill them; the equivalent of pacing the floor. There could be only one reason: Mr. Gibbs would be calling again this afternoon. But why the agitation of nerves? What would be different?

Two worrisome answers rushed into her mind. Did they plan to run away together? That did not seem probable, with the squire on the verge of dying.

The other answer sent a shiver down her spine. Today would she not find the tray and cups in the garden chair? Would they bring indoors what appeared to be more than friendship?

While running away together would be the more drastic action, there was something more repulsive and even sinister about the latter.

You don't know this to be for certain. She prayed, *O God, please let me be wrong.*

But it did not seem that way, for when she and Becky went

downstairs after Becky's nap, Mrs. Hollis *was* actually pacing the kitchen.

"Ah, there you are. I was just about to come up for you. Best be on your way . . . the squire's waiting."

This could not happen. Jewel had to say something. She ushered Becky through the door.

"Wait for me by the chairs."

"What is it?" Mrs. Hollis asked as Jewel closed the door.

Jewel drew a fortifying breath, albeit a trembling one. "Mrs. Hollis, I'm more grateful for your kindness than you can know. But I feel I must say something."

"What is it?" Mrs. Hollis repeated.

"My Norman was a simple bricklayer. But he would have died for Becky and me. And actually he did, to give us food and a roof over our heads."

"I'm sorry, Jewel. But why are you saying this?"

"Because Doctor Hollis is a kind, decent man." Jewel swallowed. "Far better than Mr. Gibbs, who pretends to love his uncle but barely looks in on him."

Mrs. Hollis's lips thinned into a disapproving line.

"I know I'm speaking out of turn. But it's so hard to stand—"

"That will be quite enough," Mrs. Hollis said softly, but with tiny nostrils flaring. "You've been listening to servants' gossip."

"I saw it for myself. . . ."

"We each handle grief in different ways." She went to the door, opened it. "Mr. Gibbs is hardly one to confide in his staff. I suppose I should appreciate your concern, but I will thank you to keep your opinion to yourself. Now, go make your visit."

"What's wrong, Mummy?" Becky said as Jewel opened the gate.

"I just needed to remind Mrs. Hollis of something important," Jewel replied with a reassuring hand on her shoulder.

"Will we move to another house?"

"I don't think so, mite." If Mrs. Hollis were inclined to dismiss her, surely she would have done it on the spot.

As they were about to turn onto Bartley Lane, Jewel heard, "Yoo-hoo! Jewel!"

In the near distance, Mrs. Raleigh waved from the side of her garden, the younger children visible through the fence pickets.

"You're visiting the squire?" she asked when Jewel and Becky drew closer. "Would Becky care to play?"

"We're going to blow bubbles with hoops!" Claire enthused.

"Bubbles . . . hoops!" Samuel echoed.

Mrs. Raleigh motioned Jewel aside as the children chattered. "My parents stopped by on their way to see the squire. Doctor Rhodes said he could go any minute. It might not be good for her to be there."

"Oh dear. You're very thoughtful."

Mrs. Raleigh nodded. "Just drop her off every afternoon. It won't be that much longer. Anyway, she's good for Claire and Samuel. They're much calmer with an older child about, but I can't ask John to give up playing with his friends all the time."

Jewel thanked her and hurried up the carriage drive. As much as it had seemed to comfort the squire to see Becky, she was too young to be exposed to dying. Vicar and Mrs. Phelps were coming down the manor house steps, toward a horse and trap tied to a post. Mrs. Phelps embraced her, and the vicar took her hand.

"At last we meet, Mrs. Libby."

"How is your health?" she asked.

"I'm almost fully recovered. In fact, I preached yesterday while you were with Loretta. It was good of you to take care of her."

"The squire's still hanging on," Mrs. Phelps said. "I've never see such strength of will."

A lightning-quick glance passed between husband and wife. They bade her farewell and moved toward the trap, but then Mrs. Phelps turned.

"We wonder if we should look in on Loretta. We don't want her to think we don't care. Philip is working so Doctor Rhodes can be here, so we've not had the chance to ask if her headache is gone. But what do you think? Would now be a good time?"

"No, ma'am," Jewel said, and hoped not to be asked to explain. As much as she loathed lies, she feared she might slip into one. "This wouldn't be a good time."

They thanked her and moved on. As Jewel knocked at the door, she wondered if she had given the wrong answer. This could possibly be the best day to visit. Surely Mr. Gibbs was with the squire. Surely even *he* would not abandon an uncle hovering on the brink of death.

∞

"In Nottingham there lives a jolly tanner,
His name is Arthur-a-Bland,
There is never a squire in Nottinghamshire,
Dare bid bold Arthur stand."

Donald sang softly, pleased with himself. He had made plenty of mistakes in the past, but all for all, if cleverness was worth as much as gold, he would be as wealthy as Midas.

He was seriously considering theatre, once his life was

reestablished. His good looks and talent would go a long way, given the right contacts. Had Ambrose Clay known Uncle Thurmond? Perhaps the actor would be caught up in the wave of sympathy soon to flow his way and agree to write letters of introduction.

For his performance before Doctor Rhodes and Vicar and Mrs. Phelps had been nothing less than stageworthy. As the clock hands had neared the appointed time, he had put his increasing agitation to good use by kneeling by the old man's bed and weeping profusely into his hands.

"I've failed him in so many ways! I can't bear the shame! Vicar, pray tell me . . . is it too late? Can God ever forgive me?"

It was like dangling a worm before a carp. He had smiled into his hands at the touch upon his shoulder, the sound of the vicar's gentle voice.

"God will forgive anyone who truly seeks repentance, Mr. Gibbs. Why don't you go off to a quiet place and pour your heart out to Him?"

Wiping his eyes with his handkerchief, Donald had sniffed and said, in a touch of genius, "It has been my custom of late to walk among the trees, where I felt His presence so strongly as a young man."

And thus, his feet trod the path to the cottage.

Manufacturing tears had been easy. All he had had to do was think of Reese.

Reese!

He blinked as new tears threatened. Reese, who would come begging when Donald became the toast of England. The thought stretched his lips into a bitter smile. He would ignore Reese's pleas for forgiveness. For a while. Show the consequences of abandoning him. Ride around London in his uncle's coach. Flaunt his fortune.

But alas, his fingertips could not quite touch the money. Because of legal steps Mr. Baker must take, the will would not be executed for at least a fortnight into the old man's stay in the ground.

There was still the issue of the August mortgage payment, due in eleven days. Though he would have enough to take the house out of possible foreclosure when his hands closed about his inheritance, there was the chance some greedy investor would have snapped it up before then.

And thus, he must step up the hints to Mrs. Hollis, though she bored him to tears with her complaints about her marriage and having to spend one whole month in Gresham. Some people had genuine problems.

Just inside the gate she stood, stunning in a Wedgwood blue gown flowing from the waist with fluid movements. She usually waited in a chair, ofttimes reading, as if she had planned to be out in the garden anyway and was a little surprised that he happened by.

"Mr. Gibbs!"

The anxiety in her face unnerved him as he drew closer.

"Is something wrong, Mrs. Hollis?" Was her husband aware of their little meetings? Had Jewel gotten her revenge after all? Not that they had committed any mortal sins, but he had heard of husbands so jealous that a tipping of a hat could invite a thrashing.

"I must speak with you of something important. It kept me awake for hours last night."

"Pray, what is it?" he said, escorting her to a chair. "You're obviously in distress. What may I do to help you, dear lady?"

Her smile was a mixture of gratitude and relief. "And yet

your first thought is for me. My doubts over this decision have vanished."

Decision? Donald thought, holding his breath. "They have?"

She leaned forward earnestly. "Forgive my indelicacy for asking, but how much longer can your uncle last?"

"You must be psychic, Mrs. Hollis. As we speak, Doctor Rhodes and others keep watch over his last breaths. I am only here because, even in my grief, I could not bear the thought of your wondering if"—he allowed himself a bashful shifting of his eyes away from hers—"if I had lost interest in our friendship."

"Dear Mr. Gibbs! I would never think such!"

His eyes met hers again.

Her face was positively glowing.

She held up her palms. "Please hear me out. You mentioned your fear of not being able to meet your next mortgage payment."

He gave her a pained look. "Did I? Inexcusable! I was in dire straits, talking out of my head. No doubt you thought I was dropping hints."

"You're too honorable for that."

He willed a blush to his cheeks. *Could the mighty Mr. Clay do this?*

"I'll ask Father to lend me the money. He never refuses me anything, as if to make up for siding with my sister. How much is your payment?"

"Your friendship is more valuable to me than money," Donald replied. "I fear I would be trading one for the other. It may be that I can buy back the house once it's foreclosed."

He got to his feet. "And, kind lady, I must return to my uncle."

She rose, as well. "Friends bear each other's burdens, Mr. Gibbs."

"Fifteen pounds," he finally said, shoulders rising and falling with a theatrical sigh. It was more than the actual mortgage, but his purse missed the feel of crisp pound notes.

"Now, was that so hard?" She smiled. "I'll telegraph my father and ask him to send a cheque at once."

Already his wisdom in requesting extra money was becoming evident.

"Dear Mrs. Hollis! Words cannot express what a difference you've made in my life!"

Impulsively, theatrically, even gratefully, he took her into his arms and held her, murmuring into her hair how he would do anything for her if she ever found herself in need of help.

At the sound of a twig snapping, he jumped back as if she were on fire. Both heads turned toward the gate. Not a soul. Donald drew closer, noticed a canvas sack propped against the fence.

"What is this?"

"Oh dear." Mrs. Hollis rushed over and began wringing her slender hands. "The boy who delivers laundry. He had to have seen us! Philip said this village thrives upon gossip."

"But we've always been aboveboard." Fatigued by all the emotion of the day, Donald wished very much to go back to the manor house and smoke a cigarette. "I was distraught over my uncle, and you were comforting me."

"Yes, perhaps." She bit her lip, gave him a worried look. "If we end up divorcing, Philip could use even a rumor of . . . adultery . . . to his advantage."

"Ah." Donald nodded understanding. "Then I should stay away. Just in case."

She was shaking her head, eyes filling. He put a finger

beneath her chin and said softly, "Remember London? Where we shall both end up very soon? I will look forward to renewing our friendship . . . Loretta."

She sniffed and smiled up at him. "Yes, of course. You're right. I'll have Jewel deliver the cheque to you when it . . ."

She frowned.

"What is it?"

"I'll have to send it another way. Jewel . . . Jewel's not so fond of you. She warned me that we shouldn't be friends."

Donald chuckled. "Indeed? And did she say why I dismissed her?"

"No."

"A small thing. Becky stole something valuable, but Jewel practically accused me of hiding it in her trunk for an excuse to dismiss her."

"That doesn't sound like Becky. Or Jewel."

"No doubt Becky only meant to play with it for a while and forgot to return it. Young children are prone to plunder. But Jewel took offense. I've forgiven her for that. Why don't you put the cheque in an envelope addressed to Mrs. Cooper? I'll ask her to keep a watch for it, and Jewel won't know what she's delivering."

"Yes, I'll do that."

He touched her cheek. "Is that all?"

She smiled. "I'll do that . . . *Donald.*"

Whistling a jolly ditty below his breath, Donald tramped the path through the woods. His house was saved, and he no longer had to work for it.

Chapter 30

The squire lay with hands folded upon his sunken chest, face as white as his pillow, blank eyes half open. Doctor Rhodes sat on the opposite side of the bed, as if to make room for callers paying their respects.

"May I?" Jewel asked.

The doctor nodded.

She leaned to press a kiss upon the dying man's forehead. His eyes never moved.

"Is he suffering?"

"He has no apparent birthing pains. I've given him some laudanum to be sure."

"Birthing pains?"

The doctor smiled tenderly. "I have sat by many bedsides, and have felt the difference in the room when a soul leaves it. My friend is being birthed into another world."

Jewel sat in one of a pair of chairs on the side of the bed nearest the door.

Mr. Toft stepped inside. They traded grim nods. He advanced to pat the squire's frail shoulder. Wiping his eyes, he asked Doctor Rhodes, "And where is Mr. Gibbs?"

"Off praying for his soul," the doctor replied in a voice tinged with doubt.

But Jewel hoped it was so.

After Mr. Toft left, Jewel nodded toward the copy of *Around the World in Eighty Days* on the bedside table. "We've but two chapters remaining."

"Vicar Phelps read Scripture," the doctor said, "and his eyes never blinked. He has no knowledge of anything going on in this room."

"How can you be sure?"

Doctor Rhodes nodded wearily. "Very well."

She took up the novel, opened it to the Pears soap wrapper that served as bookmark.

" 'It is time to relate what a change took place in English public opinion when it transpired that the real bank robber, a certain James Strand, had been arrested on the 17th of December. . . .' "

Servants stepped in for reports, to touch his hand. Jewel hardly noticed them. The squire had never said an intelligible word to her, yet in her mind she felt his companionship as they traveled through the story.

She was midway through the final chapter when Mr. Gibbs entered.

"Mrs. Cooper is sending up tea."

"Thank you," Doctor Rhodes said.

Mr. Gibbs seemed composed, serene, if indeed he had spent

the afternoon praying. He folded his long limbs into the chair beside Jewel's.

"How is he?"

The doctor rose, put stethoscope into his ears, and listened to the sunken chest. "Growing weaker."

Poised to read another paragraph, Jewel glanced at the brass clock atop the squire's chest of drawers. Four o'clock. She should have left a half hour ago.

"I shall have to finish tomorrow," she said with great reluctance.

"Very well, Mrs. Libby." The look in Doctor Rhodes' aged eyes said she would not have that opportunity.

She had hoped he would offer to read, but he was so obviously weary. She set the book back upon the table and touched the squire's hand. As she turned for the door, she happened to glance to the side. Out of the doctor's line of vision, Mr. Gibbs' long fingers drummed upon his knee, as if he were a schoolboy sitting through a boring lecture.

She realized two things in that moment. That he cared even less for his uncle than she had thought. And that she had no reason to fear him. She picked up the book again, carried it to him.

"Mr. Gibbs, please finish this for him," she said in a tone that begged no refusal. He *owed* it to the dying man. And even to her.

His mouth twitched as if to refuse, but then he shrugged. "Very well. Show me where you left off."

She pointed out the paragraph and left the room with the sound of his voice behind her.

" 'Phileas Fogg had, without suspecting it, gained one day on his journey. . . .' "

Becky skipped by her side, chirping over the fun she had had with the Raleigh twins. The laundry bag sat inside, a reminder that life goes on. She would be ironing tomorrow, no matter who passed on.

Mrs. Hollis was apparently napping.

"I must cook quickly," Jewel said to Becky. "And I don't need any help today. Play quietly."

She chopped lettuce for salad, brushed four lamb cutlets with egg and dipped them in breadcrumbs, as Mrs. Beeton's book advised, and put turnips into a pot to boil.

At the sound of footsteps on the staircase, she automatically glanced over her shoulder. Mrs. Hollis was descending, her blue gown appearing to have been slept in, her ringlets crushed on one side.

"You're back."

"Yes, ma'am." Jewel scooped a chunk of clarified butter into the skillet for browning the cutlets.

Mrs. Hollis came into the kitchen. "That young man who delivers the laundry . . ."

"Vernon Moore." Jewel struck a match, lit the burner.

"Doesn't he usually deliver in the morning?"

Jewel realized the reason for the question. She turned and saw the worry in her eyes. "I meant to mention that he was late."

"You should have."

Jewel's blood chilled.

But there was a meal to finish.

As the evening wore on, Mrs. Hollis became increasingly restless, even more so than that morning. There was blessed relief when she went upstairs. Jewel was clearing away hers and Becky's dishes when Mrs. Hollis came back downstairs in a simple dress of faded rose muslin, her hair repaired.

"The peas and salad will keep," Jewel said. "But if I hold

the lamb cutlets any longer, they'll dry. Wouldn't you care to take your supper now?"

Staring yet again through the kitchen window, she waved a hand and said, "No, no, I'm not hungry. Just put them on a platter. You can warm them later for Doctor Hollis. Or perhaps he took supper at the vicarage?"

"Probably so."

Mrs. Hollis turned from the window, eyes wide. "But surely he would have sent word, don't you think?"

"But perhaps he was called to the manor house? Doctor Rhodes was fatigued."

She snapped up that hope like a frog would a moth. "Of course."

That was the case. Doctor Hollis arrived, full of apologies, after Jewel had put Becky to bed. Mrs. Hollis helped him out of his coat, something Jewel had never witnessed. He seemed surprised, and even more so when she said, "I was worried."

"I should have sent word." He loosened his collar. "But it did seem unkind to send one of his servants out when . . ."

He glanced toward the parlor.

"Becky's asleep," Jewel assured him. "He's gone?"

"I'm sorry, Jewel."

"He's in a better place. I wish I had had the chance to meet him before his illness. He must have been a sweet tender man."

Doctor Hollis smiled. "Let's just say he was a diamond in the rough. It was kind of you to visit so often."

He looked toward the platter and pots sitting upon the stove. "And I'm sorry, but they brought up a tray."

"It's all right, sir." She would clear the things away later. It seemed best to go upstairs and allow the two time to sort out the day.

On her way up the staircase, she heard Mrs. Hollis say, "Mr. Gibbs, the squire's nephew, came here earlier, quite distraught, asking if Jewel would hurry over there. Of course I gave permission. He was overwhelmed with gratitude. He hardly seemed to know what he was doing!"

He knew, all right, Jewel thought on the landing. And Mrs. Hollis was a foolish woman. But if today's fright had caused her to realize what she stood to lose, perhaps some good would have come of it after all.

She would pray for them tonight. And she would thank God for giving her an appreciation for Norman for the few years she had him. That none of her memories were tainted by guilt.

"Are you all right?" Philip asked. They sat at the dining table, he holding a beaker of water, she mashing butter into a bowl of turnips.

She chewed, swallowed contentedly as if dining on cheesecake at the Berkeley Hotel. "I'm fine. But when you didn't come home . . ."

"You were worried?"

"Terribly." She licked a stray bit of turnip from her finger.

That reply would have sent him to his knees just days ago. But it rang flat in his ears. But why would she even say it if she did not mean it? She had never been generous with compliments, even in the best days of their marriage.

They had danced around each other for over a week. But now that she had broached the subject of their marriage—in a way—perhaps this was the best time to ask what he had wondered for days.

"Did you write to your mother, Loretta?"

"No. Or rather, I did, but I tore it up."

"Why?"

"Because I agreed to a month. It's not right to back out."

His hope dissipated, like ether in air. But why was he surprised? She had said that it was over.

So what kept him there in the cottage with her? Besides the desire to spare his family from humiliation, he supposed it was inertia. Just as after investing the time and trouble to see a play that was not as good as expected, it was easier to sit in the theatre and hope it improved than to get up and walk out.

Chapter 31

Black-garbed cheese factory workers, farmers, and shopkeepers entered Saint Jude's beneath tolling bells. Through the gap between two servants on the second pew, Loretta watched the back of Mr. Gibbs' dark head.

He sat alone, the last of his family. How she longed to provide some support and comfort, if only by assuring him that any day now the cheque would arrive that would save his house.

Vicar Phelps conducted the sermon. A woman who Philip whispered was Grace's mother-in-law sang "Abide With Me" in a sweet clear voice.

After the burial everyone trooped over to the manor house. Past the foyer, Loretta could see tables set up in an oak-paneled hall already jam-packed with humanity. Donald stood to the right, wearing a black armband. He shook hands with those entering, expressing gratitude for their condolences.

With Philip at her side, she slipped her gloved hand into his and said in sympathetic tone, "Do you remember me, Mr. Gibbs? Mrs. Hollis. You came by asking for Jewel the day . . ."

He smiled sadly at the two of them. "You must have thought me a wild man, madam. I owe you a debt of gratitude for helping me clear my thoughts."

Even when Donald's greeting duty was finished, she could not speak with him privately. Philip was always nearby, or members of his family. Only Aleda was not present, though she had attended the funeral. Jewel and Becky had disappeared afterwards, too, which surprised her, given their affection for the squire.

Finally, opportunity presented itself for her to speak with Donald. An older man who introduced himself as the late squire's solicitor, a Mr. Baker, asked Philip if he was owed any fee. As the two men conversed, she noticed a white-haired woman offering Donald a slice of cake at the end of a long table.

She threaded her way through the crowd and was halfway there when Vicar Phelps turned from chatting with a farmer-type man. Speaking over the chatter filling the hall, he said, "I'm glad you've recovered from your headache, Loretta."

"Thank you." She returned his smile while attempting to edge by.

His brow furrowed in thought. "You know, Mrs. Phelps once had a lodger who used feverfew. It's an herb, in case you're not familiar with it."

"I didn't have fever," she said as the corner of her eye watched Donald shake his head politely at the woman with the cake.

Vicar Phelps chuckled. "For headaches. It grows at the foot of the Anwyl. I should be happy to collect you some, now that I'm out and about."

Over his shoulder, she saw Philip and Mr. Baker part, and Philip move over to Jeremiah Toft and his wife.

"Thank you," Loretta said. Now, how to rid herself of her father-in-law?

"You should get some food before it's all gone," he said with a step backwards, still smiling, as if he had read her mind and had not taken offense.

"Thank you," she repeated, and resumed her mission. Donald was on the other side of the table now, moving in the opposite direction. She watched him draw aside Mr. Baker. They spoke briefly and exited the hall into some inner part of the house. When Mr. Baker returned, he was alone.

Dare she slip away and look for him? She could use the excuse of seeking a water closet.

But then Elizabeth Raleigh appeared out of nowhere. Loretta's dutiful inquiry as to her health prompted a low-voiced description of morning sickness that made her wonder why anybody bothered to have children.

As Elizabeth prattled happily about how huge she had gotten while carrying the twins, Loretta's mind traveled back to the embrace in the garden. She could feel Donald's strong arms around her. *"London,"* he had said, affirming that they would resume their friendship in a more favorable clime. If only time would speed ahead.

⸜∞⸝

When no cheque had arrived by Tuesday, worry robbed Loretta of sleep. Had the telegram actually reached her father? How tragic it would be for Donald to lose his house over a simple kink in the line. What would he think of her?

Wednesday morning, she dressed in her amethyst-and-gray silk gown and pinned on a straw hat.

"Good morning, Mrs. Hollis," Jewel said from the stove.

"Good morning. Don't cook breakfast for me. Perhaps an early lunch. I want to get my hat from that dreadful millinery woman."

"If you'll wait until Becky takes her nap, I'll go for you."

"No, thank you. A walk will be lovely. It seems a bit cooler outside."

The twins were in the Raleighs' garden, too engrossed in blowing bubbles to pay her any mind. Still, she walked quickly, lest Elizabeth come outdoors and pounce upon her with more pregnancy details.

She hoped to have children herself one day. She enjoyed Becky's winsome presence in the cottage. She adored, in a bittersweet sort of way, Conrad and Irene's fair-headed two-year-old son, Stephen. But with a future so uncertain, it was fortunate that it had never happened.

Lately, it would have been a miracle if it had.

"I smell rain in the air!" an elderly woman called from a cottage garden.

Loretta looked up through elm branches at the few benign white clouds, and wished her good day.

The woman behind the counter had yet to look up from her magazine.

Donald cleared his throat. "Miss Perkins?"

She jerked her head up, slapped the magazine shut, and squeaked, "Mr. Gibbs!"

"You mentioned that you sell men's hats?"

"Why, yes."

"I'd like to have a look at your wares."

She giggled, lashes batting as if hinged at the lids. "But of course."

She hastened around the counter, took his arm, and almost pulled him to a dressing table. While he sat on a stool before an oval mirror, she pressed assorted sizes of silk top hats, felt bowlers, and straw boaters onto his head, leaning to peer into the mirror over his shoulder so that her ample cleavage was shown to best advantage.

Donald smiled at their reflections, sick to his stomach. After the funeral, Mr. Baker had asserted that not one drop of money would be available until the will was read. That he may not even sell one silver fork, one painting, or one horse to save his house, without facing charges of thievery.

He believed in his charms, and had patiently waited for Loretta Hollis's cheque to arrive from her father. But only two days remained until the mortgage was due. He had paced a trail in his bedchamber carpet. Time for another plan.

Thus he sat allowing Miss Perkins to press her bosom into his back. Owning her own shop meant she had money.

"Sorry, won't do at all," he said, lifting a silk hat from his head and adding it to the stack upon the dressing table. Some had edged to fall to the carpet, only to be ignored. He swiveled around to face her. "I shall have to go elsewhere."

Her lips formed a pout. "There's no elsewhere but Shrewsbury. Why would you want to go to all that trouble when my hats are just as good?"

Minus those on the floor, he thought. He glanced toward the curtain behind the counter. "Perhaps you have more in the back?"

"They're all out here."

"Not even one?"

Her shoulders rose and fell with her sigh. "I'm afraid not."

Take a hint, you stupid twit. He arched his eyebrows at her.

"Perhaps you've overlooked one in some dark corner? I could help you look."

Understanding flooded her eyes. A smile curled her full lips. She squeaked, "That would be very kind, sir."

"Has the mail been sent out?" Loretta asked Mr. Sanders in the post office side of Trumbles.

"An hour ago," he said, tinkering with a stamp machine. "I sort the incoming in the afternoons, and it goes out mornings."

"Do you recall anything for Mrs. Philip Hollis?"

He chewed a lip thoughtfully. "I'm fairly sure there was nothing."

"Could it be that the telegram I sent to London last week was misdirected?"

"Sometimes problems do happen. But most times we know."

"It may have been sent to the wrong address," Mr. Trumble called from his side. "London's a big metric-polis."

At her insistence, Mr. Sanders tapped out a new message: *Please send fifteen pounds at once. Loretta.*

The *at once* was the only new addition to the message of nine days ago. But even so, would the cheque arrive in time? Mail from London took three days.

If only she had thought to bring along some money from the household account. She had directed packing in a daze: clothes, toiletries, and jewelry.

A bell tinkled and two women entered just as a thought struck her.

Jewelry.

In particular, her pearls, hidden away with her jewelry

pouch . . . just in case—after Donald had warned her that Becky liked to plunder.

She loitered before a rack of sewing notions, though she had never taken a stitch in her life. The women completed their purchases and launched into a maddening debate with Mr. Trumble over whether rain was indeed coming.

"How would you know?" one teased him. "Stuck indoors as you are."

Mr. Trumble patted his shoulder. "My rheumatism knows. Care to make a wager?"

The two left the shop in giggles.

Loretta approached the counter with a brass thimble. At least Becky could spin it on her finger. She said, casually, "Are there not places where you may borrow money against valuables? Such as jewelry?"

"Why yes. But not here. In Shrewsbury. They're called 'pawn lenders.' "

"Will they return the valuable when you repay the loan?"

"Certainly. But at a barrelful of interest."

"Then, it's safe to deal with them?"

"Yes, I think. There are laws they're bound to, just as this place. Mr. Stillman of the Larkspur . . . he goes down there on the look for military medals and war memo-randums."

There was still time. She had only to get her pearl necklace to Donald, to pawn in Shrewsbury. If Jewel balked at delivering it, she would take it herself.

She thanked the shopkeeper and scooped up the thimble. The pair who had spent so much time at the counter chatted outside the shop clutching paper bags. One said to the other, "She may be snooty, but you've promised Amelia a bonnet for her birthday. Will you disappoint her?"

My hat, Loretta thought. Not wishing to wait yet again behind the two, she dashed around them.

"Pardon me, ladies."

She swung open the door, but did have the courtesy to hold it open for them, now that it was established that she was first. The curtains behind the counter parted and Priscilla came through. She gaped at Loretta and the women, turned to close the curtain shut, and half squealed, half giggled, "Not yet, Donald!"

Fear and outrage propelled Loretta across the shop and around the counter.

"See here now!" Priscilla cried as Loretta yanked aside the curtain.

Donald Gibbs stood on the other side, looking disheveled but not dismayed. "Sorry, Loretta."

"Out!" Priscilla shrieked, tugging at Loretta's arm.

Loretta jerked away, consumed by rage. "I was going to pawn my necklace! I would have left my husband for you!"

It was only then that she remembered the women. She looked over her shoulder. Their eyes were wide, as if to absorb as much of the scene as possible.

"And I appreciate it," Donald was saying. When she faced him again, he smiled and patted his coat pocket. "But that won't be necessary."

Chapter 32

Loretta's feet could not move swiftly enough. She would have gathered her skirts and sprinted if her upbringing would have loosened some constraints. It seemed every schoolyard child ceased chasing and spinning to stare, every cottage gardener ceased clipping and digging to gape. Even the *good morning*s chirped her way did not fool her. They knew her shame! It was written on her face!

But it was nothing compared to the picture in her mind of Philip hearing the news. She had given him every reason to think the worst.

Elizabeth stood at her letter box and turned to smile. "Why, good morning, Loretta."

Loretta ignored her.

"Loretta?" she heard from behind.

On the path, she did kirtle her skirts and run. Pounding

the dirt made her teeth stop chattering. If only she could run and run and run, to a place where no one knew her. Or better yet, run back to the past and take the place of the Loretta of one month ago.

Savory aromas met her inside the cottage, but did not whet her appetite. Jewel ceased polishing a lamp to give her a worried look.

"Mrs. Hollis? What is it?"

Becky, stacking blocks with Tiger dozing nearby, looked up.

"Nothing!" The hem of Loretta's gown toppled blocks and sent the cat dashing away as her foot hit the first step. Upstairs, she threw herself across her bed. The teeth-chattering returned with a vengeance. She lay on her side, curled up into a sorry ball of humanity. Her left palm ached. She opened it, realized she had clutched the thimble until it made an impression into her flesh.

And she had forgotten her hat.

If it ever came back into her possession, she would stomp on it. It had been the source of her woes. If only she had never stumbled into Donald Gibbs.

A soft knock sounded as she wept into her pillow. "Mrs. Hollis?"

"Go away," she rasped.

But the door opened, and Jewel stuck her head around it. "May I not bring you some lamb stew, ma'am? Some tea?"

Loretta sniffed. "Can you bring me my life back? You'll be pleased to know you were right about Donald Gibbs."

"It doesn't please me at all." Jewel entered the room, went over to the chest of drawers, and brought out a folded handkerchief.

Loretta snatched it from her and blew her nose. "Now leave me alone."

"I'll answer that, Wanetta," Julia called, coming out of the water closet after washing garden soil from her hands. They felt damp, even though she had dried them. She wiped them upon her skirt, just in case a hand should be thrust at her.

She could only hope this visitor would not be one of the more chatty villagers. Dora and Wanetta were laying the cloth for lunch, and Philip would be there any minute.

Swinging open the door, her heart sank. Mrs. Hopper of Milkwort Lane stood there, her expression a mingling of pity and, oddly, excitement.

"I must speak with you and the vicar at once."

"I'm afraid he's unavailable, Mrs. Hopper." Of truth, Andrew was upstairs with Aleda, reading her latest serialization. But she had the right to determine what *unavailable* meant in her own home.

"Well, my sister-in-law, Maida, and I witnessed a terrible row between Mr. Gibbs and your daughter-in-law. I recognized her from church, with the blond hair."

After hearing the story, followed by Mrs. Hopper's lament that the younger generation had life too easy and thus were lacking in morals, Julia thanked her for coming.

Eagerness quivering her cheeks, the woman said, "What will you do, Mrs. Phelps?"

"My family will tend to the matter. You should hurry. I see some dark clouds on the horizon."

There was no use in asking Mrs. Hopper to keep this to herself. Like a wave, the news had probably swept through Gresham by now.

Upstairs, Andrew groaned into his hands over the news.

Aleda slapped her desk with a loud *whump*. "That hussy!"

Julia had thought to tell her husband in private, but Aleda would hear it the first time she connected with anyone outside the vicarage anyway.

"We can't keep this from Philip," Andrew said.

"No, we can't," Julia agreed. This was Gresham. From downstairs, she heard the door open and close.

⟡

Jewel was clearing dishes from the table when Philip entered.

"Doctor Hollis!" she exclaimed.

"Don't worry," he assured her. "I took my lunch at the vicarage."

"It isn't that." She glanced upstairs. "It's Mrs. Hollis. She's in a bad way."

Philip nodded. Becky was smiling up at him, as if hoping for his attention. Even in his tormented state, he stretched out a listless arm to ruffle her red curls.

"Will you take Becky out to the garden?"

"Yes, sir."

Loretta lay curled upon the coverlet, half of her crimson-splotched face pressed into her pillow. He felt a surge of pity for her. It was good that he had heard the news some distance away. Most of the anger had worked out of his system during the walk over. Replaced by a startling awareness.

He stepped over to sit on the side of the bed. She curled her elbow beneath her head to blink up at him through slits.

"Loretta."

She coughed, wiped her nose with a sodden handkerchief. Having spent so little time in her bedchamber, he had no idea where she kept others, so he took his from his pocket.

She blew her nose again and croaked, "I'm so sorry, Philip. Can you forgive me?"

He hesitated. It would be easier when the wound was not so fresh. "Why does it matter?"

"It matters."

"I believe I'll be able to, one day. But our marriage is over. That should make you happy."

"But we didn't do anything!" she blubbered. "He only embraced me once, and only because . . . I offered to lend him some money."

"Then why the scene in the shop, Loretta?"

Dully, she said, "I was flattered by his attention. But when I realized he was only using me . . ."

"There'll only be someone else after Mr. Gibbs."

Anger suffused through the misery in her face. "Philip . . . I'm not that sort of woman."

"You were that sort of girl, Loretta."

She gaped at him. "I beg your pardon?"

He sighed. "Your parents denied you nothing, so you never learned how to accept loss and move on. When Conrad left, you couldn't cope. You threw your hopes into me, that I could be a substitute. If I hadn't been available, it would have been someone else."

"That's not so."

"I've seen the way you've looked at him, a hundred times. When I couldn't make you forget Conrad, you had to start looking elsewhere. My parents say love should be built upon a foundation of friendship. That takes time. Yet you decided you loved me, and then I suppose Mr. Gibbs, within days."

She opened her mouth as if gasping for air, as if about to protest, when she burst into fresh tears and scrubbed at her temples with her fists. "I can't stop thinking of Conrad! It's as if he lives in my mind. You don't understand!"

"No, I don't," he admitted. "Can you not *will* yourself to stop?"

"Don't you think I've tried?" She lowered her head again to the crook of her arm, blinking dully, sniffing. "At times, he wasn't even that pleasant. He once called me an idiot. The stronger his criticisms, the more I adored him. Irene's marriage isn't as happy as she lets on. I've seen the way he speaks to her when he's in ill temper."

Philip cast about in his mind for what next to say. If only he had asked his parents' counsel when they broke the news in the parlor. The mental image of the scene brought another picture into his mind. He rested a hand upon her arm.

"Did you notice the small watercolor of Saint Jude's in my parents' parlor, Loretta?"

Her head shook, slightly.

"It was painted by a boy with a severe clubfoot. He'll never be able to play the typical boyhood games. Yet he doesn't sit around grieving over what he can't have. He's fastened his attention upon his art."

After several seconds, she said, "I don't understand."

"Perhaps by *willing* yourself to forget Conrad—as I just foolishly suggested—you must still concentrate on him. But if you fill your mind with the good things you do have, until it becomes a habit, Conrad would eventually be forced out."

"Forced out," she murmured.

"Perhaps not all at once. It would probably be gradual. Like leakage."

Another second passed. She coughed a small laugh. "Leaked out?"

"Through your ears, I would suppose. The nose would be disgusting, and you've taxed it enough today anyway."

This time her shoulders shook with her laugh. She wiped her eyes.

"I've never said how much I appreciate your sense of humor."

He patted her arm.

"Is our marriage really over?" she asked.

"Isn't that what you want?"

"No." She shook her head. "Will you not give me a chance to outgrow that willful child you so aptly described?"

He longed to take her in his arms, say how much he loved her. But the wounds were too deep to simply pour salve over and declare them healed. He needed to see evidence that she was over Conrad. That she loved *him*, before risking more pain.

"We'll talk later." He got to his feet, said gently, "I have a baby's cleft lip to repair."

She looked stricken. "A baby's?"

"A girl." Gently he said, "We're not the only people with problems, Loretta."

He could hear her swallow.

"I know you'll do your best for her, Philip."

"I'll try."

"Will you . . . come back this evening?"

"Of course." That had not been his intention, but intentions were to be servants, not masters. While staying at the vicarage would be the wisest course, it would increase the humiliation she had suffered. Yes, she had brought it upon herself, but she was still his wife.

⁂

Though the bath water had grown tepid, his fingers were

prunes, and his skin stung from heavy-handed scrubbings with the cloth, Donald could not get clean.

But he must not miss the express to London. He should have instructed the servants to pack his things before making a beeline to the water closet.

Tomorrow would not be too late. But he had spent enough time in this prison. How good it would feel to spend the night in his own house again.

He pulled the stopper chain and stood, reached for a large towel and dried himself. Mr. Baker would by law be required to inform him when the will was to be read. And Priscilla Perkins had been most generous, reaching into a lockbox and coming out with fifteen pounds.

He could hear her squeaking voice in his mind. *My parents won't miss it if you repay me next week.*

Next week, three weeks, perhaps yes, perhaps no.

Swathed in his wrapper, padding up the corridor, he barked to Mary, the first servant to cross his path, "After I'm dressed, I shall need you to pack my things."

"Yes, sir. For how many days?"

"Pack it all. Everything."

When he walked out of his bedchamber wearing his finest pinstripe suit, Mrs. Cooper was waiting in the landing. Clearly, Mary had gotten to her.

"You're leaving, Mr. Gibbs?"

Try not to look so broken up, he thought. "When my trunk is ready, have the carriage and a driver sent around."

"But it's Jeremiah's afternoon off."

"Then put Osborn to it. He drives wagons. How difficult can it be to drive a carriage?"

"Yes, sir." She hesitated.

"Well?"

"The sky is growing somewhat dark. If you're going to Shrewsbury, perhaps the coach would—"

"Yes, yes." He could see her logic. And besides, there could be an angry husband out there. Not so wise, riding through Gresham in an open carriage.

❧

Mrs. Hollis drifted downstairs, still looking a wreck.

"I've kept the stew warm," Jewel said, and pulled out a chair.

"Thank you." She held up an amber bottle. "But have we any more salicin?"

"You have a headache?"

She rubbed her temple. "A genuine one this time. There was only about a teaspoon left. It'll wear off in an hour."

Becky, only recently awake from her nap, stared at her splotched skin and pillow-matted hair.

"Am I not a beauty?" Mrs. Hollis said.

"No, ma'am," Becky said with childish honesty.

"Pick up your toys in the parlor, mite," Jewel said, and to Mrs. Hollis, "Why don't you have some food, and I'll look for some salicin."

Listlessly, Mrs. Hollis picked up her fork. She looked up at Jewel. "I never did anything immoral with Mr. Gibbs."

"Yes, ma'am." It was none of her business anyway, as she had been so told.

Some skepticism must have shown upon her face, for Mrs. Hollis said, "Yes, meeting him in secret was wrong. But he never came inside except to make tea."

"Yes, ma'am."

"You don't believe me?"

"Begging your pardon, but why would it matter?"

"It just does." Mrs. Hollis gave her a pained smile. "You're the closest friend I have in Gresham."

She seemed invited to voice her opinion, so she would do so. "It shouldn't be that way, ma'am."

Mrs. Hollis sighed. "Yes."

Jewel left her to her lunch, and searched the cottage. When she returned to the kitchen, Mrs. Hollis was pushing aside her plate. The bread was untouched, and more than half of the stew still remained.

"I'm too nauseous."

"I'll nip over to Trumbles. I'll have to leave Becky with you, or it'll take me twice as long. Let's put you in the garden. Maybe fresh air will help."

They stepped outdoors, Becky carrying her doll. Jewel noticed dark clouds hovering over the Anwyl. The sky overhead, while cloudless, had assumed a hue between blue and pewter. Still, there were no rumblings.

She helped Mrs. Hollis into a chair, and then turned another around so she could prop her feet. Leaning her head back, Mrs. Hollis looked up at the sky and said, "Perhaps you should wait and see . . ."

"I don't hear thunder. I'll hurry."

"Will you please buy peppermints?" Becky asked.

"Hmm. We shall see."

They traded smiles; Becky, because she understood what that meant, and Jewel from the enjoyment of having enough income to treat her daughter. She ran upstairs to fetch fivepence. She was meticulous about not charging personal items upon the Hollis account. On her way out, she took an umbrella from the stand.

"Take good care of Mrs. Hollis," she said.

"I will, Mummy."

Chapter 33

Jewel was not the only person trying to outrun the rain. Standing fourth in queue at Trumbles, she wrestled with herself over whether it would be rude to explain to the two customers just before her that she had but one purchase to make.

Two, she corrected herself. She would not return without Becky's peppermints, even if she got soaked.

But how could she know but that the two—a boy of about twelve, and a woman of forty or so—had any less to purchase? What she *did* know was that the elderly man at the counter appeared to be stocking up for winter.

"And some of thet Fry's Cocoa," he said.

"Sorry . . . I'm out of Fry's," Mr. Trumble said with an apologetic look toward his waiting customers. "They sent Suchard's this time."

"Is it any good?"

"See here on the box? It says *Nature's Choicest*."

"Well now, they ain't gonter write *Tastes Like*—"

"Cocoa is cocoa, Papa," Jack Sanders called from the post office side.

"What's the matter, ma'am?" Becky asked in the garden.

Loretta opened one eye and stared into the girl's worried face. She did not realize she had groaned aloud. She rubbed her temple. "My head feels like nails are sticking through it."

"May I bring you some milk?"

"No thank you."

Becky turned to look about the garden, as if seeking a remedy. "Would some berries make your head better?"

"I think not."

"They're very good."

She looked so hopeful that Loretta sighed and said, "Perhaps one or two. Mind you be careful, as your mother says."

As the boy made his purchases, the woman who had been in queue before him paused before Jewel with her parcels.

"You're Doctor Hollis's maid?"

"Yes, ma'am."

"Pity, what happened in the hat shop. We've known him for years, and he don't deserve a harpy such as—"

"Madam," Jewel said. "I'll thank you not to speak of my employers."

"Well, hoity-toity!" The bell jingled angrily over her exit.

Fortunately, the boy purchased only a tin of matches. But his eyes purchased and devoured the jar of Pomfret Cakes. His shirt sleeves were frayed, but most village children seemed to wear their worn clothes for romping, so that was no indicator. Still, he was a child.

Jewel stepped up to place a penny on the counter. "Please add some licorice to his order."

The boy gave her an incredulous grin as Mr. Trumble weighed out the black lozenges. "Thank you, miss."

"You're welcome." How refreshing, to be on the giving instead of receiving end.

Thank you, Father, again and again. She vowed that if she ever had the means, she would help those less fortunate in more substantial ways than sweets.

To his credit, Mr. Trumble did not mention whatever scene must have happened in the millinery shop. He dropped both salicin bottle and peppermint sticks into a small paper sack. "Mind you hurry home."

A brisk and damp breeze met her outdoors. The clouds had thickened, rolling in from the west, sending smaller ones scudding across a pewter sky. At the crossroads, a fat drop plopped onto the back of her hand. She was fiddling with the umbrella when her ears caught the sound of hooves clopping against the stones. Squire Bartley's coach rolled up Church Lane behind a team of horses, the driver wearing mackintosh and hood. He pushed it back to grin at her. Mr. Ramsey. She smiled and waved.

Her gaze slanted down toward the coach window, and caught sight of Mr. Gibbs. No one could mistake the dark mustache. Now that his poor uncle had passed, he had no reason to stay and pretend to care, meddle in marriages, and accuse children of stealing.

She cared nothing about the rain splatting against her umbrella. Her feet plodded along the wet stones, but her spirits danced. A low rumble sounded behind her, and she picked up the pace.

Something wet hit Loretta's forehead, then cheek. She opened her eyes just as a clap of thunder sounded. She pushed aside the other chair and hurried to her feet as more drops hit her.

"Becky?" Cobwebs crowded her mind, but she had enough presence to look over at the gooseberry bush. When the girl was not there, she scanned the garden, calling. Her doll lay on the seat of another chair, being pelted by rain. Loretta snatched it up and hurried into the cottage.

"Becky?" she called, closing the door as a rumble shook the sky.

She climbed the staircase. The garret room Becky and Jewel shared since the Hollises' arrival was empty. On her way back down she looked into hers and Philip's bedrooms.

Rain was drumming against the roof. She was starting to panic.

"BECKY?"

Water closet, she thought on her way downstairs. But the pantry was closer, and she could vaguely recall the child offering her some milk. She looked inside. Empty. She was turning when Tiger, mewing piteously, attempted to wrap herself about Loretta's legs. Losing her balance, Loretta caught the edge of the dresser with her hand. A tart pan clattered to the floor.

She recalled the blackberry tart Jewel had baked, just days ago.

Becky said berries! Not gooseberries!

But she would know better than to go into the woods alone.

She's four years old. She strews her toys. She's not perfect.

Holding her breath, Loretta looked back into the pantry. The pail was missing!

She had to get help. She'd go to Elizabeth.

But the rain's tempo increased upon the roof. Surely she had not slept long, or Jewel would have returned. Becky could not have gone far. She yanked her umbrella from the stand and plunged into the rain.

"BECKY!"

It seemed the sky grew darker by the minute. The curtain of rain blurred the cottages and gardens past the rim of Jewel's umbrella. Flowers bobbed, shrubs danced, and the branches of young trees swayed. Her boots were damp, and the back of her dress was plastered against her skin. It would be good to get to the cottage and shrug into her flannel wrapper, if only long enough to dry out before starting supper.

She was nearing Mr. and Mrs. Raleigh's cottage, and flinched when thunder roared across the sky like a cannon shot. Should she bang on the door and ask for shelter? They would give it warmly.

But this rain promised to set in for hours, perhaps all night. The thunder would frighten Becky. Mrs. Hollis needed her medicine.

Holding her umbrella with her left hand, she shoved the parcel down her collar with her right, then hitched up her sodden skirts to her knees. She did not worry about immodesty. She was the only person in Gresham foolish enough to be outdoors in this deluge.

⁓

"She's moving," Philip said softly. He had never used chloroform on such a tiny patient. Just four months old. But everything he had read in Doctor Rhodes' journals indicated that the sooner the surgery is performed, the less disfigurement the child suffers.

Even with stitches, little Amy was beautiful, with her father's wide, deeply lashed eyes, and evidence of her mother's fine bone structure.

He could only hope that these were not merely muscle twitches and spasms he was witnessing.

Five minutes later, the girl's lusty cries filled Doctor Rhodes' well-scrubbed surgery.

"Nothing the matter with her lungs," Doctor Rhodes said as the parents hurried in from the waiting room.

"She's angry, not hurt," Philip assured them. "I've injected her lip with a small amount of morphine."

On the other side of the examining table, Billy Casper put his arm around his wife's shoulders. Both sets of eyes shone, Phoebe's behind wire-rimmed spectacles. Hard to believe, Philip thought, that his former schoolfellow had been the bane of Phoebe's youth, with his teasing and tormenting.

"She's beautiful," Billy said as tears coursed down his cheeks.

"Yes," Phoebe said, weeping, as well. "But how will I feed her?"

"The same as always. It will be an adjustment, but I believe she's up to the task."

"May I feed her now?"

"Yes, of course."

Mrs. Rhodes, gray-haired and bent-shouldered, stepped through the doorway. "No one will disturb you in the parlor."

So intense was Philip's attention during the surgery that he had paid scant attention to the thunder clashes, the rain lashing against the windows, the extra lamps brought in. The darkness pressing against the glass surprised him.

But his patient was foremost in his mind. When mother and child had left for the parlor, he held out a jar for Billy's inspection. "You must rub this onto her lip four times daily. It contains carbolic acid for killing bacteria, morphine for the pain. In two weeks, we should be able to remove the stitches."

"And hold her as much as possible," Doctor Rhodes said. "It will actually help with the pain."

"As well as keep her fingers from straying toward her lip," Philip said.

Billy was beginning to look overwhelmed, so Philip said, "I'll write it all down, as well as stop in every day for the first week. But do remember what we said about holding her."

Phoebe's stepfather stepped in from the waiting room. If Billy was once the bane of Phoebe, Harold Sanders was once the disgrace of Gresham. But marriage to a widow with four children changed him into a pillar of the village, an outstanding dairyman, and tenor in Saint Jude's choir. His frame was still imposing, though the shock of straw-colored hair was dull with gray. The deep-lidded green eyes were red rimmed.

"You don't have to worry, Doctor," he said. "She will be held."

"You must all stay here until this weather clears," Mrs. Rhodes said, coming into the surgery again. "And if it doesn't, we have enough beds."

Philip went over to the window. Because of the lamps, all he could see was his reflection in a fluid sort of way. But the fury of the storm could be felt. It rattled the panes as if a creature were demanding to be let in. A loud clap of thunder startled him, and he took a backwards step.

"You can't go out into that, Philip," Doctor Rhodes said from behind.

He would have argued but for one thing. They were right. No one should be out in this storm.

The thunder was terrifying by the time Jewel turned from

Church Lane onto the path. *You should have waited at the Raleighs'. What good is a dead mother to Becky?*

She plodded on doggedly. The rain fell pitilessly. Through the torrent she caught sight of the picket fence. Home!

The gate banged open and shut, open and shut. Had she forgotten to latch it? But she pushed past, through the garden and the slick steps.

"Mummy!" Becky shrieked in the kitchen, throwing her small body against her. Her little face was almost as red as her hair, and she shivered as someone with a fever.

The umbrella rolled an arc on the floor where Jewel tossed it. She got on her knees and cradled her sobbing daughter.

"Sweetheart, the thunder can't hurt us in here," Jewel said over the wind howling down the chimney and rattling the windows. "Why didn't you go to Mrs. Hollis? Is she upstairs?"

When Becky was calm enough to speak, she held out her finger to show her a small gash. "I tried being careful. I wanted to bring her a treat."

"You mean you were picking gooseberries?"

"She said I may," Becky said with anxious expression.

Jewel squeezed her. "Sweetheart, it's all right."

"I didn't want to wake her."

"She fell asleep in the garden?"

"Yes, so I washed my hands in the water closet, but I couldn't reach the medicine Doctor Hollis showed us. So I got the berry-picking bucket to step on."

"Brave girl," Jewel said. But she was troubled. She could understand Mrs. Hollis falling asleep in the garden. Even a small dose of salicin could make one sleepy. Becky was not an infant who needed constant watching, and the thorn prick was not serious. But to then shut herself upstairs during a thunderstorm and leave the child downstairs in hysterics?

Perhaps her headache is much more severe, she thought. *Too painful to think clearly.* She should take the salicin and a beaker of water upstairs, before changing into dry clothes.

Another blast of thunder launched Becky into her arms again. Jewel held her until it was over, then kissed the top of her head. "Come with me. We shall see after Mrs. Hollis."

"She's not here," Becky said.

Terror pushed Loretta into hysteria. Hugging herself with her arms, she could not stop sobbing even to call out for Becky, though she was hoarse from doing so.

O Father, please help us. Where's Becky? I'm so sorry, so sorry, oh please, send Philip, oh please!

The tempest shrieked and wailed and howled like a thousand wild beasts, the water assaulting her face, her clothes, her eyes. It had whipped her umbrella from her hands. Barely could she see the trees swaying and rocking and snapping, lashing their branches.

Loretta had made it to the blackberry bushes, as evidenced by the stinging wounds across her palms and backs of her hands. Brambles had snagged her clothes as if trying to pull her in, and when she jerked and stumbled away, she lost sight of the path.

A branch whipped across her face. She found her voice again; one more scream in the storm.

Chapter 34

Though the sofa cushions lapped on either side of him like velvet waves, Philip slept fitfully with one ear out for a lull in the storm. He wore his tweed trousers and cloth shirt so that he could grab his shoes from the floor, his coat and umbrella from the Rhodes' hall tree, and be gone within seconds.

He was a lunatic for not allowing himself to give up and sink into sleep, he told himself. Yes, he had promised to return, but Loretta would understand, and in fact, was probably sound asleep. She could sleep through anything. Even if he was positive that she was awake, he would not tap upon her door. If they *were* to stay together, there was still much to sort out, mend or cast off, before resuming the physical element.

Not that there had been much of that after their first few months of marriage.

Still, he had hope. The first step to curing a disease was identifying it.

Sometime later, two gongs from the parlor clock pierced the fog in his mind. He sat upright, realizing he could only hear them because the storm had ceased.

His way was lit by only a low half-moon and handful of stars, between tattered remnants of clouds. But he knew these roads, could probably walk them blindfolded.

He took off his shoes and stockings at the entry to the dark path, and vised them under his arms. No sense in ruining them. He picked his way, and made a face as mud oozed through his toes. How the boyhood Philip would have laughed over his fussiness. Water dripped from trees. Passing around a silver birch, he noticed a light in the kitchen window.

The gesture touched and saddened him, for it was probably Jewel who had thought of it. He slogged along faster. As he crossed the garden, he shuffled along the grass to wipe off as much mud as possible, but he was still a mess. He ran around the cottage to clean his feet in the water closet.

Barefoot, carrying shoes and umbrella, he opened the parlor door. In the shadows made by the light coming in from the kitchen, he saw movement in a chair drawn up to the sofa.

"Doctor Hollis?"

Jewel's whisper. She rose, clad in nightgown and wrapper, her hair in disarray about her shoulders.

"Why are you—"

"Shh . . ." She touched his arm.

He looked down at the small blanket-covered form on the sofa. Just enough light revealed red hair. He followed Jewel into the kitchen and pulled out a chair at the table, quietly. Jewel stared at it, as if waiting for him to sit. When awareness dawned in her face, she sat and waited for him to pull out another chair.

He could not read the expression in her blue eyes.

"What's happened?"

"Look for her jewelry pouch," Doctor Hollis said as they entered Mrs. Hollis's bedchamber. "She would never leave without it."

Jewel opened drawers, looked under folded undergarments and nightgowns, while Doctor Hollis stood at the wardrobe opening hatboxes and sliding his hand between hanging gowns.

"No gowns or shoes seem to be missing," he said with a touch of hopefulness. His voice flattened. "But then, if she left in a hurry . . ."

She could buy a thousand new gowns with Mr. Gibbs' inheritance, Jewel thought bitterly, moving pillows. She stretched her arm beneath the mattress.

You don't know that's what happened, she reminded herself.

"Here, allow me." He came over to raise the mattress. Nothing. He even looked under the bed and pushed the wardrobe from the wall.

"I don't understand," he said, shaking his head.

Jewel's heart sank. She had hoped he could offer some reasonable explanation. That Mrs. Hollis would not actually feign a headache just to get her away from the cottage, and then leave Becky so cruelly.

She was forced to tell him about the coach.

"But you didn't actually see Loretta, correct?"

"I didn't."

"Jeremiah wouldn't have allowed it. Even at the risk of his job."

Jewel hesitated. "Mr. Toft wasn't driving."

If Philip had thought Loretta could not hurt him any more than she already had, he was mistaken. With his pillow gathered above his shoulder and heart thumping, he lay on his side and wept.

∞

Even after all that had happened, Becky greeted the dawn seeping through the window with her usual burst of energy. Jewel opened the eye not pressed to her pillow and watched her daughter stretch out her arms and wiggle her fingers to make faint shadow images upon the wall.

Jewel groaned. Tiger shifted against her feet.

"Mummy." Becky rolled to her side so that their faces were inches apart. "I woke you?"

"No, mite," Jewel said. "Your four years woke me."

She wrapped her arms around the girl and turned her so that they lay nestled. Gauzy slumber was beginning to claim her again. Becky shifted, turned and said, "Are you asleep again?"

Jewel yawned. "No."

"What does 'my four years' mean?"

"It means little girls don't appreciate sleep!" Jewel grabbed and tickled her until she giggled. Tiger leapt to the rug in search of less tumultuous bedding.

"I love my good girl," Jewel murmured, giving her a squeeze.

"I'm a good girl?"

"The best."

"I putted the pail back after I finished."

"There you are. Good as gold."

With so much joy filling her arms, Jewel felt a pang for Doctor Hollis. Had he even slept? She should cook breakfast as soon as she heard him stirring, just in case he was not up to breaking the news in the vicarage yet.

A thought pricked her mind. It probably meant nothing, but she took Becky by the shoulders and turned her to face her again. "Was Mrs. Hollis gone when you returned the pail?"

Tears welled in her brown eyes at the memory. "I looked everywhere. Even under her bed."

"Think hard, mite. When you asked permission to pick gooseberries, did you say *gooseberries* or did you say *berries*?"

"I wanted to pick gooseberries. I said they would make her feel better, and she said mind I be careful."

"But did you say *gooseberries* or *berries*?"

Becky shook her little head. "I don't remember, Mummy."

"I'm down here," Doctor Hollis called when Jewel knocked upon his door.

He sat at the table dressed in white shirt and brown trousers, and drinking from a cup. She must have slept more deeply than she thought. The shadows beneath his eyes revealed how well he had rested.

"There's more tea in the kettle," he said softly, soberly. "Becky's not awake?"

"She's playing with Tiger. I'll bring her down later."

"Was she terribly frightened?"

Forgoing the tea until after she said what was on her mind, she replied, "Terribly, sir. It was a bad storm."

"I thought I would walk over to the manor house to ask if

Mr. Ramsey has returned. If he was caught in the deluge, he would have boarded the horses and spent the night in Shrewsbury."

"You're going after her?"

"No." His long fingers tapped the handle of his teacup. "I'll not force her to stay with me. But just to know for certain."

More fearful of doing the wrong thing than appearing foolish, Jewel told him what Becky had said about the pail, and her exchange with Mrs. Hollis.

"What if she said *berries* and Mrs. Hollis thought she meant blackberries? What if she did take the salicin and wasn't quite thinking straight? What if her head really hurt? Wouldn't that cloud her thinking, too?"

He sat straighter, brow denting. "Has Loretta ever seen you and Becky leave to pick blackberries?"

"She has."

Staring askew at her, he said, "We've had our differences, but she would never leave Becky alone like that. Even if she were running away with Mr. Gibbs, she would have told Becky to go indoors, that she was going to the shops, anything. Not slipped away while she was in the water closet."

"I believe that, too, Mr. Hollis," Jewel said. But not because she needed to convince him, for he was already pushing out his chair.

"Drop Becky off at Elizabeth's, and send Jonathan to Constable Reed's to ask for a search party. Then go on to the manor house."

She got to her feet. "To speak with Mr. Ramsey?"

"No, to get Jeremiah Toft," he said on his way to the door. "He knows these woods like the back of his hand."

Heavy mist brooded about the tree trunks. Leaves dripped

in the tepid morning light. Huddled under an oak's gnarled wet branches, Loretta twined her shivering arms close, but they did not bring warmth to her drenched body.

Nor comfort. *Is Becky out here?*

"B-Becky?" she called through chattering teeth.

Please let her be home.

How would she ever be able to face Jewel, to admit she had allowed her daughter to wander off into a storm? She would rather die.

And die she might. It seemed she had slogged along for miles, tripped by vines, scratched by brambles, assaulted by branches.

Her feverish mind retraced her steps. Becky was not at the gooseberry shrub, nor behind the cottage. If she had been in any of the rooms, she would have answered her summons, obedient child that she was.

The water closet . . .

The absent pail had put it out of her thoughts. But children went to the water closet often. More so than adults.

Father, please . . . I'll do anything. Be the best wife. Send Philip to find me!

Philip. What would he be thinking? She could only hope, should she die, her body would be found before animals ravaged it. That he would not spend the rest of his years wondering.

For he would wonder. He loved her so.

And that had been the problem. He was right. Like a coddled child, she treaded over better toys in pursuit of the elusive one.

You can't be sure about the water closet, a voice inside nagged and accused. She must continue searching, calling for Becky, calling for help. Pushing against the tree trunk, she struggled to her feet.

"Wait." Jeremiah held out an arm.

Philip froze in midstep, held his breath.

"Only a dove."

Philip let out his breath, cupped his hands to his face again. "LORETTA!"

A twig snapped off to their left. The dove called again, only it wasn't a cooing noise after all, but a sob.

"It ain't a dove," Jeremiah said, to Philip's back, for he was already tearing through the undergrowth.

Around a dense stand of trees, and there she was, whimpering and staggering toward him. Her hair lay plastered to her head and shoulders, her filthy and ripped gown clung to her. But she was there and alive!

"Loretta!" he exclaimed, closing the gap between them, scooping her up into his arms.

She leaned her head upon his chest and wept, her whole body shaking.

"Don't try to speak," he said as Jeremiah caught up with them.

But she rasped out an unintelligible word.

Guessing, he said, "Becky's fine."

From the sobs pressed into his chest, he realized he had guessed correctly.

Chapter 35

Panting and snarling, wolves chased her through the rain and darkness. She could not push her screams from her chest. One beast crashed through the bushes at her feet! It bit her hands as she attempted to push it away.

She realized she was pushing against bedclothes. *A dream*, she thought as her heart ceased racing. She opened her eyes.

Jewel stood holding a tray, and gave her an apologetic look. "Sorry, I dropped the spoon. I'll get another."

"A spoon?"

"Doctor Hollis said to wake you if you hadn't eaten by five o'clock. Mrs. Phelps brought over some mutton soup from the vicarage."

"I've slept all day?"

"You were only brought here just before eleven o'clock."

Loretta eased herself up onto her pillows and raised her

hands so that Jewel could position the tray. Her hands were bandaged, leaving the fingers exposed. She touched her cheek and felt some sort of salve. Her wet clothes had been replaced by a nightgown. Warmth enveloped her, luxuriously dry warmth.

"Where is Philip?"

"He had to see about a baby he operated on."

"The little girl with a cleft lip." Was that only yesterday?

"I'll fetch another spoon."

"Will you send Becky up with it? I have to see for myself she's all right."

"Yes, ma'am." But instead of leaving right away, Jewel leaned down to drop a kiss upon her forehead. "Thank you."

It was out of the bounds of acceptable behavior for a servant. Loretta raised a bandaged hand to touch her cheek.

Philip eased Loretta's door open. She lay against her pillow. He began closing it again when she opened her eyes and said, "I'm awake, Philip."

He entered and felt her forehead, detecting no sign of fever. "How do you feel?"

"Safe." She smiled. "Alive. How is the baby?"

"She'll be fine. She has a loving family to help her mend."

"It won't stop children from teasing her when she's older."

"Yes, I'm afraid that's so. But hopefully, knowing how much she's loved will give her some armor."

He looked over to the empty soup bowl upon the tray. "Good. You took some nourishment."

"It was delicious. Is your mother here still? I'd like to thank her."

"She and Father were here only briefly, to see about you. You're the heroine of Gresham, by the way."

"Heroine?" A dry laugh escaped her lips. "Now you're teasing."

"The woods were full of men searching for you. They've told their wives, because at least eight stopped me on my way to Doctor Rhodes' to ask if you were all right."

"Incredible."

"Would you like something for pain?"

"No, not now."

He picked up her hand, gently. "I must beg your forgiveness, Loretta."

"Forgive you?" She shook her head. "Whatever for, Philip?"

He swallowed. "I could have looked for you earlier, if I hadn't believed the worst."

"You thought I left with Mr. Gibbs?"

He related Jewel's sighting of the coach, the absent jewelry and purse.

"And then my disappearance seemed too great a coincidence," she said. "I can't fault you for that, Philip. But my jewelry's in the back of your wardrobe."

"Mine?"

She sent a self-conscious look toward the door and lowered her voice. "I was afraid Becky might . . . plunder."

"You haven't said if you'll forgive me."

She smiled up at him. "I do."

Her fair hair had dried in a tangled mess that smelled of the woods. Jewel was heating water for a bath downstairs. The scratch across her cheek did not need stitches, but would leave a scar. Yet she had never looked more beautiful.

"You know," she said thoughtfully, "while I would never wish to repeat last night, perhaps it was the best thing that could have happened. For two reasons."

"And what are they?"

"Well, if it atoned for the scene I made in the shop, it was worth it. If I'm going to live here, I wouldn't want everyone believing I'm a fallen woman."

"And the second?"

"Becky was foremost in my mind, because I feared she was in danger. But through it all, I desperately wanted you to come for me." She stared up into his eyes. "You said I should fill my mind with good things. You're the best thing in my life, Philip. May we start over?"

All of his plans for caution flew out of the window. Throat thickening, he said, "Oh, Loretta . . . there is nothing I'd like more."

"Ouch!" she said.

He loosened his grip upon her hand.

She laughed, and he smiled, once he was over the shock of having hurt her.

"I've treated your family shamefully," she said. "I'll love them as my own. You'll see."

"That will make me very happy. But we'll have to love them over a distance. Visits back and forth. We need to be in London."

"But your dream . . . you're so happy here."

"There are two of us in this marriage. I was happy there during those first good months. And I can be happy anywhere with your love."

"You have it, Philip," she said, pressing his hand to her cheek.

"Will I still have it when I inform your father I wish to go into private practice as a dispensary surgeon?"

She gaped at him. "Philip?"

His heart sank. If she intended, still, to be her papa's little girl, their conversation had been for naught.

"You'll have the best of both worlds."

No bath had ever felt so good, even though the water stung her scratches. She sat at her dressing table in her nightgown, hair bundled in a towel and fresh bandages upon her hands. Surprisingly, the scratch across her cheek was not as devastating as she would have thought. A night lost in the woods could put things in perspective.

Soft knocks sounded.

"Come in."

In the mirror she watched Philip enter.

"Jewel said she'll comb your hair after she puts Becky to bed."

"Will you do it?"

"Why, yes."

As he crossed the rug, she studied him again in the mirror and was struck with the change in him. She wheeled around on the bench. "Your beard!"

He rubbed his smooth-shaven cheek. "I wasn't so keen on it anyway. I only kept it out of stubbornness. There's a bit of willful child in me, too."

She smiled and handed him the comb, and unwound the towel from her head. "Begin at the ends or you'll pluck me bald. I'm afraid it's going to take a long time to get the snarls out."

"I have all night."

A few minutes later, Jewel, also wearing wrapper over her nightclothes, brought in a pot of cocoa with two cups, along with an envelope.

"This was on the table."

"Thank you," Philip said. "I forgot it was there. My parents brought it over with the soup."

"Will there be anything else?" Jewel asked in a tone that begged refusal.

Loretta laughed. She had forgotten the previous night had been long for others, as well. "Yes, Jewel. Go to bed."

"Straightaway, ma'am."

"It's from my father," Loretta said, staring at the envelope. She rather wished he had not seen it, for even though she had admitted planning to borrow money to lend to Mr. Gibbs, the reminder could drive the pleasantness out of the room. While Philip poured the cocoa, Loretta took out the page.

"Dearest Loretta,

"That you would demand so outrageous a sum with no explanation convinces me of the notion that struck my mind after you left London; I have undermined your marriage by showering you with things not yet attainable by your husband. I have sold the horses and carriage and found another position for Tom. Most of London takes public transport. A brisk stroll down to the hansom stand will be tonic for your health."

The willful child in her rose up to say, "Mother and Father have a landau *and* coach."

Philip set her cup and saucer upon the dressing table before her. "They can afford them."

She took a sip of warm cocoa, then another, and made a face in the mirror. "We should give back the house, too. Move into some dismal little rooms in Whitechapel. That would show them."

"The house was our wedding gift. They'll be hurt if we give it back."

"You think so?"

"I know so. Besides . . . it's a fine house."

She set cup onto saucer, twisted around to smile up at him. "It's not too late to fill it with good memories, Philip."

He smiled down at her. "It's not too late."

"That's a hint to kiss me."

His eyes shone. Had she never noticed their rich blueness before? With a tender hand between her shoulders, he leaned down and kissed her, sweetly, with a restrained passion she had not realized how much she missed.

"M-m-m. Cocoa," he said.

She touched the scratch upon her cheek. "I'm glad you shaved the beard."

He was starting to stand when she caught his head with her bandaged hands and whispered, "This place could use a good memory or two."

He raised back far enough to give her a stunned look. "No. Absolutely not."

"You no longer find me attractive?" she teased, knowing from the look in his eyes that was not the case.

"You're beautiful. But your ordeal . . ."

"I'm fine, Philip."

"Jewel and Becky . . ."

She tugged on his earlobe. "They're not above *your* room."

⚬◦⚬

"Loretta and I would like to make an announcement," Philip said in the vicarage dining room three days later.

"You're returning to London," Aleda said flatly.

"Within the week. We can't thank you enough for lending

us your cottage. And we plan to visit here once a month. At the very least, take an early train on a Saturday."

"Now remember . . . you've just come from church," Jonathan teased.

Elizabeth touched her husband's hand. "That would be very thoughtful, Philip and Loretta."

"Thoughtfulness has nothing to do with it." Philip smiled at his father and mother. "We need you. All of you."

He laid out his plan to set up a private practice attached to Saint George's Hospital. "I'll help Doctor Rhodes find someone to take my place here. But already he has letters from some very qualified doctors."

Throughout his speech he tried to read his parents' faces. Sadness? Resignation? Relief?

"May I also make an announcement?" Loretta asked.

"But of course," Elizabeth said.

She stood, looked at the faces around the table. "My husband has forgotten to mention that we hope you will visit us often, as well, and stay in our home."

Mother finally spoke. "Thank you, Loretta."

Loretta stared across at her with sheepish smile. "And the next time, we will treat you . . ." She cleared her throat. "*I* will treat you as honored guests, for I behaved very badly the last time you visited."

"Not so," Father said charitably.

An uncomfortable silence followed, broken by laughter when Loretta wrinkled her nose at him and said, "Now remember, Vicar, you've just come from church."

Chapter 36

Anxious to hear from Gabriel, Aleda had taken to waiting at the letter box, usually with Becky accompanying her. Aleda was glad for her company. The girl's questions about beginning school soon distracted Aleda from checking the time every half minute.

"What if the other children don't like me?"

"They'll like you. If there are some who don't, you must remind yourself of all of us who do like you, and that eventually they let you out of school."

It was so good to have her watch again. God bless Mr. Trumble, for asking Mr. Stillman to keep an eye out for it as he visited pawn lenders for war medals. She had had to pay almost the full value to redeem it, but hopefully, that would be returned soon.

Mr. Gibbs had obviously found it. And he obviously thought he was clever for pawning it in Shrewsbury. But how arrogant, and even silly of him, to sign the ticket *Ronald Tibbs*.

The sight of Mr. Jones trundling toward them with his letter sack pushed all thought of Mr. Gibbs from her mind. She hurried to meet him.

"I believe this is what you've been waiting for," he said, handing her an envelope with Gabriel's familiar script.

> *12 August 1884*
> *Dear Aleda,*
>   *I am pleased to inform you that my editors at Macmillan's would like to meet with you on Tuesday, the twenty-sixth of August. We will have the house prepared for yours and Mrs. Libby and Becky's arrival on Monday.*
>
>   *Very truly yours,*
>   *Gabriel*

Aleda turned over the page, looked in the envelope. True, Gabriel was concise, but this was maddening. Meet with her? To offer a contract? If so, could he not spare the few extra words?

"Is it good news, Miss Hollis?"

Aleda gave her shoulder a squeeze. "I think so."

Back at the cottage, she carried the letter up to the guest room, where Jewel was putting fresh sheets upon the bed.

"How wonderful!" Jewel cried, throwing her arms about her.

"But it says nothing about a contract."

"But why else would they want to meet with you?"

"Well, yes." Aleda felt better.

"But why does it say Becky and me?" Jewel asked.

"You're to come with me. Wouldn't you like to see London?"

"We'd love to, but . . ."

"As my traveling companions," Aleda explained.

She could say more, but thought it best to allow the court-ship—for certainly this was what it was—to flow along naturally for now. And besides, Gabriel had not given her the liberty to express his feelings.

"I wish he would have said more," she said. "Did all the editors like it? Are there parts they'll want me to rewrite? He's so maddeningly concise."

Jewel gave her a wry smile. "So, you're not happy?"

Aleda smiled back. "I'm overjoyed! In fact, I'll probably run all the way to the vicarage to show my parents."

That night, with Becky curled into the curve of her side, Jewel thought again what a pity it was that Miss Hollis did not wish to marry Mr. Patterson. He would revere a wife, as Doctor Hollis revered Mrs. Hollis. As Norman had revered her.

But few emotions were set in stone. She prayed again for a miracle.

⌘

On the Thursday morning of the twenty-first of August, Aleda unlatched her garden gate and set out on the path. Notices were posted all over Gresham, asking villagers to act as witnesses to the reading of Squire Bartley's will. Unnecessary, for all Mr. Baker would have had to do was inform Mr. Trumble in the hearing of some of his customers.

She pushed back her sleeve to look at her watch. Half past nine. The meeting was to begin at ten o'clock. There were no signs of Elizabeth and her crew as she passed their cottage. She would hurry to the vicarage and walk over with her parents, if they had not left.

Dismissing Horace Stokes would be his first action, Donald thought as the coach rumbled down Church Lane. He already had buyers interested in the cheese factory. He would even make it a condition of the sale that Horace not be rehired. He would rue the scene he made twenty-one years ago over attempts at innocent fun.

The horses were slowing in preparation for Bartley Lane when he spotted Aleda Hollis. She turned her head to send a puzzled look his way. When the coach was even and his eyes met hers, she held up her fist in an unladylike manner.

Go on, behave like a pig, he thought, scowling at her through the glass. Just before her image slid from sight, he noticed a glint of metal at her upheld wrist.

Uneasily he thought, *But how did she get it back?*

Most probably, this was a new one. She should never play with cards, if that was her bluff, he thought, propping hands against the seat on either side as the coach turned.

Just because he was bound to his uncle's agreement with Miss Hollis didn't mean the person to whom he sold the estate would be bound to it. Another condition of sale.

It was good to have power.

And Reese had even returned last week, as if able to smell that power in the air. All the suffering Donald had been through made this victory all the more sweet.

Mr. Baker rose from a library chair as Donald entered.

"You're late," Mr. Baker said, not offering his hand.

Donald shrugged. This little old man could no longer intimidate him. In fact, he would hire another solicitor to handle disposing of the property.

Power.

A document that appeared to be the will, and one other page, lay upon the polished oak table before him.

Which was surprising. His parents had only owned a house,

bank account, and some stocks, and he had spent an hour signing papers.

"We must do this quickly," Mr. Baker said as Donald pulled out a chair.

"Why aren't the others here?" Donald asked, barely daring to hope. Had his uncle left out the servants? It did not seem fair, for many had worked there for decades, and deserved at least small legacies. But who was he to argue with his uncle's wishes?

"They will be leaving soon to the village hall for the other reading."

"What do you mean?"

"Your uncle has left you five hundred pounds."

The words assaulted Donald's ears like a curse.

"You jest."

"I'm aware you had hoped for more, but if you'll pay off your debts and invest the remainder, you may live in modest comfort for the rest of your life."

Modest comfort?

"You'll do even better if you find some sort of profitable employment."

Donald sneered at him. And do what? Dig ditches? He was a gentleman, from a long line of gentlemen whose forebears had had the wisdom, or craftiness, to be on the right side of some king or another. Labor was for peasants.

"There is a mistake here. Surely he didn't leave the rest to the servants?"

The solicitor uncapped a pen. "I'm not at liberty to say until all other recipients have been informed. I assure you, everything is in order with the courts."

Donald's chair fell backwards with a *thud*. He shot to his

feet and pounded his fist upon the table. "You've cheated me, you old snake!"

"I understand your disappointment. You may, of course, retain your own attorney to look over the will."

"I shall do just that! You'll not get away with this!"

Mr. Baker brushed the insult off as if it were a piece of lint. "Two small but significant liens have been filed against your inheritance. I can deduct them from the cheque I am about to write, or you may battle it out in court."

"And who are these two people?"

"Miss Aleda Hollis and Mr. Amos Perkins."

Donald barked a laugh. "Let them take me to court."

"Very well." Mr. Baker began gathering papers.

"Wait. You mean I can't have the cheque until it's settled?"

"That's exactly what it means, Mr. Gibbs."

Grinding his teeth, Donald snatched the pen from his hand.

There would be a battle over this whole fiasco. But not today. Not when he had to make the five-o'clock express to fulfill his promise to Reese of a night out on the town.

Chapter 37

More children than usual played on the green, for only adults were invited to the meeting in the village hall, in the interest of chair space and decorum. Older children or maids minded the few younger ones toddling about.

Claire and Samuel sprinted toward Julia, Andrew, and Aleda, with John following patiently.

"Grandmother!" Claire chirped, throwing arms around Julia's waist. "Father says Aunt Aleda is going to sell her book and be rich!"

Samuel, caught up into Andrew's arms, naturally opened his mouth. "And Mother hopes she'll buy some decent clothes!"

"Samuel!" John scolded with an apologetic look to his aunt.

But Aleda was howling with laughter. Julia and Andrew laughed, as well.

Inside the hall, Mr. Sykes shifted over in the second to last row so the three could sit together. Elizabeth sent a wave from across the aisle. The hum of conversations faded to silence as Mr. Baker stepped up to the platform. Only the sounds of children at play came through the open windows, but they were not intrusive.

With no preamble besides introducing himself, the solicitor got down to business: "Squire Bartley leaves the manor house with its outbuildings and orchards and parks, and the sum of one thousand pounds sterling, to Mr. and Mrs. Horace Stokes."

Stunned silence, then gasps and chatter filled the hall, followed by applause. Julia lifted a bit in her chair and followed other gazes toward Horace and Margery, weeping profusely in each other's arms. She felt the sting of tears herself. So the orphans would have room to romp and grow. And knowing the Stokes, there would surely be more of them now.

Andrew, smiling, but with a worried dent between his brows, turned to Julia and said, "But what of the squire's servants?"

"Perhaps he left them some money?"

He did better than that, for the next item was the enormously profitable cheese factory. As Mr. Baker read the names of the servants, there were whoops of joy, and happy sobs.

It was a matter of fact that the squire was wealthy. But the vastness of this wealth surprised Julia as Mr. Baker continued reading.

Cheese factory workers were left the cottages that housed them in the three rows, a stone's throw from the factory, as well as forty pounds each for improvements. Dairy farmers were left their farms; villagers who had leased from the squire, their cottages. Two thousand pounds went to the parish mission fund, and one thousand to Saint Jude's charity fund.

Gipsy Woods was left to the whole village, with the

exception of an acre surrounding the gamekeeper's cottage, which went to Aleda along with the cottage. Julia patted her back as her daughter wiped her eyes.

There were various smaller amounts. One hundred pounds for each school. Twenty pounds for the archery team. Thirty pounds for the subscription library. Ten pounds for a signboard to be erected at the entrance to the village reading *Welcome to Gresham. Home of Anwyl Mountain Cheeses.*

The latter brought laughter. Leave it to Squire Bartley to carry entrepreneurism to the grave.

The celebration spilled out onto the green, while individuals or heads of families stayed to sign legal documents. Andrew, representing Saint Jude's, took up the last spot in the queue that had formed, with Julia at his side.

They were in no hurry. They had questions.

"When was this will drafted?" was Andrew's first.

"Squire Bartley expressed the desire to change his will during one of my regular visits in early May," Mr. Baker replied. "Due to his wish for secrecy, I brought up two legal clerks from Shrewsbury four days later to witness the signing."

"But it was in early June that he asked me if it would be moral to break his promise to his sister. Just hours before he was struck ill."

"I'm not surprised. He was tormented over what he had done, as much as it pleased him to help so many deserving people. He clearly wanted absolution from you. But for having *done* it . . . not for planning to do it."

Mr. Baker paused. "How did you respond?"

"I suggested he give it all away beforehand," Andrew replied, "except for however much he would wish to leave to Mr. Gibbs."

"Clever. You would make a good attorney."

"He makes a better vicar," Julia said, taking Andrew's arm. And she voiced her question. "Was Mr. Gibbs left anything?"

"I'm allowed to tell you, now that he's been informed. Five hundred pounds. Squire Bartley could not bring himself to disown him. He did love his sister. But if anything remains of it a year from now, I will be the most surprised man in England."

Conversation over supper at the vicarage centered around the squire's legacy to Gresham.

"I doubt anything like this has ever been done," Jonathan said, and turned to Aleda. "You should write a story about it."

Aleda shook her head. "I can't. Fiction has to be believable."

Mother gave her a perplexed look. "Shipwrecked seamen battling pirates and giant lizards is more believable than something that actually happened before witnesses?"

"I'm afraid so, Mother. Readers are willing to accept all sorts of fantasy, as long as the story line follows the basic laws of God and nature. For example, I can't have my characters defy gravity and float out of harm's way . . . unless they were written about as some sort of cosmic aliens or elves with those powers already mentioned."

"How many squires in history have left fortunes to their villages?" Elizabeth asked.

"None before midcentury," Father said. "The laws of sucession were quite restricted: male heirs or the Crown."

"What a pity that it's so rare as to be unbelievable," Jonathan said.

"But we're happy for Gresham, aren't we, Mother?" John asked. He alone represented Elizabeth and Jonathan's children.

Perhaps it was her pregnancy that caused Elizabeth to realize she could not coddle the twins forever; thus the servants would be feeding them and tucking them into bed.

As much as Aleda loved Samuel and Claire, she relished this opportunity to converse without background reminders not to slurp or complain about the food.

Elizabeth smiled at her son. "You're excited about the new archery equipment, aren't you?"

He smiled and nodded, but Jonathan's face at the mention of archery equipment betrayed the greater excitement.

Even Dora and Wanetta glowed as they served the meal; Wanetta because the cottage she and Luke had rented was now theirs, and Dora, because her parents now owned their modest dairy farm.

"It's a shame Jewel wasn't included with the manor house servants," Mother said.

"She wasn't employed there when the squire drafted the will," Aleda explained. "And the servants were listed by name."

"They all say she took tender care of him the brief time she knew him," Father said.

Aleda smiled to herself. *Jewel may not own part of a cheese factory, but her future—and Becky's—seems very promising.*

Chapter 38

Jewel could barely contain her excitement as the train squealed into Paddington Station on the twenty-fifth of August.

"This is where the queen lives," she said to Becky.

Becky pressed her face to the window. "Will we see her when it stops?"

"I'm afraid not, mite," Jewel said as Miss Hollis covered a smile.

Mr. Patterson met them on the platform, all smiles and embraces. "I'm so glad you're here."

"I didn't expect you to meet us yourself," Miss Hollis told him.

"Are you serious? I've planned this for days."

They sent each other meaningful looks, and suddenly Jewel felt as if she and Becky were intruding. There was clearly some unfinished business between the two. But on the bright side, it seemed her prayer for a miracle was being answered.

With porter in tow with the luggage on a cart, he escorted them to his coach. The driver, a compact man with light brown hair, opened the door.

"Hello, George," Miss Hollis said, as Mr. Patterson tipped the porter.

He doffed his cap. "Good morning, Miss Hollis. Got yourself a fancy book deal, I hear."

"Well, it's not set in stone yet."

"That ain't what Mr. Patterson says."

She raised hopeful brows at Jewel. Jewel smiled back.

Finally, the coach joined the stream of traffic leaving the station. Mr. Patterson had kindly insisted she and Becky take the forward-facing seat so that they could see through the windows. For a few minutes, he and Miss Hollis spoke of the coming meeting, while Jewel and Becky looked from side to side. London seemed very much like Birmingham, with its buildings and masses of humanity riding and walking in all directions. But not nearly as sooty.

"What do you think of our city, Becky?" Mr. Patterson asked.

She looked up at Jewel.

"Go on," Jewel said with a smile.

"There are too many people, sir. And we haven't seen the queen. She wasn't in the big hotel Vicar Treves took us to, either. Is she hiding?"

Jewel winced and opened her mouth to apologize. Before the end of the day, they would have to have a chat about tact.

But Mr. Patterson's laughter filled the coach. He leaned forward. "I'm afraid you're probably not going to see her . . .

and, no disrespect to Her Royal Highness . . . but I can show you monkeys and tigers and elephants."

Becky pressed her hands together. "Please, Mr. Patterson. May we see them?"

He raised brows hopefully at Jewel. "After lunch?"

Jewel tensed. Surely he did not propose to take Becky on an outing alone.

"Please, Mummy?"

"You're very kind, but I'm afraid . . ."

Mr. Patterson said gently, "I'd wager you've never seen monkeys and tigers and elephants yourself, Mrs. Libby."

"Only in pictures, Mr. Patterson." She returned his smile.

"Well, I plan to spend the rest of the day browsing booksellers on Charing Cross Road," Miss Hollis said. "I'll return for supper."

She gave Mr. Patterson a mock scowl. "Not that anyone has asked."

The zoological gardens were nothing short of marvelous. With infinite patience Mr. Patterson guided Jewel and Becky to dens, cages, paddocks, aviaries, and ponds, and smiled at their delight. They gaped with awe at the lions and tigers and leopards of the Old World, jaguars and pumas of the New. They laughed at the antics of the monkeys and sea lions, and shivered at the snakes behind glass. Just as Jewel was wishing she could capture forever the joy and wonder upon Becky's face, Mr. Patterson led them to a small paddock, where for two pence one could sit upon an elephant's back for a photographer with his camera. When Becky lost her nerve at the last minute, Jewel joined her atop the huge beast, wrapped her arms around her, and smiled.

The outing wore Becky out. Back at Mr. Patterson's house,

he asked the cook to prepare the girl a little soup for Jewel to coax down her.

"When will we get our picture?" Becky murmured as Jewel tucked her into a marvelous four-poster bed.

"In about two weeks. Mr. Patterson said he would mail it, remember?"

"I wish we had a monkey. He could play with Tiger."

A soft knock sounded five minutes later. Miss Hollis stuck her head around the door.

"Gabriel said she saw every animal in the zoo."

Jewel nodded. "She'll never forget this day."

"My brother and Loretta will be joining us for dinner in an hour."

"How nice. Please greet them for me."

"Greet them yourself." She entered and whispered, "Did not Gabriel invite you to supper?"

"You don't have to whisper," Jewel said with a glance to the bed. "She's out. And Mr. Patterson was being kind. I'm content to dine in the servants' hall."

Miss Hollis folded her arms and leaned back against a chest of drawers. She stared at her, seeming to be considering something weighty.

"What is wrong?" Jewel asked.

"I've known Gabriel for over half my life. He has stayed often with my family over the years. He's a genuinely decent man."

"I believe that," Jewel said. It confirmed what she already felt, and squelched completely the earlier suspicion that he had any ulterior motive for the day's outing.

"While you've been bathing and tucking Becky in, Gabriel has been filling my ear with how marvelous the day was. This is from a man who seldom leaves his house."

Was she angry? Jewel thought back to the meaningful looks exchanged at the station. To the murmured conversation in the coach. To the *Not that anyone has asked* comment.

Oh dear. She had prayed for the miracle. And had gotten in the way of it.

"I'm so sorry. But Becky was so excited about the zoo that I didn't consider that you should be the one to spend the day with him."

"Me?" Miss Hollis shook her head. "The day worked out exactly as it was supposed to. I didn't need companions for the train. Gabriel wanted you to come."

"He did? But why?"

"Because he enjoys your company, Jewel."

Jewel's mind revisited the outing. He had not only seemed to revel in Becky's happiness but her own, as well.

"He was hurt before, and it took him a long time to recover. If you don't feel he's the sort of man you could ever love, I'm asking you to bow out gently, before his feelings grow. I could find an excuse for your not joining us for dinner. And I'll find a reason for us to return to Gresham as soon as my meeting is concluded."

Jewel put a hand to her heart. The pathway from her ears to comprehension was blocked by the old insidious feelings of unworthiness. "That's just not possible. I thought he loved you . . . and that you might . . ."

"We love each other as friends. Brother and sister. But I ask you, Jewel. Can you see beyond his wealth to the gold in his heart? And . . . can you see beyond his appearance to the beauty in his soul?"

Weak in the knees, Jewel looked about the room for a place to sit. Miss Hollis went over to the dressing table and pulled out the stool. "Sit here. I'm sorry. I shouldn't have meddled."

"No, I'm glad you spoke." Jewel swept her skirts aside and sat. She gathered her flying thoughts for several seconds, and looked up at her. "I would be deceptive if I said Mr. Patterson's wealth would not be attractive. I have a daughter to provide for."

Miss Hollis nodded. "I wouldn't expect you to answer any other way."

"But I understand what you mean about his soul. He radiates goodness. As to his appearance, his smile is very pleasing to the eyes. But looks aren't everything. Take Mr. Gibbs, for example."

"I'd like to take him and throw him in the river," Miss Hollis said. "But you haven't answered my question. Should I make excuses for you tonight?"

"No, please. But I haven't anything formal to wear."

"It's just our cozy group. Gabriel hates dressing up anyway." She smiled. "In any case, with me along, you couldn't be the worst-dressed woman at the table."

⌒∞⌒

The following morning Jewel woke in the most plush bed anyone had ever slept in, between silken sheets good enough for Buckingham Palace. Sunlight streamed through lace-draped windows to lay soft patterns upon mellow cherrywood furniture.

Memories of last night's dinner floated through her mind and made her smile. To be treated as an equal with such lovely people. And how good it was to see Doctor and Mrs. Hollis smile at each other like newlyweds.

She stretched and slipped out of bed. By the time she was dressed and groomed, Becky was awake.

"Where will Mr. Patterson take us today?"

Jewel pulled her into her arms and started unfastening her nightgown. "You mustn't ask him that, mite."

"Why?"

"Well, because he might feel obligated."

But Mr. Patterson brought a notebook to the breakfast table. "I'm glad you're awake. My list of places to show you grows longer every minute."

"Are you obligated, Mr. Patterson?" Becky asked.

He grinned at her. "Are you, Miss Becky?"

"No, sir. I want to see everything."

"Well, I want you to see everything."

Miss Hollis joined them and stated she was more than happy to take a hansom to her meeting, and so after breakfast Jewel, Becky, and Mr. Patterson were off in the coach. Mr. Patterson apologized that the day had to be divided between Westminster Abbey and the Tower.

"Tomorrow, Saint Paul's and Buckingham Palace. If you could only stay longer."

That evening, they rested up a bit, and then, leaving Becky in the care of two young housemaids, Mr. Patterson took Miss Hollis and Jewel to the Burlington Restaurant on Regent Street to celebrate the book contract.

While he was gentle and sweet, he never said anything to validate the information Miss Hollis had given her. She was both relieved and disappointed as the train carried them back to Gresham on the twenty-eighth. And she did not fully understand the reason for either emotion. She wished Miss Hollis would bring up the subject. Perhaps she felt she had spoken out of turn, or possibly miscalculated Mr. Patterson's feelings.

Back in the cottage, they settled into their daily routine, save one important change. Becky started school on the first of September.

"It's the best fun ever, Mummy!" Becky declared after her first day.

The walk up Church Lane was an easy distance, and well populated with the Stokes children from the manor house. But Jewel still felt compelled to accompany Becky that first week, watching between the elms as she was drawn into play with little girls her age.

By the next Monday, she realized it was enough to walk with her to the end of the path and allow her to be a regular schoolgirl. The pain of losing her baby eased away as the days passed.

On the twentieth of September she took a stiff envelope from the letter box, with Gabriel's return address in the corner. It was addressed to her. The photograph, of course. She took it out and smiled at the happiness on hers and Becky's faces as they sat atop the elephant.

There was a letter, as well. She carried it up the path, then sat in a garden chair to unfold it.

Dear Mrs. Libby, I hope this finds you well. . . .

"Four pages?" Miss Hollis said, turning from her desk. "Are you sure Gabriel wrote it?"

"Quite sure," Jewel said, holding the folded letter in her hands.

He had written about everyday things, such as the novel he was just finishing, and his decision whether to begin another or go with a long-standing whim to write a collection of short stories. He wondered what she would advise. He also asked about her days, and Becky's new venture into schooling.

The final paragraph consisted of one sentence.

I would enjoy very much hearing back from you, if you would care to write to me.

"Well, let's see it," Miss Hollis asked.

"I'm sorry, but it's private."

"You're serious?"

"Yes, ma'am."

"But I showed you his letter to me."

"Again, I'm sorry."

"But why?" Miss Hollis raised her eyebrows. "Is it passionate?"

Jewel thought for a second. "Yes, I think it may be."

Chapter 39

The Severn Valley Railway carried Julia and Andrew and Aleda eastward on the sixth of May, nine months after Philip and Loretta had moved back to London. Julia carried in her trunk several gifts from others, including a soft white blanket Elizabeth had knit in the rare quiet times between nursing little Noelle and tending the rest of her family. Having a busy household had taught Elizabeth to plan ahead.

Julia and Andrew's gift was shipped ahead last month; a cradle fashioned of cherrywood by the Crofts. Loretta had written to say how beautiful it was, how she hoped it would cradle many children through the years.

Philip threw his arms around them in the waiting room at Saint George's Hospital. "You're here! Thank you for coming."

"As if we would miss it," Andrew said, pounding his back.

The soft hums of conversation floated around family and friends. Doctor and Mrs. Trask. Loretta's sister, Irene. Gabriel.

And Philip. Pacing with hands in pockets, not able to sit, clearly with his mind in the delivery room.

"Have you chosen any names?" Aleda asked him.

He gave her a blank look. "Hmm?"

Finally, an older man entered, wearing a doctor's coat. "She came through fine, Doctor Hollis. You have a healthy eight-pound boy."

Julia's eyes teared at the sight of her son, gulping down a huge sigh of relief, lifting up a silent prayer before following the doctor.

"Are you all right?" Andrew whispered.

Julia smiled through her tears. "Yes."

An hour later, a nurse entered to announce that Mrs. Hollis was awake and that visitors were limited to two at a time. Naturally, Doctor and Mrs. Trask went first. When they returned, all smiles, Julia took her husband's hand and followed the nurse up the long hallway.

They passed several beds in the ward. Loretta, flushed and smiling, sat up on her pillows with a swaddled bundle in her arms. Philip sat at her side, radiating pride. He stood and took his son from his wife.

"Here, Mother. Sit. Get acquainted with your grandson."

Julia sat and took him. With fresh tears and Andrew leaning at her side, she smiled at the blue eyes staring up at her. Love welled through her.

Philip leaned to push the blanket back, revealing baby-fine strands of auburn hair.

"Was mine that color, Mother?"

She smiled up at him. "It was."

"What will you name him?" Andrew asked.

Philip and Loretta exchanged smiles.

"We've already named him," Philip replied. He nodded to his wife.

"His name is Andrew," she said.

Chapter 40

On a mild morning on the fourteenth of May, Miss Hollis sat in the garden, penning the start to another novel, while Jewel dusted the parlor furniture. Voices drifted through the window. Jewel assumed Vernon Moore was there, and indeed, she heard the door open and close.

Gabriel held a parcel, wrapped in brown paper.

"It's a book of Lillie Lane paper dolls for Becky. My cook says her granddaughter enjoys hers very much, but that you should cut out the dolls and clothes yourself, as she's still so young."

"How very kind of you."

They stared across at each other for one second, two, and then he dropped the parcel onto the cushion of the nearest chair and advanced.

Jewel dropped the dusting cloth onto a table. His arms

went around her and lips met hers with an intensity that buck-led her knees.

When they finally came apart, she rested her head upon his chest as he stroked her hair.

"Will you marry me, Jewel? I'll be a good father to Becky, and you'll never want for anything."

"Yes."

"Truly?"

Happy tears pricking her eyes, she raised her head to smile at him. "I will."

His voice thickened. "I prayed for a wife."

"And I prayed for a miracle."

"I love you, Jewel."

"I love you, Gabriel."

Planning a future took a long time when interrupted by kisses. When they walked out into the garden, hand-in-hand, an hour later, Miss Hollis stopped pacing and advanced.

"I thought you'd never come out! And I didn't want to spoil the moment by going indoors."

Gabriel opened his arm. She took a step closer, to be gently pulled into a sideways embrace. "The fifteenth of August."

She stepped back. "Three months?"

"If your father would be so kind as to perform the cer-emony. We want to give Becky time to get used to the idea. And Jewel insists on giving you time to find a replacement for her."

"A replacement?" Miss Hollis smiled at Jewel. "You don't look for people like Jewel. God drops them into your world."

"Will I go to another school?" Becky asked in Jewel's arms that night. The framed photograph from the zoo was barely visible atop the chest of drawers in the dim light.

"You will. And there will be nice little girls there, too, just like your school here."

"Will you have to clean Mr. Patterson's home?"

Jewel held her tighter. "It will be our home, too, mite. And no, the maids will continue to do that."

"And he really said I could get a kitten?"

"No, he said you could get two kittens."

Becky sighed contentedly. "What will I call Mr. Patterson?"

"You'll call him Father."

"Father."

A space of silence followed. Jewel assumed Becky had dropped off to sleep, until her small voice said, "May I call him Papa?"

Jewel smiled. "I think he would like that."

She could imagine, somewhere in heaven, Norman smiled, too.

Don't Miss These Other Charming Stories From Gresham!

Julia Hollis' opulent life in Victorian London shatters when her husband passes away. Now the family's hope rests on renovating an old inn in the quaint village of Gresham. But troublesome boarders, quirky townspeople, and the eligible new vicar are only the beginning of the memorable events in store for Julia, her family, and all of Gresham.

GRESHAM CHRONICLES

The Widow of Larkspur Inn, The Courtship of the Vicar's Daughter, The Dowry of Miss Lydia Clark